Gilded Summers

Gilded Summers

Newport's Gilded Age Book 1

Donna Russo Morin

Other Works by Donna Russo Morin

GILDED DREAMS
BIRTH: Once, Upon a New Time Book One
PORTRAIT OF A CONSPIRACY: Da Vinci's Disciples Book One
THE COMPETITION: Da Vinci's Disciples Book Two
THE FLAMES OF FLORENCE: Da Vinci's Disciples Book Three
THE KING'S AGENT
TO SERVE A KING
THE GLASSMAKER'S DAUGHTER
THE COURTIER OF VERSAILLES

Praise for GILDED SUMMERS

"GILDED SUMMERS by Donna Russo Morin is a lush and evocative novel of the distinctive period known as Newport's Gilded Age, a period brought vibrantly to life in this powerful work. Ginevra and Pearl, unique in their own way yet equally sympathetic, are captivating from the start and never let go. The passages and chapters are exquisitely and uniquely intertwined, like the young lives of its characters, sewn seamlessly with the mounting mystery and suspense. Vivid descriptions evoke the setting and period with such mastery, one feels like a 'fly on the wall,' living there with these young women who are so well crafted and developed. A genuine 'can't put it down' novel, a triumph by a masterful writer!"
   -Anne Girard (Diane Haegar) author of Madame Picasso

"Author Donna Russo Morin has a knack for both character and historical authenticity, making this journey into Newport's Gilded Age a fascinating and fulfilling tale. From the well-described details of the surroundings and costumes to the social structures at play and the strictures of upper and lower class lives, Russo Morin captures an era where women are ready to break out. Pearl and Ginevra have the same spirit for freedom and choice, but they are distinctly well presented and developed as very different women who compliment one another's misgivings. Gilded Summers is sure to suit fans of the likes of Downton Abbey, but it delivers far deeper emotional connections and realistic portrayals and is a highly recommended historical read."
   -Readers Favorite

For the man on the end of the couch;
I hope you played for me.

There is no such thing as a perfect life,
unless we make it so.

In that split second when the gunpowder bursts...the next second when the gun at the end of my hand blasts the room with light, jerking my arm back...in that time out of time, I cannot say whom I truly aim for.

GINEVRA
1899

The air reeks of gunpowder...and fresh blood.

I push the limp body off me. Someone's sobs, mine no doubt, I hear as if from far away. Dropping my skirts, my eyes skirt the room, to the body on the floor, to her standing in the doorway. I've never seen her so pale, so...blighted. I see the gun on the floor. Tendrils of smoke snake upwards from the barrel as if beckoned by the notes of a magic flute.

I hear the voices, the footsteps. They're coming. I hear my heart in my ears; I feel the snuffs of air from my nose.

What I do, I do without thought.

It takes me only a few steps to snatch the gun from the floor and cross the room to her side.

"What?"

Eyes glazed with fear find me.

I reach up and tuck a stray strand of her gleaming raven hair back into her perfectly coiffed Gibson Girl.

"Go."

"What?" she asks again, this time her luminescent brow furrows, growing awareness in the moment returns, a spark of denial simmers.

"You must get out of here, Pearl." I take her hand; one I remember having held more than any other in my life. "You have far more to lose, too much to lose."

I shake my head, tangles of thoughts rattle. The words accusing me, the voices that will say I somehow brought this on myself, part of me

1

believes. That part knows I cannot let her take any blame, for this, for him.

I lie to her for the first time in all of our years together.

"They will believe me. They'll believe I could do such a thing, why I could do such a thing. Look there is blood on my clothes, but none on yours."

Her gaze flits over my dark uniform before resting on her bright, silk gown.

I look at her face, I flash to the memory of the first time I saw her face, the young one, one so like mine.

"My papa is nothing in this world, and yours is devoted to him. Mine cannot be hurt by this. Your *famiglia* ... it will disgrace them forever."

"No. No, I must tell them," Pearl shakes her head. There is little focus in eyes that try to focus everywhere. "I came to protect you. It's my fault. If I had believed you, trusted you, he wouldn't—" she babbles. I understand it all.

Now both of our almost black eyes drop to the floor, to the body slumped upon it, to the growing puddle of blood around it, to the face so dashing even in death.

"They'll execute you," she whispers.

I grab her by the shoulders and shake her. "You did protect me. You came. You gave me time to..." I shudder, the words I must say—fleeting through the sliver of mind still capable of thinking—feel as if they are a rag shoved down my throat, and I gag on them. "...we didn't have time to finish." My gaze grabs her harder than my hands. "He always wanted me more, you know that don't you—"

Pearl shakes her head, covers her ears with trembling hands.

"He desired me." I slap her with a thin thread of truth. It is enough.

The slap of her hand spins my head; the sting of it stays long after her hand retreats.

I clench my eyes tightly.

"He always desired me more than you."

This time it is no slap. Curled fingers and knuckles meet my face. All that I had done to her feeds the strength of her arm.

I stammer back from the blow. My shoulder collides with the wall. The corner of the table digs deep into my buttock. I drop to the floor.

Pearl is blurry through my teary eyes. I can feel the sadness in the wane smile I force upon my face.

Hers creases like crumpled paper.

"My bruises," I totter back upon my feet, "these bruises will tell their own tale."

The shutters flap open; Pearl gasps.

"You made me..." She wants to speak of it. There is no time.

The voices from above grow louder, the stomping upon the stairs insistent.

"You came in time; it is all that matters." I pull her to me; hold her close. "Now we must act quickly."

With a graceful movement, grace acquired from the dance lessons she herself had given me, I twirl our bodies round, open the door, and push her out.

"Ginevra—!"

I shut the door on her face. I turn to the dead man who had ruined our lives, lives that had been better, truer, and richer, for the existence of the other, and await my fate.

PEARL
1895

If that afternoon was different from the many others that came before, I could not tell.

My father, mother, and I sat in awkward repose in the Conservatory, sipping afternoon tea, waiting for the hour of the coaching parade to approach. I detested coaching almost as much as tea. I sat apart from them by the fountain, apart from them in this room. We were all just pieces even when together, never a whole.

Thin, silk curtains fluttered in the salty breezes off Newport Harbor. The smell beckoned to me, whispering softly to me in the waves of air wafting toward me, that I was still young enough to play in it, to run in it, bathe in it. Those days had passed, or so they said, but not in my mind.

Water trickled brightly from the rouge fountain tiered with cupids, filling the heavy pauses, so many of them. I loved this room, where house fused with garden, but only when alone. I was rarely alone.

My brother, Clarence, was off playing tennis at the Casino or gadding about town with his friends, as he did more and more often of late. He still 'played.' While I, caught in the nowhere between childhood and adulthood, was rarely allowed to go anywhere without my parents. I so longed to go somewhere without my parents. But what would they be without me, the small piece of jetsam floating untethered in gloomy thickness of their marriage?

My mother prattled on and on, savoring her gossip with the same relish as she did her tea.

"Alva refuses to speak of anything but the additions to Marble House, how very grand it will be. She doesn't say it, but we all know. She expects it to be the grandest of all the cottages."

Whenever my mother spoke of Alva Vanderbilt, her voice chirped with admiration, her face twisted as if she'd bitten into a lemon. How she reminded me of the catty girls from school, the girls who made fun of me for my dedication to my studies as if that made me inferior to them in some way. How happier my mother would have been with one of them as her daughter. How often I wished one of them were.

Mother pestered my father, invisible behind his newspaper.

"Orin, we must think of expanding. The Beeches has been at the top of the list for a year. We cannot be usurped." She sat bolt straight, spine never touching the back of the chair, the lace of her day dress unfurled precisely from her small lap, and not a single strand slithered out of place from her upswept crown of red hair.

I slumped lower in my chair, crumpling my skirts in my fists.

"We will do no such thing," my father mumbled from behind his wall of paper. "It is perfect as it is. Do not forget our agreement, Millicent."

Their agreement. How it plagued Mother to have conceded to it. Father had made it plain to her; I remembered it well. Her pleading for a summer 'cottage' in the newly chic island off the New England coast, his own desire for how it should be built rising out of his love for art and architecture. He had put it to her straight, if she wanted a home in Newport, it would be constructed to my father's specifications. He demanded; she surrendered.

I sipped, gazed down in my cup, wondering why my mother could find no joy in this glorious building. Perhaps she had had little say save for the wall coverings and the furniture and such, but it was still one of the most splendid places I had ever seen, and still one of the grandest places I had ever lived. Our tour of Europe two years ago had had a profound effect on my father; and it was here, in every curved banister, coffered ceiling, and marbled column.

"But Orin, dear…"

She called him 'dear.' *Oh, here it comes,* I thought, my eyes rolling to the painted ceiling. It didn't.

With his characteristic throat clearing, Mr. Birch took a single step into the room, denying my mother her cajoling.

"There is a man here, Sir, and a girl." Our butler, as stiff as his shirt, proclaimed as if he announced the delivery of a parcel of manure.

5

"They claim you are expecting them. Costa, I believe she said their name is."

My father jumped up; newspaper scattered with a rustle to the floor. My mother and I balked at his quickness, at the rare glimpse of his smile beneath his bushy mustache.

"Wonderful, Mr. Birch," said he, rushing from the room.

Spilling tea as I quickly dropped my cup in its saucer, I rose and followed.

"Pearl, stay. It is your father's business."

I ignored her. Monotony had become my most constant companion. No matter how inconsequential, I ran toward anything to run away from it.

I stopped at the top of the white marble stairs leading down to the grand doors of our summer home, half hiding behind one set of double breche marble columns crowned with gold capitals. Just inside the small vestibule between the arched wood doors and the inner ones of grill and glass, I could see only their silhouettes against the bright afternoon light, so very small in the massive aperture. I saw Birch had left the outer doors open as if he would shoo the visitors out like pesky insects at the first opportunity.

The man was tall. A short hat and long suit jacket enshrouded him. The girl was no girl, at least not a little one. The slight curves of her body, sheathed in what I could only see as a dark-colored, single-layered dress, were those of a young woman, or a girl on her way to becoming one.

"Welcome, Mr. Costa, Miss. Welcome."

My head popped farther around the marble pillar, not to see the visitors, but my father. To see if this enthusiastic man *was* my father. He rushed toward the man, hand held out, a swath of his black hair, hair he had given me, falling upon his slightly wrinkled forehead. Reaching behind them, my father closed the doors. I could see them more clearly now.

The man looked my father's age, perhaps older, or perhaps simply more aged. It was the face of the girl, an older girl as I had thought, which held me. If not for her deeper complexion, olive I believe such skin was called, we could be sisters, for her eyes were the same nut-brown as mine though more almond-shaped, cheekbones high, mouth full, chin narrowed her face to a point.

Mr. Costa replied with a hesitant good day, but upon his tongue, it came as "gooda day." The distinct addition of a vowel gave them away. Italians. I had never met any real Italians. I studied them as I would a painting I had never seen.

My father pulled the man deeper into our home by the hand still in his, beyond the grilled doors, and into the marble foyer. He straightened his shoulders, gathered himself. Zeal still beamed from him; a bright spark glinting in his dark eyes. His voice dropped to its normal deep timbre, words spaced ever so, with aristocratic nonchalance.

"How was your journey? Fine, I hope."

The man turned to the girl beside him with a particular look I could see she read well.

"Fine, Sir," she replied. Better than the man's, the girl's English was a trifle more fluid.

"Glad to hear it." My father was a man of intelligence and pride; he could see it in others. Though the girl had answered, my father directed his reply to the man. "I hope you will be comfortable here. It is a fine house."

As the girl softly translated my father's words, I smirked. *A fine house, Father, really?*

Would he tell these people the ocean was but a puddle?

To them, our summer home must have seemed a palace, a fantasy functioning as a home, a four-story mansion designed after the chateau d'Asnieres in France, the home of the Marquis de Voyer, sitting on ten acres of land. A 'house' indeed.

"Mr. Birch, please show our new guests to their quarters, if you would." With a gestured hand and a small dip of his head, my father encouraged these 'guests' up the few steps and into the grand gallery spanning the entire length of the house from north to south.

They followed slowly. Their eyes widened at the grandeur, the enormity of our 'cottage,' the thirty-foot-high walls of white Caen stone, the ancient oil paintings, the length of the walls framed by gilt moldings that greeted every entrant. How pretentious such opulence must have looked. Their slight bodies cried out for good meals, not flamboyant affluence. My cheeks burned as I looked at them looking.

"And which would those be, Sir?" Birch sent a blast of cold through the warm room.

"Mr. Costa here is to have the luggage room. I've had Mr. Grayson refurbish it into a living space and a workshop. This is the man who has come to teach Clarence violin and to make us some one-of-kind furniture. Aren't you, Mr. Costa?"

The man nodded, but it was to my father's ebullience. His expression blank, hesitant; he understood little of my father's words.

"He and his lovely daughter will also be staying over in the winter as members of our off-season caretakers." My father turned back to Mr. Costa. "And for that I say *grazie.*"

"T…thank you, Mr. Worthington," the young woman said. "My papa, he is excited, to work."

My father took her hand in both of his.

"Ah, Geenahva, so glad to have you here as well, of course."

She smiled, and it was lovely. "It is Ginevra, Gin-*eh*-v-ruh," she pronounced her name correctly, slowly, for my father's behalf, and perhaps for mine, for I had seen her gaze flash to me with the same curiosity with which I perused her. Gin, like the drink my mother would say; emphasis on eh; rush through the v, to end low with the ruh. I said it over and over in my mind. I would say it correctly when the chance came. I swore to myself the chance would come. I would banish monotony not just from this moment.

"Yes, Ginevra," my father did a passable imitation of her name. "You will be housed with other young ladies such as yourself…" servants, he meant, of course, "…on the top floor. I'm sure we will find something productive for you to do soon."

"Sew," she said without hesitation. I smiled. "I sew."

I saw my father's grin. "Wonderful. There is plenty of sewing to do in this house. Isn't that right, Mr. Birch?"

Birch nodded. It looked as if it hurt him to do so. He held out a hand, pointing toward the right, toward the back stairs, those belonging to the servants.

"*Vieni*, Papa," Ginevra put a hand on her father's arm as she reached down for a battered valise. Mr. Costa nodded silently, picked up the two beside him, having never released a glossy leather violin case from beneath his arm, and followed Birch's lead.

As she brushed past, our eyes met. Did she see it in mine, or I in hers? Regardless, it was a fine beginning.

I feigned a headache to dismiss myself from the coaching parade, illness being the only acceptable excuse. We came to 'summer' in Newport, but our lives were as rigid here as they were in New York.

My head did throb, but with thoughts of the newcomers. I tried to whoosh them away with my reading, but they refused to depart. I lay upon my bed until it was time to get ready for dinner.

* * *

It was a rare evening during summers at Newport where we neither entertained nor were entertained, for doing so was the sole purpose of this small colony of the very rich.

It was only the family for dinner that night, just the four of us at the vast square table for ten. The large room and all its grandeur swallowed us, or so it felt to me at the time, but my mother insisted we dine there, rather than the intimate breakfast room, whether we entertained or not.

I lost myself to the light of the chandeliers and the paintings they illuminated; the ancient figures that hovered over me, over us, ever listening. More than once, I wished they would shower their wisdom down upon us. Their presence was my panacea, or perhaps it was merely the art itself. Like my father, so much of what fed me was art. Fitting that the room where we ate should be so full of it.

I missed many a tiresome conversation in the study of these paintings. Not that evening.

"Really, Clarence, is it so very difficult for you to arrive on time?" My mother chided my brother as he rushed in, still straightening his cravat, no more than two minutes past seven.

Clarence, eighteen and dashing, fulfilled his role as my mother's pet with relish; he scudded a step at her tone, one that did not typically belong to him.

"Darling, Mother, I'm only late because I wanted to look perfect for you." He glided to her chair beside mine with elegance. He had my father's height and my mother's thinness, my father's thick hair, tones of dark and light gold, like Mother's used to be. He leaned over and plucked a kiss upon her cheek.

The magic wand flicked; her earrings, much like the shape of the lights above her, tinkled and glittered, though far truer than she did.

"Don't be silly, dear, you always look lovely," she twittered like a nuzzled bird. It would have been my pleasure to stick a cracker in her mouth.

My brother came around and sat opposite Mother, to my father's left.

"Pop," he greeted my father with the stylish slang becoming so popular among the young men of his set, the young and newly on the marriage market, the athletic and always busy sparks that crowed about Bellevue Avenue like the roosters they were. Father nodded in silence, as was his way. Clarence sat, catching my eye, tossing me a sly wink. His practiced charm, so like the many other young men, had little effect on me. He should have been my hero, as he had been when we were little. I should have looked up to him with worship and adoration. Resentment was far more powerful.

He looked at the opulent façades of our homes and those like it and believed. It was more than the color of our eyes that differed. He and my mother were a matched pair. My father and I, a pair ourselves, but of a different sort.

Clarence pulled in his chair and Birch, having been standing guard at the small door leading to the pantry, gave a nod of his balding head.

The footmen entered the room, silver trays balanced perfectly on perfectly manicured hands. James, the first footman brought the soup, while Charles, the second, brought the wine. Both were amazingly handsome. I always asked for more of whatever James was serving, bringing his dazzling smile and sparkling blue eyes closer to me again and again, though I squirmed in my seat every time he did.

It was a peculiarity, of the life here in Newport, that the footmen were undeniably attractive, not only of face but of physique, for oftentimes they wore livery with breeches and stockings. They must possess, then, a 'well-turned calf' as the silly saying went. And they must be tall, six feet being the minimum height.

It became a social occasion, a real cat's party, when a woman of any house had to hire a new footman. Friends were invited over, drinks were served as handsome young men walked by, displaying their features. The women spoke of them as if they spoke of jewels, of how they glittered, how they were desired. They laughed and giggled as little girls did over their dolls. As was my way then, I hid in a secret hallway to watch and listen. My mother always enjoyed the occasion in a fine mood, enjoyed it a great deal. Admitting my own enjoyment was something I denied, even to myself.

Mother was not in such a mood at this moment. She took one silent sip of her soup, dabbed the sides of her mouth with a starched serviette, and then it started.

"Orin, please explain to me these new servants you've brought into our home. It was never part of our agreement." She put her spoon down with deliberation; she would not pick it up until he answered her to satisfaction. In truth, she had a valid point, the hiring of all the servants—as she called them, my father called them the staff, it was a telling distinction those days—was under the purview of the woman of the house.

My father didn't lower his spoon save for another helping of soup. "I told you all about them, Millicent, when we were in Italy."

"Tell me again. I don't remember."

I thought she did though, from the look on her face. My mother's face always gave her truth away. Did mine? I hardly knew my own truth then, but I knew I wanted no one to see it. I wanted nothing of my mother, that truth was irrefutable.

"Felice is a violin maestro. Not only does he play like...," my father did look up from his soup then, a bit of rapture on his rough features, "...like a virtuoso. He is also a master artisan. He makes violins, violas, as well as magnificent furniture. Don't you remember my promising he would make you furniture none of your friends would have, like nothing they could compare it to?"

He knew how to mine my mother for gold. I hid my smug smile behind my napkin.

My mother picked up her spoon. "Oh, well, yes, that part I do remember. But I thought he would make the furniture in Italy and send it to us."

My father looked like he would throw his spoon. It was a mean notion, but it would have given me quite the chuckle if he had.

"No, that was never discussed. He is primarily here to teach Clarence how to play."

"The violin?" I hadn't heard my brother's voice crack in many years.

"Yes, Clarence. It is a wonderful talent to have." My father spoke to Clarence much as he did my mother, always with a sigh in his words.

"I have no interest in playing the violin," it was my brother's turn to put down his spoon, "or any instrument for that matter."

My mouth fell open, words needing saying hung there. How could Clarence not be thrilled at such an opportunity? How could he be so ungrateful for it?

"I'll do it, Father." I heard the words for the first time myself; they came without thought. I heard too the squeak in my voice; it thrummed through me like the slide of a bow down taut strings. "I'd love to learn to play the violin."

The silence appalled. I would have preferred it stayed that way rather than be assaulted by my mother's response.

She laughed.

"Oh, Pearl, don't be ridiculous," she chuckled with cruel dismissiveness. She dismissed me often unless I served her purpose.

"Why? Why would it be ridiculous?" My hands balled into fists in my lap. The fragrance of the fresh lobster bisque suddenly smelled like rotted mushrooms.

Mother's face twisted tightly; her sneer devoured me. In that moment, I hoped my face did reveal my truth. I hoped I held up a mirror to her. "Such things are for men. Have you ever seen a woman play in the symphony?"

"No, but that doesn't mean there couldn't be."

"Clarence is so busy, after all, Orin." Mother carried on as if I hadn't said a word. It wasn't the first time. "He has his tennis and his sailing, and so many other activities. Isn't that why we bought a membership to the Casino?"

The Casino had been an establishment in Newport for ten years before we arrived. I had heard a little of the silly tale that brought about its creation. James Gordon Bennett, the man who owned the New York Herald and another newspaper in Paris I think, was the man who built it and made its rules. Before the Casino, and even now, most of the Newport men went to the Reading Room, a 'gentlemen's club,' they called it. I'd heard it was a very serious, a very stodgy place. I had walked past it, of course, for it was just down Bellevue Avenue, not far from our home. Past it, never to enter.

The rumor, as it went, claims Mr. Bennett invited one of his friends to the Reading Room. That friend, an Englishman by the name of Captain Candy, a name which sounded quite fake to me, Mr. Bennett had challenged to do something outlandish at the Reading Room, wake things up a bit. Captain Candy complied. He jumped on his horse, rode it up the stairs, and into the hall.

Imagine the outcry, the madness; I imagined the hilarity. The Board of the Reading Room censured Mr. Bennett and retracted Captain Candy's guest privileges. Mr. Bennett's response...the construction of the Newport Casino.

This club was far from stodgy. With much more modern architecture, it took up the entire end block on Bellevue Avenue on the northeast corner of Memorial Boulevard. There were tennis courts and polo courts and lovely porches where, wonder of wonders, women were welcomed to sit and socialize and watch. There were balls and banquets and musicales held there as well; I loved those most of all. Membership was exclusive but no match for my mother's determination or my father's credentials.

"I have no wish to deny Clarence all those past-times, Millicent, but a well-rounded man possesses other talents than the ability to hit a ball well over a net or excel at other sorts of sports." My father gave my brother a look; there was something in it I didn't understand at the time. Clarence blushed. "He should know of music and literature and art. Such things are what make a man a gentleman."

It was quite a lengthy speech for my father, an impassioned one at that, though, in that moment, I could find no joy in it.

"Well then," Mother said between spoonfuls, "as long as he has time for his other pursuits, ones that will bring him into the good graces of our neighbors, I suppose it wouldn't be terrible." She reached across the table to take my brother's hand, quite the stretch at this table. "Perhaps you will be able to serenade our guests sometime soon. That would make quite the impression. Wouldn't it, Orin?"

My mother brokered a deal with the high craftiness of any of the wealthy industrialists who populated our small summer community. My father knew it as surely as I did. He made the deal; he, too, was a master businessman. Clarence was quick to agree but I caught the look that passed between him and my mother; only they knew the code to decipher their message. Yet I knew my brother would still spend more time at the Casino than at any other place. I believe my father saw it as well, as I saw the ends of his bushy mustache hang lower.

I knew then there would be no violin lessons for me. It didn't matter. I knew what I truly wanted. I stopped listening, stopped eating, and remembered.

* * *

I remembered that day as if it was yesterday, not four years ago.

We were in the home of Henry Havemeyer. Miss Mary Cassatt's dearest friend was married to one of his cousins and the occasion was a homecoming of sorts for the woman painter. It was a showing as well, for her astounding works stood on easels propped up around the circumference of the room. I must have walked round at least five times.

My father, so much taller then as I stood by his side, spoke to her. He preferred the work of the grand masters of the Renaissance, but I could tell he was curious about this woman.

"Your style, Miss Cassatt, it is very unique," he'd said to her upon proper introduction.

The round-faced woman's thin lips almost broke into a smile, almost. My lips tried to form the same knowing, slight curve.

"Not so, sir," she said. "Perhaps here in America, yes. Nevertheless, it has been flourishing in France for some time. It is called Impressionism."

My father tilted his head at the unfamiliar term.

"When I traveled to Paris in 1875," Miss Cassatt continued, "the technique was burgeoning. Especially by Degas. I used to go and flatten my nose against an art dealer's window, a window full of Degas' work, and absorb all I could of his technique."

She looked up at my father; simple features no longer simple as they bloomed. "It changed my life. I saw art then as I wanted to see it."

"And your family, Miss Cassatt," my mother had chimed in with what she thought was an important question. "Do they encourage your...work?"

Miss Cassatt's face returned to its stoic self. It broke only for a moment, when her gaze turned down to me; I saw her smile for the first time that day. The smile faded like the moon with the coming of dawn as she returned her attention to my mother.

"I will tell you this, Madam. I enrolled myself in the Pennsylvania Academy of Fine Arts at the age of fifteen." She said no more, but her eyes held my mother's with a fierce grip.

Mother laughed her tinny, fake laugh. "How courageous of you," she said flatly. "Well, we will let you greet the other guests."

My mother had yanked my father away then, me with them, and brought her mouth close to his ear, but not so close I didn't hear her disparaging condemnation, "A new woman."

I didn't know then what she meant, but I learned. I didn't know what a tangled path would lay before me for it, but I, too, wanted to be a new woman. Most of all, I wanted to be an artist. I thought I had the talent, as Miss Cassatt did, but did I have her courage?

GINEVRA

The man called Birch led us through the marble hall. I walked on tiptoes. I walked as I once had through a grand cathedral back in Italy.

He hurried us along. I had only seconds to glimpse a dining room, one so large it could have served as a great hall in a castle from long ago. It glittered; gold sparkled everywhere. Across from it, an alcove, each end flanked by glass and gold cabinets. On display were more treasures of silver and gold, china and porcelain. I slowed; if I could, I would have run.

The man hurried us along.

We passed through two dark, carved doors; we passed into another world. Inside these doors, we entered a small landing.

"This is a ladies' powder room," Mr. Birch finally decided to speak to us. "The Beeches has some of the most modern plumbing in all of Newport." He turned hard eyes on me. "Family and guests only."

I returned his look. Nothing more.

The snobby man spoke with such pride; you would think this enormous place belonged to him. I suppose in a way he thought it did.

Everything about Birch was stiff, his perfectly pressed cut-away, pristine white shirt, large black puff tie with its big, fancy knot bobbing as he spoke, but especially the stiff tone of his voice. Did he speak to everyone with such cold flatness or did such a chill frost only my father and me? Time would tell.

My father nudged my arm and gave me 'the look.' I translated.

Such looks came constantly during our journey to America. I saw more of them than I did the passing ocean.

Mr. Worthington had paid our fare, thirty dollars each... thirty dollars to travel in the bowels of one of the great steamships crossing the ocean faster than the wind. It was a week living in hell.

Not allowed on deck, I had begun to dream of fresh air before the journey ended. They fed us little else but soup or stew, we slept in huddled masses on the floor in our clothes beside our luggage and had only salt water to wash ourselves.

Few of the others understood the sharply delivered instructions of the ship's crew given only in English. I was one of the few.

My role as translator had started then, and though I tried to teach Papa the language through the long empty hours on the ship, he had learned to say only a few words; he understood even less. Instead, he would give me 'the look' and I would translate as best I could.

The ship docked in New York. We rose up from our burial place and saw the sky, breathing deep. The sight of the giant lady and her torch overwhelmed us. We had heard of her, her welcoming. The people who worked at her feet were not so kind. I feared, despised, and pitied them. Their jobs were difficult; they could not show us too much kindness. To them, we were no different from the colored, what Italians called *mulignane.* The nastiness of it became my reality. They stripped away our humanity; we could have been heads of lettuce. Yet they were just doing their work.

They tagged us like cattle, put us in rooms to stand, waiting. We stood in lines for hours, herded through, telling our names over and over.

So many lost their real names. If they couldn't write, those who registered us went by sound alone, mangling many, wrong names these newcomers would carry for the rest of their lives. Worse were the ones they sent back. They had endured for nothing.

Then the inspections...our clothes, our hair, our mouths, our bodies. Endless invasions making us feel less than human. The constant questions, the same again and again. Thorough and hurried at the same time. They hurried us so fast, often I didn't have time to understand myself. They hurried us, as the butler did now, as if they couldn't wait to get us to a place where they could not see us.

Birch pointed to his left.

"This pantry here serves both the breakfast room just behind it and the dining room. A marvelous convenience for the family."

He said mahvelous as if he were one of them.

He opened another door, plain wood and frosted glass. Into another foyer, a simple if bright one of windows and white tile. The floor, the walls, the ceiling, all of small white squares of tile. Then to the staircase.

It rose and fell away from us. I looked up and down; I could see the white grillwork and polished wood banister spiral away in perfect symmetry. I stood in the middle, moving neither up nor down. It was a landing named nowhere.

"This is the servants' staircase. It is the only staircase you shall ever use."

Birch stopped and turned to us. "Ever."

My father needed no translation to understand.

"They may use it from time to time." He said "they" as if the word referred to a king or a queen. "But rarely. Downstairs, if you please," he instructed.

I had known we traveled to a rich man's house, but I never imagined a place like this. I became aware of our ragged appearance, clothes old and worn before the hard journey, now so very much worse, our ragged suitcases holding only more ragged clothes. The coarse wool scratched me for the first time in my life. My foot shrunk away from the top step; I could not see where they led.

Before he closed the door to the marble hallway—though I didn't know then it must never be called a hallway—I looked back.

The girl still stood at her place by the pillars; she could have been a sculpture at its feet. Her clothing was so fine. Her dress was short, hem falling between knees and ankles; it puffed all around her from something that lay underneath. It seemed to hover about her, fabric as fine as angel's wings.

Something nameless, a creature I had never met, was born in me that was to live within, eating away, for many years.

She stared at us still, but it wasn't a mean stare. Curious, yes, and something else, I thought. Perhaps that something else was just my own hope.

"Wait right here." Birch instructed me, pointing to a distinct spot at the bottom of the stairs in a large foyer of the same white tile.

"Right...here." He pointed again. I did not know which I was more compelled to do, curtsey to him or slap him.

He took my father by the arm and led him through another frosted door and then another, their footsteps growing ever fainter, their silhouettes fuzzy as if they walked out of this world to another. With each step they took, the churning in my gullet twisted tighter. I found myself standing alone amid people in constant motion. My feet once more pestered me to run.

Most were women, some middle-aged, most young. Their features as alike as their uniforms: fair-haired, light-skinned, blonde or soft brown hair, most with blue eyes like pieces of glass with pointed edges. I stared too.

All wore black blouses buttoned to the top, sleeves puffed at the shoulders, and full black skirts. All wore crisp white aprons; some aprons covered their whole body, others only their skirts. Atop their pinned hair, some white caps covered whole heads, while others wore dainty lace headdresses. The differences were small. I thought them particular to a precise position in the household. I did not know which was which. They were as strange to me as this new country—new world—I found myself in.

They hurried past, carrying all sorts of items: dishes, linens, mixing bowls. To the one, all stumbled a step at the sight of me. I shivered beneath cold glares. Eyes racked me from top to bottom. They were uniform in their quick dismissal.

A few men passed me. Like the women, their clothes told of their positions. Two men, one young and one old, wore dark suits, full jackets, and pants, while three others, all young and handsome, wore waistcoats and fancy shirts and ties like Birch. One of these men, really a boy not much older than me, winked as he walked past. I pursed my lips as I tilted my nose up and away from him.

Two others stood out, incomparable to the rest, as was Mr. Birch.

I glimpsed the man through a wide archway into a kitchen as large as a cavern filled with a huge wood table topped with copper, cast iron ovens all in a row, and everywhere copper pots and pans, and strange devices I had never seen. He stood, vibrant, in all white, a double-breasted white jacket, a white kerchief tied about his neck, and the strangest hat I'd ever seen; it had no brim, just a band of white circled about his head. The rest rose high, a pleated puff of fabric, like a crown. This man issued orders; he did not yell but spoke strong and firm. His accent was strange to my ears. It wasn't Italian but there was something similar about it. Those he spoke to jumped, with a quick, "Yes, Monsieur le Chef." Their response explained his speech.

"And who might you be?" She stood before me, hands curled fists on near non-existent hips. She wore all black as well, yet no apron. Her blouse boasted sharply pressed pleats, her skirt was fuller; both had a shine to the fabric, clearly finer than those of the other women. From her waistband hung a circle of keys, a huge ring of them, more than I had ever seen.

She spoke as Mr. Birch did, with such emphasis on the 't's' and the long 'o' sound. English.

While northern Italians disliked southern Italians, no one disliked Italians as much as the English and the Irish. Hope, what there was of it, fluttered out the window as quickly as a trapped bird once released.

This was my introduction to Mrs. Briggs, the housekeeper. She was as thin as a fire poker and just as hotly sharp. I learned quickly that she ruled this roost as well and as cruelly as any general ruled an army.

"Well don't just stand there, girl, ansah me?"

Squinty black eyes bore into me; lips pinched into a tight line.

"I'm-a...," My clipped nails dug into my palms, my legs beneath my tattered skirts quivered. "I am..." I rushed to correct my mistake. Too late.

"You ah an I-talian," she announced, face twisting with her displeasure. "Why are you in this house?"

I opened my mouth, nothing. Yet salvation came.

"Not to worry, Mrs. Briggs," Birch called out to us from the doorway, striding fast, my father no longer with him. My relief had a sharp bite of worry to it.

"A word, if you will, Mrs." He called her Mrs. though she wore no wedding ring. Mr. Birch motioned his large head to a room just off the hall to my right. He unlocked the door and they rushed inside; I had only a glimpse of what looked like a nice, simple sitting room, the kind I grew up playing in back home. The twang of loss and longing struck me as the clock does midnight; it stung my eyes with tears.

At first, I heard nothing, then murmurs that grew to voices raised, none too pleased. Then, finally, unhappy acceptance.

They rushed out as fast as they rushed in. They stood before me. The woman's face was far more curdled than it had been when she went in.

"So, you ah to be a new seamstress," Mrs. Briggs didn't say my name. I'm sure she knew it by then, knew all about me. "You had better be good, for the mistress and our young lady wear only the finest."

"Good, *si*, I am." The words flew from my lips. Too fast. Nerves flapped my mouth faster than my mind could stop them.

"Yes, well, we shall see about that." Mrs. Briggs turned to Mr. Birch. "I'll show the girl to her room then."

"Thank you, Mrs. Briggs." Mr. Birch blustered air, shoulders dropping.

"Up with you," the sharp-boned woman waved a hand at the stairs.

I hesitated. I wanted my father, wanted to know where he was. If I took a single step away, it would be a step away from him.

Mrs. Briggs's bony fingers pinched my shoulders, clamping, she turned me and nudged upward. There was no heaven waiting for me there.

When Papa and I had first stood outside this mansion they called a 'cottage,' we stood shivering from cold fear. Scrolled columns and statues surrounded us, beside us, above us. They threatened, guarding even though they were stone. It looked like the *palazzos* of the wealthy *signori* built on the mountainsides of Italy. From our home, we could see them hovering on the horizon like clouds. Like clouds, always out of our reach.

My father's shoulders had turned, turned back toward the path on which we approached. If minds had hands, mine would have pushed him there. He faced the door once more. I held my silence. As we looked at what would be our future home—no, that wasn't right. It would never be our home, but the place we lived; my true home would ever haunt me, becoming grander as each spectral memory invaded my mind. As we looked at it, we thought it was a two-storied building. It was not.

The basement, from where Mrs. Briggs and I started to climb, hid from the outside, and there was another subbasement below the first, she told me so, as if this *were* her home, though I hoped never to see it, just as I hadn't seen it from the outside. Yes, the floors where the most work took place lay beneath the ground's surface.

As we continued upward, Mrs. Briggs took it upon herself to inform me of all the servants in the house. I couldn't keep up with such a list.

I stopped listening and started counting; there were more than forty people here to serve four. If she meant to overwhelm me, she succeeded. If she meant to make me feel like nothing, she succeeded there too.

I grew dizzy, nauseous, as she rattled on as to who did what, or more importantly, what some didn't do.

"Mr. Birch, Chef Pasquel, and I rule this roost. Howeva, the personal maids and valets are far superior to the footmen, the stable boys, or the upstairs maids. Mr. Birch does not serve dinner or empty ashtrays, nor is he expected to answer the door. The mistress's maid does not clean her room, does not even make the bed."

She babbled, layering rule upon rule like frosting on a cake. Too many to remember; too confusing not to break. It would only be a matter of time. Did all of America live by such rules?

As we climbed, I found yet another surprise, another hidden floor. Here were the servants' quarters. From the outside, this floor looked like a row of carved vertical indents held up by carved brackets, all of the same peach-colored stone, a parapet not to keep marauders out, but the servants hidden.

As we hurtled the last step, I stopped mid-stride. I found myself not in a dungeon as I expected, led there by the fiery dragon that was Mrs.

Briggs, but in a simple dormitory of rooms. I didn't know then that the constant juggling and fighting for good servants were part of the life of the rich, 'the servant problem,' I would later hear it called. Mr. Worthington had built a nice servants' floor, hoping to keep his staff pleased and in his employ.

A wide hallway with polished wood floors stretched the length of the house. In two places, my head dropped, eyes widening at the large rectangles of glass squares etched with stars. I saw the light of the sun and my gaze flew upward. Above them, windows in the roof matched their size and shape. Sunlight flowed through the very floors and ceilings as if the owner could command the sun above him as well and as easily as he did all the people beneath him.

On each side of the hall, numbered doors led us on.

Mrs. Briggs brought me into the one that would be my room.

"All the single rooms are occupied," she informed me. "You shall have to share." Were a single room available it would not be mine to have. I knew which rung on the ladder I stood; I had not yet stepped off the ground. Whenever she looked at me, her eyes started at my face, but always moved downward, always darkened with distaste.

The room was far larger than I expected. Two beds hugged the walls, each with a large white steel headrail, a smaller one at the foot. There were two closets, two chests of drawers, two chairs, and a large dressing table that sat before the window between the beds. It was far more than I had ever had at home; it did not make me miss home any less. Home was not a place or things.

The windows were a surprise, the secret of this floor revealed. Through the mullioned panes, I spied a small roof, level with the bottom of the window, a roof of small rectangles of stone. Just beyond, a grey high-shingled wall, the wall that on the outside appeared as carved stone, the wall hiding us away. At least the windows let in the natural light, but it came from nowhere. I could not see the sun or it me.

"You shall be sharin' this room with Greta," she told me, accidentally dropping her 'g,' not so superior in truth after all. "You shan't see her much. A kitchen maid works the longest hours."

She turned her back to me, yet I heard her mumble, "And that's what you should be."

I pretended not to hear, though I did it badly. I would become a master at it soon enough.

Greta's side of the room was bright and alive. A merrily squared quilt covered her bed, pictures hung from the wood rail circling the room painted pale yellow, a lovely, embroidered pillow sat on the chair. The other side looked barren and empty; my side.

"Put your things away." She pointed to the chest and the closet. "I'll be right back with bedding and something decent for you to wear." She looked offended as her gaze scratch over me.

She left me there. I sat on my bed, wondering if I would ever breathe again.

My father had promised me this would be a better life for us, as he had promised my aunts it would be. He had filled my head with the wonder that was life in America. I did not know them then as the fairy tales they were. This room was to be "my home" for the rest of my days. My skill with a needle put to use keeping the fancy clothes of the very rich in perfect condition.

I heaved a gulp of air.

In Italy, I would not have such a fine house. I would have married a simple boy from our simple town, and we would have lived in a simple house. But it would have belonged to us, to me. I would have made clothing for my husband and myself and, if blessed, our children. The clothes would have belonged to us. I would have earned a few *lira* sewing for others in the village, money for my family.

Here nothing would belong to me. I would take no pride in my work, for the people who wore the clothes would never notice it. I would make a little money, but with no family to share it.

I could no longer call my life my own.

* * *

When I finally saw my father again, he was sitting at the far end of the long table in the servants' dining room just off the kitchen, another small and cramped rectangle. He sat alone. There were at least three empty chairs on either side of him; the other servants bunched themselves together at the other end like grapes.

There was another table, a small round one, in the back, right corner. At that table sat Mr. Birch, Mrs. Briggs, the chef, and another man whose face I hadn't seen yet. No one need tell me why. One day I would learn they—the rulers of the ruled—were called the "Swell Set;" I would have another name for them. The real "servants" belonged at the long table. There were ranks within the ranks; I was in a maze with no clue of which path to take.

I rushed to my father, but his guarded look buffeted me. I slowed, sat beside him. In hushed Italian, we told each other of our day. He had fared better than I had. He had his own small room to sleep in and work in, a space of his own, filled with the incredible tools and wood Mr. Worthington had waiting for my father and his talented hands.

As he told me of it all, his eyes gleamed; he rubbed his hands together in anticipation. I hated Papa for a sharp moment—a sharply jealous moment—hated he should be so pleased.

Yet I couldn't break him of it; I hadn't seen him happy since before Mama grew ill. What sort of daughter would I be to deny him this? One that would surely and sharply have displeased my mother.

I told him of my room and that I would share it with another girl. Though I hadn't met her yet, I was sure she sat somewhere along this table. When I told my father of the sewing room Mrs. Briggs had shown me, my enthusiasm—what there was of it—was true, a truth I found easy to exaggerate; a small gift to him. The equipment was the best I had ever seen, some I had never seen. My fingers, so skilled with a needle, guided and trained by my mother when I was a young child, longed to begin work, which I would in the morning.

I watched my father's eyes as they took all of me in them.

"Your clothes, they are fine," he said in Italian.

My uniform would be the same as most of the other women: a simple black, puffed sleeved blouse, a simple black full skirt, both of cheap cotton. I would wear no apron or cap of any kind. My short-heeled, ankle boots were my own. Though their cracks and worn spots had insulted Mrs. Briggs, there were no others in the house to fit me.

"Shine them up," she had ordered me, telling me where the shoeshine room was. "I'll get you new ones when I have the time."

Who knew when that would be? I had rubbed my boots for a half-hour with some linseed oil and a rag.

"Yes," I responded flatly, hearing my own indifference, "fine."

His thin lips drooped at the corners until he opened them. Before he could say more, the staff room maid began her parade into the room. In and out, in and out she came, with dish after dish, simple fare of chicken and potatoes and peas. It was the best meal my father and I had eaten since we left Italy.

We sat among the rest of the house staff, as we would at every meal, among them but not with them. They were all there, all the inside servants Mrs. Briggs had named, yet I had no idea who was who. I knew my father hated to reveal his thick accent in the few words of English he could speak. Though one of the most talented and creative people I had ever known, he would not let his speech reveal a false truth. How strange it was for a man with such a great mind, and me, who possessed one as well, to be thought of as simple, simply because we spoke with an accent. Accents sit upon the lips, not in minds, but small minds could not know the difference.

For his sake, I followed his lead, eating without a word. Though I did not speak, I did more than my fair share of listening. I convinced myself it was to learn the language better, a feeble disguise. I fed upon their gossip as I did the meal. My naughty eavesdropping would make my yenta aunts proud. The thought almost made me giggle.

"The mistress has instructed me to find out what the Astor woman has ordered for her fall gowns." I heard Mrs. Briggs say to Mr. Birch. With a quick glance, I saw she ate her fill, more than I would have imagined from the look of her. Perhaps her meanness devoured the food long before her body.

"You cannot wear that dress at yer wedding, Edna!" The outcry came from a parlor or chambermaid. I knew them by then as those who wore the dainty lace on their heads.

"What?" The sweet-looking girl beside her, Edna no doubt, grew paler, though I didn't think it possible. She looked to one of the footmen closer to my end of the table. He shrugged his shoulders, a groom-to-be unaffected by such nonsense. The bride turned back to the woman. "Why ever not, Beatrice? You know I cannot buy my own."

"It is bad luck, thas what it is," the outraged girl, Beatrice, hissed.

"But dear Mrs. O'Brennan has made such a kind offer."

"Indeed, I have," chimed in one of the older women, by her all-white clothing, the assistant chef.

A gasp came from the other table. Mrs. Briggs grew ever-sharper dripping in overly dramatic horror. "You cannot do it, Edna. It will be the death of you."

With her sharp tongue, she told a tale of her niece, one who was to wed on the very day some man shot the president named Lincoln. The ceremony canceled; the bride gave her dress and veil away. The woman who wore it to her wedding died within a week.

Old world suspicious came into the room, beside it fear in a range of tones bouncing off the hard stone like church bells. Their voices told me another tale as well.

We were in a company of mostly English, Irish, and a few Germans. They came from countries where service had been an accepted form of occupation for hundreds of years, where accepting one's rank was a natural order of life. There was not another Italian among them, nor a single American.

I whispered softly to my father who listened with no expression. I'm not sure if it was the story or his shame that he could not understand which kept him so stone-like.

"Ya'd best believe it," this from another woman.

"I knew you'd agree with me, Nettie," Mrs. Briggs garbled, her mouth full. They said Italians had no manners.

Nettie sat tall in her chair. Her uniform was much finer than those of the other women, even that of Mrs. Briggs. Her silk black blouse was edged in white lace and cut with fine tailoring. Her black skirt wasn't nearly so full and yet, when she moved, I thought I heard the swish of a petticoat or whatever these women wore as fine undergarments. Her hair was done up smartly and her hands were clean and without callouses. A ladies' maid; *the* lady's maid.

"Doon' ya know the story of Mrs. Belmont's wedding dress?" she asked the table at large, her voice thick with Ireland. When all at the table shook their heads, she almost seemed to smile as she began to tell.

"Well, Mrs. Belmont had ordered her dress from Worth's, of course."

I did not know who Worth was, so I did not understand her "of course." I felt pulled into her tale no matter. I felt I should know more about who this Worth was.

"She ordered it late though and feared it wouldn't arrive in time. So," Nettie waved a hand, "she had another made in New York. Which she ended up wearin'. When the exquisite Worth dress arrived, she gave it to a friend, I forget which, who had just announced her engagement."

She paused, whether for effect or breath I couldn't tell.

"And...?" one of the footmen prodded her. The men too were well into the story, but they had no patience for her dramatics.

"And the woman accepted it. Within a few days, the engagement was broken."

"No!" Edna gasped. She thought twice now about accepting Mrs. O'Brennan's offering, the wariness ran all over her face. I looked upon her heartbreak with sad eyes.

"Oh, but it doesn't end there," Nettie enjoyed herself now. "That poor broken-hearted woman gave the same dress to another friend. Hers was a sad, unhappy marriage."

"So are a lot of marriages," a man whose name I didn't know muttered with a nasty grin.

"Doon' be smart with me, Silas," Nettie scolded. "For that is not the worst of her story. Not only was she unhappy, but she died. In childbirth. Within a year."

Nettie sat back in her chair, her pleasure at shocking the room as evident as the shine on her skin.

The room filled with noise once more, allowing me to translate to my father without much notice. They chattered like the *gazza*, the, how you say, magpies, that filled the cypress trees back home, their never-ending chirping a constant sound, a wonderful sound there. Was this the entertainment in these servants' lives? As if there was so little true living in them, they filled the holes with the lives of others.

"Do you believe in such silliness?" I asked my father at the end of the tale.

He turned a gloomy gaze on me. Nodding, in his low voice he told me, "I have heard such tales before. Never doubt, Daughter, either bad luck or good."

He called me daughter, as he always did—my name rarely touched his lips—but it was few occasions when I heard him speak so seriously, gave me advice of any sort.

Mr. Birch stood and everyone at the table followed. My father and I hurried to do the same. "Ten minutes, ladies and gentlemen."

It was a call to order. I would quickly come to learn the privileged lived an odd sort of free, even when it came to their hunger. Staff ate dinner at six, the family at seven. If there was a dinner party, service was precisely at eight.

My father patted me on my shoulder as he left, returning to the workshop he already loved. A pat here and there was all I received, no matter my need for more. I knew it should be enough, knew it was the best he could give, but it was sparse to the many hugs and kisses my mother had gifted me with during our years together. How I longed for them now. I shivered in my skin.

I stood at my place as others rushed into action. I had no idea what the second seamstress did during the family's dinner.

"Back to the sewing room with you," Mrs. Briggs was quick to educate me, even as she walked away, Nettie at her side. "And wash your hands and face. The mistress or the young lady may come to you if they spill on themselves. I surely hope you know how to treat stains."

I nodded, though I didn't. The other seamstress was also a laundress. I had washed my fair share and more of coarse wools, but never of silks or satins.

Mrs. Briggs grunted at me and turned to her company. She leaned down, closer to Nettie's ear, whispering. Not quietly enough.

"How many nights has it been?"

I heard. I listened, taking my time to leave the room.

Nettie rolled blue eyes. "Every night since we arrived. He in his bed, she in hers, every night."

Mrs. Briggs clucked her tongue. "It's not good."

"It's worse," Nettie hissed. "They bicker, collie shangles for hours, almost every day."

I had no idea what *collie shangles* were, but they did not sound a good thing.

A pucker-faced Mrs. Briggs shook her head in small, tight snaps. "A man of his prestige should not be with such a vulgarian. She has no idea how to behave." Her hands tossed her frustration in the air. "She has no idea how to run this house."

"All the better for me." Nettie snickered.

"They *have* to work it out," Mrs. Briggs sounded fierce. "If they split, who knows where we would end up?"

I left them then, hurrying by. The words made me sad. What a pity to hear Mr. Worthington suffered a bad marriage. A part of me, the part longing for home, felt a small spark of hope. I saw a way back. I couldn't have been more wrong.

* * *

I saw nothing of my roommate that night—I was already asleep by the time she came into our room, exhaustion overpowered the fearfully unfamiliar, the roiling of thoughts and emotions—and she was gone before I woke up. Just as well, for I would not have wanted her to see the sweat of my dreams—running after my mother but never catching her, trapped in the bowels of the ship as it sunk, locked in a room with no latch.

I got up and lit the lamp by my bed. My room on the back of the house, the west side, was as dark as it had been when I went to bed. Little light found us here in the service tower. Even with the window shutters open, the barricaded wall deprived us of the sun's cheery light until it traversed its path over the top of the mansion.

Or did I see only gloom? Like a silly little girl, I thought I would wake once more in my bed, where the sun streamed in as it crested the rolling hills along with the smells of the waking earth, rich and thick, full of life.

I left my room for my turn in the bathroom; there were three in all for the servants.

I stumbled down the hall as I passed one of the male servants, his body clad only in his robe. My eyes sought the floor as fast as I could force them, though they fought me. Heat burned upon my cheeks. I had never even seen my father in such a state of undress. I did not expect to find the men and women's rooms so intermingled as they were here. I didn't realize what it meant. How could I? My world, the one I still longed for, was a well-guarded one, especially for young women.

Mr. Birch roomed at one end and Mrs. Briggs at the other, in large rooms they shared with no one. I hoped any sort of misbehavior, despite such moments as these, might be difficult to do. Difficult, but not impossible. A person may be young and inexperienced, but it doesn't make them a fool.

I scurried along and gratefully shut myself in the bathroom. One large, well-equipped, and always spotlessly clean bathroom. I dropped myself against the closed door finding my breath, eased by the soft pale pink of this women's bathroom at the north end of the hall. It washed my discomfort away as I washed.

Mrs. Briggs had been strict in her instructions for the use of this room.

"We are allowed to use the facilities only when it is our scheduled time." She said the word oddly, sheeduuled. "Get your business done quickly and get out. Most importantly, you must always, always clean up after yourself. Dry the tub, the sink, and the soap."

Drying soap was by far one of the silliest things I had ever done. I saw my head shake in the glass above the sink; my lips formed a smirk.

I dressed and sat on my bed, a lifeless statue chiseled by fear and uncertainty. Shadows of loneliness surrounded me. I was untethered, adrift in a house—a world—I knew nothing of. Tears tickled the back of my throat, but I swallowed them away. I stared at the wall, seeing the rolling hills of home in the streaks of paint. The sight did not cheer. My leg bounced; my hands wrung. I needed to do something.

When the bell rang in the hall, I jumped up, opened my door, and poked my head out, eyes wide and searching.

"Come along with ya'." Beatrice fluttered a hand at me. "Thas the bell for breakfast."

I followed her; relieved someone had spoken to me, relieved to learn something of the ways of the house. There were three bells to tell us what to do. A cowbell to start the day, a jingle bell for meals, and a tea bell alerting us if a family member needed service. Shrill and jarring, one would jump whether they needed to or not. The bells sat atop a box, a strange contraption with squares and flags.

If the silence and stillness of my room was a crypt, below stairs was a storm of frantic life. So many of the servants went about their work, lighting fires, as they would through the day, though a glimpse through the many windows on the narrow staircase showed the sky hinted at coming sunshine through the fog, promising some warmth. Summer mornings by the sea were a different kind of daybreak.

Farther below stairs, I heard metal tinkering, gruff male voices barking brashly.

The kitchen was as busy as a hive. Chef Pasquel gave precise instructions to the crowd of scullery maids helping him prepare breakfast for the families and the servants.

We had fifteen minutes to eat a bowl of porridge, some tea—a strange pale drink in comparison to the espresso I used to start my days with—and some bread and butter.

"To your sewing room, girl."

I jumped, turned. She stood behind me. I hadn't heard her come near me, not a step. I'd barely had a few bites.

"Yes, Ma'am," I stood, gave my silent father a silent nod, and rushed off.

I climbed two flights of stairs back to the sewing room, entered with a surprising rush of pleasure... it was empty, save for its magic tools... and me. This room seemed to hold me within it, the me I knew. In there, I looked at it as mine. My ownership was short-lived.

The large woman rushed in, the bunch of clothes in her arms almost as big as she.

"You can sew, can ya'?" she asked, a lovely greeting.

"I can," I said, giving back the gruff I got.

"Well, there's plenty, so get on about it."

On the table against the wall, she plucked down the pile she carried with a sigh of relief.

"There's some simple work here," she hurried on as she separated the clothes, throwing them in smaller piles here and there. "Some buttons missing, some socks need darnin'. But..." here she stopped her busy hands and turned to me, her round, pale face was flushed with pink, wiry red strands poked out of her faded blue cap "... one of the mistress's dresses has lost some beads and must be replaced." She pointed a chubby finger at me. "This work requires great care. She will see, oh you can bet she will, if it's not done right. Believe you me."

Her plump face puckered; it looked as if she tasted a bad memory. I quaked, never stopping to think why they entrusted me with this task.

"You'll find buttons and beads in that cupboard there." She pointed at a tall piece of furniture set in the back corner; there were at least thirty small drawers in this large oak piece. "They must be perfect."

"Yes, Ma'am," I said, again, feeling sure they would be words I would say often.

With a clipped nod, chins appeared in the plump flesh of her neck. She spun on her heel and made for the door, a busy woman.

"*Scusi.*" I could have bit my tongue. "Excuse me, please. Who you are?"

I knew that wasn't right either, but it was too late.

"I'm Mrs. Brown, head laundress and seamstress," she said, chest rising, a quirk of a smile. "Well, I guess I'm simply the head laundress now."

She looked over her shoulder into the hall and skipped back to me faster than I thought a woman of her size could move. "And between you, me, and the wall, I'm mad as hops that you're here."

My lips opened and closed; a fish caught in a hook. Her words confused me. They were not the first, would not be the last, to make me feel like the foreigner everyone saw me as. The wall could hear us? No, that couldn't be right. "Mad as hops" frightened me. Was she angry with me? I hadn't done anything yet. She looked anything but angry. She read me well.

Mrs. Brown pinched my cheek. "I'm glad you're here, gel, the work was too much for me." She smiled then. I had never seen a smile belong on a face so well. "Mind me, do good work or I'll hear about it."

At the door, she flung her last words over her shoulder, "When you're done with the Mrs.'s dress, just lay it on her bed."

With that, she was gone. I was on my own. This tiny room with a window facing the small front garden was mine, all mine. I volleyed between fear and excitement.

I set to work. The buttons, the darning, went fast and smooth. I saved the dress for last, a treat for myself, wanting my fingers limbered up before I tackled it. I put it on the curved, dress form. It was wonderful, perhaps the finest dress I had ever seen; never had I worked on such a garment. It was nothing like the simple, rough-clothed dresses I had learned to make by my mother's side. It was a frock like those that filled my daydreams; the fantasies where I designed and made such dresses. For more moments than I should, I simply stared at it, walking round it to see all its glory. I circled it as I would a great piece of art.

It was all silk, lace, beads, and pearls. It hugged the form tightly through the bodice and the upper legs, then flared wide and long, draping the floor. The puffed sleeves, much larger versions of those I wore, were sheer and had the trickiest design of beads, a floral pattern on the largest part, the stem and leaves flowing down to long cuffs buttoned with more pearls. It was there, in the long curling stem, that I found the open spaces, the beads' missing places.

It took me ages to find the right beads to match, even longer to sew them in perfectly. My pace slowed by my eagerness to do the work perfectly. The sun rose above the tree line, had started to make its way to my window, and the room grew brighter and brighter as I worked. I was as thankful for the window and its glimpse of sky and trees as I was for the work my hands did. The noises in my mind silenced by purpose and gratitude.

I finished and stood back, pleased. Not the slightest stitch revealed where the new joined with the old. I wanted to carry the dress through the house. I longed to show Mrs. Briggs and everyone who doubted me—which was probably everyone—that I was true to my word. I could sew, and very well. I wanted to scream at them. Though I spoke with a heavy accent, spoke slowly, my mind was quick and sure, as were my hands. I had been the smartest girl in school, the most talented sewer too. I longed to be that girl again, known as that girl here. Vanity and pride are not virtues, but they were mine in that moment. I claimed them reluctantly. If no one here would know me, at least I would, the all of me, good and bad.

I knew I couldn't parade the dress, parade my prideful self through the house. I knew I had to return the dress to Mrs. Worthington's room and nothing more.

I took the dress off the form slowly, draped it delicately across my forearms, and poked my head out the door. I saw no one and entered the small foyer outside the room and through another door into the hall. Through all the sewing, my hands were still and sure. Now they shook. My pride and vanity and the sureness they gave me betrayed me and stayed behind. I was once more the lost, uncertain girl. I had no idea which room belonged to the woman of the house.

The doors across from me stood closed, but I didn't think Mrs. Worthington's room would be so close to the sewing room, or the servant's stairs beside it. Along the wide hallway, of the same cream marble as on the floor below, across the wide foyer at the top of the double staircases, those the family used, I saw doors opened at that end.

I tiptoed to them, past tapestries larger than I had ever seen, older still. I smelled my own sweat along with the fresh flowers blooming on every table in every room I passed. I peeked in the first door. It opened to a narrow hall, long and dark and secret, and then two more doors. Both stood open. The first room was rich and dark, deep maroon silk covered the bed, the walls, the curtains. A man's jacket hung on some sort of contraption in the corner. Mr. Worthington's room, I thought, or the son's.

I saw a bathing room at the end of the hall, the door to its foyer and the door to the inner room both open. Inside was a bathing room like none I had ever seen. My unworldliness slapped me good and hard; knowing there were those who lived better lives was one thing, seeing it another. Within its square dimensions lay a deep tub, pure white tile, a marble sink painted with a garland and topped with a faucet of gold, and the strangest toilet, hidden by a cane-covered box. Another basin stood next to the toilet, something shaped like a miniature tub, though I had no idea what it was. The dressing table held every sort of grooming device, delicate ones—combs, brushes, mirrors, and more—all made of tortoiseshell. My mother had a tortoise comb; it was all she had. It was now mine. I held it often but never used it.

I couldn't go in, couldn't keep staring, though I wanted to. Such a bathroom belonged to a woman.

The door closest to it stood opened too. I stepped in and knew at once it was Mrs. Worthington's room. Never had I seen such a place. Rich, thick, light green silk was everywhere, delicate furniture, scrolled and gilded, and lace, lots of lace.

I could have stood there forever staring into this room, this world, unlike anything I had ever imagined. Delight and envy tangled with anger, a knot of rough yarn. How could so few have so much when so many had so little? I criticized it even as I longed for it.

The voices stopped me.

They echoed up the stone stairs, bounced against marble walls, coming closer.

I laid the dress carefully on the bed, as instructed, and rushed out.

I slipped to a stop. The voices were upon me. I heard footsteps now too.

I ducked out a side door by the main door. I found myself in a tiny hallway leading to another tiny hallway. I turned 'round and 'round, not knowing which of the three doors would lead to the best hiding place. The voices grew closer. I spun like a top, the string one of dizzying confusion.

I found a narrow corner, a cubby of space. I jammed myself in, back to the wall, and slipped down. I huddled in a ball as the voices grew louder and closer. I stayed there even as they grew softer and farther away again. Lost became redefined in so many ways. I couldn't stop the tears then.

PEARL

I was up early, eager for the day. Barefoot and in my nightdress, large windows in my large room thrown open for the warm, salty breeze to greet me. I stood before my easel, as I did most days. I know now that I did not see the glory of it all, all which was mine. I never questioned its beauty or my possession of it, not as I should have.

My gaze drifted out those large windows, my mind followed, across the vast lawn of rolling slopes that led to the grove of feathered trees. My trees. I closed my eyes then, opening my artistic vision. With it, I saw a small child, a girl, barefoot and giggling, ringlets bouncing and flying behind her, pudgy hands flapping with the freedom.

I opened my eyes, turned back to the self-portrait—that portrait—before me on the canvas.

Mother had grudgingly allowed me the "hobby," an appropriate one for a young lady of means. "Appropriate" from her meant acceptable to society, her most critical gauge. Little did she know I had no intention for it to be a hobby. Not since that day. Not since I had met Mary Cassatt. Was there a part of me that set my course simply because it would upset my mother? I would not be the first daughter to rebel in such a manner. I only knew the burning passion compelled me to it—my art. Denying it would be to deny myself.

As I brushed on broad strokes of vibrant colors, pigments pure and unmixed, I remembered Mary Cassatt's indomitable expression in the face of my mother's barely concealed disapproval. I strove for more than her talent.

I put my brush down, pleased with the morning's work. Perhaps the memories had helped. I turned my attention then to my next project.

I hoped I might catch a glimpse of the new arrivals to our home.

They were so unique to my world. Filled with such people, people who lived to serve us, Mr. Costa and his daughter were the only Italian people I had ever seen in one of my homes. That sounded dreadfully snobbish, I know that now, but there it was, the truth of my life. Though Mother and her friends, indeed all of the powerful women who ruled domestic life, complained about the lack of good servants—the opening of factories and shops had found many of those who thought servant life worthy before, now found it was no longer worthy enough—few looked to Italy and other countries to fill the void. Did they carry some disease? I thought that unlikely. Did they smell? I giggled. I thought that simply foolish.

Their novelty intrigued me. Ginevra with her sharp eyes and her quick tongue, particularly so. There was more to her, I had seen it in the fleeting few minutes I had to study her. I wanted to learn more. I suppose it was not well done of me, to think of her as an object of curiosity and not as a person. How often we strive to break the shackles of breeding. How very difficult it could be.

It would be a feat to spend time with her as I had few interactions with the staff, but I would try my best. It would be a little easier as I walked through my life so unnoticed. My father had his work; like the other men of this summer colony, he would often be here only on the weekends, perhaps coming back on a Thursday rather than Friday. My brother had so many activities, I rarely saw him. My mother had her events, tons of them throughout the day, all of which she would change her clothes for. Mother rarely sought me out save for the times she longed to look like a doting mother or when, even at my age, she aimed to put me in front of the eye of eligible men.

"It's never too soon to make an impression," she said to me so often it was like a prayer.

We were an incestuous bunch of a sort; it was rare for anyone of the "set" to marry outside it. We played together, bowed to each other as we took dance lessons together. It seemed only natural to find a mate with those we spent the most time. Yet, if one should become a widow or a widower, it was often that the surviving partner married the deceased partner's dearest friend. It was like the quadrille, the most popular dance of the time; they changed partners in life with the same ease and frequency that they did in the dance. My nose crinkled at such couples. I turned from them and such couplings that made me long for a bath.

I knew most of the morning would be mine, especially if Mother chose not to go to the Casino. As the fog still hung thick around the house, clinging to the trees, shrouding the statues all over the grounds, the typical morning spent seeing and being seen would not be in the offing today. For the first time, I was quite glad for it. All the better for my hunting about.

I would not wear his distinctive hat or carry his pipe, but I relished with childish delight playing the role of Sherlock Holmes. It had not been so long ago that playing, pretending, was something I did all the time; the freedom of childhood is hard to relinquish. I confess I was more than a little smugly pleased to do something my mother would absolutely detest. Doing so had become as important to me as 'fitting in' was to her. We were equally misguided and wholly oblivious to it.

As I was not yet old enough to wear a corset, I was allowed to dress myself for I had not yet been assigned my own maid. My governess, nearly obsolete in my maturing eyes, supervised my choice of morning dress when I called for her, helped with the long line of buttons down the back, checked my stockings and my low-heeled slippers.

"You'll do," she said as I stood before her for the final inspection. It was all she ever said.

Thank you ever so much, I longed to respond with a dash of my mother's stinging sarcasm.

A spinster who had never known much of life, Miss Jameson seemed excessively concerned with my education, my father's doing I was sure, but not so with my grooming, though she tolerated it, my mother's instructions no doubt.

Many of the girls my age had wonderful relationships with their governesses, asking questions about life as well as about their studies or comportment. I was never sure whether I was glad or sad I had no such familiarity with Miss Jameson. It would have been wonderful to have a grown woman with whom I could confide, to whom I could ask questions, questions growing increasingly more complex as I grew older. There was only emptiness there, a void of womanly wisdom, a terrible void for a girl trying to become a woman.

On the other hand, our distant relationship allowed me more freedom than my friends enjoyed. Freedom I was especially thankful for that morning. I rushed from my room and her.

As I surmised, I was alone in the breakfast room. Nonetheless, Birch stood guard at the pantry door, a door hidden behind a black and gold Chinese screen matching the exotic décor of the room. He looked less formal in his morning suit, though the informality never made its way within him, while James piled the sideboard with enough food for ten people. One can truly see abundance only if they have seen its lack. I never had.

I ate a few bites, wiped my mouth with the thick linen napkin, and pushed back my chair with a squawk against the parquet floor.

"Thank you," I chirped to the men as I scampered from the room.

"But Miss…" I heard Mr. Birch call out. He rarely saw me eat so little; he may have thought me unwell. The staff knew so much about us, so much more than we would ever know about them.

"I'm fine, Mr. Birch, not to worry," I called as I rushed out into the gallery, my low-heeled ankle boots clicking upon the cold stone floor, disturbing the silence of the house.

Ginevra had said she could sew, but I doubted if the indomitable Mrs. Briggs would allow her to, or if the housekeeper would put the new girl—a foreign girl—to work at some other menial job. I thought the latter more likely, so set I out to find chambermaids and kitchen sculleries at work.

I searched room after room. Ginevra was not in a one.

* * *

Her quiet sobs, thick with sadness, helped me to find her at last.

It had taken far longer than I expected. I had even made a most fictitious excuse to go below stairs to the steamy laundry room—knowing if my mother found out it would not go well for me—but Ginevra was not there either. Nor could I ask for her. I knew, even then, how the staff would look down on me if I did.

These hard-working people, ever at the whim of others who deemed themselves better, had as many notions of what was proper and what was not as those they served. They could be as ruthless about the rules of this life as the wealthiest of families. Anyone who had lived with servants for the whole of their lives knew we were great fodder for their spiky tongues, though my mother ever denied it. She did little to worry about what they said of her. She revealed too much of what should never be revealed.

They must have allowed Ginevra to fill the position of seamstress after all. I ran through the hall, up two flights on the main stairs. I ran like the child I had been, enjoying myself far too much, or like the boys who enjoyed sports whom I envied so. No one saw me, thankfully.

There was no one in the sewing room, but there had been. The lone gas lamp was on, a sure sign of detailed work, drawers were open, needles and thread and scissors littered the room, tools of the trade looking recently used.

When I heard my father's soft voice, with Geoffrey, his valet, a quiet sort of man as well, I hid behind the door of the sewing room. Should they pass this way, though they had no reason to, I had no desire for them to see me, to answer the questions that would surely come. In truth, I had launched myself into the role of spy and had no desire for the gambit to be broken, for the juvenile amusement of it to end.

They spoke of trivialities, of coming and going, of what to take and what to leave behind.

They moved on quickly, into my father's room, and back out, back down the stairs. The quiet, the most common sound in my house, ruled once more. That's when I heard it, the crying. Any game I played ended abruptly.

There are many sorts of crying. Joyful tears had laughter mixed with them. Deep loss, the pain of grief, came from a dark, desperate place. I had heard that sort of crying only once—had heard my mother crying only once—when her mother passed away. The quiet sobbing I heard now was not like either; they were the tears of a lost child.

I followed the sound toward the south of the house, near the rooms of my parents and brother. The sound was as muffled as the pain they evoked. Melancholy spoken without a word. To cry was a release, as much as was laughter and affection. To contain it, whatever sort, was to deny it. Without release, there could be no overcoming. I may have been young, but I had cried enough to know.

I stood at the end of the hallway, hearing it, but not finding it. It was as if I played another game, one of hide and seek, though the one hidden clearly had no desire to be found. She played no game. A few steps this way, and suddenly I knew.

The odd construction of the house, with its individual foyers and hidden hallways, created a wealth of small empty spaces. I found her there, in the hall within the hall between my parents' room.

Huddled in a ball, her dark dress enveloping her, her head hidden beneath a shield of her arms, she didn't hear my approach.

"Ginevra," I said quietly, as I might to a small animal I had no wish to frighten. She flinched but didn't look up. She retreated further into the narrow corner in which she had lodged herself.

"It's all right, Ginevra, I've not come to chastise you," I cooed at her. "I've been looking for you all day."

At last, her eyes found mine. Almond-shaped yet red-rimmed and swollen, the beleaguered depth of her nut-brown eyes belonged on a life-weary adult, not a child. She looked no more than twelve or thirteen though I would soon learn she was older.

"Tell me what's wrong, dear?"

She stared at me.

I scrunched down, squatted beside her, wrapping my skirts over my legs as she had done, crooking my arms just like hers. I said not another word.

Ginevra stared as hard at me as I did her. I waited. I would wait as long as need be. I don't know what she saw on my face, but it was enough.

Her words came then, hesitant at first, then like from a faucet at full open. Her sobs faded as she found release in the telling. Her knowledge of English was greater than I expected, though she stumbled and mangled the words in odd arrangements. She told me of Mrs. Brown. She told me of the work she'd done that day, how proud she was of her work on Mother's dress, of finding her room, of the voices, of how she came to be where she was.

She told me nothing of her tears.

"Then why are you crying, dear girl?" I asked her, unable to see as she did. "You've done nothing wrong. In fact, it sounds like you've done quite well for your first day."

Her full bottom lip began to quiver. "F...father, your father."

I shook my head at my revelation, chastising myself for not seeing it sooner.

"My father would not have been angry with you." I tried to assure her even more. "Nor even my mother. It was your job. Servants are in and out of our rooms at all times of the day and night."

Ginevra blinked; eyes wide. "It true?"

"It is true," I corrected without making it obvious. "As long as you have a valid reason to be there, you will never be in any trouble when you go in any room."

Her chest rose and fell with a deep breath, her shoulders shook with its quivers. She leaned her head down, but not to hide in the valley of her arms, but to rest her chin upon them. She looked better. I was so glad of it, for I had made her so.

We sat in silence for a few more minutes. I dared to reach out, to place a hand on her shoulder, to rub it softly. A stray tear, a leftover, trickled down her cheek. She turned to me.

"I lost, very lost."

If she meant in the house or in her life, it made no matter to me. I knew how she felt.

She was a servant, a member of the staff, a non-entity my breeding decreed. It was the pervasive attitude of my set. Yet if I was more than who I was born to be—allowed to be—as I believed I was, couldn't she be as well? Could a lifetime of habitual integrations be nothing less than habit? Mary Cassatt thought so. I vowed then to help Ginevra find whatever she felt she needed. I knew exactly where to start.

"Come with me." I took her by the hand and pulled her up. She answered with a drawn-out moan. I ignored it.

Peeking out the door to the hall, seeing no one, I pulled her again, even as she uttered soft mutters of protest that I continued to ignore. With the same excited energy with which I had searched for her all morning, I pulled her through the house, to the south end, down the back stairs, through the Conservatory—ever so grateful we passed no other member of the household—and out onto the side terrace.

Ginevra no longer moaned. The resistance of her arm voiced her hesitance. I smiled back at her, hoping to reassure her. Enjoying myself too much at the sly mission I had undertaken, one so very not in keeping with the decorum of my world, I was blind to her. I did not once ask myself whom I served, her, or me.

Our destination was one I had been to so many times since we had moved to The Beeches. I spent more hours there than I did in the house. I had fallen in love, fallen for its magic, from the very first moment I stepped into it. I knew she would as well. I knew it was exactly what she needed at this minute. As if I could know what resided in another's mind. The arrogance of my world was contagious.

I pulled her to me at the back corner of the house, flattened us against the wall as I looked over the two terraces running the entire width of the building, across the vast lawn stretching from the terraces to our destination, falling further into the delusion of espionage I played at. I would have laughed with the joy of it would it not confuse Ginevra more. It was a huge open space, grass-like green velvet flowing in low rolls away from the house, those I attempted to recreate upon my canvas. Usually, I would simply walk straight through. I couldn't be so flagrant with Ginevra by my side.

I saw no one on this side of the estate. I spied a few men at the far side gardens tending to the hydrangeas and rhododendrons. But there was no one on our side.

"Come. Quickly," I hissed, once more pulling her along.

She pulled back this time. This time she found her voice. "I find trouble. Mrs. Briggs, she…"

"She won't be looking for you at this time of day. She'll be far too busy with my mother, planning menus and other such nonsense." I bounced on my toes, grinning ear to ear, believing I could infest her with what I felt.

I pulled again. She came. We ran.

From the terrace, we ran straight north, until we ran through a line of maple trees. Behind them, a small path ran the length of the property, between the high stone wall that kept others out. I often averted my eyes from the sight of it, for it gave me the shivers.

As the carriage house came into view, I stuck my head out from between two trees, once more looking for prying eyes, once more finding none.

With one more pull, I led her onto the end of the vast lawn and into the trees, the weeping beech trees.

"Duck," I called as we came to one of the small entryways of branches and leaves. I crouched and as did she behind me. We were inside.

I stopped, as did Ginevra. Her hand dropped from mine; her mouth dropped as well as she raised wide eyes at the cathedral within. My cathedral.

GINEVRA

I entered a world not even my imagination had ever taken me to, not even in the words of a fairy tale. I couldn't stop myself from staring up and around, seeing the branches twisting and tangling over my head, reaching far up as if to touch the sky. There were so many others curling right down to the ground as if bowing to us, as if asking us to step on them, to climb up them.

As if not allowed, any thoughts of duty or Mrs. Briggs slammed against the hidden entry, barred from this magical place.

Pearl stepped upon a lumpy root without a moment's hesitation, her face changing; for the first time, I thought I glimpsed her unmasked truth. As if a monkey trained to dance, she climbed. To watch her lithe movements was a gift in itself.

She looked back at me, a mischievous wood nymph.

"Well, come on." Her hand waved me toward her.

I couldn't stop myself from following, couldn't even if I wanted to. I didn't.

She led me up and around, but not too high, until we came to a branch sticking out straight and sure from the thick trunk of the tree. Now both monkeys, we used hands and feet as we made our way to the middle of it. It was a tricky act, especially for me with my floor-length skirt, but we both wore low-heeled boots, so our footing was sure. There we perched, birds on a clothesline. It was the most charmed moment of my life. It was a moment that has, that will, stay with me forever.

PEARL

For a while, we said nothing, for nothing should be said when first entering such a place as that. The spirit of nature precluded all words, glorified by one's silence. That same spirit engulfed us as did the trees. They grew as tall as a grand cavern, a cave for giants, yet its delicate, almost ethereal leaves flowed down to the ground like trickles of water into the ocean. Unseen creatures scurried upon the leaf-strewn ground. Birds fluttered, though few chirped; even they honored that sacrosanct spot with their softness. I'd learned here, beneath the weeping beeches, that there are greater sacred places in nature than in any building man could construct. Ginevra broke the silence.

"*Bellisimo,*" it was a whispered prayer. "B…beautiful," she stumbled on the English word. "You lucky…you *are* lucky living here."

I didn't know how to answer her. For all the things in my life, I thought there was little luck to it. It had just always…been, been what it was, filled with all it was filled with. Did I feel lucky? Most often, it felt as if the skin I was born in didn't quite fit; perhaps it had been tailored improperly. But the why of it eluded me. Was I truly just "difficult," as my mother so often called me? I didn't know. Here I knew myself or at the least had no need to scramble for my name. Yes, for *this* place, I was indeed very lucky.

"Have you seen any of the other cottages, Ginevra?" I asked a question devoid of emotion, neutral ground upon which to start.

She nodded, eyes still wide. "We walked, from corner." She pointed north. "There was other…cottages?" I understood the question in the word. It was a silly word the community used. They lived in mansions. "But none like you…yours."

I patted her hand. She tried so hard to use proper English, but it was not an easy language to learn, and I had a feeling she had taught herself most of it.

"Someday soon, we'll walk up Bellevue and on the Cliff Walk," I promised her. "You'll see more cottages." My lips fell in a cynical frown.

"They only call them cottages because the Europeans do, to label them as their summer homes. There are some just as grand as this, if not more so."

"No?" Her brows rose crookedly upon her moist brow.

I nodded, smirking. "Oh, yes. Much more grand." Though she hadn't explained what she denied, what she questioned, I had understood immediately. It had been easy.

Ginevra's shoulders rose to her ears. She lifted a hand from the tree and made a circle round her head. "Why? Why here?"

"Well, as I have overheard the tale, there was this man, a tailor named Smith, born and raised here in Newport, who believed so much in the beauty of this place, that he and another man started buying up all the land. This place was very famous; men of the Revolution came here, came from here, one who even signed our Declaration of Independence. But there was also a great deal of slave trading that went on here as well." I looked out of my history books and back to Ginevra. Her eyes seemed stuck upon an unblinking gaze. "Well, sure enough, this Smith fellow was right. Somehow, many of those rich, southern plantation owners heard about the place, from the slave trade no doubt, and they started traveling here in the summer to escape the awful heat of their own climate. One plantation owner, Daniel Parrish, came first and built Beechwood. Then Mr. Wetmore, a very rich man who trades goods with China, built Chateau-sur-Mer, By the Sea," I translated for her, my hands fluttering like the wings of the birds that flew over our heads, adding their soft twitters to mine. "And then it all grew faster and faster. More families built cottages, each one larger than the last, the Astors and the Vanderbilts, the Van Rensselaers and the Stuyvesants."

I turned a serious gaze upon her. Could I trust her with my thoughts, even the darkest of them? I stared at that lost girl I had found in the cubby who had shared her fear. Yes, I could trust that girl.

"They are like children, I think. If one has a toy, the other must have a bigger, better toy, and the next, and the next." She watched my mouth as I spoke. "Do you understand?"

"*Si*, yes, I think, yes," she said, her words hesitant, but not her tone. I didn't know, or perhaps I didn't want to tell her, the full truth of things. At least the way I saw them. These powerful men, some of "old" money, some of new, who had made their riches after the War of Secession, had made their fortunes in coal mines and the spread of the railroad across the country. They made so much they didn't know what else to do with all their riches. They gave their overbearing wives—women who were the true power of this small, remarkably privileged community—carte blanche. It became a hobby, in truth a convoluted competition of sorts, the creation of these miniature palaces. Those who lived in them became the chess pieces upon the checkered board of a highly structured way of life.

"The men spend millions of dollars—"

"M...millions?" Ginevra gasped, almost slipping from our branch.

I grabbed her, steadied her, and huffed a laugh cynical to my own ears. "Yes, millions, to build these cottages. And they give even more millions to their wives, to decorate, to entertain."

I looked off to the west. From this high up, I could see the lowering sun glinting off the harbor away down the hill. "I know this world is run by men, Ginevra, but this place, Newport? Here women rule. You will see."

She looked away, a furrow on her brow, a frown upon her lips. "I do not think I want...to see."

I laid a hand softly upon her shoulder. "I do not think you have a choice."

Ginevra turned sad eyes on me. There was something in them so familiar I could have been looking in a mirror. She simply shook her head.

"It is entertaining, I will tell you that," I said lightly, as lightly as I could. "Especially thanks to Mr. McAllister—Ward McAllister. He's a snooty little man who has deemed himself the king of good manners. He hisses in the women's ear, and they listen." I plucked a feathery leaf off the tree, released it, and watched it float to the ground below us. "Oh, yes, thanks to him life is all very scheduled, very coordinated." I no longer knew if I spoke to Ginevra, if she understood. I only knew I said thoughts I had longed to say for so long, with no one to say them to.

I had many acquaintances but far fewer true friends. Among them, there was not a one who was not enraptured with our privilege, our opulent life. None who questioned it. They danced merrily to the tune forever played, marionettes on their strings. They would not understand the things I said to Ginevra. They would, in truth, shun me for them as the girls in school shunned me. Except perhaps Consuelo Vanderbilt, but she had far too much to deal with herself. I couldn't burden her with my confused and contrary thoughts. Here, with Ginevra, the lock upon them was broken.

"There is so much to do, but every day they are the same things to do. In the mornings, everyone gathers at the Casino to show off their latest fineries. Then we go to the beach, then luncheon, which can often be with fifty people or more. Then for me, there are still lessons with the governess, though I am the smartest in my classes during school term."

Ginevra brightened, poking her chest with her own finger. "Me, too. Smartest of all." She grimaced at her own words, at how far from smart they sounded.

"I can tell, Ginevra, do not worry, I can." I could. It was there, plain to see, as though someone had painted intelligence upon her face.

The creases upon her skin smoothed, a churning sea coming once more to rest.

"And then we go coaching, a grand coaching parade." I continued.

"A p…parade? Whata is parade?"

"We all dress up—very fancy—get in our coaches and all drive up and down the streets, Bellevue Avenue and Ocean Drive, and then we drive back."

"Up and back," she repeated, but not because she couldn't understand the words.

"We do it every day. Everybody does," I giggled. "I don't know why they started it or why they keep doing it. Don't tell anyone, will you?

You will see. We do many things for no reason at all. No good reason." These last words slipped from my mouth before I could close it.

Ginevra's hard stare burned my face. My hands twitched to cover it, but it was far too late for that.

"And we leave our calling cards. Well, we don't deliver them. We drive to each other's house and send our coachman to deliver them to each other's door." I blathered on as if I was not unmasked. "There's teatime in the afternoons. The women call on each other, taking turns at each other's cottages, and then return home for a rest. Then dinner. For my parents and Clarence, it is often at someone else's house, sometimes with over a hundred people in attendance."

"No? Hundreds?" With each response, each question, Ginevra's voice pitched higher and higher.

"Oh yes, sometimes hundreds," I said, and then muttered, "The Four Hundred."

"Eh?"

I put my hand on hers. "That, I will explain another time." I did not want to speak of it now. "It is all rather gay and fun and light. Two months of play before we go back home."

Ginevra pulled back her chin. "Back home? This not home?"

I shook my head; not only at her question, but at the answer I must give.

"No, Ginevra, we only stay here during the summer. We arrive a little earlier than most, so we can celebrate my birthday. It's only a few days away."

Her eyes lit up and with them her face. "Mine too is soon."

"When?" I cried.

"The third of *Luglio.* Ju...Ju...,"

"July?" I blurt, incredulous. "Mine is the second. How old will you be?"

"Eh...*sedici*...eh." She held up one finger, then six.

"Sixteen?! Me too!"

We smiled together then.

My smile stayed with me as I finished telling her of my living arrangements.

"We have another home in New York City. Do you know where that is?"

"*Si*, we came," she closed her eyes, looking for the English words she needed as if they were written in her mind, "our ship came there."

"Oh, yes, of course it would," I said quickly. "We live there most of the year."

I could feel the frown form on my face. I didn't like to think of New York. Our house there was not nearly as grand as The Beeches, but then again, every house on the upper east side of Manhattan was grand, just of a different sort. I shook New York away. The summer was just beginning.

"But here is where we come to play. And you will play with me."

Ginevra grinned through her head shook. "No, I not play. I must work."

I sighed. "Yes, I suppose you must."

It was my turn to look at her, peer into her. I had been talking of myself, of this privileged way of life far too long. It was not well done of me; it was not in keeping with the manners drilled into me. I cared not for propriety, but I did for how I treated Ginevra. Did I seek this girl out only as an outlet for words I could not say elsewhere? Was my intent only to use her so? To shatter my bored monotony?

"Enough about us. What about you? Where in Italy did you come from? Why are you here, Ginevra? Your father, you? Where is your mother?"

I had gone too far. I saw it immediately. I wanted to know all about her, but like so many people in my life, they didn't want me to know. I thought she would leave. Instead, she began to talk. She told me her story.

GINEVRA

Pearl shared so much with me, it was as if she had taken off all the layers of her clothing. It was a simple act and yet not. How strange the only gestures of kindness should come from one I was to serve. She was of a rank so far above me in a country where rank meant everything, I knew in truth I shouldn't even be there with her, talking with her. Ours was a smudged line from the start.

When she asked me, "Tell me about you, Ginevra. Where in Italy did you come from? Where is your mother?" I had to answer her; I wanted to, wanted someone in this place to know, to care enough to want to know. Those we live with are more than companions or colleagues or even those we serve; they are a witness to our lives. Until that moment, I walked invisible with not a witness in sight.

GINEVRA
1886

My aunts had always come and gone as they pleased, barging into our home, entering without a knock, barging into conversations between Papa and Mama, never a thought to what was and wasn't their business. It was the way of us, of life there. Until they started coming more often. Until my mother's stomach started to expand. The innocent child I was watched it grow gleefully, a child hoping for a brother or sister.

Mama started changing, eyes sunk, skin turned grey. She seemed to be losing weight, arms and legs becoming spindly sticks, even as her stomach enlarged.

As the doctors started coming, as my mother's beautiful young face grew old, forever pained, I knew there would be no baby.

She took to her bed and still they told me nothing. They passed me as they did the small oil lamp and table in the corner by the door.

They came to our house day after day. The women brought food by the armfuls. The men sat beside my father, all as silent as he. They filled our small home, but it still felt empty. I sat on the floor beside my mother's bedroom door, watching the doctor come and go, my aunts as well. They looked down on me, offering me forced smiles, light pats on the head. Their touch turned me cold. They wouldn't let me in to see her. Until that day.

"Ginevra." The voice of my Zia Domenica, my mother's sister, woke me as I dozed, though such sleep had crept up on me unnoticed. When I opened my eyes, I found her knelt down before me. Her red-rimmed eyes told me. "Come, Ginevra, come see your mama."

I had been longing for such words for days. It was the last thing I wanted to do. I knew what it meant. My cowardice was a shameful thing.

I took the hand she offered, felt my own tremble as I took it.

Shadows blanketed the room. Closed shutters blocked the sun, the air. I could barely breathe. I could barely see the small being my mama had become. Her skin lay thin on her cheeks, fell in the deep hollows of her sunken face. Her swollen stomach protruded from her body. Whatever lay in there grew ever stronger as she grew weaker. I closed my eyes to the sight, my mind replacing it with the beautiful woman who had smiled with the twinkle of stars whenever she looked at me.

My aunt nudged me forward and I moved on feet brushing the floor. I sat in the chair by her bed and stared, wondering where my mama had gone, where she was going, for I knew she was going.

Reaching out, I put my small hand in the unmoving one lying on the bed in front of me. The cold of it was one I had never felt before. My hand trembled as it took hers and gave it a squeeze. My fingers sank into her skin like toes in the sand.

"Mama?" I thought I shouted but knew it was no more than a whisper. I swallowed; my tight throat hurt. "Mama?" I tried again.

Her head moved, barely. Her eyelids fluttered, opened only to slits.

"Ginevra," her voice was a pale sound of the one I had always known, yet my heart warmed to hear her say my name. "You must take care of Ginevra. He—" she coughed, frail body quaking with it. My aunt rushed to the other side of the bed, held mama's head, and held a cup of water to her lips. Most ran down Mama's cheeks. Only a few drops made it past her dry, cracked lips. The coughing stopped.

"Ginevra," she said again.

"I'm here, mama, right here." I squeezed her hand harder. She turned her head toward me.

"You must take care of Ginevra," she croaked. "He doesn't know how."

She spoke of me, but she didn't know me. She didn't know me but in her frightening words, I knew she loved me. I had little as a child, little in the way of clothes or toys. Though my father's talent as a musician was great, there was little place in this small town on the east coast of Italy for it to shine. He made the most beautiful violins. His hands made magic out of wood. Few here could pay much for them. What I always had was her love. I would have it still. She had just told me it was so.

Her sick face swam in my sight. Her eyes closed as breath rattled in her chest.

Zia Domenica came to me. Her hand on my shoulder pulled me. I shrugged it off, leaned over, and kissed my mother's cold cheek. Our last kiss.

After she died, he left all her things exactly where they were: plain dresses hung limp in the wardrobe, small trinket boxes stood open on her bureau, her few simple pieces of jewelry gathered tarnish.

I would find him, sometimes, staring at the boxes and their lowly treasures. Did he look at them with regret, hearing my mother's unspoken desire for more, or perhaps his need to have given her more? Or did guilt hold him there, relieved that he would hear such silent need no more?

For months, my father and I simply existed, living together in a purgatory of nothing. We ate at the same table, slept in rooms beside each other, saying only words that needed to be said.

"Dinner," he would announce as I sat at the table doing schoolwork. I cleared my papers, placed the dishes, and we'd sit over them, feeding our bellies but nothing else. Not the grief eating at us both.

I wanted—needed—him to help me through it. I know now he simply didn't know how.

Like dreams that kept repeating, so were our days, days that stretched to months, to years. Until the fancy man came.

I had been in my room reading…or trying to. Mostly I stared out the window. I spent many hours this way since I lost her. I thought I saw her in the sky, the clouds, in the trees, in the sound of the ocean in the distance. I searched for her in every waking moment. I dreamt of her as I slept.

The tie binding me to the world was gone, and I floated aimlessly. Did I want to return, or did I want to let go? I was so young, only eight, and yet I knew my loss would be a part of me for the rest of my life. I didn't know if I could live this.

I heard someone come in but didn't care who it was. Until I heard their voices grow louder, harsher. I snuck out of my room, sat on the top step, and listened.

"We are going to America. A very rich man wants me there, wants me to work for him. He is paying good money, a lot of money, for me and Ginevra." They were more words than I had heard my father speak in months, and with more strength and determination than in my whole lifetime.

"Who is this man?" Zia Domenica sounded just as determined.

I listened as my father told my aunt of the man who had come to our home before…when mother was still well, or so we thought. I remember the man's clothes, like nothing I had ever seen, a coat and a jacket and a waistcoat, some sort of scarf wrapped intricately around his neck, a hat tall upon his head. So fancy and precise. My father told her of their conversation, of the money he had paid for one of my father's violins. I remember the meal that night, more meat than I had ever seen on our table.

"He has sent me a letter. He wants me to teach his son the way of the violin now that he is old enough. To make some for him. He believes I could make other things too, furniture."

"Furniture." It was a huff. "You are no simple furniture maker."

"I don't believe he wants simple furniture. He is a grand man. His home, he says it is quite grand."

Silence settled until he broke it, shattered it.

"He believes in me, Domenica."

A sigh. "Ah, so, yes. I know what that must mean to you. She believed in you too. Always."

My father said nothing. He knew my mother had always allowed him his work. Never once did she pester him to do something else, something to make more money. Never once did she question him as an artist, though it kept us always struggling. Her family was not always as kind.

"And what of Ginevra?"

"He said there will be a place for her always, as long as I am there. Even longer should the need arise. He has promised me of it."

"She will be a servant then?" I could taste the bitterness of my aunt's thoughts on the matter.

"A servant in a very wealthy household. It is better than I can do for her here. What would she become here but a servant to whichever man she married? It is all that is here for her."

"And what is wrong with such a life?" huffed my aunt who lived one. "She needs us, her aunts. She needs women to grow into a woman."

I heard his low grumble. I'd heard it so many times before. In this meager way, he would voice his displeasure.

"There will be women there."

"What? Other servants? *Dio mio*." My aunt did not hide her irritation as he did. "They will not love her."

"I love her."

My hands gripped the railing. How strange to hear him say those words about me. I can't remember when he had said them to me.

"*Si*, you do, I know you do." Her voice softened as a chair scrapped on the floor. Did she stand beside him? "But do you love her enough?"

She asked the question as if she stole it from my mind.

"It is the best I can do for her."

I heard footsteps, a door opened, sounds of birds entered.

Before it shut, I heard, "Promise me, Felice, that when she is old enough to decide, if Ginevra wants to return, you will let her."

I didn't breathe as I waited, as I wondered whether this life my father spoke of in America would be better than the one I lived now. I wondered, when the time came, what I would want. I could not know.

"I promise," he'd said. My fate had been sealed.

GINEVRA
1895

"He kept promise." I shrugged a shoulder. "He think he kept promise."

"I won't ask you if you're happy to be here," Pearl fretted. How silent she had been through my story, even when I floundered and grasped for the correct words. Her face had changed many times. Each change spoke its own tale. "How could you be?"

She did not speak as if she gave advice to a servant; we spoke as travel mates on a winding, bumpy road. To be understood by someone else is sometimes the best we can hope for in life.

"My papa, he happy, is happy," I told her. I did not want her to feel badly about my life in her home, in this home.

Pearl looked at me; her eyes were so like mine, as was our hair, though hers was not quite as curly. She smiled with half her mouth. "Fathers and mothers."

I nodded. The day grew long, but there was no time within our leafy cave.

"They make us who we are," she said, to me, to the tree. "In the good and bad ways."

I nodded again. I understood her as well as she did me.

"Your papa, he is happy?" I remembered the conversation I had overheard last night. I wouldn't tell her. Such things would pass between us, but not yet.

"In his way, I suppose he is, yes." Was she trying to convince herself or me? I thought she wouldn't say more about him. I was wrong.

PEARL

The moment had come. Would I trifle with this girl or truly befriend her? My eyes closed for a moment, my stark vision drawn inward, seeking truth, looking for what was right, what I wanted against the consequences of wanting it. With my words came the answer. No one reveals their dark truths to trivial acquaintances.

"My father is a railroad baron, as so—"

"Bar-ron?" Ginevra said the word strange to her as if it were two.

"A businessman, a very successful businessman, like most of the men who come here in the summer. But he is also a descendant of..." I would have to watch my language, not because of Ginevra's mind, but because of her lack of knowing all the words. "He was born into a great family, with a descent that can be traced back to the Mayflower. They became very rich. But my great-grandfather had somehow—Father has never told me; I think he is ashamed—lost the family fortune. My father earned it back, doubled it. Now he is on both sides of the line."

Ginevra lifted her shoulders. I scoured the branches above to see if the words I needed sat upon them. In the end, I shrugged and spoke plainly.

"Not a real line, there is a line, among the people, an invisible line, marking where their money came from. Does that make sense?"

"*Si*," she rolled her big brown eyes as she nodded. "Mr. Birch, Mrs. Briggs, Chef," she raised a hand and drew a line in the air, "me and the others."

"Yes," I laughed a little. There were all sorts of lines in our lives in those days. Ginevra learned about them quickly. Perhaps there were lines everywhere, even in Italy. All of life seemed a blurry line as I dithered for my dot upon it. "Well, this line is drawn in the roads and in the cottages. On one side, there are the 'Nobs,' people who inherited money, came down in the family. 'Old' money, they call it."

I looked at her. She nodded, still with me.

"On the other, there are the 'Swells,' people rich now, but not before, people who made their money in business and industry. 'Nouveau riche,' they are called."

I didn't bother to explain that it had been Mr. McAllister, *again*, who had made such distinctions, and such distinctions important, who had, somehow, become judge and jury of all. I judged harshly those who judge others. I was too young to see my own contrariness.

"Because my father came from money *and* made a lot of money, he stands alone in a way, in the middle."

"It not…it is not easy for him." I heard tenderness in Ginevra's voice as she summed up her father so well.

I shook my drooping head. "No, it isn't. And she doesn't make it any easier for him."

"She? Mother?"

I sniffed an ugly little laugh. "Yes, my mother. She is twelve years younger than he is, you know. I think she was his prize for making the family rich again. They met before he went off to serve in the War of Secession."

"Ah," Ginevra breathed, "the scars."

I frowned. "Yes, the scars. They had married when she was only sixteen, but she made sure they were bound together before he left, securing his affections lest he fall for some southern belle. I think she meant to secure his fortune for her own. Her family had had money once, but not very much when they met. She was, is I suppose, one of the great beauties of Society. Beauty is as powerful as money here."

I stopped for a moment, my mother's words buzzing in my ear, a bee with a harsh stinger, *You will have beauty and money, Pearl. You know what Ward says, 'beauty before brains, brains before money.' You will move us even higher up.* I didn't care about climbing as she did, save perhaps in this tree.

"Well, she never imagined he would return 'deformed.' Her word, one she bandied, threw at him, cruelly," I continued. The words rushed from me as if they were in control, not I; to say them was a need I did not know I carried. Here, with Ginevra, they seemed to know better than I, know they were safe. "The scars are shrapnel marks—bullet pieces—dotting his left cheek like stars on a clear night. When he talks to people, he always looks over their left shoulder, showing them mostly the other side of his face. My mother always stays on his right, at the table, standing at social gatherings, or on afternoon strolls, if she stays with him at all."

This time Ginevra took my hand. "He handsome, manly."

I stared at a face that I had only just met, yet one I knew. She did not speak words merely to pacify; she said what she thought was true. Gratitude warmed me like the shafts of light sneaking through the leaves. I would feel more of its warmth.

"I think so," I said with truth. "When I sneak into his study or slip through the dark to climb into his bed for a reassuring cuddle," my head dropped sheepishly, heat crept up my neck, "I know I'm too old to keep doing it, but he doesn't seem to mind." I waggled my head as if to waggle away my childishness. "When I do, he is so very generous with them, with his cuddles. I always do so on his left side. I often reach up and touch his scars." I giggled, head tall upon my straight neck once more. "I remember one time I took a little finger and traced a line, connecting the dots on his face."

" 'I've made a giraffe, Father,' I remember saying. I remember most his soft smile."

With a shake, I came back to this place beneath the beeches. I looked at my attentive listener with a sidelong glance. Sympathy etched her face, the chisel one of my own sad making.

"But then he brought her here," I said, my tone rose as did the tide. "She's better here. It's such a small community. She gets to rub elbows with queens nearly every day."

Ginevra's face opened, brown eyes flashed and hid as her eyelids opened and closed, open and closed. "Queens? You have queens here? Queen of America?"

I laughed, taking her hand as I saw the hurt my laughter caused her.

"No, no, of course not. Not real queens, only those who think they are. Those women I told you about."

I picked another fluffy leaf from a nearby branch, picked at its fronds as I tried to explain these people, "The Four Hundred" as the world knew them, to this unworldly girl. How did one explain the three unusual women—rebel, perfectionist, loose cannon—who sat on their thrones, Alva Vanderbilt, Tessie Oelrichs, and Mamie Fish? Of course, the true leader was Mrs. Astor; no one dared rival her decisions. Between the three of them, they could not knock her off the one true throne.

I straightened my back until I was almost bending backward, puffed up my cheeks, stuck my nose in the air, and tightened my throat, "If you want to be fashionable, always be in the company of fashionable people."

Ginevra laughed a real laugh. It sounded like the seagulls forever wafting above our heads while on this tiny island.

"Who that?"

I laughed too, knowing my imitation was a laughable caricature. "*The* Mrs. Astor," I told her through our giggles. "She thinks she really *is* the Queen of America."

"But how," Ginevra struggled. I sat quietly, encouraging her with stillness and a smile. "How these women come to...?"

She was stuck. I helped, but I did so with a bit of a laugh. "Rule?"

"*Si*, rule," Ginevra, though she didn't fully understand our language, she understood queens rule, by whatever means, in whatever forms.

It was my turn to pull my shoulders up to my ears. "I really don't know, Ginevra. I haven't figured it out yet." Oh, how youth misinforms us of our own knowledge. Yet there were things beyond my keen then. I saw them even through my own self-importance. "I only know when they started coming to Newport, when they started building their 'cottages' here, my mother had to have one too. Of course, Mrs. Astor had to approve of our taking a residence here."

Ginevra gave me that look, one I would come to recognize. She tilted her head to one side, one brow rose on her smooth tawny skin, her mouth puckered as if she'd eaten something bitter.

"Yes, these women rule. They decide who can and who can't have a cottage here."

"Where do others go?"

I pointed west as if we could see across the harbor. "They have lovely homes in Narragansett, near a long, long, beautiful beach." I hesitated. I had been to Narragansett once. In some ways, I thought it prettier than Newport, simpler, more elegant and the enormous stretch of beach could have come straight from the Riviera. "*If* they are ever invited to an event here in Newport, and that is a very big if, they take the ferry over from Narragansett Pier."

I took a hard look at my cottage, the palace that was my summer home. In comparison to some of the other mansions, it was rather austere, just as much marble but far less glittering gilt. My father's words came back to me, as they did yesterday at dinner, "If you insist we build in Newport, then it shall be where and how I say."

"I was shocked, almost as much as my mother," I told Ginevra. "It was one of the few times I had heard him so decidedly firm. Nor did he back down, even when Mother screeched that this plot of land was on the wrong side, on the landside of Bellevue Avenue, not the side perched atop the rocky bluffs, overlooking the Cliff Walk and the sea."

" 'We shall be a laughingstock,' " Mother pined with tinny trucu-lence.

My father grabbed Mother's hand and walked her along the thin dirt path leading left around a thick grove of oaks and maples. On the other side, the trees thinned. A clearing sloped gently away before us, striking for the punctuation of its end by three magnificent beeches, these beeches. Their spindly branches intertwined as if they embraced while others arched and twisted, reaching for the ground, their feath-ery leaves fluffy as cotton. Even then, I could see the cubbies of space beneath them and longed to enter its haven.

My father stopped, turned west, and pointed.

"Look," he said simply.

"And there it was... the sea my mother craved. Over the tops of the beeches, we saw Newport Harbor."

Yachts at anchor bobbed on little waves. The orange summer sun dipped down drawing ever closer to the deep blue sea, glowing brighter with each tick of descent. Its glow lit the thin wisps of clouds daring to draw near, turning them to licks of flame.

In the face of such beauty, my mother became mute.

I shimmied closer to my father, tucking my small hand in his, smiling when he gave it a squeeze.

" 'What shall we call it, my Pearl?' "

"All the cottages have names, Chateau Sur Mer, Marble house, Wakehurst, Rough Point."

As the lowest tip of the sun slithered beneath the ocean horizon, its tangerine rays struck the beeches, filling the cave-like spaces with light. They glowed as if lit from within. I was captivated.

"The Beeches," I said.

My father grinned as he does, with a nod and a grunt.

"Beeches," he repeated. "One might know it for the trees, for we shall write it that way. But others might think it's for the beautiful shore all around us."

He looked down at me with his somber brown gaze.

" 'How very clever of you, my Pearl. Well done.' "

"Though I had not thought of the double meaning of the word, I felt clever nonetheless. I always want my father to think of me as a clever girl, not the kind of girl my mother is."

"Your mother, she is…snotflea," Ginevra attempted. I laughed. She said it wrong, but she got it right. I didn't want to speak of my mother. Or Ginevra's mother. They were both absent in our lives, though a different sort of absent. I'm not sure if it made a difference, or which was worse.

"The first thing we need to do is to improve your English," I announced, then immediately felt sorry for my words. Had I insulted her? It was the last thing I would wish to do to this new friend of mine, for I did feel that we would become friends. We can never know when a similar soul will pass our way, or what sort of dress it may hide behind. My fears fled with her rapid nodding, the spark bursting in her dark eyes.

My taut shoulders dropped; I breathed again. "I think you should start with reading. If you read out loud, it will help when you speak."

I saw the truth then in the slump of her shoulders and the slow slide of her features lower down her face.

"You don't know how to read, do you?" I asked softly.

"*Si*, Italian." She screwed up her shoulders along with her pride.

"Well, that's wonderful," I praised. She needed me to. "Then I shall teach you to read in English and to write, of course. Would you like that?"

"Yes. Very much." Her words were simple; her smile was so much more.

* * *

I scampered down from our perch on the tree. I ducked out, like Alice from the rabbit hole, and onto the lawn. On my own, there was no reason to hide, and I made for the house, crossing the vast yard at a leisurely pace. I skipped as I did so often when I was younger. The shadow of Ginevra, the smiling one, skipped beside me. Her ethereal, unsuspected place beside me made the summer sun brighter. Summer had just begun. I looked forward to the days of it quite differently than I had done when we first arrived in Newport that year.

Was I silly to think of Ginevra so fondly already? Perhaps. Was I wrong about the affectionate connection so quickly forming between us? No, not at all. The resemblance of us—not of the physical sort—was far more powerful than the contradiction.

I looked up to the house, past the two sets of stone stairs, the two wide terraces, the statues rising up at the ends and anchoring the middle. I looked up to the windows, the windows to my room. I saw a curtain fall back into place.

My steps quickened as I groaned.

I rushed into the house, through the Conservatory, and up the main stairs to my room.

She stood there waiting.

"You've kept me waiting, again." Miss Jameson stood with her fisted hands on her narrow hips. "This time for more than an hour."

"I'm dreadfully sorry," I said, and I was. For all that I treasured the time beneath the beeches with Ginevra, my manners were ingrained. To keep someone waiting so long was simply not done.

"Do you think I have nothing better to do than to wait for you?" she demanded.

From across the hall and through the foyer I heard voices, words spoken with the same sharp tone. Ginevra, in the sewing room, received the same sort of greeting as did I.

"No, of course, not Miss Jameson," I lied. In truth, she didn't have anything better to do. She was there to teach me, to add to the regular lessons of school, nothing else. The nothing else, reminded by my absence, was where her anger truly lay. "I do apologize. I will try to do better."

"Oh, you will do better." There was a threat to her words. "What were you doing?"

"I…I…," I stumbled, "I was out in the gardens sketching."

Miss Jameson knew of my love for drawing, for painting. My façade was a believable one.

"Where is your sketchbook?"

I looked down at my empty hands. I was a terrible liar.

I laughed. I didn't fake that any better.

"Well, silly me, I must have left it in the garden," I tried to laugh again. Again, I failed. "I'll go get it."

"You'll do no such thing."

I knew that would be her answer and sighed with relief. My sketchbook was in the small desk, in front of which she stood, statue-like, with arms crossed, a foot tapping.

"You will sit yourself down and work on these math problems." She pointed to my desk chair and the papers waiting there for me.

I quickly did. As I struggled with the numbers—for working them didn't come easily to me—she paced behind me, watching me work, sharply instructing me when I did my figuring wrong.

Her patience, already worn thin, nearly disappeared.

"Such a waste of time," she muttered as she paced, lips so tight all she could do was mutter, arms crossed equally as tight across her scrawny chest, "these girls have no need for such knowledge. They'll never use it. No, not these girls."

It was a condemnation not only of me, but of all the girls of families such as mine, girls whose only goal in life—decided for them—was to marry the right man, have children, and become the next cog in this exclusive machine that was the social life of the rich. They told us this truth, verbally beat it into us, from the moment we could start listening. I listened, merely listened. We choose what we truly wish to hear.

I was smarter than my brother…my brother who was pushed to learn about business and railroads and running large companies. Learning he had no interest in. His was a life so full of promises, of potential. He took for granted what I longed for.

"How dare you?!"

The thunder raged not from the sky, but my door, and my mother standing in it.

I jumped up from my chair, my feet twisting on themselves, stumbling as my words did. "I…I'm sorry, Mother. I lost track of time. I've apologized to Miss Jameson."

My governess stood casually, her fingers tapped merrily upon her folded arms; a smirk slithered across her lips, splitting her face. She showed no surprise to see my mother.

"I saw you!" Mother screamed, lunging toward me with a pointed finger. I backed away, my buttocks slamming hard against my desk. If I could have climbed over it, put it between us, I would have. "I saw you with that girl, that foreign servant. How dare you?"

The monster of anger that was my mother chased away my thoughts, my words. I was the fox, and she was on the hunt.

"Do you know what they would say if they saw you?"

"They" could be any number of people.

"You could ruin us. I will not allow it!"

A gust of wind blundered through the open window, pushing against my back, pushing me forward.

"But, Mother, she is…she is in a strange land. I thought only to be kind and—"

"Do not speak to me." Mother's face was just inches from mine, yet I hardly recognized her. "You will only listen. You will never, ever, see that girl again, never spend a second with her. Do you understand me?"

I understood too well; such understanding did not serve her cause.

"You're being cruel, Mother. Such people deserve our—"

"Enough!" Mother bellowed; her gentile veneer, one she practiced with such constancy, broke like a thin crystal champagne flute under the crunch of a heavy boot. "You refuse to listen to me, don't you? As you always do."

Her enraged gaze scoured my room. Fiery eyes latched and held.

"Well, I shall make you listen."

Faster than I ever saw her move, Mother flashed across my room, grabbed my kit and paints and brushes, grabbed my canvas, and made for the door.

Grief did not belong only to death.

"Where are you taking those?" Desperation plunged me toward her.

Mother stopped at the door, turned back. Evil shattered her beautiful face into grotesque shards.

"If you spend time with trash, then to the trash these will go."

"No!" I pleaded. It didn't matter.

"The rest of it, Miss Jameson," Mother instructed, "be sure it all goes."

That woman's pinched face lit with satisfaction. "Yes, Madam."

Far too happily, Miss Jameson quickly gathered what was left of my supplies and made her way to the door, stopping at the threshold.

"You, return to your work."

I fell into my desk chair, battered as if beaten. Mother had never gone this far to bring me in line. Or had I stepped too far from it? I dropped my face to the papers before me but could see nothing past my tears, nothing but the loss of my most precious items.

* * *

Another night, another dinner alone. I sat in the dark room, lacquered black walls made glorious by the use of gold fleck paint and bright reds of the colorful Chinese figures. My only companion was my pain. I was as dark as the walls, with not a speck of gold in sight.

Mother and Father walked in, both resplendently dressed; he in his waistcoat atop his white shirt and tie, swallowtail coat cut short in front, top hat in hand. She with a beaded frothy dress whose tail shushed along the polished floor, her wide-brimmed laced and flowered hat perched at just the perfect tilt upon the pile of her red hair.

My fork stopped halfway to my mouth.

"I hope you have learned a valuable lesson today." My mother stood by my side, looking down her straight, pert nose at me.

I put the fork down.

"I have." I lied. "I'm sorry, Mother," I said truthfully. I was, very sorry she had seen me with Ginevra; sorry I had not been more careful.

I looked to my father knowing he knew, knowing my mother had informed him of every little tidbit of the day. I searched his face, looking for what I needed, not finding it.

He said nothing.

Mother sniffed at me, unconvinced. "You've lost your painting, and I'm not sure you should continue your lessons either." That dig was for my father, not me.

She circled away from me as she drew on one long satin glove, head shaking, but just slightly, so as not to upset the creation on her head. "Dancing, etiquette, managing a household, now those topics should command your attention, not math, or science, or art."

I longed to pick my fork back up and poke her with it, not hard, just enough to prick some sense into her. My fingers gripped it until my knuckles turned white.

I turned to my father. The frustration returned. I knew it was by his instruction I partook in such lessons, why would he not defend them, defend me.

I closed my eyes and sighed. Father did all he could not to anger his young wife, not to feed the fire of her ire.

He looked at me, at my thunderous thoughts darkening my face. My skin was pale but worse ridiculously opaque, no matter how I practiced the stony countenance of my set, of my station. It was nothing but time wasted. I didn't know how to be anything but me, a me of confusion and contradiction.

"I see no reason to go that far, Millicent." Finally, Father spoke, softly but firmly. My frozen heart melted, a drip. "I do believe the Vanderbilt girls are receiving the same tutelage, are they not?"

It was rare for Father to speak against my mother's dictates; thoughts created fewer arguments. When he did, he did with great keenness. I would have rather he fought for my painting supplies to be returned, but this was enough, for now. He had hit her tender spot, for my mother cared about nothing more than doing what the leading families did, including my brother and me.

"Well, yes, Orin, I do believe they are." Mother's face, blackened like a storm cloud, turned to look out the window. I could see the hold she had on her other glove; the white knuckles of her grasp were just like mine.

"Then I believe it best…," my father began.

"Yes, yes. It is best." Mother pulled on the glove with sharp irritation, the same clipped edge in her voice.

"Continue on then, Pearl." She could not have said my name with more disdain. "But if I catch you with that peasant again, you will lose all. Am I clear?"

"Yes, Mother." In truth, I did not want to lose my lessons. I treasured learning as my mother did her jewels. I simply wanted more.

"Come along, Orin." Mother sashayed quickly from the room. My father lingered. He stood by my chair and leaned down to me, a hand on my shoulder.

"I understand you, my Pearl, I see you," he spoke softly, whether to offer me solace or so that Mother would not hear, I didn't know. "But I can only protect you from her so much. I can't protect you when I'm not here."

He stopped. Closed his eyes for a moment.

"And I can't protect you from the world. Our world can be a hard place. Do you understand?"

I nodded, though I didn't understand fully, not yet. I understood only his comfort.

My father gave my shoulder and squeeze and left me.

* * *

I woke from the nightmare gasping. My face wet from tears and sweat. The shadows in my room had taken on the shapes of the awful dream. I needed my father.

I slipped from my bed, shivering from the cold in the stillness of the hot summer night. I didn't knock but entered my father's room in a rush. His bed was empty and as cold as I. I couldn't bear searching for him, too afraid of what lay in the dark parts of the house, there were so many of them, too many and of all sorts.

I would go to my mother. Is that not where all children go when in need? She could give comfort when she wanted, though she rarely wanted to. Perhaps I needed it from her especially. I knew her door to the corridor would be locked, it always was. I hurried through my father's room, through the bathroom between, and reached for the door connecting her room to his.

The doorknob would not turn. This door too was locked. She locked out not only me but him as well.

GINEVRA

I slipped away from Pearl, slipped away from our place beneath the beeches, though I didn't want to. Everything looked different—felt different—after being in there with Pearl. Surprises came in the strangest of packages. There were no words, in my language or hers, that could describe it. I no longer walked through life quite as alone, though I was very alone as I followed her directions to the side of the house and the servants' entrance there.

As I wandered into the circular drive, its canopy of wisteria and wrought iron, though beautiful, felt like a trap closing down on me, but now I could see the holes in its teeth. Happiness seemed to die when Mama died. Beneath the Beeches, I thought I had glimpsed it again, at the least the shimmering promise of it.

Pearl promised me, before I left, that this was not the first and last time we would be together beneath the beeches, rather it would only be the first of many. She promised to find a way to let me know when we could meet, if I could get away to meet her. A promise such like that of the buds of spring.

I slipped in the door to another white tiled foyer. I could see the cold kitchen just beyond another frosted door. I could hear the voices of many at work. But no one saw me. I quickly stepped to the stairs on my left, the servant stairs, pleased with myself for slipping back into the house unnoticed. Too soon.

"*Figlia?*" My father was there, just as I rounded the landing to the next set of stairs. "Daughter," he said again in Italian, there was none of his sparse affection in his tone or upon his face.

"Where have you been? That Mrs. Briggs came to me, looking for you."

"I...I...," I stumbled. "I had to put a dress, in the lady's room. I got lost." It was the truth, but only some. I lied poorly, whether this was a bad or good thing, I wasn't sure, I was only certain it was my way, a way beyond changing.

"Tell me the truth." He was as stony as the statues posing everywhere in and out of this house.

I told him everything, fixing the dress, hiding, and being found. I told him of Pearl and my time with her beneath the beeches. Happiness chirped in my voice. None of it showed on his face.

He said nothing for a very long time. When he spoke, I wished he hadn't. His words fanned the sparks of my own doubts.

"It will never last," he said flatly. "We will never be friends with these people. Do your chores and stay out of sight."

It was a cruel scolding. He walked around me, walked away from me, and back down the stairs.

Stay out of sight, he had said.

Stay out of mine, it was cruel thought my mind flung at him, but I didn't put it there. The little between us, the little I received from him, with such coldness, it almost chased away the joy Pearl had given me. Almost.

I hurried up the next flight of stairs, through one door, to the sewing room.

She stood there, waiting.

"Where were you?" Mrs. Briggs' pale face turned as red as the walls in Mr. Worthington's rooms.

"I...," I started, stopped, not knowing my way.

"Never mind, shut your bone box. I really don't care. And I don't care how young you ah. In this house, everyone works."

From the foyer, the yelling reached us. Mrs. Briggs fell silent, listening, as I did. We heard every word. My heart ached. It was my fault. Nothing Mrs. Briggs could do to me now would punish me more than what had happened to Pearl. Though she tried her best.

Her long bony fingers grabbed my upper arm and with a hard yank, pushing me down in the chair before the long sewing table. For the first time, I saw what was on it.

Socks. Piles and piles of socks.

"These are the servants' hosiery, almost all of it. You are to match them up, see which needs fixing, and fix them."

There were enough socks to keep two sets of hands busy for hours. I sat before the piles unable to say a word.

A bony finger poked my shoulder.

"Get to it," she sneered, "and don't come out until you've finished, not even when you hear the dinner bell."

* * *

For hours, I sat there until my hands hurt. The flickering light of the gas lamps showed every painful, red pinprick dotting my hands. My stomach grumbled, angry with me for not tending to it, but I still had so much to do. I wanted to cry again, like this morning, but within my empty gut, only anger grumbled.

Without pushing back my chair, I slipped from it. Stopping at the edge of the opened door, I peered out, seeing no one. I slipped downstairs, past Chef Pasquel and the kitchen maids, still hard at work.

I had missed dinner long ago. Not another servant was in sight, not a sign of Mrs. Briggs either. All had made for their beds save those who waited to serve their masters—the valets and Mrs. Worthington's maid, and those finishing the kitchen cleaning. I slipped past them unnoticed.

The long, narrow workroom they had given my father smelled like the forest I played in back in Foggia, and the idea of tears came back to me with the memory. Fresh wood of every sort and size stood in piles against the wall. In the corner, on a table of polished oak, my father worked, making the violin for the young man of the house. He stroked the wood as if it were alive and could feel the caress of his hand.

"I need help, Papa," I said in Italian.

Without looking up, my father shook his head, light found his skin through the thinning grey hair. "English."

My jaw jutted forward. I struggled for words in my own language that would convey my struggles.

"H…help, Papa," the word came to me on the memory of Pearl and her offer of it.

At last, he looked at me, his gaze as dead as my mother. He shrugged. He didn't understand. It was an admission he hated to make. In our language, I told him of the housekeeper and the socks and the lack of dinner.

He turned to me. Nothing in his features gave me any hope.

In Italian, he told me, "Do what they tell you. Finish the work. You will eat tomorrow."

I shivered at the cold, in his words, in this house. I turned without a word.

"Ginevra." He called me back and I turned out of duty.

He thrust his head to a small table in the opposite corner. "*Pane.*"

My mouth watered at the sight. On the table sat a chunk of bread, large beside the crumbs of what looked like cheese and perhaps some sort of meat. I ran to it, and with two hands held it to my mouth, tore at it with my teeth.

With my treasure in hand, with at least ten more bites left, I made for the door. I turned to thank him, but my father had already turned back to his work, to the sanding of wood, the stroking of it. I left him, still devouring my bread, focused on the food hitting my angry belly. But not so focused that I didn't see the trash bin in the laundry room and what lay in it.

* * *

My mission complete, I slowly climbed the stairs, my aches my only companions.

The hall was empty, almost dark. I slipped into my room, for the first time so grateful for it.

And for the first time, I found Greta in her bed. From beneath her nightcap, I could see thick curly red hair, a deep, dark red. Beneath the covers, she faced the wall, her small body curled in a ball. Her hair and her small build I remembered as one of those at table, one who had not said a word to me, though she must have known, both last night and that day at breakfast, who I was, that I was to share her room.

I tiptoed in, not wanting to disturb her, and began to unbutton my dress, each press of my punctured fingers bringing another stab of pain.

"She don' want ya here."

I jumped with a small gasp and spun round.

Greta's startling blue eyes pierced me; hatred glowed brightly in the gloom. She'd turned under the covers to face me without a sound.

"None of us do, ya know, no really." Her accent was as thick as her meanness. "But I'll tell ya this, do what she says, or we'll all pay fer it. Then you'll really see what it can be like here, fer the likes of you." She turned her back to me once more.

With such a tender "good-night," I silently shrugged off my dress, and in my chemise, slipped beneath the covers of my bed, shivering in the hot night.

PEARL

But often through the singing broke
A burst of laughter gay,
So young were we, so glad and free,
That happy Summer day!
And hand in hand would linger long,
As through the dance we moved,
For some of us were lovers then,
And some of us were loved.

I lay back on my bed with a sigh. Such beautiful words and written by a woman. I had obtained a copy of *Verses*, a book of poetry by a Newport resident, a young woman by the name of Edith Wharton. She was only sixteen when she wrote them, the same age as I was now. Her proud father had had them privately published fifteen years ago, but I had found a copy in the Astor library a few years ago, while there for the birthday party for Pauline, *The* Mrs. Astor's daughter who was near my age.

I had smuggled it out, snuggled it near me ever since. Read it when I should have—

"What in heaven's name are you doing?"

Mother's voice shattered my reverence. I jumped up, shoved the book of poetry beneath me.

"I...I was just about to get ready."

It was a glorious summer day and the hour for the beach had fast approached.

Her grey eyes narrowed. She held out a hand. Though she did not admire intelligence, hers was sharp. There was nothing for it. I slipped the book out from beneath me and handed it to her.

"How many times must you read this?" Mother tossed the book on the floor as she would a piece of rubbish. "Aren't you supposed to be reading another book, the one I gave you?"

Now I wanted to squint at her. I didn't.

I scrambled to pick up the ignored book—*The Ladies' Book of Etiquette, and Manual of Politeness: a Complete Hand Book for the Use of The Lady in Polite Society,* by a woman named Florence Hartley. The title alone repulsed me—before she could see the turned-down corner clearly marking my place, still stranded in the middle.

"But I am, Mother. It's always right here, by my bed." Yes, always there, always forgotten.

She snatched it from my hand. It fell open, the traitor.

"This is the same page you were on when I asked you last week."

This book she also threw, at me. It landed on my lap, far heavier than it actually was.

"There will be no beach for you today. When I return, I expect to see progress made. I *will* question you."

Oh, I was sure she would. What she didn't know was the punishment she adjudged was no punishment at all. No beach, the whole family gone, I could think only one thought...more time with Ginevra beneath the beeches. Mother had already taken my most treasured possessions. In my mind, I had little else to lose and far too much to gain by being with Ginevra.

"Yes, Mother." I did my very best act of contrition. It worked now as it always did.

She left me with a huff, thankfully, before she could see the smile beginning to blossom on my face.

I listened as I heard her agitated steps wander away from me, growing fainter as they trudged down the stairs.

Like a child, I bounced on my bed. In the joyful frivolity, I wasted precious time. I picked up the dreaded book, and another, and made for the door fast.

It was a portent, in my mind, that my room, on the other wing of the house than my parents, was just steps away from the sewing room. Through one frosted glass door and into a foyer, I stood beside the door.

Ever so slowly, I peeked my head around the threshold.

I had never noticed how dark the room was before. Dark brown, textured cloth covered the walls, the furniture, the rugs. All dark—save her smile—when she saw me there.

"Are you alone?" I whispered to Ginevra.

She nodded, pulling her needle and its tail of thread.

I held the book up before me, grinning like a little girl, my brows dancing up and down on my forehead. She grinned as well.

Ginevra lifted her shoulders, splayed her hands to show me the piles of work before her.

I rubbed my stomach and made a ridiculously sickly face. *Maybe I should be an actress*, I thought, *my mother would die of apoplexy.* I choked back the guffaw longing to be barked.

Ginevra bit her lip, bit back her own laughter I could tell, nodded, and dropped her face back to her work, but not before I saw another grin.

I made my way back to the family portion of the house unhurried. My mother was gone; there was little need to hide. Reaching the first floor, I heard the sound of drawers opening and closing from my father's library. Servants were to clean in there, but never to invade any of it. I strode off, ready to reprimand the offender. I've since heard it said that no matter how hard we try, we eventually become our mothers. I fought against it even then. My righteous indignation in that moment was hers, all hers.

But there was no offender, only my father.

"Hello, my Pearl," he greeted me with the endearment that had been mine since before I could remember. I stepped into the room forever thick with wood, leather, and man.

"Hello, Father." I tossed back casually, a camouflage. I didn't know if my mother had told him of my continued wayward behavior. She hated when I did not attend the days at the beach. At my age, she already paraded me before the sons of like years from the best families, already tried to push us together. She must have complained to him. She was always complaining to him.

"What are you up to this fine day?" he asked, still rummaging in his desk. Mother hadn't told. "No beach for you?"

I shook my head. "No, not today. I have some studying to do." He didn't need to know more.

"Study is always good," he said with half his attention.

My father valued education and learning. The thought struck me like a hammer blow. Would he approve of what I was about? That it contradicted my mother so grossly could swing him decidedly one way or the other. Once more, I dared to push against one of the many fences that surrounded me.

"Actually, Father," I stepped closer to his desk, he looked up at me, "I'm going to teach Ginevra to read and write in English."

He stared at me with his sad brown eyes. The sadness he could not hide, everything else hid behind it. After what had happened, I wasn't sure he would still be on my side.

"Can she read and write in her own language?"

He surprised me. It was a surprise whenever he did.

"Yes. Yes, she can," I said happily.

Father studied me for the length of a breath. "Good. It will be easier to teach her then."

He gave his form of approval, as he had learned to do safely, given but not outright. It was enough, more than enough.

I leaned down and squeezed his hand. "Thank you, Father," I said, squeezing harder at the sight of his pleasure.

I dashed away and out of the house, filled with joy, to await my friend beneath the beeches.

"My Pearl?" Father stopped me cold. I turned. "Don't get caught."

GINEVRA

It had been a few days since we were able to meet again. Though Pearl would sometimes pass the sewing room, an unnatural path for her to take when coming from the downstairs ladies' bathroom, but one easily explained if she had to.

For my needs, I had to climb either to the third floor or down to the basement.

On days when we could meet, she would flick her brows up, flick her head out toward the trees, but I dared not go again at first. I worked very hard for a few days. Red pinpricks on my fingers told the truth of it, as did the ache from an always bent neck. That day–having become an established part of Mrs. Brigg's well-run household–found me courageous.

I waited a few minutes after Pearl disappeared from the door and made my way to the laundry room. I told Mrs. Brown I felt unwell and needed to use the facilities, holding my stomach while holding my face in a scrunched way–the way the Pearl had done–silly but convincing.

Instead of making my way to my room as I told her I would, I slipped down the stairs, out to the side terrace, and ran the path behind the maple trees to cut across to the beeches.

Stepping through the curtain of flowing leaves and branches, I stepped into that other world once more. Here, no work would bend my body until it ached; no harshness could reach through the softness.

Pearl had brought books, one by a woman and one by a man. She flapped them in her hands as if they were wings and their words would give us the power of flight.

"Let's start with this one on etiquette. It's dreadfully boring but the language is a little simpler than Mr. Twain's is, though not nearly as interesting. But I think it a good place for you to start."

Start we did. Slowly, ever so slowly. With the tip of her finger, she scrolled across each line, only moving it when I had learned the word. The movement marked our passage through the work, my passage into the language. The shadows shifted upon the pages beginning to look less like gibberish and more like words.

Don't hold your parasol so close to your face, nor so low down. You cannot see your way clear, and you will run against somebody. Always hold an umbrella or parasol so that it will clear your bonnet, and leave the space before your face open, that you may see your way clearly.

I read it well, happy with my progress. Comprehension filtered through recognition, the meaning ridiculous.

"Do you not understand it?" Pearl asked me, her face florid at whatever she saw upon mine.

"No, I understand." I shrugged with a shake of my head. "But this, this how you live?" I stabbed the page with an accusing finger.

She frowned. When she frowned it was like a dark cloud passing in front of the sun. Such a frown—and one I put there—put something new in our floral cavern. It was an awkward, uncomfortable thing.

"Well, this is how we are made to live."

I began to understand even if she did not.

"Believe it or not, how you hold a parasol is seen as a sign." She lectured with words she spat from puckered lips.

"A sign-a?" I shook my head at the added vowel sound, the part of my accent I had so much trouble erasing from my speech.

"Oh, yes." Pearl chirped, the other Pearl. "Let's say a young lady is walking down the street and she sees a man she likes approaching her. Raising her parasol as he passes tells him she's interested." Pearl taught me much more than how to read and write. "If she wants him to follow her, she would close the parasol and hold it in her right hand. One must be very careful though, the wrong signal can lead to the most dreadful misunderstandings."

I stared at her. She studied my scrunched face.

"Women are not alone in such things." She plucked at her skirt as if she plucked words from an out-of-tune violin. "The men do as well. They must know the right flowers to send and to whom. Red roses, of course, are a sign of true love, while yellow speaks of jealousy or of favor once held lost. Yes, the men must know the language of flowers and how to speak it with…their…florist."

Her words fell away beneath my lengthened stare. She shrugged dismissively, though not without her pale cheeks blushing pink. I couldn't stop myself, though I wish I had.

"These things are…are…*importante?*" I faltered for the English pronunciation.

"Important," Pearl corrected me kindly, as a friend, not a teacher.

"Ah, *si,* important." I held the book out toward her. "These things are important to you?"

To this day, I'm unsure if it was the question or the cynical way I asked her that offended, or whether seeing it through my eyes allowed her to see things all too clearly.

She snatched the book from my lap.

"Well, yes, of course they are important," she said, imitating her mother. "One must live gracefully." She faltered. She didn't like the sound of her mother's voice coming from her mouth any more than I did. "Well, you know."

I grabbed her gaze with mine and held it. She lowered her face against its penetration. We had journeyed to places better left alone, places that disrupted ourselves, and what we were becoming together. Such a journey needed to end.

"Maybe they important, are important," I said, barely keeping the smile from my face. "But not to you. I know what important is to you."

This time I grabbed *her* hand, pulling her down the tree clumsily.

"You will make us fall," she warned as her free arm pin wheeled like a rudder to my engine.

I kept pulling, straight out of our hideaway.

"Ginevra?" Pearl sputtered, stumbling along behind me, gaze flashing this way and that, looking for lookers. I took us into a run toward the carriage house.

No one was there. The grooms were either driving the family or exercising the horses. It was the perfect time.

"Ginevra?" Pearl stammered on thickening confusion, scudding to a stop, pulling her hand from mine. "What are we doing here? Yes, I like to ride but it's not that important to me."

I laughed. I couldn't help myself. I took possession and pulled her again, pulled her up the side stairs on the outside of the carriage house, to the small loft above. I opened the door, stepped back, and thrust her in. Her gasp echoed upon the rafters.

Pearl slapped her hands to her cheeks, walked into the room with slow deliberate steps. She spun to look at me, then spun back. She couldn't take her eyes off the items in the corner by the back, bay window. There stood her easel, a canvas already on it. On a table at its side lay all her paints and brushes.

She spun back again, her face slack with wonder. "Goodness gracious. Ginevra, what have you done?"

It sounded like she scolded me. She didn't. Her smile brimmed and quivered, as did her tears.

I scuffed my toe into the roughhewn wood floor. "I only did what you would do for me."

She came to me and wrapped her arms around me. It was our first embrace. It would not be the last. I had been in her world only a short time, but even then, I knew how rare such an embrace was, an embrace between the privileged and those who served them.

With me still in her arms, Pearl jumped up and down. I had no choice but to jump with her, laugh with her. She jumped and laughed her way to her paints and her easel.

The next time we met, when Pearl came for our reading time, we read *The Adventures of Huckleberry Finn* by Mark Twain.

* * *

I whirled through days in a haze of work and salty breezes. Each day a little of the strangeness of this strange place became familiar. Every morning I woke up to a different me, no matter how tightly I held onto the old.

I saw people of such riches come and go, carrying their wealth with little thought of its treasure. I saw meals served to crowds and intimate parties, food fit for a king's table and his court.

I saw little of Pearl. She had the whirl of society and I my work and my studies. I did both to my best. I almost came into Mrs. Briggs' good graces. Almost.

"Turn the light out already," Greta grumbled at me that night. It was not the first time; it wouldn't be the last. The late-night hours were often the only time I had to do my reading, practice my writing. A servant's day was ten to twelve hours long, even a seamstress, even if all she did was sit in a room in case she was needed, back growing stiff, fingers actually longing for work, and a mind unoccupied to wander adrift. I preferred the nicks of needles in constant motion to the tedium. I didn't know what bothered Greta more, the light or what I did within it. The louder she grumbled, the louder I turned pages.

"Just a few more minutes," I muttered without looking up from my book.

With a huff, she threw off her thin summer bed linen and stomped out.

"I need a wee," she announced as if I asked.

I heard her stomp down the hall. I forgot her as her outraged footsteps faded to soft thumps, becoming as faint as the tick of a clock.

The pictures in the magazine, a copy of Harper's Bazaar I had stolen from the trash bin, set my mind on fire. The glossy pages were filled with fashion, articles on fashion, pictures of fashion, I lost myself to it. I learned who Worth was. I studied each picture, each sleeve, each skirt, picturing how I would change things, imagining how I would design such creations. I left this room, this world, and went to the place of my dreams.

The dream shattered.

"What do you think you are doing?"

Mrs. Briggs stood in the threshold. I hadn't heard her steps, hers and Greta's, hadn't heard the door open. My body and my face tightened, almost painfully.

"Well, I-a reading." Nerves invited back the accent I tried so hard to lose.

She marched across the room to my bed; robe wrapped and tied as tightly around her as her anger, dark ash blonde and gray hair falling in a frazzle down her back. Mrs. Briggs grabbed the magazine from my hands with such force, without warning, the page in my hands ripped. The sound made me flinch.

"Harper's Bazaar? Hah!" she laughed at me, so did Greta, standing behind her, smirking with satisfaction. "Why does a girl like you need to be reading such a thing?"

"I thought...good for my work."

"Your work is to mend and fix, nothing more. Your kind will never be anything more."

My gaping mouth snapped closed. Pain stabbed my jaw as my teeth ground together. I longed for a sharp tongue in full possession of English with which to whip her.

"Go to bed, go to sleep this minute," Mrs. Briggs ordered, stomping out of the room with the same anger in which she had entered, taking the magazine with her.

Greta slipped back into her bed, "Nighty, night, Geeneeva," she twittered at me.

I stared at her back. There was an English word for her, I had heard the men in the basement use it. It began with a 'b,' though that was all I could remember. In my language, under my breath, I called her a *puttana*.

* * *

Somehow, one of Mrs. Worthington's day dresses, one of her favorites, had become ripped at two seams, long stretches of them. I spent the entire morning fixing them, every stitch I made, I made with the best of care.

"Ah you done yet?"

I jumped. Once more Mrs. Briggs stood in the threshold.

"Almost," I replied, unable to keep a note of pride out of my voice.

Within a flash, she stood before me and my table perched before the window. Mrs. Briggs picked up the dress, scoured it with mean eyes. Her two hands traveled down the length of one seam, all the way to the hem. She pulled.

The rip was like a scream, it screeched through my head. In seconds, she destroyed hours of my work; in truth, she longed to destroy my strength.

"Not good enough." She dropped the dress on the desk. "Do it again. Better this time."

She left as she came. I barely noticed.

The clanging in my head wouldn't stop. My hands shook. I gripped the edge of the table until my knuckles blazed white-hot. She had made the damage worse; she had made my job harder. I almost thought to throw it away, almost.

I picked it up and began again. If the battle continued, I would not fall to it.

* * *

I had had no lunch, thanks to Mrs. Briggs and her destruction. I skipped it to finish the work, just barely making it to the dinner table in time.

I sat beside my father as always. He rarely saw me, saw my truth, for he rarely looked for it, but not that night. He raised his shoulders at me, face scrunched by question and confusion. I just shook my head, sat, and began to eat.

As my hunger ebbed so did my anger. Not for long.

"Faleece!" From the senior staff table, Mrs. Briggs bellowed at my father.

He sat upright, stopped chewing.

"The sideboard door has broken, again. You will fix it after dinner. Do not go to your bed until you do." It was an ungracious order, in truth, one Mr. Birch should have given. Mrs. Briggs brought her displeasure with me crashing down upon my father. Hatred is a poisonous thing; we do not often have the antidote for our own. My back stiffened. My fingers turned white as I strangled the fork in my hand.

"It is Felice, feh-LEE-cheh," I said with more force than I had said anything in my life.

"Eh, what's that you say, girl?" Mrs. Briggs grumbled, nearly growled.

I didn't even turn my gaze to her.

"My father's name is Felice," I said with the correct pronunciation, my softer exclamation did not diminish my stern intent. "We been here almost two months. I think it polite you say it right. I believe he has, eh, earn it."

Before she or anyone could say more, I thrust my chair back and stomped away.

In the quiet I left the room in, I heard her bellow, "Why you...come back here, girl!"

I neither went back nor turned back. I never heard my father's name pronounced incorrectly ever again.

* * *

I didn't go far. I sat in my father's room waiting for him. He came in for his tools to fix the wretched sideboard.

"You should ask for more money," I said in English as he took a step in the door.

He hesitated, whether by my presence or my words, I don't know. In the few moments we had here and there, he had started speaking more and more English, though his accent was still heavy, heavier than my own. Only with me, would he practice it.

"*É basta*. It enough," he answered, stepping to his tools, picking through them. "We have home, we have food, what-a more you want?"

I didn't blink. "Freedom."

For one of the few times in my life, his eyes found mine with a snap. "I have my pride," he said in Italian.

Without letting him go, I said, "Pride is a luxury."

I stood. I would try no more. If he had answered me differently—if there had been but a smidgen of empathy, of support—each day that would come after this day might have been different. The fight ebbed out of me as water swirls down a drain, leaving the sink empty.

I went to stand by him at his worktable. I saw huge pieces of mahogany set beside smaller, already cut pieces. In one of those, I glimpsed the basic figure of a woman, the start of scrolls.

"This is not for violin, Papa." My voice squeaked with surprise. "What are you making?"

He picked up one of the pieces, his hands caressing it lovingly. Without looking away, without releasing his hold on the wood, he said in Italian, "The master has asked for a cabinet. He called it something else, an English word for it...broken front?" It wasn't a question, merely his unknowing. "A display piece, for the violins I make for him."

I was pleased for my father. I could see how this newfound purpose did much to bring him back to life, out of the limbo he had been stuck in since my mother's passing.

I meant to tell him, tell him how happy I was for him, but his absorption with his work, his caressing of the wood, had commenced once more. I longed for such a touch from him. A longing never to be fulfilled, save for one time yet to come.

"You don't belong here, girl." Once more Mrs. Briggs had found me, once more her cruelty slapped me. "Get back to work."

"*Buona notte*," I whispered to my father. He nodded silently.

* * *

My father shuffled into my room the next afternoon, head hung low, hat still in hand. He said nothing but quirked his head outward.

I stood in the same murky silence.

"*Cofano*," he muttered and turned from the doorway.

I grabbed my bonnet as instructed and followed.

He took me on a rare outing that Sunday afternoon. It was our turn to have this particular time off, one so coveted by every servant in this gilded world. Every servant was allowed one evening and one afternoon off from work; my father rarely stopped working.

It was his apology, though I had to listen to the underneath of the silence to hear it.

Though my father rarely took days off as the rest of the staff did—on a regular, rotating, strictly followed schedule—there were a few times when we had ventured from the estate, mostly when something was happening my father deemed worthy—an historical re-enactment on the commons, a performance by the small orchestra Newport boasted. I'm still unsure what prevented him—something deep within him—from simply having fun.

I could still remember our days back in Foggia, when a festival filled the small piazza, burst its seams with music and laughter, food and wine.

My father would stand on the outskirts. Not alone, but with a few men of similar reserve, little more than a few words passing between them as we played and danced. Perhaps he simply loved to watch my mother, the beauty in the center who charmed us children, who danced with such grace her limbs moved with the same magical floating as her long, dark hair.

Yes, perhaps he wanted nothing more than to watch her, for his eyes hardly ever left her.

I accepted his apology in the same silence that he offered it.

PEARL

The summer was passing quickly, too quickly. I wanted more time, time with Ginevra under the beeches. Yes, her strangeness had infatuated me at first, but soon, very soon, it was our likeness that captured me, a deeper likeness that broke the boundaries of our shallow differences. I longed for our unique conversations, teaching her, learning from her. I blessed her presence in my life every time I snuck off to the carriage house loft. Thanks to her, my hands still knew the tingle when I held a brush. I still dreamed; it didn't matter that it was in secret.

The cottages on Newport took up but a small tip of the small island, and yet it was a whirlwind, a prevailing vortex that sucked us in, holding us there with its intangible but potent seizure. My youth did not exempt me from it. It had been days and days of events, days without any time with Ginevra, yet I dared not make excuses for not attending today's event. In truth, I was intrigued.

Alva Erskine Smith Vanderbilt, one of the leading ladies of Newport, one of three that formed a powerful trio that determined not only proper behavior but who would and would not be accepted into our world. She was a woman I took pains to avoid. Yet when Mother informed me that Mrs. Vanderbilt was hosting a party where a special speaker would attend—a speaker for women *and* young women—I was eager, for once, to accompany her.

I had been in Marble House before, yet it never failed to amaze me. Considered the most striking of all the cottages, Mrs. Vanderbilt reminded everyone whenever possible. I remember my father talking about it when we were in Paris, how it was modeled after the Petit Trianon of Versailles. I had heard others compare it to the White House or the Temple of Apollo as well. Regardless of its origins, it was the very essence of opulence and grandeur captured by the cottages of Newport.

As was Mrs. Vanderbilt herself. She dominated Newport society with willpower and boldness, not beauty or charm, for she possessed little of either. Frizzy mouse-brown hair sat atop a plump face, a roundness matching her body, her bulbous nose turned up at the least provocation.

What she did have was a sophisticated French boarding school education and a lineage of southern aristocracy. She had been summering in Newport since before the Civil War; perhaps that's why she thought it belonged to her, and none of these Yankee newcomers. There were rumors about the hard times of her life, when her father lost his money, when her mother lost her life. A gruff exterior builds a great wall for shielding pain, for hiding it in a world where truths were so often hidden. What she also had was her husband, one of the richest men in the world.

Mother and I entered the Gold Ballroom, not the largest in Newport but by far the most ornate, to find every woman—young and old—of standing in attendance. The buzz of excited voices echoed off the carved gilt wall panels and huge painted ceiling.

"Well, how odd," Mother said sotto voce, whether to me or herself, I wasn't sure. "Alva is not greeting her guests."

She wasn't. Instead, the indomitable presence of Mrs. Vanderbilt stood grandly at the front of the room. Beside her, a very serious-looking woman, the speaker, no doubt. She wore a simple black dress, though corseted, it bore none of the frills and lace and embellishments *en vogue*. Even her hair spoke of her; it was not curled and piled but flattened and held back in a tight bun. I was already curious.

"Ladies, ladies, to order please." Mrs. Vanderbilt clapped her hands with a crack, her voice boomed over the twittering. Mother and I quickly sat in two of the sea of chairs, as did all the others. The room fell into an abyss of expectant silence.

"I'm so pleased to see you all here today," Mrs. Vanderbilt began. I almost laughed, as if we had a choice. When Alva Vanderbilt called, everyone answered, or they would know her chill for years to come. "And I am so proud to introduce you to a new friend of mine, Miss Lucy Stone."

As a small round of applause ensued, the serious woman stepped up beside Mrs. Vanderbilt.

"Miss Stone, here, is the first woman from Massachusetts to earn a college degree."

Lighting struck me; the tips of my fingers tingled. Mother released a huff. I sat up straighter.

"With others, she helped organize the first National Women's Rights Convention as well as the formation of the American Woman Suffrage Association," Mrs. Vanderbilt continued her introduction. My mother continued her mews of displeasure. "And she is a regular contributor to the *Woman's Journal*. You will all find a copy of the latest issue beneath your seats."

Like many, but not all, I reached quickly for the slim broadsheet beneath my chair as Miss Stone began to speak.

"Thank you, Alva." Miss Stone's voice was a whisper in comparison to her sponsor, yet most ears hung on every word. "And thank you all for coming today. I know there are some here that may not be receptive to the things I have to say. To those of you, I first want to say that I do believe that a woman's truest place is in a home, with a husband and with children. However, their lives should also include large freedom, pecuniary freedom, personal freedom, and the right to vote."

Murmurs of all sorts shuddered through the room. Lucy Stone was not daunted.

"Half a century ago women were at an infinite disadvantage in regard to their occupations. The idea that their sphere was at home, and only at home, was like a band of steel on society. But the spinning wheel and the loom, which had given employment to women, had been superseded by machinery, and something else had to take their places. The taking care of the house and children, and the family sewing, and teaching the little summer school at a dollar per week, could not supply the needs nor fill the aspirations of women. But every departure from these conceded things was met with the cry, 'You want to get out of your sphere,' or, 'To take women out of their sphere;' and that was to fly in the face of Providence, to unsex yourself in short, to be monstrous women, women who, while they orated in public, wanted men to rock the cradle and wash the dishes. We pleaded that whatever was fit to be done at all might with propriety be done by anybody who did it well; that the tools belonged to those who could use them; that the possession of a power presupposed a right to its use."

A few of the older women stood, their noses thrown into the air as they left the room. Mother pulled on my arm; I shook it off with a vengeance. Miss Stone continued without a care for those departing; clearly, it was not the first time she and her message had received such a reaction.

"We believe that personal independence and equal human rights can never be forfeited, except for crime; that marriage should be an equal and permanent partnership, and so recognized by law; that until it is so recognized, married partners should provide against the radical injustice of present laws, by every means in their power."

"We are leaving, Pearl, this minute. You should not hear this nonsense," Mother hissed at me as she stood, pinching my arm until I stood up beside her. She grabbed the journal in my hand and tossed it on the floor. I had no choice but to follow. The room was long, and we were at its front. It was impossible not to hear more as we made our way out.

"A wife should no more take her husband's name than he should hers. My name is my identity and must not be lost."

They say lightning never strikes the same place twice, yet I was once more struck. "My identity." The words followed me, came with me, stayed with me, as they would for years to come. Mother might have taken me from the woman's presence. She might have robbed me of the journal I so wanted to read—though I knew I would find a way to reclaim it. She may have tried to renounce all I had heard, insist I give it no credence as she did the whole ride home, but I gave no credence to my mother's words. That belonged to Lucy Stone and those of her ilk. I couldn't wait to share them all with Ginevra.

* * *

The footmen packed the line of carriages to overflowing. The high heat and humidity of August had given way to cooler nights and foggier mornings. It was time for us to leave. Last year, I packed my personal bag with a rush, hurried to the carriage. This year, I dallied and lingered.

I was eager to return to school, to regular studies of depth, unlike those of the irksome Miss Jameson. Yet the thought of not seeing Ginevra again for ten months tainted my eagerness. Our conversations beneath the beeches had only grown more intense after telling her of Lucy Stone, as we read the copies of the *Woman's Journal* I had had her purchase and secret away to our spot. We were Pearl and Ginevra, the same girls who had met beneath the beeches, but that Pearl and that Ginevra were no longer.

"Come along, Pearl," my mother called up the stairs to me. In the quiet already taking up its winter residence, I could hear the tap, tap, tap of her fancy shoes upon the marble floor of the foyer.

"Coming, Mother," I called out from my door, but instead of heading to the family stairs, I snuck across the hall, and into the sewing room.

I found her there, back to the door, standing at the window looking down at the carriages.

"It is time," was all she said.

I said nothing.

Without thought, I went to her and wrapped my arms around her waist. She put her arms around mine.

"Will you go the whole way in those?" She pointed down at the carriages, said 'those' as if they were something she despised. I suppose she did.

"No," I replied, though I smiled at how well she spoke, how far she had come in just our short time together. "We'll sail home on the steamer, out of Fall River."

Her brows crinkled as she looked back at me. "A falling river?"

I giggled. It made her smile, a little. "No, dear, Fall River. It is a town in Massachusetts, the next state from here. They have ships that go back and forth between New York and Newport. It is how all the men travel from week to week, back and forth."

"Ah," she said, nodding.

Ginevra turned. We faced each other.

"I am but a breath of time away. You'll see," I whispered.

I ran out, not from her, but our sadness.

GINEVRA

She was gone. Life became pale as the winter sun, marked by the dry, scraping sound of dead leaves as the wind rattled them along empty streets.

I kept busy. Only four of us stayed behind. The general caretaker, Bruce Grayson was a crabby and sullen man who saw to things such as the plumbing and the heating, as well as the grounds. Staying seemed to suit him just fine. He rarely strayed from his rooms in the carriage house, joining us only for meals, still sitting at the senior staff table, though he was the only one remaining.

Mrs. O'Brennan stayed behind, the middle-aged widow who, during the season, served as second to the chef. She cooked for us as well as taking on housekeeping chores, as did I. What there were of them.

At first, our days were a rush to return all to perfection, though the perfection would stand unnoticed, a woman dressed beautifully to stay in her room, unseen. We covered the furniture with yards and yards of white fabric. We shuttered the windows of all the family's rooms as if we closed our eyes to them, blocking out the sight of them.

As the winter stretched out, the months like years, I often snuck onto the family floors to walk about the ghosts, the beautiful furnishings and sculptures covered in their protective linens. I feared and worshipped them.

They were so like the ghosts in stories I read with Pearl, like those Charlotte Bronte wrote of in *Jane Eyre*. Yet they gave me hope, for their very presence insured that they—that she—would be coming back. Their company was far better than the silent sullenness of Mrs. O'Brennan.

She swept floors every day, one floor a day from bottom to top, and then started again. I helped her, dusting away the cobwebs. I helped with meals as well, and though we were side by side for many hours, an ocean lay between us, never to be crossed. She stayed within the emptiness of her life. Any attempts to bring her out of it was like trying to pull out a weed whose roots were buried far too deep in the ground.

I remember the day she was making tarts, delicious tarts I found irresistible, eating seconds even when my full belly told me not to.

"These is…are wonderful, Mrs. O'Brennan." I went and stood beside her by the nearly empty countertop. "Where you learn to cook so well?"

She kept on kneading the dough. "Here and there."

She might as well have not answered. I tried again.

"You from." I stopped, corrected myself, Pearl's voice in my ear. "Are you from here, Newport?"

Mrs. O'Brennan nodded. "A Rhody, born and raised."

"So, your family, they are here too?"

Her hands hesitated their manipulation. It was so quick I was lucky to see it.

"I've been in service to the Worthington's since I was a child," she said in an accent I had come to learn belonged to the people of this region. The "Rhody," a mixture of the English so many were descended from, but far less lyrical. "They are my family."

What a sad statement; what could I say in response? I said nothing. Nor did I try to talk with her again. I had made my attempt, told her I would be a companion, should she want one. I could do nothing more. Day after day, we spent side-by-side draped in silence as the cloths draped the furniture.

I continued my studies, reading with the thirst of a dried sponge, conjuring up headaches as I tried to improve my cyphering skills. I made great headway in the uninterrupted world that had become my life, with no Greta to grumble at me, no Mrs. Briggs and her reprimands.

Other servants, the others left behind in other cottages, came to visit now again. They talked much about the lives of their masters rather than their own lives.

There was so much rain. Minute drips clung to everything like a dotted web; colors—flowers, lush lawn, stone beauties—were a grayer shade of themselves. As was I.

Then came the snow. My father and I had never seen snow. I found an old coat in the carriage house, a man's far too big for me, but I put it on anyway and went out in it. It looked so different from how it felt. It looked like a layer of thick icing, but when I picked it up, it fluttered through my fingers. Yet, after a big storm hit, when the snow came up to my knees, walking through it was like walking through thick mud. I laughed every time I went out. It was one of the few joys of winter in Newport.

Once, I caught my father watching me. That once, I saw a real smile on his face.

When May hit, it hit like the storms of winter.

The house woke up. The same was true for all the cottages. Everywhere there was rushing in preparation for the return of the families. Such madness for four people, when a different four—the four of us—had been living so simply, without any fuss, for so long. Mrs. O'Brennan kept me busy from dawn to dusk and well after. The beds were made, fresh towels put on the racks, lampshades dusted. We freed the furniture from their slumber beneath the draperies.

In the final days before the Worthington's return, fresh flowers—purple hyacinths with their deeply floral scent...the prickly beautiful forsythia and their waxing aroma—filled every room in the house, bunches and bunches on every table, sometimes four or five to a room. Fresh fruit sat expectantly in bowls beneath. We polished everything to a glittering gleam.

I polished myself as well. For her.

PEARL

1896

Nothing had changed, and I had never been so grateful.

The hectic life in New York had pushed through the months with a fury. As I watched them flitter by, I felt nothing but gratitude.

The frantic activity of arrival erupted in the house on Bellevue. The staff brought in trunk after trunk, even their own, which they had to haul up to the hidden third floor.

I entered my room, breathed a sigh. Contentment awaited me in my pale green room with its silk linens and its pink accent lace. I sat primly while my trunks were brought in, while one of the chambermaids unpacked for me.

There was so much more to unpack this year. Just a few days away from turning seventeen, I put away forever the short pinafore dresses of a child with their sailor collars, and the plain bonnets, and now wore the long dresses of a woman. True, they weren't as adorned or as flamboyant as those of a true adult, a woman of eighteen who had had her coming out. Nor was I allowed to pin my hair up in the twisting, complication coifs so in vogue, but the long dresses brought me to the beginning of a crossroad, one that lay many divergent paths before me.

The chambermaid retreated. I counted her steps. As soon as they were gone, I made for the door, for her.

She was already there.

Ginevra's head poked out the frosted glass door separating the family quarters from those of the staff. On her face was the sweetest smile I had ever seen.

I rushed out my door, she out of hers. We threw ourselves together.

GINEVRA

With summer, she came, and my life filled with color. With her arrival, I leaned out to the floor forbidden to me, daring to bring the
disapproval and scorn from the others below. I didn't care at all.

To feel Pearl's arms around me was as if to feel my mother's, one
arm of tenderness, one of belonging.

"Come, let me show you my new gowns," she cried, her first words
to me after she hugged me. I smelled her expensive perfume and hoped
it would stick to me as the smoke of the kitchen always did.

There was no showing off in her showing, only the thrill of fashion we both shared. I inspected every garment, seeing the change in
designs to the more-sporty looks I had studied all winter.

The postman had continued to deliver *Harper's Bazaar* to the cottage and there was no one to read them but me, no one to stop me from
reading them. I had practically memorized the designs as I had the new
words I discovered in the books I borrowed from Mr. Worthington's
library.

Mrs. Worthington had her own library as well, but it was a children's library compared to that of her husband. Like many women of
the day, she abided by the practice of separating the books by male
and female authors, not allowing one to touch the other. That alone
squashed any enthusiasm for the tomes I might have found there.

"They are beautiful, Pearl," I said. "And you will look even more
beautiful than ever wearing them."

"Ginevra!" The dress in Pearl's hand fluttered to the ground; her
head spun. "Your speech! You sound wonderful, almost American."

I glowed beneath her praise; a longed-for thing so absent in my life.
We mirrored each other's smiles.

She hadn't changed much in our months apart. Pearl was a little
taller, but then so was I. Her face had thinned. I could see a true change
in it, a true glimpse of the woman she would become. I wondered if
my face had changed in any way. The three people I had been alone

with for all these months would not have told me if it had. My mirror showed me only what I thought I could—should—see.

"Thank you, Pearl. I am so very glad you are home." To her, this was her summer getaway. To me, it was her home as well as mine. "You should hear me read."

"I must," she chirped with delight, "right now. You know where we must go."

The beeches. I sighed.

In the months of spring, I had watched their spindly skeletons grow fuzzy with buds then burst with fluffy leaves. I imagined they grew thicker and thicker for us, to make our hiding place more hidden than ever. I never went, not even in the warmer months. Her absence there would have made her absence too complete.

"I...," I wanted to go there with her, more than anything. Such desire could not erase my truth. "Mrs. Briggs will—"

"Mrs. Briggs will be in a frightful tizzy," Pearl said, putting her gowns back in the splendid wardrobe of dark wood and white porcelain trimming. "Come," she insisted, grabbing my hand, pulling me through the house and out to the trees as she had the first time. She truly was home.

PEARL

My long dress tangled around my ankles, my feet stumbled and slipped, my balance tested.

"Now you know how it is for me," Ginevra giggled behind me as I struggled to hold on to my skirts and hold on to the tree. I laughed with her.

Ginevra read to me for a bit, astounding me with her progress, she barely faltered, and when she did, it was on words many Americans would stumble upon as well. She changed my opinion of her intellect to fact. She grasped our language quickly, making me laugh with her few bumbles and misses, for she laughed at them as well. How I loved people who could laugh at themselves.

She was my Ginevra, but she wasn't. She was a year older, yes, and her physical form had changed a bit: her cheekbones were so much more prominent as were her budding breasts. Her voice was different; it was no longer a whisper.

As we had made our way to our beeches, she didn't hide behind me, didn't seem to care about hiding, about slipping unnoticed through these trees, this life. Her eyes didn't dart about; she looked straight ahead. She was no longer a dog fearing its brutal master. It made her even more beautiful. All my life I've known women for whom another's beauty would make friendship impossible. I wondered how the footmen would look at her now.

"Oh!" The thought of Ginevra and men brought another thought, another something to share. "I met a boy, well, a young man."

Ginevra's smile ran up her face, into her almond-shaped eyes. "A boy?! Tell me, tell me everything."

I did. I told her how I had met Frederick Havemeyer at the opera.

"His mother is an Astor, so you can imagine how happy that makes my mother."

I laughed as Ginevra rolled her eyes.

He sought me out at other affairs, always chatting with me, asking me about school. He was a friend of my brother's and much like him.

I gave that little thought, for they seemed reserved for the strange feeling he wrought from the pit of my stomach, how shy I became in his presence.

"You, shy?" Ginevra squeaked. "I do not believe."

I dropped my chin though I grinned. "Well, he is four years older than I, a real young gentleman. He could have his pick of girls already out."

But he didn't. He chose to talk to me more than any of them. He crept into my thoughts far too often.

"He is here?" Ginevra asked with still a hint of her accent, its sound now exotic somehow. "Will you see him here, in Newport?"

I nodded, again dropping my chin, hiding the flush warming my face.

To speak of him gave flight to whatever it was that fluttered in my stomach so. "Oh, yes. His family has a lovely English cottage, right at the start of the Cliff Walk. I've heard it has the most amazing view."

"Perhaps you will get to see this view." Ginevra waggled her brows at me. I giggled.

"I think I will, I hope I will," It was my truth, and it was safe in her keeping.

Her open heart and mind opened my own. Friendships among the set were puddles, shallow and reflective of what lay only on the surface. Friendship with Ginevra was a deep ocean, full of exotic creatures and life, full of things to discover.

"The last time I saw him was at a musicale. Just before he left me, he leaned down," I leaned toward Ginevra as he had, my lips close to her ear. "He's very tall, very broad, with sparkling blue eyes beneath golden hair—and he whispered, 'I'll see you again, my dear, soon.' "

Ginevra sucked in her breath. It brought it all back with a hiccup of my own. I shivered as if I could still feel his warm breath on my skin. Never had a boy—a young man—affected me so. It felt much as it had when I put on my very first full-length dress.

I did not share the dreams of a pristine white wedding dress, of running a home, as did all my other friends. After listening to Lucy Stone, reading more of her articles, I knew there was the promise of more on the horizon. In his presence, I forgot all those words I had read.

I looked up. Her eyes were waiting for mine.

"Have you been reading *Women's Journal?*" she asked, quietly as if it were a sin.

I simply smiled, as did she. But then...

"Oh!" I cried as I pulled the folded and creased bit of newspaper from my pocket. "I know you didn't see this; you couldn't have, it was in the *New York Times.*"

Ginevra snatched it from my hands, ever hungry for more reading, for more news of the hurtling journey women seemed to be traveling. I read with her, leaning over her shoulder:

WOMEN CAST MOCK BALLOT

New York, Nov. 3—Women will today have their first opportunity to voice in New York. Of course, their votes will not be officially counted, but they will vote just the same.

The suffragettes have arranged for receiving ballot boxes and polling places in various theaters, and the suffragettes will have their own voting places.

"To vote?" Ginevra kept her gaze firmly upon the tatter of paper in her hands.

"Yes, Ginevra," I whispered, as one did in church. "To cast a vote is to decide which man will be president, or senator, which man the voter wants to make decisions on government issues. To vote is a right and a privilege only men have had." I tapped the paper in her hand. "If this continues, it may not be much longer until we get the same rights."

"Until we get to decide," she whispered as I did.

I nodded. Our eyes locked; together we looked at the future. "I have heard rumors that there may be a mock vote held here, right in New-port."

"Would you do it?" she asked me.

"Would you?"

"Yes," we answered together.

Her gaze dropped back to the powerful words immortalized on the paper. "It changes much," she said.

I shook my head, "It changes everything."

We chewed on that for a while, but it was like taking a small bite out of a feast for four hundred.

"Do you want to marry, Ginevra?" I asked her after a time.

She said not a word. She looked up. My gaze followed hers. The sun had reached its apex. Through the straggle that was the beeches' limbs, its form, bright warm rays scurried through the gaps, dappled our faces with its light. We both stared at the limitless sky.

"Yes, I think I do." Her eyes remained upon the sky; she shared a thing we see in the firmament.

"You think?" I prodded.

"I want children and a home. I want love, yes." She turned to me, her lovely features twisting; her thoughts, like mine, resembled the branches of our beeches. There are few thoughts that did not twist upon others. "It is what we are meant to do, *si?*"

I looked to the ground below us. Down there was where we lived; the sky was where we dreamed.

"Yes, it is what we are told we are meant to do."

Her head bobbed slowly. "The world, it shows us our, eh, path, yes? But what if we want another path or a wider path?"

"A wider path?"

"*Si,* I want a husband who loves me, children to care for, a house to call my own. But there is something in me that wants more. Something mine alone."

"Mine alone," I murmured. She was a thief skulking through my mind. We were of an impressionable age in an age of change, change especially for those our age. "If only there could be a man to love who would let us have such a thing." I looked at her dead on. "Do you think there is something wrong with us?"

Her face crinkled. "Wrong?"

I nodded with dispirit. "Yes, wrong. Is it wrong that we want other things than simply marriage and children? My mother says it's wrong, says these 'new women' are wrong."

Ginevra chewed on my words. Her gaze dotted my face, but I did not think it was my face she saw.

"It's no wrong, it's different," she said.

Ginevra raised her face to the crepuscular rays of the sun finding us through the patchwork of the beeches, brushing the long, thick chocolate hair from her face. She closed her eyes; her full lips had just the slightest upturn at their corners. Without moving, she spoke the truth, a hard, irrevocable truth, "Yes, different. It is a good thing, no? But I think we will pay for it anyway."

The changing way of life, of women, was a part of us, as we were a part of it; another tie that bound us. We would try to have it all, the "more" that itched at us, and love, just as Lucy Stone had said. Neither of us knew how we would, only that we had to try.

She took my hand. "To find such a man, a man that could support us, the true us, that would be the best, but I am no sure there are such men."

"Oh!" I cried, thinking of Frederick, wondering if he was such a man. I suddenly remembered I might see him that very afternoon. "I have to go. Mrs. Fish is throwing a party for Marion, her daughter. She's a few years younger than I, but it should be a wonderful party."

"Maybe he will be there," Ginevra said. Her eyes sparkled as the corners of her mouth twitched upward. She made my hope her own.

I took her hand.

"I'm so glad to be back with you." Truer words I had never spoken. She squeezed my hand and nodded.

"We will spend more time together this summer," I promised her. "It may be a struggle," I warned her. "Mother is fanatical about my push into society. She's obsessed with plans for my birthday party. But I will not let so many things take away from our time. It is too precious to me."

"And to me," Ginevra said softly. "But you are right, it may be hard. I saw Mrs. Briggs for a few minutes earlier. She made it clear she will work me to the bone. Your seamstress in New York, she was no good?"

"She was fair," I answered truthfully. My first long dresses had been purchased from the House of Worth. Englishman Charles Worth had become a couture phenomenon in Napoleon Paris. Anyone who was anyone wore his clothes. Any alternations, any repairs, were left to the woman's seamstress.

"Mrs. Briggs said she was not, eh, up to standards."

My eyes bulged. "What a wonderful compliment."

Ginevra stared at me; one brow raised in silly cynicism. Oh, how I had missed her.

"Don't you see? She was implying, though I'm sure she would cut out her tongue if she knew she did so, it was *your* standards the girl in New York couldn't live up to."

Ginevra's eyes flew open, blinked rapidly. Her small smile was a gift I had not received in far too long.

A thought—a seed—was planted in my mind then. I sniffed a laugh as it grew.

"There may be a way we can see each other more." I leaned over and planted a kiss on her smooth cheek. I picked up my skirts and made my way down. "I shall see you soon."

I hurried away before she could ask the questions writ upon her face. I left her in perplexity, shrouded in my mysterious words. I would say no more, not until I was sure.

GINEVRA

I returned to the house, made my way to my room to change before dinner. Try though I might, I could not seem to force the corners of my mouth downward. They dropped as I walked in the door.

There was Greta returned once more, once more to share the room I had had all to myself for so many months. She hadn't changed. Her freckled face still pinched with displeasure at the sight of me.

"Oh," she said, "it's you."

"It is me," I said, pleased to see her surprise at my diction, "and it is you. We are together again. But no worry, I do most of my reading out there now."

I pointed to the small landing between our window and the inside of the false outer wall.

As winter had warmed to spring, I had found myself there more and more. I had seen many of the staff do the same last summer but had never found the courage to go myself. With them gone, I had made it mine as well. Sometimes I climbed out the window instead of using the door at the far end of the hall. I followed the sun around the landing as it made its way up and over the house, like a flower following its glowing warmth. I couldn't see over the false wall; it was taller than I was. The sun and the tops of the trees and the smell of the ocean, those found me. Contented by their company, I would sit and read, and pretend I was back in Italy. It was a place almost as dear as the place beneath the beeches.

Greta laughed her mean laugh, shook her head at me. "Still reading. Whatcha' doin' all that readin' for? Ye don' need it sewing buttons."

I didn't answer. My words would be as lost in her mind as a guppy is in the ocean. I could think only of what Pearl's last words could mean.

PEARL

The day was so extraordinary fair, so warm and brilliant with sunshine, the non-conformist that was Mrs. Mamie Fish, decided to stage her daughter's party on the front lawn of Crossways, a Colonial-style mansion overlooking the harbor. How her peers had teased her, in their biting way, for not building on the more fashionable Bellevue Avenue rather than on the west side of the tip of the island, on Ocean Avenue.

"We're not rich, pet," she called a lot of people "pet," mostly because she was terrible at remembering names, "we only have a few million." It was a statement only one of the great trio of women could make. Women, who, besides Mrs. Astor, sat at the top of the social pyramid of this life defined by where one sat.

As soon as we arrived, my mother swiftly ran off to find our hostess, to kowtow, to praise. She should have just begged; it would have been faster for the truth to find her.

I should have done the same, simply greeting Mrs. Fish, but I didn't. Nor did I seek out any of my acquaintances, not even Consuelo, my true friend among a set of those who pretended to be. My eyes scanned the jubilant crowd for Frederick and none other. I needed to see him, his true self, removing the blinders attached to me since birth. I did not know how often I wore those blinders were it not for my conversations with Ginevra. Frederick was everything my mother would wish for me. That thought alone made me question my own.

The crowd of people milling about the lawn, dapper in their frothy day dresses and striped blazers, was in fine spirits. The sun here was different from in the city; its glow and warmth penetrated deeper, finding the us deep inside, the us that hid behind heavy coats of pretension and pomposity. The smell of the ocean and the sound of waves crashing on shore infused us with their potent energy. The rules of our lives didn't change, but the happiness to be in this remarkable place changed how we lived within them.

I wandered about, merrily returning the many merry greetings cast my way, looking, always looking. Just when I had given up hope, there he was. He looked even more dashing in his casual navy-blue sack coat and striped pants, his white shirt, collar pressed pristinely down over the matching navy tie. His blue eyes blazed beneath his straw boater.

He saw me then, too. His roving eyes passed me, returned, and stopped on me, stopped and smiled. He offered me a wink and, once more, my stomach tumbled, like the children tumbling down the hill of grass.

In a circle of other such young, dashing men, including my brother, his hands flew, his lips turned up and down as the surf came in and out, his laughter joined theirs as it crashed onshore. Frederick could have been any of the others he stood with; perhaps he wasn't or perhaps that was simply a wish.

Another within this circle, a handsome one I had to admit, locked his gaze upon me as well. I could not hear his voice, though I saw his lips move, nor could I hear his laughter though his head tipped back with the boisterousness of it. His clothes, clearly expensive, did not flash as the others did. His was not a gaze I had experienced before. I pulled from it, its unfathomable hold upon me, demurely nodding my head at Frederick—hoping it was demure—letting him know, without a word, I would be waiting when he could detach himself.

I could dally no longer; it was time I paid my respects to my hostess. Mother would hunt me down if I did not do so soon. I made my way to the front of the house.

There they sat, the three who would one day be known as the Great Triumvirate.

Like queens on three high-backed cane chairs, they perched and possessed the shade beneath the front portico held aloft by four giant Corinthian columns, their pastel afternoon dresses vivid against the pure white house.

Alva Vanderbilt sat in the center, for she was the core of them.

As I approached, my steps growing shorter the closer I crept, I remembered Mother's drilling of how, and how not, to address Mamie

Fish. She would oust anyone who said, "pleased to meet you," instead of "how do you do," "pardon me" instead of "I beg your pardon," or "I presume" instead of "I suppose." Those who faltered would never step a foot near Crossways again.

I was only a few of those steps away from them when I heard her voice—her low, raspy sort of voice—speak my name. It was a closed door that magically appeared, stopped me cold. I turned my back, not taking a single step away.

"I see the Worthington girl is here, Pearl, I believe it is," Mrs. Vanderbilt said in that practiced tone of hers; it was both flat and haughty. Did she really think I couldn't hear her though I was only a few steps away? Or did she think herself so above me it didn't matter?

"Yes, she is. As well as her brother." Marion Graves Anthon Fish—known to those whom she allowed as Mamie—cast her sharp, deep eyes set in her long, dour face about. "Just there."

She was the strangest of the three, I thought. At times her behavior bordered on the outrageous, kicking sand in the face of the milieu in which she surrounded herself, yet known for the most innovative and extravagant of parties. Her balls and dinners were often the highlights of the season, and yet she deigned the whirl of teas, card-calling, coaching parades, operas, and musicales that were so much a part of this life. A true dichotomous personality, though perhaps I think there were other words for it, words not so polite.

Her rudimentary upbringing and limited education resounded in every one of her, "Howdy-do, howdy-do", her favorite greeting. Yet her ambition was a force to be reckoned with—that few dared reckon with—determined to not only reach social prominence but to rule it, all the while appearing as if she detested it. There were many faces to Mamie Fish, as they were to most who summered in Newport. They exchanged them as they did calling cards.

I often heard my father talking to Mr. Fish—Mr. Stuyvesant Fish—calling him an angel. For all of Mamie's outward acrimony, theirs was a love match, one that endured, as he endured, her fluctuating moods with patience and unruffled manners.

Mrs. Fish, however, was best known for her mouth, not its beauty or what she put it in, but what came out of it. My mother had actually heard her call Alva Vanderbilt a toad once, but that was the least of it.

We had been in the receiving line of one of her parties once, and I had heard her sharp tongue for myself.

"Make yourselves at home," she told the couple entering before us, "and believe me, there is no one who wishes you were there more than I do."

I shuddered to imagine her turning that tongue upon me. I held my breath as I waited for the next words.

"You surprise me, Mamie." Mrs. Vanderbilt sipped her lemonade without a sound.

"Well, yes, I suppose it would surprise you," Mrs. Fish's cackle dripped with the same sarcastic tone. "But they are dear children. My Marion adores Pearl so. And their father is utterly mahvelous."

"Oh, I agree wholeheartedly about Mr. Worthington," Mrs. Oelrichs, the final point in the triangle, said her piece. "His war record, his quiet grace, his intelligence. Yes, a wonderful man is our Mr. Worthington."

Of the three, Mrs. Herman Oelrichs, formerly known as Theresa Fair, called Tessie by most, had the most mundane heritage of the triumvirate. While she was now mistress of one of the grandest cottages on the island—Rosecliff—she was born in a California mining camp, the daughter of an Irish immigrant, an immigrant who made millions at Comstock, the famous silver mine. The man who made the American dream come true was also a debauched womanizer. When Tessie's mother divorced him, though a scandal, it was the best thing that could have happened for Tessie and her husband Herman, son of a wealthy German shipping magnate.

One of her brothers had committed suicide, another—with his wife—perishing in a high-speed accident in Paris. Tessie and her sister inherited their father's fortune. They purchased Rosecliff just a few years ago. Herman Oelrichs was more than happy to let her. He was also more than happy to let her have her full social life; he had his own. It was lively but far from public. They performed their pretense of intimacy with a skill worthy of any Shakespearean actor.

Tessie had married a man much like her father. Many wondered if she filled her bed with others as well and as often as her husband did, for she was the beauty of the group, a classic Irish beauty, crowned by regal grace. Hers was a true hourglass figure, with or without a corset, displayed to perfection beneath her huge hats and lace dresses, her creamy skin, and luxuriously thick chestnut hair.

"Yes, yes, yes, Mr. Worthington can be all that, but he can be such a bore," Mrs. Vanderbilt vomited cutting words as she so often did, never once stopping to wipe her mouth. "A gracious bore, I will give you that. But that…that woman."

As if suddenly struck with the same illness, the triumvirate groaned as one.

"She is so, so very…crass," Mrs. Oelrichs struggled, but not more than I did. It was hard enough to hear them call my father a bore, no matter the other things they said of him. I knew anything they said of my mother, "that woman" as they called her, would be scathing. For all my own condemnation of my mother, I loathed hearing these women speak of her so poorly. Only I could, for she was my mother.

"She must have read every one of those silly how-to guides and puts on a ghastly performance of their suggestions," Mrs. Fish pursed her lips, looking heavenward for salvation from my mother and her antics.

"And all at once," Mrs. Vanderbilt quipped, chortling with amused condemnation. "Did you see her the other night in New York, when she twirled her parasol, fluttered her fan, and dipped her hat, all at the same time?"

"Or tried to," Mrs. Oelrichs chimed in on the demolition of my mother merrily. "And the way she throws herself at young men. A horrible flirt."

"Are you sure all she does is flirt?" Mrs. Fish's dribbled snidely.

"Deplorable, simply deplorable," Mrs. Oelrichs muttered as a snake hissed and lashed out its venom. Perhaps she had cause.

"You can put a jeweled gown on a dead body," Mrs. Fish suggested, "but it doesn't mean it isn't a corpse."

Mrs. Oelrichs tittered into her cup. "We shan't be taking her up then?"

Mrs. Vanderbilt slapped the small white wicker table before them with a gloved hand. "Honestly, Tessie, must you even question it?"

"No." Tessie hung her head a bit, but just a bit. "But what of Mr. Worthington and the children?"

"Humph." Mrs. Fish clearly deplored her friend's obvious mixed feelings. "Well, we won't shut them out. Stu would be furious with me. Mr. Worthington is one of the few he truly enjoys. We shall simply have to tolerate the hen for the rest of the coop."

"More like a crow," Mrs. Astor said. The women applauded her with the scandalized laughter she craved.

I had heard enough; I heard too much, no matter who these women were. I spun round and stabbed her with the disgust fuming inside me. If she saw it, she gave no sign. I walked away, my back ramrod straight, just as Mother had taught me.

* * *

We returned home at teatime and the four of us sat in the wicker chairs of the Conservatory, almost as still and stony as the nine statues perched in the sunroom, their hard grace somehow apropos in the full windowed walls and the delicate lace curtains. I sat with my back to the view. I could see it just as well in the two mirrors on the inner wall, mirrors reflecting the panoramic vista of the yard. The reflection of the four of us stripped us of our social disguises.

Anger still seethed in me, pumped by the women's words that echoed in my head as if it were an empty cave. Though I had spent some time in Frederick's company, my good manners, and whatever acumen of flirtation I possessed at the time, were as flimsy and elusive as a single layer of chiffon. Or perhaps it was his friend who joined us, Butterworth his name was. How off-kilter his presence made me;

he was so unlike the other young men. Perhaps something within me knew, even then.

As I sat and sipped my tea in the awful silence that was a family fractured by more than just actions, but philosophies, I realized the true source of my anger was not the pretentious women or even their words, but the truth of their words. Mother was everything she shouldn't be, didn't need to be, in the abundant world we lived in. She could have simply enjoyed it with gratitude. She never did. That truth both grieved and strengthened.

"I would like Ginevra to become my personal maid."

My declaration shattered the silence as if I had hurled a rock through one of the windows.

My brother's laughter broke the silence.

I gave him a look that was as good as a slap.

"You're serious?" he sputtered.

"I am."

"You are not," my mother said, no, she declared.

"I truly am, Mother." I heard it; the disrespect emblazoned in my words. "You said yourself as we were leaving New York that it was time I had a maid of my own. Ginevra is the perfect choice. She knows all about fashion, is a wiz with her needle, and she's quiet and lovely and polite." Which was more than could be said for the catty, self-important Nettie, my mother's maid. Ginevra had told me all about her, her true self below stairs, how Nettie told all my mother's secrets, laughing about them with Mrs. O'Brennan and Mrs. Briggs. Ginevra would cherish my secrets as if they were her own, the very best feature for a lady's maid.

"It ish ridiculusss." Mother slurred her words. It was only teatime, but I knew, as did we all, she was half-rats already, as she was so very often, more often of late, earlier and earlier.

"It is not." I put my cup down, sat up straighter. "Mrs. Briggs herself acknowledges Ginevra's talent. She said so. She told Ginevra her work was better than Agnes's." The sloppy seamstress in New York.

"I will not have—" my mother began.

"Perhaps she is right for you, my Pearl."

My father spoke, spoke against my mother's wishes. I could have jumped up and thrown my arms around him. Could have, if such a thing was done in our family, in our gilded cages.

"Her father is one of the hardest workers I have ever known. His talent is beyond compare. Don't you agree, Clarence?"

My brother looked up, caught in a rabbit trap. His shoulders dropped, shrugged. "Actually, I do."

"Clarence!" my mother snapped. He had always taken her side, no matter the topic. Her face blanched beneath her fine powder.

"It's true, Mother," Clarence continued, slouching in his chair with the arrogant indifference that was a daily part of his wardrobe. "The violin he made me is quite something. And his teaching, well, it has actually made me want to learn—to play better."

My mother's mouth opened; nothing came out. A miracle.

"She has the right look for the job," Father continued, touching on Ginevra's beauty, a must for a lady's maid in a world where beauty is the greatest of all attributes. "And I know she is well educated, and well-read."

I bit my lip. He knew of Ginevra's education and literacy; knew I had given it to her. Our secret was safe in his keeping.

"Mr. Birch?" my father called out.

Birch stood just outside the door, always there, always listening. With but three steps, he stood in the Conservatory threshold.

"Please ask Mrs. Briggs to join us," my father requested of him.

"Right away, Sir." Birch bowed out of the room.

"You cannot allow thish, Orin," Mother whined at him, her head, grown heavy, slumped into the cup of one palm. "What will they say?"

The omnipotent "they;" the aristocratic, snobby "they." "They" were always there, always defining who and what we were. "They" were far too elusive, far too "them," for me to ever care what they thought.

"I *am* allowing it, Millicent." My father turned his full face to my mother. He looked at her as I imagined he must have looked on the battlefield.

"But Orin—"

"You called for me, Sir." Mrs. Briggs entered the room, dashing away my mother's tantrum, delaying it. Her dark storm clouds hovered over the horizon, drawing ever near.

"Ah, Mrs. Briggs, thank you for coming." My father greeted her respectfully. I wondered if he knew her true nature would he be as generous. "It's been decided my daughter is of the age where she needs a personal maid."

Mrs. Briggs nodded; she took the news in stride. "I'll make inquiries."

"No need." Father waved a hand. "It has also been decided that Ginevra will be promoted to the position."

"Ginevra!" The mask dropped; the true Mrs. Briggs revealed. "Ya cannot be—"

"It's been decided." My father stopped her; respect replaced with undeniable demand simply with the drop in his voice.

"But…but the girl knows nothing about being a lady's maid," Mrs. Briggs argued, though now she sputtered softly.

"Well then," I chirped like a bird gifted with a worm, "we shall have something in common, as I have never had one. We will learn together."

Father bestowed a pleased glance upon me.

"Have Nettie give her some speedy lessons," Father said. "From what I hear she is a bright girl, like her father no doubt, she will learn quickly."

"But…"

"That will be all, Mrs. Briggs, thank you," my father dismissed her swiftly but with his understated politeness ever at hand.

"Yes, sir." She left, but not without a backward glance at my mother, each face replicated the other's frustration.

"Orin, this is simply madness." As soon as the housekeeper was a foot out the door, my mother's storm came crashing in. On unsteady feet now, she stamped her foot, hands fisted by her side, shoulders pitching.

Who is the child now, I thought.

"She is from below stairs," she derided as if Ginevra came from the bowels of the earth.

Somehow, through lips pulled thin, a jaw clenched painfully, I corrected her.

"She is from Italy."

I did then what I should have done the rest of my life, to her and the way of life she championed to the point of cruelty. I turned my back on her.

GINEVRA

It was hard to remember a happier day, though I knew there were some, back before mama died. Their memories skirted my mind, tickled my dreams, sprinkled themselves throughout my days as salt is at a long meal.

This was the happiest day I could remember in this new world.

When Pearl told me what her plan had been, told me her father encouraged it, told me the truth of the change of my life, it was like a Christmas morn when I was still a child.

"You won't feel...strange?" Pearl asked me, eyes lowered as she twisted the ribbons that circled her small waist. "Well—serving me—will you? I want to give you some freedom, less drudgery, but I don't want our friendship to change."

Fondness turned to love then, as it would remain. I imagined why she would have such a concern, but it lived only in her imagination.

"I won't be serving you," I bubbled, smile so wide my face hurt, "I'll be helping you, as you have helped me."

Her gaze flicked up; it sparkled even as her shoulders slumped, as she expelled a breath so hard, she must have trapped it tightly.

Such feelings did not belong to Mrs. Briggs; I could practically see the smoke from the fumes of her fire when she confirmed the authorization of my new appointment from Mr. Worthington, when she showed me my new room—my private room.

It was more than a room. It was the key that unlocked the door to me, a door I had shut tightly, to all others save Pearl.

I could decorate it and arrange it in any way I wanted. I could read all night without any bitter words and huffs of frustration from someone else. As I took ownership of the room, I took ownership of a portion of my life lost to me since we walked through the grand doors of The Beeches.

Carrying the last armful of my possessions, a few more now than when I had arrived, I turned back to Greta staring with fire in her eyes at my back. I brushed her off as I did the heat off my back.

"Bye-bye." I trilled my fingers at her, speaking in that singsong tone of superiority she had used so often on me.

I barely had time to finish putting my clothes away when Nettie came for me.

"Come along wich ya' then." Such words said more than their true intent; they told me whose side she was on, not that I expected her to be any different.

I smirked away her disdainful displeasure. Though they may try, nothing she, Mrs. Briggs, or anyone could do to dump water on my flames of joy.

Nettie hurried me to the family side of the house. I walked tall and smart in my new uniform with the ruffled blouse at collar and cuffs, and a new skirt, not one worn by another before.

"Ya' will wake the young mistress every morn', bringin' her breakfast upon a tray. Also in the morning, you will treat her skin with the proper creams, as well as her hair. It is your job to see to her beauty, do ya' understand me? I amn't gonna' be telling ya' all tis agin." I nodded, followed her, her instruction, but not so much that I did not notice the change in her speech; she was Nettie from Ireland below stairs, the maid to the mistress above. Which one was real? "Pearl will need to change five or six times, depending on whether there's a ball or a banquet. Our women, even if they be young ones, must adhere strictly to the right dress for the right moment of the day."

Nettie talked fast and walked fast, but not too fast. I kept up, easily. Her lips thinned; her voice sliced. I nodded with a small smile. I would chide myself later for my enjoyment of her annoyance.

"Pearl will have a dress for morning calls, for receiving calls, for visiting, and for being visited. There are morning street dresses, at home morning dresses, riding dresses," she stopped to huff. "Now tere are those new walking suits," she was as displeased with the new fashion as she was me. "There are their evening dresses, those for home, for a dinner party, a ball, the opera…"

I stopped listening. I knew all about all these dresses, had been studying all about them throughout the long, cold, lonely winter. To help my dear Pearl into each and every one of them would please us both. I would get to wear them in spirit as I longed to do in life.

* * *

They all stopped talking as soon as I entered the servants' dining room. They may as well have put up signs, some would read angry, others disgust, many envy.

I held my head high as I took my seat beside my father.

"What is happening," he whispered to me in Italian between bites of his watery stew. "I hear them speak your name, over and over."

I leaned toward him. In our language, I told him, everything. The look he gave was not the one I expected. He would disapprove. He would tell me my grasp was further than my reach. He did none of those things.

My papa put down his spoon and sat back in his chair. He stared at me for a long time, or so it felt to me. He stared at me as if he didn't really know me, but as someone he would like to know.

He reached out his hand, took mine in it, and gave it a squeeze, a hard squeeze saying all he couldn't, all he didn't know how to say. My heart fluttered as I blinked back tears.

When Papa let go, I almost reached out to hold his hand again, longer, more. I didn't; I couldn't. I would hold the feel of my hand in his, in that moment, in that way, for the rest of my life.

We took up our spoons and ate our dinner.

The rest of the staff resumed talking, forced talk of unimportant topics. As they began to finish and scatter, to return to work or their evening off, I lingered. It was a meal to savor. Yes, the beef was a bit tough, the broth thin and a bit tasteless, but it was the finest meal I had had in this house, as I sat there in my new uniform, as I lived in the skin of one who would better herself. It was a comfortable fit.

My father gave my shoulder a quick pat as he left me. Most of my other fellow domestics passed me without a word, save for three.

"Good fer ya', gel," Mrs. Brown said, she didn't whisper, as her large form bumped my chair.

"Thank you," I said, thanking her for more than her words.

"Congratulations, Ginevra."

I turned, surprised.

Charlie, the second footman, stood in the doorway. His pleasure for me, clear on his freckled pale face beneath his slicked-back red hair, shone brightly with sincerity. I had denied his flirtations, both this year and last. Yet he stood there, happy for me as few were. He was a better man than I thought.

"Thank you, Charlie," I beamed. "Thank you very much."

He tipped his head and left. I smiled into my bowl.

"Don't be so pleased with yourself." Mrs. Briggs, the last to leave the room, was the last to speak to me. "You ah far too friendly with the young mistress already. Why do you think so few of the others like you?"

I let her talk. I kept eating. She would not sour the meal I ate upon with such relish.

"Don't be acting as if you ah too good for them. I'm warning you," she bristled and huffed off.

I may not be too good for them, or most of them, I thought, wishing I could say the words to Mrs. Briggs' face, *but I know I am far better than someone like you.*

* * *

We laughed loud and often—that first night as I helped her dress, helped her with her hair, getting ready for an intimate dinner party at the home of the Langdon's—laughter filled the room as surely as her expensive perfume.

"We must stop," I sputtered, nearly doubled over in laughter. "Your mother will anger at our fun."

"Oh, let her fuss," Pearl dismissed as I buttoned her long cuffs trimmed with just an edging of delicate lace. "I've never been happier, thanks to you."

I gave a tug on a strand of her long hair. She only laughed more.

We picked out her jewelry, just a ring and small earrings suitable for her age, and we completed her ensemble, my first creation.

She stood before the long pedestal mirror; her eyes moved up and down and back again. "Ginevra, you're a genius. I never would have thought to put the purple ribbon round my waist. It works perfectly with the dress."

It did. It set off the yellow silk and her creamy skin to perfection.

"It works because you are so lovely," I said, and she was, in part thanks to my work, but that I would keep as a gift to myself.

Pearl preened as I gathered the discarded clothes from the afternoon, the mess of hosiery and undergarments. As I whirled round. A glimpse caught me, froze me before the windows of Pearl's room. There, in the distance, the Newport Harbor glistened as if diamonds floated on the surface.

PEARL

"You can't see it from your room, can you?"

Ginevra spoke not a word. Her gaze remained upon the vista.

"Can you?"

Ginevra shook her head.

"My father didn't mean to do it, you know. He didn't mean for there to be no windows up there. The architect, well, he thought it brilliant," I rushed to defend my father. Someone had to. I always would. "And my father, well, my father is sometimes too far in his own thoughts...I don't think he realized."

"No to worry," Ginevra turned, the smile on her face one she put there, not one that came to her, a trace of her accent slipping through on the crest of emotion. "I can come here now, to see you and it."

"You know," I said, suddenly remembering, knowing the happiness it would bring her, "as my personal maid, you may have my dresses considered out of style and unwearable in society."

Ginevra's dark eyes gleamed. "Dresses? For me?"

"Oh yes." I ran to my wardrobe and pulled out a few garments worn last summer, or lighter ones worn through the winter season in New York. No more than a year old, they would be deemed out of style. A green and white striped dress with a high lace collar and short cuffs, a lovely yellow polka dot number with a box pleat skirt and an apron drape all trimmed in black silk. I pulled them out, one after the other, and threw them on my bed.

"They're all yours if you want them," I said. I turned.

Ginevra had not moved an inch, not made a peep.

"Do you want them?"

Ginevra didn't answer me, not with words. She ran to the bed and scooped them up in her arms as if they were a newborn babe. She held them close, an embrace, one she pulled me into. Simple words of gratitude fell short. I didn't need them.

"Don't let anyone take them from you, Ginevra." I knew the realization of what I had done, making her my maid, was not all good, there would be a price to pay, perhaps for both of us. She had overcome so many obstacles since we first met; I knew that in raising her up, I had raised more of them up as well. My teeth bit upon themselves; what kind of world was it where a young woman bettering herself would be looked down upon, by many, too many?

"Don't let them take any of this away from you."

* * *

Ginevra bustled about my room, putting away discarded dresses, unused hairpieces.

"Leave that, Ginevra," I impatiently instructed. "It is not your job, and we must go."

Her brows flew up her face so fast I thought they would fly right off.

"We?" she squeaked, a hand upon her chest.

"Of course, we, silly." I took her by the shoulders, patting the tips of her collar down, tucking in the back of her shirt. "You are my personal maid. You must accompany me should I have need of you."

She hadn't moved. "What do I do?"

"There will be a room, not far from the ballroom or the dining room or wherever the party is anchored." I shrugged. "And you will wait."

"Wait?" Her head cocked to the side. "Wait for what?"

I tapped my foot. I saw a discussion between Nettie and me in the near future. This was for her to have told.

I heaved a breath, expelling my frustration at Nettie before Ginevra thought it belonged to her.

"Me, Ginevra. You will wait for me. In case I need you to fix my dress should I spill on it, should a heel catch and rip it."

I had seen the maids often, crowding in a small room, all dressed in black, a murder of crows. I had rarely seen them do anything.

What I saw was Ginevra's creamy skin blenched, her fingers tied and knotted themselves. I took them in my hand; I freed them.

"It will be the most tedious time you've ever had. It is very rare that something happens." My words prodded; I saw a crow now as a dove.

"I'm sorry, Ginevra, you should have been told about this. I am sorry it will be so very boring for you."

Her stoic face cracked like the shell of an egg. Ginevra rushed to the mirror, pushing back any loose strands back into her bun. Satisfied, she returned to my side.

"Not boring," she preened, "I am going to a party."

We left my room, our laughing trailing behind.

We didn't get far. Mother waited on the stair landing.

Her hard eyes racked every inch of me, searching, hoping, for something to criticize. She found nothing to bite on. She bit herself with such ire, ate away whatever softness lay deep inside if there was any left.

"You must watch your behavior with your maid," she sniped, not speaking Ginevra's name as if Ginevra didn't have one or Mother didn't know it, as if Ginevra weren't but a few steps behind us. "They will call her a parvenu, the other servants will, mark my words. What they will call you, the servants, our friends, will be much worse. I will not have it."

"I really don't care what they call me, not below stairs or anywhere else," I assured her, echoes of her own nasty determination, locking my eyes firmly with hers. "Ginevra is my friend as well as my maid. If they cannot deal with it, it is their problem and yours, not mine."

With that, I walked away from my mother, frozen on the wide landing of the wide white marble stairs, Ginevra just a few steps behind. The late evening sun, streaming its tangerine rays through the high arched windows, fell into the cracks beginning to show on Mother's face. I knew I would paint them one day.

"Come along, Mother, we mustn't be late," I called back to her. I bit my lips together before my laugh could wiggle out of them.

GINEVRA

We looked so similar; we were faceless. Dressed alike, no one could tell one from the other. It was the way "they" preferred us to be, a necessity in their lives but not in possession of lives of our own.

It did little to spoil the newness of this experience for me. I had never watched them, them all together as they were now, this closely ever before. In the watching, "they" became simply "them."

From the small hidden room just off the cloakroom, I could see them nodding to each other in the same way, walking the same, talking the same. I never knew so many words could mean so little. They laughed the same, as practiced as any performance, save for Pearl's mother. She had an array of laughter; which one she bellowed through the room seemed to depend on the sex of the person igniting it. Each held different notes; few were not off-key.

It did not take me long to become, if not bored as Pearl had warned, at least unimpressed. I watched Pearl instead. Her added flair, that I gave her with my touches upon her clothes, that came from within her, radiated about her as if the sun shone forever upon her back. She smiled wider when she gave someone her real smile. She walked fluidly, not as if her back was flat to the wall.

I knew her eyes as well as I did my own. I knew that though they latched here and there, they did not find what she sought. I did not know what he looked like, but I knew who she looked for.

As Pearl made her way out onto the porch that wrapped itself about the house like a comforting blanket, my gaze followed her through the windows. As her path led her off the porch and onto the backyard, my link to her broke. I was a seamstress intent upon repair.

"Come back here," one of the faceless others hissed at me as I slipped to the threshold of our cubby, as I set one foot out of it.

"I thought my mistress waved me to her," I lied.

I did not go far, but two more steps, just enough to see through the ballroom instead of into it, to see the backyard through the back windows.

There she was, glowing in the marching dawn, still looking.

"Do you know who she looks for?"

I gasped, clamped my hand upon my mouth. The man's voice poked me sharp and quick like the needles I plied, a needle with a high dose of masculinity.

With my hand still upon my mouth, my gaze sidled away, finding a pristine white shirt and perfectly knotted tie.

I raised my gaze to find his, the color of a glittering jewel.

I moved my hand away, wiping the sweat upon my skirt.

Full lips twitched.

"You are her maid, are you not? Pearl Worthington's maid?"

He knew me for what I was and how I was, but his kindness remained.

"Yes. I am, yes." I finally managed, knotting my hands behind my back.

His chin ticked ever so slightly at my accent. That and nothing else.

"Well then, do you know who she is looking for?"

I did not know if this was 'the' Frederick. If I spoke his name to him, it would not do well for Pearl. If it was not, I would reveal her secret, those I kept as well as my own.

"I no kno..." I cleared my throat of its bad grammar with a cough. "I do not know."

He sniffed as he smiled. I did not fake my lack of knowledge well.

"Then perhaps I shall have to go and find out for myself," he said.

"As you wish, Sir." I gave a bob of my head. When I looked up, he stood beside me still.

The edges of his face rounded; he looked at me for me.

"Why is it the most beautiful girls have the most beautiful maids?"

Did I suddenly stop understanding English? Did he really just say I was beautiful?

I hoped he had. I hoped he was not Frederick.

With a nod of a dark-haired head and a jaunty smile, he left me.

PEARL

It wasn't a largely attended affair. There were only about one hundred of us at the modest mansion, Gravel Court, of George Tiffany and his wife, Isabella. It was one of those sedate, family affairs, the kind my mother detested, and I thoroughly enjoyed. Good, but not overly rich food accompanied by quiet, sincere conversation. Peaceful.

Yet I wanted more. Not the more my mother wanted, but a more that surprised me.

As I strolled about the Italianate villa, in and out again, along the porches festooned with merry guests, down the lush, rolling humps of lawn, this "new woman" searched for a man. I searched for Frederick, longing for his eyes to see me so splendidly attired, longing for the look in his eyes when he did. With each step I took, discontent darkened me as the setting sun did all of Newport.

"You look splendid, Miss Worthington."

I whirled at words snatched from my mind. I caught my face before surprise and more disenchantment ran off with it.

"Thank you, Mr...?" How dreadful I was for forgetting his name. He seemed to hover on the outskirts of everywhere these past few days.

Full lips turned up at one corner, the corners of his eyes crinkled. I had to raise my eyes to find his. When I did, I found the most distinctive brown eyes I had ever seen, warm and amber, like Father's brandy.

"Butterworth. I am Herbert Butterworth, we met at—"

"At Crossways, yes, of course, I remember you, Mr. Butterworth," I reassured him and myself. Could one handsome face truly make all others invisible?

He bowed slightly as some gentlemen still did with enchanting chivalry. Slim but muscular, his clothes conformed elegantly to his broad shoulders, his slim waist.

"Thank you, Miss Worthington. It pleases me to hear you say so."

Who was I looking for a moment ago? I can't remember.

"Is this your first time summering in Newport?" How I detested those etiquette books my mother forced upon me; how grateful I was to have read them. They put words in my mouth when my brain could not find any.

"It is my first time in Newport, yes," Mr. Butterworth replied. We began to walk without either one suggesting it. Our stroll was a natural one among nature's beauty, stars began to twinkle in a sky still magenta with the echoes of the setting sun. Lanterns hung on trees and porticoes lit our way, as if we traversed from one star to another. "But I fear I shan't be summering. I'm only here for another week. A short visit, I'm afraid."

I did not know this man save for this passing acquaintance, but the ring of disappointment was a familiar one.

"Do you wish you could stay longer?" I asked.

He stopped walking, as did I. He turned to me; those eyes held me in their grasp.

"I do, Miss Worthington." His eyes never left mine. "I do indeed."

* * *

As Ginevra readied me for the next afternoon's coaching parade, we chatted about last evening; I chatted, she nodded and 'eh hemmed' as she contrived the upper part of my hair into a twisted curl on the right side of my head and perched my hat tilted to the left.

"So many of the girls praised my outfit," I told her truthfully, hoping to banish the darkness. "They adored all the little touches you added."

She grinned. "*Si*, sometimes it is little things that make us special."

Ginevra stopped brushing the rest of my hair, the long lengths that would fall to my waist in silky waves, smoothed by her ministrations. She came 'round to stand before me.

"Why you frown?" She stared hard at me, too hard, for she saw me as others didn't or couldn't. I knew I couldn't lie.

"Frederick," I said flatly.

"He was not there?"

My head shook, but only slightly. "No, he wasn't, but…"

Glowing amber eyes reflected in my mind, a reflection that softened the firm line of my lips.

One brow rose up Ginevra's face. "But...?"

"Well, there was a fine, that is," I floundered needlessly. From Ginevra, I could not run. "A Mr. Butterworth was there. He was rather...engaging," I hedged, foolishly.

"Hmm, engaging, was he?" Ginevra looked away, back to her tasks, though she saw right through me. "And who is this Mr. Butterworth?"

It was my turn to turn, to spin away from my vanity to the woman standing behind me.

"You know," I pondered, surprising myself, "I don't really know."

Her brow quirked again; one corner of her mouth matching it.

"Seems to me you do not need to know."

Before I could deny her words, she took my shoulders and twisted me, my back once more to her.

Ginevra returned to brushing my hair. She knew how it soothed me.

GINEVRA

As I had the summer before, I snuck down to watch them, though the need to sneak was no longer mine. As long as I had done my duty to Pearl and her bedroom, my time was my own, as long as I was always at the ready should she need me. Yet what I did I felt strange to do in the open; the need for invisibility, that still wore my name.

I stood just behind the stone pillar to the left of the gravel drive. In my dark uniform, I was unnoticeable behind the high scrolled iron gate, as notable as the flowerless box hedges growing beneath the carved tops of the beams of stone. I watched them, every day I watched them, cold in the shadows even on hot days.

The men sat tall; their silk stovepipe hats even taller. Leather-gloved hands held reins and whips. Boutonniered chests puffed up, chins stuck high. Their topcoats matched the vivid green of the trees lining the avenue, their yellow-stripped waistcoats as bright as daisies. This place, this world belonged to the women, but this strange parade was men's delight. The women sat behind them, dressed and laced in pale colors. Their large, fancy hats sat on their heads like mushroom caps, their stiff, upright necks the stems.

Some carriages were bigger than others. Phaetons, barouches, victorias, four-in-hands. Pearl taught me about them with as much detail as she did reading and writing.

"A 'whip,'" she told me, "was a coaching master. He will always observe the proper protocol while driving. They must know who they may pass and who they may not." She had rounded a downturned gaze upon me. "We are ranked you see, and if someone of a higher standing is behind us, we must give way. We must all know our place." Her words were so bitter they must have stung her tongue. She shook herself as if she shook off the cold of winter. "But some," she had giggled, "like the Belmonts and the Bennetts, well, their howling swells, are they not?"

"Howling swell?" What a frightening person they must be. "It is some kind of beast?"

Pearl rolled her eyes as she did a lot at my questions, but her smile held her patience. "A howling swell is more, much more. They deck out their coaches so much more elaborately, flowers everywhere, on the horses, on the carriages. They're so much showier. Mother always wants Father to fuss up our carriage."

"Does he?" I asked.

Pearl shook her head. "He couldn't be bothered, dear. If he had his way, we wouldn't coach at all." She had stared out the window. "I wish he had his way."

She never saw me in my hiding place. I was as unnoticeable as my simple dark uniform. At least she never showed she did. She wouldn't, for both our sakes.

I watched them, every day I watched them, my nose full of the fecund scent of the flowers all around me, my mind saw me on one of them, dressed in one of the frothy, delicate dresses I so longed to wear, pictured myself as one of them. I knew the truth, even then. My station had been improved, as had my clothes, but there were heights one such as me could never scale.

Pearl passed, but it brought me little joy. Her dress as fine as any, her small, tasseled parasol fluttered prettily until she would become old enough to wear a wide-brimmed hat. Her back was as straight as the stone pillar I stood behind. All was as it should be, save that the small smile she allowed to sit upon her face looked as if it hurt.

What she never told me was why. Why at the same time every day did all these rich folk put on their fancy clothes, get in their carriages, and parade up and down Bellevue Avenue? Their horses crunched out a rhythm, bells jangling. Their wheels clattered on cobblestones. Their horns tooted. They never actually went anywhere. They drove up and then down.

They nodded to each other as they passed, small movements, the same gesture. I did not understand. Their eyes did more work, scouring each other's clothes, each other's carriages, and who rode in them. The air changed, thickened, as it always seemed to when they gathered.

I looked for him in every carriage, though I did not know I did at the time. A whip or a howling swell; that was the question.

Often times the villagers climbed the hill leading from their small houses and shanties down by the water, and stood along the fences and high walls, watching, like me. To those in the carriages, they were nothing more than rails in a post, not worthy of a glance.

So many days I watched, I came, ever so slowly, to figure it out. Yes, it was to see and be seen by each other that brought them out, lining them up with such precision, leading them from one end of the avenue to the other and back again. But I knew, I came to know the real reason.

They needed to see each other done up and perched up to know who they pretended to be was really who they were, who they thought they were. These coach parades were daily reminders, their fairy tale was real life, or was their real life a fairy tale? Out in the air, on the road, no one could see the dirty clutter of their lives shut away behind the gates and mammoth doors of their "cottages."

The carriages rumbled past, like me, going nowhere.

PEARL

"It's going to be the party of the summer," Mother preened as she opened the few replies to my birthday celebrations at the breakfast table, all of us around her. Intimacy in this intimate setting was still as elusive as ever; if we reached out our hands, they would grasp only empty air. "I'm still so enraged that I had to do them myself. Damn that Miss de Baril."

"I really don't need a grand affair, Mother, just something with a few of my friends..." It was all I wanted; all it should be. The days of the huge balls, my coming out, were just around the corner. I held onto the days of a small group of giggling girls, of silly backyard games, and lovely little remembrance gifts for as long as I could, if I could. I could not.

"Well, of course, Pearl," Mother didn't deign to look up, at me, the party's guest of honor. "But there must be a few of my friends as well." Ah, the truth of the matter, for her. Her truth was bent, if with nothing more than how few of the ladies of Newport were really her friends.

"Ouch!" she cried, sucking a finger. "Another little paper-cut. Oh, how many I have suffered with these invitations. Damn that Miss de Baril."

Not a one of us spoke. It was a subject sure to charge up of my mother's inner beasts. None of us dared remind her that Nettie, not her, had addressed the hundreds of invitations, had seen to their distribution, not her. All Mother could fixate on was that *the* Miss de Baril hadn't done them. If my mother cut herself, it was on her own misplaced frustration.

Miss Maria de Baril had been one of the chosen, a member of an original Newport family who had lost their money and their social status. The wise young Maria had turned her years of being in the game—and her claimed Inca ancestry—to her benefit. Stout, dumpy, forever over-plumed with beads hanging from neck and wrists, her handwriting was the finest on the island. She had become *the* social secretary after creating masterpiece invitations for one of Mrs. Astor's great balls. Her fame—her skill—had become so *en vogue*, in such demand, that she became the chooser, deciding for herself for whom she would or would not complete work. My mother fell into the latter category. She could have been thrown off a cliff for all the screaming she had done about it when the letter of rejection arrived from Miss de Baril.

Our silence was not a hindrance to her ranting.

"She claimed she was far too otherwise occupied, but I know better." Mother threw down the envelope in her hand and turned to my father as if she would stab him with the jewel-encrusted opener still in her hand. "I am not fully accepted; we are not fully accepted."

So it went, another breakfast, another meal trapped in the cage of my mother's tantrums.

Her rant lasted nearly an hour. My father and I suffered in silence. Our appetites diminished as her shrill grew sharper. Only my brother fed her obsession, for he too seemed to be growing as obsessed. He played tennis and polo, belonged to all the right clubs. He was handsome as ever, there can be no doubt, perhaps more so as his face cut with the sharpness of manhood. Something had changed though, changed in him that changed the outer him.

To me, he had lost the cherub sweetness of his youth, innocence lost to cravings, though they would find him little satisfaction. He wanted only the prettiest girl, trifling with hearts as if they were the ball on the tennis court, bouncing them back and forth, to him and away. He who was once my hero on the mount had shrunk before my eyes.

"I've tried my best with Mrs. Astor and Mrs. Vanderbilt, and of course, with Mr. McAllister. They smile ever so prettily to my face and then never accept our invitations. We must do something. You must do something, Orin."

"Eh, what's that you say?" My father came back from his mental distance at the sound of his name.

"You must do something to get the Astors and the Vanderbilts to Pearl's party." She slapped her hand on the table. We all jumped.

"I know exactly what to do!" Her loud exclamation sent the birds from their perch on the statues just outside the open windows. "I need some money, Orin, perhaps a good deal of it."

Father looked at her without a word. Still in her silk dressing robe of pale yellow, hair loose and tumbling down her back, she was another woman—a different woman—until she opened her mouth. Intelligence burned in her pale eyes; if only she set it upon a worthy task would it find its true purpose. It never would. If she made such a demand, he would make her do so fully; he would not prod her along.

"We must pay *Town Topics* to cover the party. They will not give it any mention unless we do. And it *must* be mentioned. All those who declined the invitation must see just how fabulous it will be."

The society journal, *Town Topics*, was *the* social news source in Newport. The good, the bad, and the fictionalized became ever more so—so often exaggerated, distorted, and even extorted—if its writers covered it. No wonder they called them rags.

"Will its success not be gratifying enough?" my father asked. He would rather allow the horses to defecate on the rag than read it.

"Oh, Orin," Mother pleaded, ever so sweetly, leaning forward to allow him a view of the assets she brought to the marriage, "how can it be a success unless everyone knows about it?"

My father peered at my mother as if he looked at someone he did not know, or care to know. He squinted at her, perhaps looking for the woman he had married, though I don't think she was that woman anymore. Pain mottled his face. He turned his gaze to me. The darkness dispelled.

"For my Pearl, I will do it."

Like a switch thrown, Mother became herself, all sweet cajoling gone like the morning mist on a good wind off the land.

"Must you still call her that? She is almost a grown woman."

She had gone a step too far.

Father glared across the table at her as I imagined he would at a particularly difficult employee. He jabbed the air with a pointed finger.

"She is, and always will be, *my* Pearl." The finger thumped upon the table, an exclamation mark upon his words.

I looked quickly down at my plate, quickly shoveled a forkful of food in my mouth before it could reveal its smile.

"Speaking of my Pearl's birthday," my father continued with a strange note of amusement in his voice. I looked up. The hint of a smile played at lips hidden beneath his bushy mustache. "I know it's still a few days away but considering how fair the day is I think I should give you your present now."

"You have a present...for me?"

My fork clanged upon the dish; my eyes bulged as my voice squeaked. My father had never gotten me a gift, purchased something for me without the involvement or approval of my mother, ever. That in itself was the best gift he could give me.

"I have two gifts for you," he leaned toward me. How I longed to paint the jubilant mischief brushing across his face. It would be as rare a depiction as the Mona Lisa. He charmed me, utterly and completely. He rose from his chair and pulled the cord by the door. Unheard on the third floor, a bell chimed, a flag dropped. Within minutes, Geoffrey, his valet, stood at the door.

"That box, if you would, Mr. Tobin," my father requested. "And please alert Mr. Grayson to have the other item readied as well."

"Very good, Sir," Geoffrey backed out of the room with the smallest tilt of his head.

My mind whirled. What could my dear father have gotten me that came in a box *and* required the assistance of Mr. Grayson, the grounds superintendent? It couldn't be a horse; I had a fine one, had had many already in my life. Those he had given me as my right and for his enjoyment as well, for my mother never cared to ride with him. She hated what it did to her hair.

"Orin," my mother hissed, "what have you done?"

He looked at her, all pretense of patient condescension surrendered.

"I have done nothing but acquire my dear Pearl a special gift for her birthday. Ah." He forgot my mother and her narrow-eyed suspicion as

Geoffrey returned, a large box topped with a glorious pink and green ribbon in his hands.

My foot waggled beneath the table. How I longed to reach for it like the child I had been not long ago. I waited, allowing my father to make his presentation.

"This, my Pearl," he said, standing, taking the box, and delivering it to my lap, "is only part of the gift, but you must have this to enjoy the other properly."

I removed the ribbon slowly, wanting to keep it, rather than rip it as my mind prodded me. I lifted the top off...

"Oh, Father," I whispered, wonderstruck.

"Oh, dear Lord, Orin," my mother's voice hissed with venomous displeasure.

I stood, allowing the bottom of the box to drop, holding the outfit up by the shoulders and against me. Though I felt its fine fabric, its unique form pressed against me, I couldn't believe it. To see it for what it was, gave the rest away.

"Really, Father?!" the words burst from me. I threw myself in his arms.

As he wrapped his strong arms tenderly about me, he whispered in my ear, "Truly, my Pearl. I hope you never grow so old you forget to have fun." He held me away from him, staring deeply into my eyes, bore into them. "Don't let this life stop you from having fun."

I stared up at him. He had never spoken such words to me. It was always implied, though never said, his disapproval of the privileged life we had, of the freedom and imprisonment it caused. I thought it had to do with his father, with what had been done by the grandfather I had never met.

"I promise, Father," I said. Truer words I had never spoken.

"Well, go on then, go put it on and come outside when you're ready." Father smiled childlike.

I threw the clothes back in the box where its accessories still remained, pressed the whole bundle to me, and ran to the door.

"Ginevra!" I shrieked, knowing I would need her help donning the very strange clothing.

"How could you, Orin?" I heard Mother say as I left them behind. Opening that box was like opening Pandora's.

"Actually, very easily, Millicent," Father replied.

I laughed as I ran up the stairs.

* * *

With Ginevra's help, I donned the ever so fashionable, ever-so-scandalous clothing.

Ginevra took one look at the clothes, one look at me, and said, "You must remove your corset."

"I must?" I questioned, dubious, but so filled with hope it astounded even me. The corset upon me came off with all due and joyous haste. With her help, I wiggled into the newly designed corset, one with stretchy material down the sides.

"I can breathe!" I chirped, doing so deeply, feeling my ribs and their new ability to expand, and flouncing about with the freedom of an uncaged bird.

The prim button-down white shirt enhanced with a tie, short and not nearly as fancifully knotted as those men wore, but a tie, nonetheless, gave me a dashing flair. The jacket was of such a lightweight material...

"It is sailcloth," Ginevra said as she helped me into it. I strained my neck to look at her over my shoulder. The question formed, needing to be asked, but my longing for what lay ahead was a greater need.

It barely felt as if I wore a jacket. What a jacket it was. Bright with blue and white stripes, it had the tightness along the forearms and the large leg-o-muttons at the top, as did most of our clothing in those days, but it stopped...at my waist. There was nothing of the cumbersome knee or floor-length coats about it.

Yet the jacket was not shocking when compared to the bottom half.

"Bloomers!" Ginevra and I cried together. I saw how she looked at them...like a starving man looked at bread. It wasn't the first time I had seen that look. Strange how easily I recognized it.

"We shall get you pair," I said. Joy is never so great as when it is shared.

Ginevra waved a hand at me. "I will make myself a pair."

I stopped. This day was full of surprises. "You can do that? You can make clothing, not just repair it?"

"Oh, *si*, yes," Ginevra nodded as she turned the bloomers this way and that, studying them. "I can make many things, fine things."

I grabbed her by the hand, the clothes. What must be waiting for me outside, forgotten if only for a flash of time. "Make me a dress, Ginevra. Make me the finest gown for my birthday party."

Deep brown eyes scrutinized me as if it were a first glance. "Do you mean it? You, you would wear it?"

"Yes," I cried, swinging our arms and the clothes held aloft between them, "of course, I would, as long as it is nothing too outrageous. With your sense of style, I would imagine it will be quite different."

Her face bloomed, roses on her cheeks, hibiscus in her eyes. "Not quite different. Maybe a little." She giggled, as did I.

"Come, get these on you." She returned us to the moment, my moments she gladly gave me.

"These" were named for Amelia Bloomer, a grand lady who had been working for women's rights, another "suffragette." Ginevra and I still read about them voraciously in the paper and magazines, each time ticked us forward, like the second hand of a clock.

The bloomers hugged the waist as a skirt would, they had yards and yards of fabric around the upper portion of my thighs, until just below the knee, but there they were cut in two, like men's pants. Well, they were pants...women's pants! They cuffed tightly below the knee. Ginevra fluttered through the tissue paper in the box and pulled out the most darling short hose, patterned in diamonds of light and dark blue, as well as flat-soled shoes of thin leather with tassels at the end of their laces.

Ginevra finished primping me and stood back.

"*Magnifico,*" she breathed. Then held up a hand. "Eh, how your mother would say…mahvelous."

We shrieked with laughter and fell against each other.

"Pearl!"

My father's voice from below.

"Come along now, my Pearl, the best is yet to come."

They must have heard our laughter, oh how my father must have loved it. I was certain of it, as certain as I was that my mother cringed at each peal.

With one last squeeze, I pulled Ginevra with me.

* * *

It stood at the bottom of the front steps, held up by the ever-tweeded Mr. Grayson.

"Oh, Father." I stood before it, mouth agape. It was the finest bicycle I had ever seen. It was the new sort, the safety bicycle it was called. Gone were the penny-farthings with the enormous front wheel and the small back one. These wheels were almost the same size, the back being just slightly larger. Nor was there a bar running from the padded seat to the handlebars. It had been dropped much lower, to just above the chain that connected the two wheels.

"It is so you can step through." My father showed me, with great delight in doing so. "The man at the shop told me it made the sport so much more ladylike. Is that not so, Millicent?"

My mother stood at the top step, arms entwined so tightly across her chest like a protective shield. Her creamy skin was blotched red as if every speck of blood in her body lay livid upon it. Ginevra, standing behind her, caught my gaze with a bulge of fear.

"Tell me you do not mean for her to ride that…thing…along the avenue, Orin."

My father laughed, spite-tinged laughter. "That's exactly what she will do."

"But what will they say?" Mother ran down the steps, her voice reaching a tone only dogs could hear.

I pulled away, but my father's hand on my back stopped me. I stopped listening as well, as much as I could, turning their acrimonious words into nothing but a hum in my head. His determination rendered her fury impotent. Their arguments were the background noise of my life. In that moment his subdued voice, while still restrained, echoed with a resilience I had never heard him use when speaking with her. Something had changed. I found I became more concerned with whatever that was than with how this argument would end. His victory—my victory—was a certainty, of that I had no doubt. The why frightened me.

"Enough, Millicent, enough," my father demanded, commanded. My mother's lips clamped together tightly until a line of white appeared around her mouth.

"Off we go, my Pearl. Come, I'll help you."

Help me he did. He showed me how to put one leg through, one foot on one pedal, and push off.

I yelped as the force of my legs drove the machine faster and faster. I jig-jagged as my arms chaotically joggled the handlebars. He ran beside me, grabbing one handlebar, steadying me. I found balance.

"You've got it, my Pearl, you've got it!" he cried, releasing his hold.

I did. Off I flew.

GINEVRA

I followed them down past the gates. I stood behind the stone statue that was her mother, behind her father whose pale chuckles sparkled with joy. Pearl wobbled for a bit, but soon she became this beautiful creature gliding down the street. Her long dark hair streamed behind her like a kite's ribbon.

We watched Pearl fly down the length of Bellevue Avenue, past the mansions and their haughty, haunting occupants. It was the perfect street for such a device, mostly flat and smoothly packed dirt, the cobbles ended just after the Casino farther north.

"Oh, this really is the worst, Orin," I heard her mother complain sharply. "Look at how she is being stared at."

Mr. Worthington never took his gaze off his daughter. "Must we always care what they see?"

"Of course we should," she bit at him. "However, will we move up if we don't?"

He turned to her then. I shuddered, grateful such a look was not pinned on me.

"You don't always care, Millicent, do you?"

I had no clue what he meant. I didn't want to. She offered him no answer; her silence was her answer. I saw it in the bitter twist upon Mr. Worthington's face.

Pearl came flying back to us, cheeks blooming as pink as the roses in every garden, her face alight with exertion and pleasure.

"Come, Ginevra, come with me," she called out.

I didn't move until Mr. Worthington looked back at me over his wide shoulder. "Go on, girl."

It was enough.

I brushed past Mrs. Worthington, shivering as I slipped by her coldness.

I stopped beside Pearl and her new contraption. "I do not know how. I no have the right clothes."

"Just sit on the seat," Pearl instructed me, "I'll do the rest."

Thoughts and worries fled in fright at what awaited me. I bunched my skirts about my legs, straddled the small seat, and put myself into her keeping. We wavered a bit as my extra weight sent Pearl off-kilter. Soon enough she adjusted, and soon enough we were off.

I became a bird flying through the sky, the wind washed over me like the freshest water, cleansing my face, my mind, my soul. I closed my eyes, surrendering to it.

"Look at them." Pearl laughed the words flying back to me on the same wind.

I opened my eyes and saw two women—statues captured—sculpted by disbelief and disgust. Mrs. Fish and Mrs. Vanderbilt stood on the steps of Marble House. A vast lawn away, their shock and revulsion blossomed as clearly as the deep blue hydrangea blooms just behind the iron fence.

I laughed along with Pearl. We cared for nothing but the freedom, the feeling of it.

We turned 'round in the wide corner where Bellevue Avenue became Ocean Drive and made our way back. Pearl waved to the women still frozen in distaste. I turned my head, hiding my unshrinking smirk.

I jumped off as we turned into the path to The Beeches. Pearl's parents still stood there waiting for us, together but apart.

"Enough, Pearl," her mother's command drenched us like a bucket of cold water. "You must return. And you," the frost in her voice chilled my bones, "you are to serve her. That's what you are paid for."

It was a sting, as she meant it to be, but not one sharp enough to spoil the moment. Side by side, Pearl and I walked the bicycle to the carriage house where Mrs. Worthington insisted it reside.

"Have you ever felt anything like it?"

We shared wonder as if we had dreamt the same dream.

"No, never," I agreed. I put my hand on one of hers that steered the device. "Thank you," I said, without saying for what. Her lips spread wide. I could see every one of her teeth. She knew.

PEARL

The morning of my birthday came with the birth of golden light.

Ginevra brought me breakfast in on a tray, though I rarely lounged, rarely simpered in my bed. It didn't matter that it was the fashion, it was a fashion that did not fit me well. She set the tray about me, opening the heavy draperies, and threw open the windows. As if the walls fell, my room now sat outside amidst the brilliant sun, hot breeze, and chirping birds.

Then, without a word, she left me.

"G...Ginevra?"

She should have stayed with me. It was part of her job, yes, but a treasured one, treasured by us both. We'd plan the day's outfits, all of them, and talk, our talk, not that of a mistress to a maid. She had left, left me on my birthday. It couldn't be. She wouldn't. She didn't.

Ginevra returned in a few moments, her hands full.

I became one of the birds, a crow for I crowed. I jumped up, nearly tumbling my breakfast tray and all its contents onto my bed. In Ginevra's hands was quite the loveliest evening dress I had ever seen.

"It's pink and green!" I blurted, slipping the tips of my fingers over the soft fabric, making it real with the touch.

Ginevra beamed, holding her creation as if it were an infant, and brought it to my wardrobe, hanging it against the outside of the doors. I fell back upon my bed, staring at it.

In so many ways, it was much as the evening dresses of the day were. The bodice was fitted tightly, the skirt, though still bustled, was narrow, straighter than was the fashion a few years ago. What she had done with ribbon and lace, green ribbon and pink lace, I had never seen. It was remarkable, remarkably gorgeous. The short, puffed sleeves made of pink chiffon were pleated at the top and cuffed just above the elbow, but the cuffs were made of braided green ribbon, a trimming I had never seen, and ended with just the hint of scalloped pink lace.

Along the bottom of the skirt and its slight train, ran another row of the twisted green trimming, as did the waist, though there were three rows of it. Those rows came together at the back and flowed freely over the small bustle, just past the end of the small train. The precision of her stitching was as fine, if not better, than anything from Worth. It was art—art I would wear.

From the ribbons encircling the waist, Ginevra had brought them upward vertically, striping the bodice. Where the bodice ended in a scoop neck, the ribbons continued, on their own, meant to lay against my skin. They gathered together, connected to a choker made of three rows of the pink lace. I had never seen anything like it, not on any woman or in any magazine.

"Ginevra!" I gave a whispered shout. "It is...you are...magnificent."

I jumped up and pulled her to me. Her cheeks plumped against my shoulder.

"You like it?" she asked with a need, uncertainty plaguing her pride.

"Like it?" I held her away from me. "I adore it. You are so...I didn't know you could..." words failed me. "When did you learn to design like this? How did you learn?"

Ginevra lowered her chin in that charming way she had, charming for its freedom from affectation. Peeking at me through lush lashes, she grinned.

"From reading."

Our laughter rang in my ears for all of that day and night. Almost all of it.

* * *

As was the fashion, I walked into the ballroom on the night of my birthday party a half-hour after the last guest arrived. Here, white stucco relief decorations were everywhere, on the doors, the paneling, and the cornice, moving on to form an elaborate ceiling frieze with a center medallion of winged cherubs. Light from the crystal chandelier, ormolu wall sconces, and Louis XV andirons glittered off the richly carved woodwork of cream and white, and the gilded mirror frames. It was, perhaps, the most stunning and tasteful room in our cottage.

When I stepped in, every eye turned, every flapping lip stilled. Gasps rose up like fog, especially loud from the gathering of women and the girls, at the sight of my ensemble, my hair.

Ginevra had tried to talk me out of it, warning me of tempting trouble. I would not be daunted. To wear a dress such as the one she made me insisted I wore my hair up, to reveal it and me as they should be. But, to wear one's hair up proclaimed females as women, no longer girls; a privilege that awaited those turning eighteen. It had become a marker along the path of women's lives. It was a sign, as bold as any written on a board, that a girl had reached marrying age. In my mind, I was a woman, one far wiser than my mother. Conventions and consequences be damned.

Self-pride is a road to ruin.

They gathered around me, crowded me, asking about the dress as if it hung on a mannequin—where did it come from, who made it—turning me around and around as they gawked and sputtered surprise and praise.

Only one woman made her distaste plain, though I imagined there were others of the older set who felt the same.

With her porcelain smile firmly set, Mother came and took me by the arm.

"Yes, yes, dear girls, she looks quite…extraordinary," she said to my friends, detaching me from within their protective circle, "but Pearl must make her way about, must greet all her guests. I know you understand."

She didn't care if they did. Her fingers pinched my arm; a bruise would be in full bloom by morning.

"That…is *not* the dress I bought you." Her frozen smile didn't thaw a bit. I thought she would draw blood with her icicle teeth. "Where is that dress and where did this…this…thing come from? And how dare you wear your hair up! You've humiliated me."

"Do you like it, Mother?" I pushed, safe in the milieu. "It was made especially for me."

"You will march yourself upstairs this minute," Mother hissed at me, mouth so close her spittle pinged my face. "You will change your dress and put down your hair."

A year ago, I would have done just that.

"This gown is perfect for me, and this hairstyle belongs to this gown. And like it, it will *not* be changed." She had taught me ruthlessness; she had only herself to blame for being my first victim.

"It's bizarre," she condemned me for condemning her, for that's how her eyes saw it. "It's—"

"Pearl, you glorious girl," Consuelo Vanderbilt, such the dearest of friends, scampered to us, taking my mother's smile for a real one. "That is the most amazing dress I have ever seen. Is it by Worth?"

"Hello, dear Consuelo." I tugged my arm, a small tug. My mother released me before anyone could see how tight her grasp was, and I hugged my friend. "No, it's not. It's actually by a new, up-and-coming designer, I'll tell you all about her. You'll excuse us, won't you, Mother?"

Mother's hot glare flicked between Alva Vanderbilt's daughter and me. She had no choice in her answer.

"But, of course, dear," my mother said, her voice came out of her nose with a discordant twang. "Be sure to pay your respects to Consuelo's mother. And Mrs. Astor, of course." She pointed in the corner where, wonder of wonder, the queen of Newport society sat enthroned, her courtiers around her. I was almost sorry to see her here, sorry my mother's tactics had worked. It would only encourage her to do more.

"I will, Mother, in just a minute. I promise." I meant it. To have Mrs. Astor in our home was a feat. It mattered a great deal, though I despised that it did, loathed that one woman could have such power over others. Yet there was a part of me—the small part of me who wanted Frederick to pay me more attention—that knew the value of having her here.

Consuelo and I chatted, strolling around the room, greeting other guests and friends, whirling on the social merry-go-round. Dizziness found me in the whirl of my thoughts on the carousel of my mind. How could I both revere and despise, long to run to and from, with the same need?

As we came back 'round, to the corner just to the left of the main door with its glittering gold grand piano, I squeezed Consuelo's arm.

"I must do my duty," I whispered to my fellow conspirator. I ticked my head in the direction of Mrs. Astor just beside the piano before the cold fireplace where she had taken up reign.

Consuelo hid her pale smile behind her gloved fingers. "Best of luck," she whispered and took herself off.

"Dear Mrs. Astor, how wonderful to have you here," I exclaimed softly, feigning the confidence that spoke the words, confidence that should have owned naturally. I felt an odd notion to curtsey. "And you as well, Mrs. Carey." That would be Mary Astor Carey, *the* Mrs. Astor's sister-in-law.

Caroline Schimmerhorn Astor, known simply as *The* Mrs. Astor. Her ever-present partner in censorship, Ward McAllister, forever blathered about the importance of beauty before brains to someone who wasn't. In my eyes, and others as well I think, Mrs. Astor was nowhere near beautiful. She had a large jaw and far too prominent a nose. She was short, and dare I say, dumpy. Yet the climbers forever compared her to Queen Victoria; she dressed and acted the part, embracing it completely.

According to Mrs. Astor's gospel, it took three generations of wealth, acquired not through work but through birth, to attain social acceptance. Her husband, William Backhouse Astor, Jr., was the grandson of the John Jacob Astor, he who had made his fortune investing in real estate, a pursuit deemed acceptable. She could trace her lineage back to New York Dutch aristocracy, a true "Knickerbocker," as they were called.

Husband was never very close to wife, not in spirit or location. He was far more dour than she; he possessed none of the refinement and ambition his wife demanded in others. He cared more for his horses, yachts, and—if rumors were to be believed—other women.

I didn't believe they were rumors; they were just more tales of another philandering married man in this cloistered community, tales rooted in fact as deeply as our beeches are rooted to the ground. Of all the things these people thought of themselves, the most harmful was that they were, or thought they were, above reproach.

With such credentials, she felt justified in dictating the rules of this society, a notion I could not accept. Who was anyone to judge another? Yet judge she did.

The ladies greeted me warmly and invited me to sit on an ottoman at their feet. Where else.

To my surprise, our conversation was lovely. I wondered whom exactly I conversed with, the true woman or the truth she allowed. She was, after all, the bastion of this elegantly macabre way of life I struggled to embrace.

I rose, excusing myself to see to other guests, the only correct excuse. I had done myself proud; I'd said all the right things at all the right times and in just the right manner. In the eyes of these women—upon whom so many fates depended—nothing but an approved impression gleamed. Staying too long in their company, as my mother did so often, could undo it all, untying slips of knots just tied. I had little care to be a knot along this particular rope, but it was the only one in my hands at the time.

"I will take my leave of you, ladies." I rose with perfect grace, imitating a manner studied for years, and with a small bow of my head, made my departure from them. Their salutations of their enjoyment of my company followed me like the train of my dress.

Nerves I had held at bay now rushed upon me. I could only keep my composure and my graceful gait into the next room, where—thankfully—punch, wine, and champagne waited. I took up a glass of the latter and leaned against the wall, just the other side of where the social autocrats sat.

I should have walked further away.

"What a lovely young woman," I heard Mrs. Astor say and I sighed relief into my glass.

"Indeed," agreed Mrs. Carey, "she is a fine tribute to her father."

"And what a surprise considering her mother, though I suppose it explains her appearance."

The wine in my mouth turned bitter. I should have walked away but couldn't.

"We really should take her up," Mrs. Astor proclaimed, their idiom of acceptance, that which every man, woman, and child strived for, the crowning achievement for anyone in our circle.

"Do you not think her too...too modern?"

Mrs. Astor huffed. I think it was a laugh. "Perhaps a little modern is not an entirely bad thing. It shows spunk. I like spunk."

"However can we take her up when we haven't the mother?" Mrs. Carey lowered her voice, yet not her displeasure.

"Taking up that girl will be quite easy," Mrs. Astor assured. "Taking up *that* woman will never happen, not as long as I breathe."

There it was, my mother's irony.

"I suppose it is not right to punish the daughter for the mother," Mrs. Carey insisted. "And the father is such a dear man. He has suffered enough, I think. Seeing his daughter done well will surely comfort him. Relieve him of the pain his wife causes him."

Of what pain did they speak? They could not know how my mother harangued my father, her coldness to him. Or was it that evident? Was it some other pain?

"Quite right," Mrs. Astor agreed. "For the father's sake, we will ignore the mother."

"She may take it as a sign of her own acceptance."

Mrs. Astor laughed outright. "I hardly think so, dear. Accepting the daughter will not find me anything but cordial to that awful woman."

"Nor I," Mrs. Carey concurred.

"It's settled then. Be sure to include Pearl on your guest lists, my dear. She will have to deal with her mother's disappointment, not us."

I could hear no more. Taking up another glass, of what I do not remember now, and did as I should have done. I moved quickly from the room, from the nearness of these sitting magistrates, and made my way to the farthest room I could find.

In the library, I sat at a bridge table that had just lost its fourth, but it was not this ever more popular game of cards that I pondered, but this tenuous game of society in which I existed. At seventeen, I was finally deemed old enough to learn and play the game taking society by storm, ousting whist from its lofty position as the favored card game where it had sat for centuries. These days it seemed no matter the occasion, someone would demand a game of bridge. I was never more grateful for the trivial pursuit as I was in that moment.

I felt so very grown up as they allowed me a seat at the table. The cards in my hand trembled; I held them tighter. I partnered with Herbert Butterworth, and we played against my brother and Frederick. I floated between two worlds, one dark and sultry, the other golden and dashing. I played more than one game in that moment.

Herbert, as he insisted I now call him, taught me a great deal that night, as if I hadn't learned too much already. Would I have played differently if I knew that night was the last night I would see Herbert that summer? Perhaps. But the path of life called "what if" was too fatiguing to traverse. I strayed from it as much as I could.

Within a few deals, a few tricks, I had the nuances of the game down pat. Within a short span of time, the glow of its novelty dimmed as quickly as a candle snuffed out for the night.

If this was the glory of adulthood, I would readily choose the normality of childhood, for in comparison, its peace and idleness were surely more enticing.

GINEVRA

From the hidden corners of The Beeches, I watched her sail into the room. My eyes closed as I heard the gasp of wonder over her gown, my sigh released my held breath. It was as if the clock had already struck midnight and it was already my birthday and not hers.

This small group of Pearl's friends gave her the gift of their company and their genuine well wishes. She whirled from one to the other, chatting and laughing, and beaming.

I watched her dance many a dance, most often with just two men. One I recognized as the charming man that had called me beautiful at Gravel Court. In my mind that was his name, The-Man-Who-Called-Me-Beautiful. When they danced, I watched him more than her. Before these men, her face changed, a similar change, one of blooming cheeks and sparkling smiles.

It was as it should have been, a night that belonged to Pearl and her alone, no matter how often her mother pushed herself into the center of the room, she could not achieve the center of attention. That belonged to her daughter. Mrs. Worthington's face showed pleasure and displeasure in equal amounts. I understood; it was an understanding that frightened me.

Yes, Pearl owned the night. It should have been a night of nothing but delights, but there it was again, the bitter stab of jealousy. This night it bore two names. I envied those young women, envied their freedom and their beauty, their dresses and their jewels. And I envied them Pearl. She should belong to me and no one else.

I walked away then, fairly certain the dress wouldn't need me. I knew she didn't. I could not watch any longer.

* * *

I lay in my bed listening. Even from two floors above, the sounds of laughter and music drifted up to me. I listened to the sounds of the crickets chirping in the warm night air. I listened to the clock tick its way onward until it tolled midnight.

It was my birthday.

My father had made no mention of it, no mention of plans or gifts. I didn't expect he would. My birthday was too full of shared remembrances of my mother, shared grief.

I knew the servants knew of my birthday as well. I knew they would do nothing at all, and they hadn't.

Listening to the tolls, I heard the quiet of my life. The tolling stopped long before the loud silence of my mind, long before sleep found me. It didn't find me for long.

* * *

"Ginevra!" The insistent hiss came from the door.

I opened eyes heavy with sleep…or did I dream.

"Ginevra, wake up!" It came again.

I bolted upright, looked around, found the sliver of light from the hall lamps slipping in my door.

It was there I found her. Pearl.

"What are you doing here?" I whispered, jumping from my bed, jumping to the door, grabbing her hand to pull her in, but she wouldn't allow it.

"Put on your robe," she commanded, pulling her head out the small space, checking the hall, up and down as I donned the garment. With it on, I went to her again. I saw the small sack she carried in one hand.

"What have you—"

This time she grabbed my hand, "Come on!" she giggled. I shushed her even as I followed her.

I should have known where she would take me.

* * *

We didn't climb the beeches that night. She was still in the dress I had made her, swearing to me that she never wanted to take it off. I was robed but barefoot.

Beneath the great canopy of the beeches, we sat. Pearl opened the sack and pulled out her treasures. A lone candle on a silver stick. She struck a match to it and the canopy beneath the beeches glowed from within.

I swallowed back a lump of tears as she pulled out a piece of cake, a piece of her birthday cake, but it was to me she sang, it was my birthday we celebrated.

We wrapped ourselves together in the beautifully embroidered and fringed shawl, the last of her treasures, the one that became my greatest treasure, her gift to me, and talked.

We didn't talk about her party, the fabulous clothes, the equally fabulous people. We chattered about our bicycle rides, about our dreams, and little else.

The greatest gift Pearl ever gave me was herself.

PEARL

The heat wave hit us the next morning, but it was frigid in the breakfast room.

Mother sat ramrod straight, as always, yet the kinks in the rod began to show. Veins pumped on her forehead. She snapped at her food rather than bite it delicately from the tip of her fork. I hung from an unraveling thread; it was just a matter of time before it snapped. Silent trepidation screamed from my father and Clarence. We held our breath. We didn't need to wait long. She shifted her pose in her chair ever so slightly.

"I've instructed Mr. Grayson to give Pearl's bicycle away," she said and sipped her coffee.

"Mother!"

"Millicent!"

Father and I chorused outrage.

Clarence quickly dabbed the corners of his mouth with his serviette and stood. "I must be off. I have court time with Henry." He was out of the room before his words.

I glared at his back, despising him for his cowardice. A big brother's place should be beside his younger sister—not during a card game or a party—but when the chair she sat upon tipped, daring to tip over.

I reached my hands across the table; hers were just out of reach.

"You can't do this, Mother," I pleaded without shame.

She glared at me, "And you can't do many things, but you do."

Mother stood and threw her napkin on the table, anger contained set loose.

"Did you really think you could defy me in so public a manner, humiliate me as you did last night, with no consequences?"

I gaped up at her open-mouthed. "But...but everyone complimented me."

"So they said to your face," Mother jabbed me with her words. "You have no idea what they said to each other, behind my back."

"Don't you mean...," *my* back, I started to say. The brightness of epiphany, wrought by the slip of her tongue, strangled me.

She knew. My mother knew how the community spoke of her. For her it was a mortal wound, I understood. But this anger—her anger—did not belong to me alone. Part belonged to 'them,' those she idolized. She would deny any ownership of the status she herself created.

"You throw away convention without a thought, without consulting me. Why should I not throw away your toy?"

I knew crow must become a part of the breakfast I must eat.

"You're right, Mother." My voice softened with contrition. It echoed in my head as desperation. "I should have shown you what I was wearing, how I planned to wear my hair. I, well, I thought to surprise you."

"That was no surprise. That was rebellion, against me."

"No, it wasn't." It was rebellion against so much more. She did not need to know it.

"You're right, Millicent." My father spoke. His words drained my blood. My head wobbled on my weakened neck. "But I think the punishment should fit the crime. This was a mere infraction. Besides, Pearl looked stunning last night. I'm quite sure that is all that is being said."

Relief sailed into sight, but it had not yet landed.

"This was no in-frac-tion." Each syllable of the last word contained even more bitterness.

"I think we shall refrain Pearl from riding the bicycle for two weeks. As long as her behavior during that time is suitable, it will be returned to her."

They glared at each other, two generals at the front lines. The ticking of the foyer clock matched my heart pumping in my ears.

Mother's top lip curled. I had never seen such a beautiful woman so ugly.

"Very well then. Have your way, you always do."

Father's face contorted with sarcastic laughter trapped within. I could not blame him. Mother held on to delusion as a drowning man does a life raft. In it, she saw their marriage as if it existed as Father would have it. It was a grand delusion indeed.

Mother stomped away from us. Not a backward glance as she left the room. She left us stewing in the heat of her anger.

Father spoke to me then, even as his gaze stayed upon Mother marching away, "I think that might be the last time I saved you, my Pearl. The last time I can."

I swallowed hard but could not swallow away the lump in my throat.

Father looked at me. For the first time, I knew the incredibly successful and ruthless businessman he was. I glimpsed the core of him, a man who would do whatever it took to break his own bonds, of rebuilding, of regaining respect. I saw how much he wished me to be like him.

"The rest is up to you."

I remember when I was a child, my mother's hair had been a lovely sort of light brown, dark blonde mix. The strands of each tone flowed together in her long hair, adding richness and depth to the elaborate coifs so popular in those days. From the moment she met Alva Vanderbilt, it was no longer enough. Like Mrs. Vanderbilt and Tessie Oelrichs too, my mother had to become a redhead. Her need to be one of them led to the most awful of grueling ordeals, every month, a two-day ordeal.

The closely guarded formula from Paris required several complicated and messy steps. They dyed the hair black first, then green, then finally the desired hue of red. No woman dared be seen in such a frightful state—and she looked frightful indeed—so those who chose the practice were prisoners of their own making, prisoners in their dressing rooms during the long unsightly process.

I confess those two days every month became a blessing for me. Mother could not be out and about, could not see where I went nor with whom I went. As much as her obsessive need to change herself to fit in revolted me, I took full advantage of this nasty habit.

Ginevra helped me don a walking outfit that morning. Though it was warm, storms threatened, the booming sort only the heat of summer brought on. It was no day for the beach.

"Run upstairs and grab your bonnet," I told her, shooing her with my hands as she gave me her one brow raised, quizzical look. "Go on. Let's take a walk together, shall we?"

There was nothing untoward about a young lady taking a walk with her personal maid as her chaperone. There were no rules, those unwritten ones, against it. They would not know I walked with my friend, not my maid.

Ginevra hurried to do my bidding, hurried to enjoy such a trivial thing as a walk, a simple pleasure of life that had been denied her all last summer. It was only minutes until we were out on Bellevue Avenue, me with my parasol, her with her bonnet.

The moist warmth slowed our pace. The dust of the road tossed upward as the carriages past us had no strength to fight its oppression and fell back to the ground quickly, defeated.

"Have you been painting?" Ginevra asked once we were safely away from The Beeches, safely away from prying ears.

My lips spread without effort.

"I have, a great deal," I said. "In fact, I've done much to further my career as an artist."

"What? What have you—?"

"And you, Ginevra," I put her off, not yet, not just yet. "Have you been designing?"

"I have," she nodded, clasping her hands together, curiosity distracted but not entirely. "I have sketchbook with so many of them. I must keep it hidden, though. I think Mrs. Briggs looks in our rooms."

I stopped. My arm in hers, jerking her backward.

"That's deplorable. You are a hard worker in the employ of the Worthingtons. She has no right to invade your privacy in such a way." Outrage held me in its pinching grasp. I would do something about it, though I didn't know what or when.

Ginevra shrugged it away. "It is her way. I do not think she is alone. I have heard others, other staff from other cottages, say same happens to them."

Pain stabbed my jaw; my body told me of my anger. No wonder there was such dissatisfaction among staff, so many escaping from their posts to find employment in the mills and factories. Work in the mill might have been harder, but often hard work is an easy price for self-respect.

I threw off my rage as best I could and commenced our stroll. I did not want it to shadow our time together as the dark clouds rolling in attempted to do.

"Well, you must keep on," I insisted, "I look forward to wearing more of your wonderful creations."

"You do?" Her voice rose until the last note flew up skyward.

"I most certainly do. In fact, perhaps you could think about designing day dresses, something a bit more subdued, less frothy. I may have need of them."

It was Ginevra's turn to stop, her unspoken question clear, in the tilt of her head. We were knit too closely to keep a single strand of my truth from her. It was time. I told her of my future hopes, knowing she would breathe not a word of it to anyone.

"Oh, Pearl, how wonderful, for you it is the perfect thing," Ginevra cried, her enthusiasm overtaking her quiet nature. "But, but your mother—"

"Oh, Mother be damned," I bit the words out with a snap of my jaw. "I don't care a whit for what my mother may think." I stopped. The thought stopped me. I put a hand on Ginevra's arm. I held her gaze with mine. "I don't want to be like her, Ginevra. I don't want to be her."

I said it aloud. Relief cleansed me.

My sad demons, ones she saw clearly, darkened her gaze. She put her hand on mine. "And you never will be, Pearl. You are not made...like her."

There was little grace to her truth, there did not need to be. The astonishing truth served better.

We walked on, arm in arm.

"Lispenard Stewart lives there," I pointed across the avenue, to a lovely white colonial-style mansion, small for Bellevue, with a columned porch that wrapped around the entire front and north sides.

"Lis...pee...nard? That is a name?" Ginevra croaked on laughter. I joined her.

"It is, actually. And oh, what a rake he is."

"Really?"

Gossip. We told ourselves we were above it when, in truth, no one was. Everyone savored a taste of it now and again.

"He's near to forty but still not married. Some consider him the most eligible bachelor in Newport this season. He's very tall, very trim, and *very* flirtatious, a grafting machine. With every female, woman, or girl—"

A crack of thunder boomed, though only I heard it. The crackle of lightning bolted through me.

I had seen him work his magic on my own mother, not that it was rare for men to flirt with her. It seemed different with him, looked different.

"And that's Oakville Villa. It belongs to the Osgoods. After that is Lyndenhurst. Mr. Hodgson built it as we were building The Beeches. He was an officer in the Navy." I kept a running commentary about our neighbors and the splendid homes as we moved along at a leisurely pace.

Time passed and so did the street beneath our feet.

"Here's Marble House, the Vanderbilt house," I told her. "This is where Consuelo... Consuelo!"

Even as I spoke her name, my friend appeared, as if summoned by my words of her. She was just coming out her door. She waved to us, jumped back in, and came back out, parasol in hand. She called back into the house with a frown on her lips and creases on her brow. She came anyway, no matter what the words were.

With her sweetness, she embraced me. I returned it in kind.

"We're on a stroll, Consuelo, can you join us?" I asked.

"It would be my pleasure," she said. She had that aristocratic diction so common among our set, but hers was neither forced nor contrived. It danced off her tongue; one could close one's eyes and be soothed by it. In that shy way of hers, she turned her huge dark eyes, like stars with their thick fringe of curled lashes, to Ginevra.

"Oh, dear me, where are my manners," I said quickly. "Consuelo Vanderbilt, this is Ginevra Costa, I've spoken to you about her. Ginevra, please meet Consuelo."

Consuelo held a long, delicate hand out. Ginevra hesitated but took it.

"*Buon giorno,*" my clever Ginevra said. Somehow, somewhere along her journey from last year to this, from stranger to onlooker, she had already learned that among some, her Mediterranean background was an admired attribute, not a despised detriment. How proud I was of her, the way she held herself tall and straight, the way she let her own beauty show through her servant's uniform. Yet I could see the way she looked at Consuelo. I had, after all, seen so many other people look at my fabulous friend in just such a way for so many years.

Tall and willowy, she had what they called a piquant oval face atop a swanlike neck framed by thick, luxurious dark brown hair. Perfect, porcelain skin, long-legged, and full-lipped, her beauty was hard to miss, and yet it affected her not at all.

"You are Ginevra?" Consuelo asked with quiet excitement, her form of it. "You are the talented dress designer?"

Ginevra blushed, glimmered at Consuelo's words.

"No, Miss Vanderbilt—"

"Oh, please call me Consuelo, and, if I may, I will call you Ginevra?" Consuelo's manners were as impeccable as they were amiable.

"Consuelo," Ginevra dipped her head, "I am no…not a designer. I am merely a maid who can sew."

Consuelo shook her head. "Do not toy with me, Ginevra. I saw the dress you designed and made for our friend. It was a masterpiece. You had all the men fawning over her."

"The men weren't—" I tried to hide my pleasure behind modesty.

"They fanned, eh, no, fawned, over her beauty," Ginevra stood taller with possessive pride, "not my dress."

Consuelo twirled her parasol toward Ginevra. "Well, I won't argue over her beauty, but your dress most certainly framed it."

"No one fawned." I stamped my foot at being ignored, being praised. I had little experience with it.

"Oh dear, Pearl, you cannot fool us." Now they conspired together. "If I recall two men, in particular, did a great deal of fawning. Frederick was one, and who was that other?" Consuelo tapped fingers covered with thin lace upon her mouth. "The dashing fellow with the black hair and golden eyes."

Did I stumble or did Ginevra? I couldn't see it clearly. Not then.

"His name is Butterworth, Herbert Butterworth," I stated plainly, or thought I did.

"Oh yes, that must be him. Look at her blush, Ginevra?"

When I turned, I saw Ginevra as I had seen her the very first day she came to The Beeches, pale and fearing what lay ahead.

"Are you all—"

"I am fine, *si.*" Ginevra dropped her chin, pulled her bonnet lower down her face.

"Do you wish to return?"

She shook her head without taking her eyes away from the dirt street beneath our feet.

"Well, I have a wish," Consuelo saw nothing of what I did, "I long for you to make something for me."

Ginevra's head snapped up then, eyes owlish. She struggled with her enthusiasm before it walked ahead of her. Two years in Newport and already she knew the power that was the Vanderbilts. I could not imagine what such a request must have meant to her.

"*Grazie,* Consuelo, it would be an honor," she said. I did not hear the gusto I expected.

"Good, that's settled then." Consuelo hooked one arm about mine, the other about that of Ginevra. We continued our constitution.

"Speaking of dresses," I said. The conversation needed to be steered in a different direction, though for who I wasn't certain. "Mother has said Worth will be here soon, visiting us all, dressing us all, all alike." My note of displeasure was as clear as the robin calls all around us.

"I'd rather look like the rest. It makes it so much easier not to be seen."

If Consuelo could have thrown off the mantle of being a Vanderbilt, no matter how grand and bejeweled, I believe she would have. Her life had been one in constant control, not her own, but that of her governess and her mother.

The woman who called Consuelo her child commanded every room in which she was present. Alva Vanderbilt was a mighty force to reckon with as an acquaintance. I cringed, imagining myself as her daughter.

Consuelo served as an accessory to her mother's grandeur; she preferred it, learned how long ago. Her lesson was much like mine. I had learned from my mother as well, learned who I didn't want to be.

We chatted more as we walked, now a trio. Consuelo's undeniable inner grace kept Ginevra in the conversation whenever possible, no matter Ginevra's station or her changed mood. We rounded Bellevue onto Ocean Drive and stopped at the top of the bluffs overlooking Bailey's Beach.

The waves churned in, pounding the shore. The ocean was angry, angry at the clouds that made the water dark, that kept us from our daily frolicking, angry as if it missed us.

"I feel like the ocean," Consuelo said, or did she think it aloud. "It's crashing in on me, wave after wave of it, I fear."

"Whatever do you mean?" I asked. I had never heard her speak so despondently. Consuelo was intelligent and educated, as curious as I, as Ginevra. A serious girl, yes, but this gloominess was not her either. On the other side of me, Ginevra nodded, her own eyes upon crashing waves.

Consuelo shook her head and forced a smile. "Oh, don't listen to me, Pearl. It's just one of those days," she answered. It was no answer.

I would not pry. I could only hope she would share her worries with me if there were truly any. As I hoped Ginevra would.

GINEVRA

When my next afternoon off arrived, I remembered my walk with Pearl and Consuelo. It encouraged me to take a walk of my own, taking my new freedom as a lady's maid out for a walk. It was perfectly acceptable for me to do so alone as I wasn't one of the chosen and didn't have to conform to their strict rules.

I needed separation, space to think.

I had taken the lovely yellow striped dress Pearl had given me and reduced it down to something more in keeping with who I was. I had no wish to look like—or pretend to be—anything more. Would I *be* one of them if I could? There was more and more of me that thought I would, an itch I couldn't scratch. Yet I knew it as a young girl's silly dreaming, at least I hoped that's all it was.

At the bottom of Memorial Boulevard, I stopped before turning right.

The ocean lay in front of me, on its daily progress of forward and back. The sun glinted off the peaks of the waves, reflecting pure golden light at me. Golden, as were his eyes.

Moving fast, the world blurred around me. I let it.

It couldn't be true, I told myself. I had been telling myself the same thing for days. Pearl had only ever spoken of Frederick. She couldn't have feelings for the man who called me beautiful.

She must not, I commanded, but of whom?

"Pardon me, Miss," the gentle singsong voice of an Irishman brought me out of my tumbling thoughts, as he almost tumbled me to the ground.

"No need. My fault." It was. I could not stand like a block of stone on such a busy street. Driving my thoughts onto safer ground, I straightened my lovely new, old dress and continued.

I couldn't change, not a stitch, of the dull uniform I must wear whenever I was in service, which was every minute save two afternoons a week. On those days, I craved some of the style I longed to create, to plume myself in at least a few of the feathers forever worn by the grand birds of this community. I felt quite fashionable, quite pretty, as I headed north on Bellevue then down Memorial Boulevard to Thames Street—in my head I said it as Pearl, as the chosen, said it, with the English pronunciation—"temes"—running along the waterfront, lined on the other side by shop after shop.

Though paid each week, I spent little. I saved my money, for something special. I just wasn't sure what that something was yet. I did enjoy looking in all the windows, seeing all the trinkets and such the Townies sold to the summer elite. Many of them did very well. They had no problem gouging the snobs who lived up on the hill in their mansions, sometimes charging triple what they would to a neighbor, a fellow Townie.

In turn, though they bought from them, the families on Bellevue detested the Townies, only they called them 'footstools,' for it was on these people's backs they lived. Their fresh food came from Townie farms, their goods moved on Townie ships, their trinkets came from Townie shops. If they would not offer gratitude, it seemed right to me that they paid for it.

I was off to the Redwood Library, the oldest in Newport, a place of great esteem, a place an American founding father, Thomas Jefferson, had once visited. Renowned not only for its books but for its looks, designed to resemble a Roman Doric temple.

I hoped to find more magazines or books on fashion and design, more things to keep hidden from Mrs. Briggs, more things to keep me busy and hide others. What I found was an article about a mysterious place, one right in Newport, one just around the corner from where I sat.

It took me no more than three minutes to arrive at its base, though it was a bit of a climb as it stood atop a grassy hill where once a mansion sat, one owned by a man named Benedict Arnold; the article did not paint a pleasant picture of this man.

Struck dumb by its presence, I could think of nothing save the words I had read. The Old Stone Tower was, or so the article claimed, citing a study of the mortar by a Reverend Dr. Jackson, was of Viking origin. Supported by eight pillars, four of which faced the main points of a compass, the upper portion was round, well not really round as some parts were wider than others, and rose nearly thirty feet. Between the pillars were rounded arches one could walk through. Of course I did, and I was not alone; people in groups and pairs circled around me as I circled the tower.

Within its shade, I shivered, though the day was frightfully hot. I chided myself with a giggle; I carried myself away on words of temple and pagan and otherworldly worshippers. Unearthly or not, I could see why so many made it a point to walk by it to see it for themselves.

With goosebumps still upon my skin, I stepped out of the shade, taking my first steps back towards The Beeches. They stopped before they began.

He was there. And he was not alone. Two young, beautifully dressed women walked with him, one on each arm.

They could be Pearl and me.

The thought jumped into my head of its accord. I didn't know what it meant; not my thought or his presence with them. I would. One day.

PEARL

Leaving Ginevra this time was both easier and harder.

We had spent so much more time together this summer, not only under the beeches, but in my room, riding my bicycle once it was returned to me, and on our walks, which we had taken to doing more and more often. Her presence by my side seemed to unlock a room hidden within me, hidden even to myself. That summer I explored the room I had never entered. In that room, with her, I laughed truer and confessed more than I ever had.

I knew when I returned she would be there, as much in my life if not more. As I grew older, as she did, there would be more occasions for her to accompany me, more times we could spend together. I clung to those thoughts for they made the leaving easier... if only a little.

In silence, Ginevra packed my trunks, shrouded in the sadness I had placed about her shoulders. It would take me a long time to erase the look on her face when I told her she would be staying in Newport.

"Mother won't let me take you to New York," I explained as we sat upon our limb last night, our last night that summer under the beeches.

The wind had turned, coming out of the north rather than off the warm ocean. We huddled close, wrapped once more together in the shawl I had given her for her birthday, the shawl she wore even over her nightgown.

"She said, if I am to have a lady's maid in New York, it must be a New York maid," I did a passable imitation of my mother's annoying annoyed voice. It made Ginevra smile, but only a little. "I had to agree, or I wouldn't have any maid. At my age, it would be, well, it would embarrass me. I had to agree, you see that, don't you?"

Ginevra had looked at me then, taking her eyes off the stars hanging so close above us, so many more stars we could see as the beeches had already begun to weep away their leaves.

"Of course, yes, I understand."

I don't think she did. Perhaps she understood why I did what I did but not the actions of my mother. She was not alone.

Mother and I warred, and Ginevra was the battleground we fought over. Promoting Ginevra to my ladies' maid had been a battle I won. Mother's counterattack was her refusal to allow Ginevra to accompany me to New York. Knowing a truth and understanding it are two very different things. I couldn't understand a mother who intentionally wanted to hurt their child.

"I made her promise, though, that the New York maid would stay in New York. That here you, and only you, would ever be that to me."

Ginevra had smiled a real smile then. I breathed deeply of the chilly air and my relief.

"Do not worry yourself," Ginevra had said softly. "I will sketch and make many beautiful dresses for you while you are away. I will go to the library." With Mother and Mrs. Briggs away, she could be the Ginevra she truly was; there was solace to be found there and she knew it.

"That will be well then," I had said, but I needed to say more, I leaned down, resting my head on her shoulder. "You know you are more to me, more than a maid, or a seamstress, or even a designer. You are so very much more."

I had never known such a direct gaze as hers that was upon me in that moment.

"You are…," she had grinned again, "*famiglia mia.*"

I had understood her perfectly.

GINEVRA

Pearl's leaving didn't feel as bad this year. The ghostly shadows didn't haunt me as they did last year. I missed her more, more than ever. Yet, I accepted it; acceptance is a great ointment.

PEARL

1897

We weren't back in Newport but a few hours when I took Ginevra beneath the beeches. I had to tell her of the great Alva Vanderbilt, how she was—it was rumored—an adulteress.

"The Vanderbilts went on a cruise with a few friends, including OHP. Well, it seems—"

"OHP?" Ginevra asked on a thin breath. She was spellbound, astounded that the great bastion of proper behavior was nothing more than a loose woman.

"Oh, sorry." I was in such a rush to get it all out I didn't stop to think. Gossip will do that to you. "Oliver Hazard Perry Belmont, he owns Belcourt, up Bellevue, just a bit past Marble House. His first wife, Sarah Whiting, was already pregnant when they married, but they divorced the same year."

"No!"

"Oh, yes." We were deep into it now, safe within the beeches. "And there were rumors, for years now, about the amount of time Alva spent with OHP." Only here did I dare call them by their first names. "He's a very handsome man, outgoing like Alva. But of course, no one could prove it. We are all so incestuous here, aren't we?"

Ginevra agreed once I defined the word for her.

"It seems, as the story going around proclaims, that OHP joined the Vanderbilts on the *Alva* for a summer cruise to Europe." I leaned closer to her, voice a squeaky whisper, words coming fast. "One night, Willie took himself off to some resort. When he came back..."

Ginevra pinched my arm. I toyed with her, but she would have none of it.

"When he came back...he found them...together!"

Ginevra's eyes popped. "Together, together?"

"Oh, yes, together. In *that* way!"

"*O Dio mio,*" Ginevra breathed.

"Oh my God is right. It's really rather ironic." I mused. Ginevra nudge me to do my thinking aloud. "Well, they were never a good match, Willie and Alva. Everyone who's anyone knows he spent all that time on his yacht, named *Alva* no less, to get away from her. But he was rarely alone."

"With friends?" Ginevra panted, hungry for more.

"No, with women, lots of women."

Ginevra nodded slowly. "Ah, *si*, ironic." Then she shook her head. "I cannot believe that such a woman would, that *that* woman would…"

"She did. And now they're getting a divorce."

"A divorce!" Ginevra cried out, slapping a hand over her mouth. The birds squawked complaints as they flew out of the trees.

With her deeply rooted Catholic faith, such an action must have seemed even more scandalous. We sat in silence for a while, a good long while. If I could reach into her mind, I would see a reflection of my thoughts, ones of pretentiousness and hypocrisy.

For all that we disapproved of the force that was Alva Vanderbilt, she was a fixture in our lives, an impenetrable stone, no matter that we chafed at where such a stone sat. Her disgrace unnerved, made the immovable movable, chinked away at what we thought we could depend on.

In our quiet contemplation, we heard the voices draw close.

It happened now and again, when we were secreted beneath the beeches, when people—groundskeepers, my brother and his friends, my parents—would come out to the grounds, whether working or taking a stroll.

Usually, we would abandon our haven beneath the weeping beeches, for what good was it if others were near, their voices intruding, breaking the illusion of our existence in another time and place. We would sneak out from the far side of the commotion, our minds shifting away from our alternate reality, like waking from a dream with the disappointment of its untruth. Though there were times when we stayed when others were near, times we shouldn't have stayed.

The small octagonal teahouses marking the entrance to the sunken gardens sat upon marble stair daises punctuating the rise at the end of the vast verdant lawn. Like small little palaces, with their copper dome-shaped roofs and their gleaming white stone. Ginevra thought the wrought-iron balustrade ring on top with the eight urns set at all the corners, made it look like a crown.

I liked the doors. French doors, of course, my mother would have no other kind, with round over-doors set atop each of the four entrances. I loved the sight of their delicacy centered amidst the hard stone. Like me, in this "cottage" my mother had demanded, fragile within its sturdiness.

There were times when Ginevra and I snuck into them, when my mother entertained no one, no small tete-a-tetes. Those times were rare. We made our place in the vast foliage cave beneath the weeping beeches. Freedom and segregation, no matter how disparate, were ours there, as we wanted it to be.

On the warmest days, such as this one, the doors of the teahouses stood wide open on all four sides. Here my parents, though in truth rarely my father, had afternoon tea sheltered beneath these small cupolas, the women perched primly upon the scrolled iron chairs, the men flounced with an elegant flop, everyone grateful for the shade and the strong breeze the wide-open space of the yard conjured up. The wind swept through, clearing away the heat, taking with it any words sprinkled about haphazardly.

On the same breeze, the voices came to us, especially if the intruders—as we always called them—chose the one nearest to us, nearest to our world beneath the beeches, the one closest to the carriage house.

Far too often, Ginevra and I would stay perched like mute monkeys on one of the lower, horizontal branches and listened. Far too often, we heard things we shouldn't have.

If we had heard this conversation a few years ago, it would have had no power, its impact lost to our innocent ignorance. We were older now. Their words became brutal fists with our comprehension.

"I really don't know how long I can stand him. I can't bear looking at him." Mother's voice was a shrill complaint. It scattered frightened robins from a nearby maple.

She spoke of my father, I knew. Ginevra knew as well, she told me so with the drop turn of her head.

"You could leave him, my dear. Alva has paved the way."

Her words plunged a dagger into my heart.

I wasn't exactly sure who encouraged my mother to do such a heinous act. I wish I did so that I could hurt her in some way, as she hurt me. The ever so practiced, haughty diction could have belonged to any of the privileged women who made Newport their summer home. The way she pronounced "we" had all the arrogance of superiority so rife in this small world. Whoever she was, she was cut from the same cloth as my mother.

Mother sounded wounded and suffering. Not the sort she feigned with such practice so often, but real pain. "Yes, but unlike Alva, I would most probably lose everything, possibly even the children." She lowered her voice. Ginevra and I craned our ears.

Ginevra's hand took mine. I didn't know until she did, how much it shook.

"But you know there are ways, many ways, of finding happiness away from him." The other woman laughed then, salt on the wound she had opened in my heart. "I have seen the many sways who pay you so much attention. I'm sure any one of them would help relieve your...dissatisfaction."

Innocence does not equate to stupidity. I had a vague notion of what the woman encouraged.

"It is just like that article said," I whispered, unsure to whom I spoke, Ginevra or myself.

"What article?" she hissed back.

"Remember, the one by the 'woman' named Belle, who turned out to be a man. The one who wrote for *The New York Mirror*. Remember he wrote—"

"Don't." Ginevra squeezed hard on my hand in hers.

"I remember exactly what he wrote." Ginevra was no longer with me, or I was not with her. *They bring money and gaiety to the town, but they have introduced a very serious evil. I mean an expensive lifestyle and a too great fondness for convivial entertainments. Older women pursued younger men. Younger women chased older men. Fortune hunters of all ages ran after anyone with money. And some highly unconventional women took up with each other and were spied kissing on the lips."*

A tight-lipped grimace sat upon Ginevra's mouth. She remembered. How she disapproved of us.

Mother laughed then, a sound I had not often heard. I had no care to hear it—that laugh—ever again.

"Perhaps, my dear, perhaps you are right. Perhaps it is the thing to do." she snickered. "Perhaps I already have. And perhaps Orin already knows."

A gale-force wind overtook the sweet summer breeze drifting through the leaves; I gripped our branch lest it fell me to the ground.

Ginevra turned and gripped me, held me on the branch. Upon her sun-spackled face, lay true sympathy.

"What? What has she already done?" she whispered.

I had no answer for her, not a sure one, or the depth of the act.

"Things are changing," I said, it was all I could think to say.

"What…things?" she asked.

"The world," I said, believing it. How right I was and how sorry I would be for it.

* * *

As had become the fashion, Mother insisted we take a family photograph every year. Since Father built The Beeches, it became the backdrop for this picture. In truth, there could be none better.

We gathered together, the four of us. On the top step of the second terrace, Mother and Father stood close but not together, shoulders touching but nothing else, nothing that mattered. The imposing, almost frightening statue of *Le Furie di Atamente*—The Madness of Athamas—behind them, somehow appropriate. Clarence and I stood on a step below, I before my mother, he before my father. Father rested a hand on Clarence's shoulder; Mother did the same on mine. I shuddered at the touch.

"Smile brightly, everyone," Mother chirped, as she always did at such moments. My father never smiled for these pictures. I offered what I could, a grimace.

The photographer hunched over his machine, hiding himself with a heavy drape of dark fabric. The flash popped and smoked. The moment captured.

When I saw the finished product some days later, I thought it should be a painting. Photographs captured truth; paintings interpreted it. This photo captured little of our truth.

GINEVRA

Each morning's awakening seemed brighter than the one that came before. I hated Mrs. Worthington more every day. The reunion with Pearl that should have been nothing but one joyous day after the other was dark and cloudy, no matter how bright the sun shone.

Pearl took her breakfast in her room more and more, as much to be away from her mother as to be with me. If she heard her mother's voice, the clack of her mother's low-heeled, kid-leather calf boots, Pearl ran in the other direction. Should Mrs. Worthington be out of doors, in the garden or a teahouse, Pearl remained inside.

I watched Pearl changing before my eyes. At eighteen, we both had begun to look like the adult women we would soon be, but she looked older, older than she ever had. My helplessness toward her kept slumber away many nights. All I knew to do was to be with her whenever I could, as much as I could.

She rarely left her room those first few days after hearing what we heard as we hid beneath the beeches, and when she did, I was by her side, or as close as I could get.

Worse, so very much worse, Pearl didn't paint, hadn't since that day.

Now she seemed only to wish to read, to escape into someone else's words, someone else's life.

She sent me to her father's library for her, for a particular book.

"I'll get it," I told her, as if I spoke to a child, "but only if you promise we go to the beeches to read it. The day is very fine, and your mother is not at home. You need some air."

I shuffled back a step when Pearl agreed.

I had been pretending to be my stern grandmother, putting on a show, never imaging she would take my threat seriously.

As Pearl slowly ate, slowly roused herself from the half-awake state she barely existed in, I left her for the library.

I had to circle the room to find it; one book in a room filled with glorious books. As I did, I passed Mr. Worthington's desk. Two photographs lay on it. One already in its frame, the new one the Worthington's had just taken a few days ago, *that* day. The old one hung off the edge of the massive desk, naked without its frame, already forgotten. I almost walked away, but something in it—two somethings—caught my eye.

On the corner of the house, where visitor carriages entered, the corner where the Worthington's guests were dropped off, the gleaming wood of the family's crest could be seen in its place on the wall, the shield-like crest my father had made for Mr. Worthington. I smiled to think the photographer had captured, in a way, my father's image as well. It was his imprint on this family moment. He wasn't alone. I was there with him.

I could barely see myself. I had to squint my eyes and hold the thick, heavy paper close to my face. But there I was. I was the ghost behind the sheer inner curtains in Pearl's room. It seemed fitting.

I took Pearl's book from the shelf, taking it from the room to her. The picture I took for myself.

PEARL

I stood at my window and watched. She thought she was being so clever, so furtive, but she didn't know I had been watching her, as much as I could, every day since that day. I knew *this* day—*this* moment—would come. I needed Ginevra.

It took a while for Ginevra to arrive. It was past eight o'clock. I had dismissed her an hour ago, thinking I would read in bed and fall asleep. I felt so very tired these days.

In the quiet of the house, I heard the carriage wheels crunch on the gravel path, and I knew.

I didn't need to see my mother, dressed to the nines, to know it was she, though see her I did. She jumped in the carriage, snapping her hand at Mr. Morgan, to go, to hurry. I didn't need to think too long or too hard to fathom where she was going. I had a good notion.

"Pearl?" Ginevra knocked on my door but didn't wait for my call to enter. Fear thinned and riddled her voice. She had been looking at me with a gaze full of it for days.

"We have to go," I said without a greeting. I reached into my wardrobe and grabbed two long coats, one for each of us. It was a warm night, but the coats had wide collars; when turned up, they would hide much of our faces.

"Go?" Ginevra's head bobbed like that of a turkey. "Go...where?"

I stopped though I didn't want to, but she deserved to know.

"My mother has gone out. She told no one. But she was dressed...," I hesitated. How startling it was that Mother's couture had been the final clue.

"...she was dressed to impress, but there is no party, no dinner or ball for such finery."

Ginevra said nothing; I sighed, relieved.

"We are going to find her. I think I know where she is going."

Ginevra knew then too.

It was no secret that the men and women, both young and old, in this cloistered community—the rarified among the rare—defied the rules, both legal and moral. The newspapers were forever filled with the tawdry stories of our tawdry lives. When I was younger, when I knew no better, I thought they had all been made up; people's jealousy will do such things. How foolish I was. Illicit trysts were as much a part of the summer activities on Newport as was sailing and tennis.

Ginevra said nothing as I took her hand, pulled her through the family portion of the house and out of it, through the Conservatory. I hurried her to the carriage house, gave a hurried explanation to one of the groomsmen—I couldn't remember his name, I don't now—for why I needed a buggy.

"My dear friend is ill," I said climbing on the sidebars and onto the driver's seat, thrusting my head for Ginevra to sit beside me. I grabbed the tasseled snapper and the reins from his hand before he could gain a tighter hold on them. "Pull up the top, would you, good man?"

I used my father's pleasant authority. The young man did as I instructed. Ginevra and I were now faceless bodies, the folding canvas of the buggy covering our heads, sheltering us, at least on the back and the sides.

"Thank you. You needn't wait up. I'll tend to the horses when we return, though we may be gone all night. I wouldn't want to deprive any of you hard-working men of your sleep."

"But, Miss..."

I snapped the reins, the horses responded, and his words were lost in the sound of the wind rushing past my ears, the crunch of the wheels on the gravel.

Ginevra held on tightly, silently.

She said nothing until we came to Memorial Boulevard and took a right, not a left. Those who lived on Bellevue Avenue and Ocean Drive never turned toward that part of the island. Almost never.

"Where are we going?" Ginevra had to yell for me to hear her over the crashing of the waves, the sluicing of the wind.

Without looking at her, I said, "Hanging Rock."

GINEVRA

A few people—couples, loud groups of mafficking young men—walked along Memorial Boulevard. A few more passed us in carriages. More than a few stopped, staring at two young women alone in a carriage, driving themselves. It was a sight out of sorts.

Once we made our way past Easton's Beach, where the Townies and the staff went to swim—the poor people's beach—less and less stared at us, we were less oddly out of place.

Pearl scared me. Her driving was uneven, and she had a way with horses, I had watched her many times. Her face was not her own, but an ugly version of her, one twisted with hate and anger. I wanted to scream at her to stop, that she didn't need to see what we both knew we would see. She knew the truth of her mother, as I did, as her father did, as most of the cottagers did. To see it would make it too real, the pain of it too real.

I turned to her; the wind snatched my hair, slapping the side of my face. I opened my mouth and shut it just as quickly. If this was what Pearl needed to do, nothing would stop her. If I tried, I could lose her. It wasn't worth the risk.

She turned off Memorial onto Purgatory Road. When I saw the street sign posted on the corner of the stonewall of the fire station, I slapped a hand over my mouth, trapping in bitter laughter. Pearl whipped the carriage around recklessly as we turned again, as all the people and the buildings faded away, as we plunged onto a rutted forest road, the trees rising, writhing in the wind above and around us.

"Whoa, whoa, slow now," Pearl whispered to the tall brown stallion pulling us along. He shook his long head, his shaggy mane whipped and stilled. Pearl slowed us to a trot, and then a walk. The four-beat gait of the horse's feet matched that of my heart.

The woods swallowed us. Owls hooted at us, angry at the presence of more intruders.

In the thick gossip that was a dish served at every staff meal, I had heard of Hanging Rock, heard all the nasty things the nasty women of the house said about it. I always thought they spoke out of desire, what woman wouldn't long for, if even a little, the romance of a secret meeting in the woods.

A river ran through the trees, we heard its gurgle. A pond was not too far off; I could smell that odor particular to fresh water, a greener smell than the ocean. It was a beautiful place, even in the dark, or especially so.

According to Mrs. Briggs, Nettie, Greta, and the rest, this was where the cottagers came; here a husband from one cottage and a wife from another came to meet when their spouses were in residence, when no other place allowed them to be together.

"Pfft, pfft," Pearl made the strange sound with her lips and pulled back hard on the reins.

"Look, there," she pointed, whispering.

I peered round the edge of the canopy, over my right shoulder. A loud groan filled my head. I left it there.

There was one of the Worthington's finest carriages. Next to it, another, equally as fine. I followed Pearl's finger and saw Mr. Morgan, off his driver's perch, walking a good distance away from the two carriages. He walked in a circle, one arm across his chest, the other stroking his doorknocker mustache. It looked as if he'd been walking the circle going nowhere for a while. It looked as if he had walked this walk before.

Pearl slithered down from the seat.

"Where are you going?"

"Ssssh!" she hissed at me, a finger to her lips. The same finger pointed to a group of tightly clumped birch trees.

I wanted to scream out, loud enough for Mrs. Worthington to hear me, for Mrs. Worthington to stop doing what we both knew she did. Pearl waved at me to follow. I did. If she must see, she would not do it alone.

Lifting our skirts, stepping high but soft, twigs cracking, leaves crunching beneath our feet, we made it to the cover of the birch trees without notice. Pearl bent sideways, peered around the tree trunks, and gasped.

"What, what is it?" I tugged on her sleeve.

She turned to me. Bright in the darkness, her eyes blazed with a white-hot anger.

"Lispenard Stewart!" her whisper was a scream.

O Dio mio, I said again, in my head this time.

I remembered all the awful things she had said about the man. I think Pearl had hoped, as I had, that if her mother was stepping out on her father that it was for love. Unrequited love was a pitiable thing, a thing that broke hearts with its tender pain. This man knew nothing of love. What he and Mrs. Worthington did had nothing to do with love.

I knelt below Pearl so I could peek around the trees as well. I shouldn't have. I couldn't stop myself even if I tried.

They kissed and groped and fondled to their heart's content, touching each other only where a husband and wife should, touching each other as if Mr. Morgan was not just a clearing away. I heard Pearl's angry breath above me, felt the shaking of her legs against my back.

"We should go," I muttered.

Pearl didn't move.

The man with the ridiculous name was kissing her mother's throat under the ear. He moved his lips across to the front, moved his lips lower, and then lower still.

I heard Pearl hitch a sob, the revolt loud.

"*Basta!* Enough," I grumbled, stood, and grabbed her arm. I pulled her, had to pull hard, but I pulled her away. She had seen enough. She had seen too much.

We made it back to the buggy without discovery. Pearl turned the horse's head, turned us 'round, and the moonlight found her face drenched with tears. Somehow, she brought us safely out of the woods, back onto the hard-packed dirt of Purgatory Road. There she stopped. Her arms dropped, as did her head. Her shoulders shuddered. I wrapped her in my arms and held her until they stilled.

"These people," she spat, I knew in her mind she was no longer one of them. How could she be? "How great they perceive themselves to be. All their money, their mansions, their fineries. It is all a false life."

She looked at me, her face twisted with pain, looking at me for an answer I did not have.

"It is not what life should be."

I couldn't disagree with her. I had watched them for three years, the grand parties, and the new clothes, every year more stunning, more elaborate. I watched—helpless and disgusted—when I saw the perfectly good clothes thrown out because they were no longer "in fashion." I had stared, astonished, in the kitchens as the footmen brought down huge trays of uneaten food. The staff would help themselves to the leftovers, as I had done on more than one occasion. And yet there was still so much of it, it filled bin after trash bin, food tossed away when there were so many going without. It seemed that for all they had, they always wanted more. They tossed people away with the same ease as last season's clothes.

"Take us home, Pearl," I said in her ear for I held her still. "I must get you in bed."

Pearl nodded, raised her head, and raised the reins.

"Heehaw!"

Before we could move again, the howl burst behind us, the carriage sped past us.

"Is that…is he…," I stuttered, astounded.

Even as a servant, I had heard what a coachman James Gordon Bennett, Jr. was. Everyone had heard about the races he organized, raced in, and bet on heavily. But this…

"Hah!" Pearl barked, a guard-dog bark. "Yes, that's him, that's Bennet."

We saw him race away, in all his glory, all of him. He was completely naked.

Pearl started laughing, kept laughing as she drove us back to The Beeches, laughed still as I changed her, and put her to bed. There, the laughter turned to tears as sometimes laughter can.

PEARL

They called Newport the playground of America's rich. We had made it so. With palace dollhouses and circus balls. For a brief, shining moment, it was the grandest place on earth. But, if it was a playground, then we, all of us—the Astors, Vanderbilts, Stuveysants, Belmonts, and those whose names may not be so well remembered—we were its children.

Every childhood must end, too often with toys broken and hard lessons learned and more than a tinge of regret and longing for what was…what could have been.

* * *

I didn't ring for Ginevra the next morning. It was not really morning yet at all, but still dawn. My eyes felt heavy and swollen; the rest of me felt numb. I threw my combing coat on over my nightgown and wandered out of my room. Directionless in so many ways.

The house had just started to wake. I could hear vague noises from two floors below, the kitchen workers no doubt.

Here, on the family floors, the only sounds were the ticking of the clocks, as out of sync as my family. I floated, my feet not touching the ground, a translucent specter of myself. The sight of my mother broke my connection, images I could not erase from my mind no matter how hard I pushed.

I made my way down the wide, white stairs. At the bottom, I began to turn right, heading for the Conservatory, heading for the little solace the room brought me. A noise to my left stopped me. I turned to it, creeping down the hall toward my father's library.

I stopped just outside the door, peeking in as I had so many times before.

I saw him then, saw him standing, staring out the window.

I watched my father as he stood at the edge of the cliff. Everything about him reeked of his despair, his unbuttoned coat, unruly hair, wrinkled trousers. His shoulders drooped. I had never seen him like this. I looked at a man I did not know.

* * *

Ginevra dressed me that night, holding my limbs, twisting my body, as she would a rag doll. I readied for one of the fabulous parties given by the Wetmore family at Chateau-sur-Mer, one of the first, one of the finest, cottages of them all. Though I had been there a few years ago for a birthday party for William Wetmore, Senator Wetmore's youngest, I had attended as an "adult." Mr. Wetmore, a two-term governor of Rhode Island, and now a Senator, was one of the more gracious cottagers, and Chateau-sur-Mer embodied his demeanor. This evening's fete was to honor his daughter Edith's engagement. I had looked forward to the event for weeks. I wanted to be anywhere but there.

"Just do your best to get through night," Ginevra nattered at me, only a few of the words finding their way into my consciousness. "Find Consuelo and stay with her and all will be well."

Ginevra took my face in her hands, putting her face inches from mine. "You can do this, Pearl. Be yourself, not your mother's daughter. I will be a room away, always."

I put my hands on hers. Gratitude swept through me for her giving, loving heart. I nodded and slipped away, not a thought to what I wore or how I looked.

* * *

The castle by the sea was alive. A dazzling shoal of fish swam beneath the atrium-like central hall, swayed beneath the forty-five-foot glass ceiling. Those not in the stream watched from above, from the balcony encircling the entire hall. I was drowning.

We did as we always did. My mother shot off like an arrow loosed into her "group" of friends—a group including Lispenard Stewart. My brother swaggered off to a bevy of young men and flirtatious young women. My father turned away.

I stood alone. I floundered about, my greetings curt but mannered, looking for some hook to be caught on. I found Consuelo in a deep conversation with Edith, the Wetmore's oldest daughter, a lovely woman seven years my senior, aglow with new love.

"Are you saying that women... *women*," Consuelo emphasized the word as if she had never said it before, "women are playing tennis?"

"I saw them myself," Edith responded with a bright smile on her long, but not unbecoming face. Edith wore her fine blonde hair bigger, her brocade skirt narrower, her bustle smaller than was in fashion, but knowing her—in the acquaintance manner that I did—I wondered if she wasn't *making* fashion rather than following it. At this moment, though, her words held me spellbound.

"Where... where did you see such a thing?" I barged into the conversation like a steamship coming into port. So astounded, I forgot all my manners. Luckily, Consuelo didn't.

"Pearl!" she chirped, greeting me with a quick embrace. In the squeeze of her arms, I remembered protocol and made the proper greetings to the small group of women around Edith, including Mrs. John Jacob Astor IV, Ava Willing, a dark-haired beauty in her thirties.

Formalities attended to, I had to have the answer to my question. The words overheard, now planted in my mind, forced the others out. I turned to Edith. "You saw women playing tennis? Where?"

"Indeed, I did. Ava was with me. It was at the most prestigious tennis club in England. Wimbledon, it's called," Edith explained, Ava concurred.

Captivated, Consuelo and I couldn't ask enough questions: how well did they play, what did they wear, was it a true tournament? We talked for far longer than we should; we should have been socializing with others. There was something in the conversation, a bonding of like feminine minds, which could not break apart. It held me together.

Until I saw him.

I had only seen Frederick once since we returned to Newport, though I had seen him often in New York. He swaggered into the room, beside him, Herbert Butterworth. Herbert didn't swagger.

If I lied to myself, I would say that men didn't matter; only my education and my painting mattered. If I lied to myself. I didn't.

Other young women my age were either already betrothed, engaged, or at the least had a steady boyfriend. When I thought of all those varied layers of relationships, I thought only of two men—these two men.

Consuelo took me by the arm, "Excuse us, ladies," she said to the group around us, or at least I think that's what she said. "I want to show Pearl the lovely Tree of Life."

I vaguely remember her hold on me, her leading me through the crowd in that crooked sort of fashion people must walk through a room full of other people. Consuelo pulled me into the alcove below the stairs. There *was* a tree of life here; I had never seen it. The painting rose the full three stories of the back of the stairs, all the way to the ceiling where bright birds fluttered against a deep blue sky. I longed to join them.

"I called on you Tuesday," Consuelo whispered, but she never let go of me. She held onto my hand. "But your mother said you weren't accepting visitors."

I laughed. It tasted as bitter as it sounded. Did I ever tell Consuelo about Frederick and Herbert and my growing feelings for them both? I couldn't remember. It didn't matter. She would have seen.

In that moment, Consuelo looked at me as if she didn't know me. She didn't, not the true me, the me I was becoming.

"Is that what Mother said? Remarkable." I pushed away thoughts of my mother for they made my head spin, my stomach ache. "Tell me."

"I just heard about it myself, the very day I came to call," Consuelo spoke softly, tenderly, as if speaking to a wounded child. She did. "Apparently they met at some college event. Herbert is staying with the Havemeyers."

The ache in my stomach twisted.

"For the entire summer." Consuelo put on the finishing touch.

I raised my eyes, brows high and stuck upon my forehead. "All summer? Here? In Newport? Together?" Sentences were too complex to form at the time.

Consuelo simply nodded.

I laughed again, an ugly sound of reckoning in a summer full of it.

"Are you quite well, Pearl? Should I call your mother?"

"No!" I snapped, too quickly, too harshly. "I'm sorry, Consuelo," I said, immediately contrite at the hurt on this dear girl's—this sensitive girl's—face. "No, I'm not feeling my best."

"And such news as this can only make it worse."

I looked at her but didn't see her. I thought of my parents, of their marriage, of what marriage would mean to me among these people who were so grand and so awful all at the same time. Had I been saved from such a fate by being forced to make a decision I didn't know how or want to make? Or were such thoughts only those of my battered heart?

"Thank you, Consuelo. Thank you for telling me."

She embraced me again and we returned to the party. I stood by her side the whole night. Most of it.

* * *

I could have been a child in a playground, trapped on a titter-totter. I sat in the middle. On one end sat Frederick, on the other Herbert. All through that night, and long after, they took turns, up and down in my attention, in and out of my heart.

I didn't try to get off. If I did, I would have to walk to either one end or the other. It seemed easier, safer, to stay in the middle. I couldn't stay there forever.

GINEVRA

I watched Pearl watching the two men as they made their way into the ballroom.

Pearl and Consuelo disappeared from my view, and I flit this way and that to find them but couldn't. I took the moment. I watched only Herbert Butterworth, the man who called me beautiful. He followed Frederick around. Where Frederick was loud, he was soft. Where Frederick was flirtatious, he was only amiable. I knew which choice Pearl would make. I put my head against the doorjamb I hid behind, wondering how I would live with it.

As soon as Pearl and Consuelo returned to the room, Frederick cried out her name.

"Pearl! There you are." He left a conversation in its middle and strode to her, Herbert right beside him, no longer behind.

I couldn't hear their conversation from where I stood. They were too far away, and the musicians had struck up the first chords of the evening as servants laid out pastries, coffee, and tea. Both men looked to Pearl. Lips moved and I imagined the words they spoke.

Pearl shrugged a shoulder, a pretty grin across her face. I couldn't tell if it was real. She reached out a hand...and took the one Frederick held out to her. Together they walked to the refreshments. I dropped my head again and sighed. My prayers may have been silent, but they were mine.

"Hello again."

That voice found me. He had found me. It was not what I prayed for, yet it seemed an answer.

"*Buona notte*," I answered in Italian as I had with Consuelo last summer. It would be foolish to deny its effect on some people, the right people.

It was only a moment, but it stretched on and on. We looked at each other in silence.

"It is a pity you are not allowed to dance," Herbert finally said. "You do like to dance, don't you, Miss...?"

I forgot my name for a moment.

"C...Costa, Ginevra Costa," I gurgled, perhaps giggled a little. I despised myself for it.

Until he smiled.

"Well then," he held out his hand for me to shake. I took it. I would never feel the same again. "I am Herbert Butterworth."

I know.

"Pleased to meet you, Mr. Butterworth." Our hands remained entwined.

"Oh no, Herbert, if you wish."

I do.

"Then I am Ginevra," I replied. I released his hand; I had to, or he would have felt mine shaking.

He bowed his head, tossing back a gleaming swath of black hair as he rose up.

"Do you like to dance, Ginevra?"

What could I do? I was helpless.

"I do," I said truthfully.

Herbert tilted his head to the side as he looked down at me.

"Then it truly is a shame," he whispered this time, and, with another nod of his head, stepped away, away from the room where all the maids sat in the nowhere of waiting, away from me.

I escaped as far into the small room as I could. I could see no more.

* * *

I sat at the staff dinner table the next night, barely eating, barely saying a word to my father. All I could think about was Pearl. Pearl and her mother. Pearl and Frederick. And Herbert Butterworth.

It had been weeks since we learned her mother's truth, since we saw it. She hovered in a fog of confusion and brought me with her.

I barely stirred even as someone sat down next to me; no one ever sat next to me before. The others—well some of the others—had come to be nice. Perhaps that wasn't the word. Perhaps they had come to accept me, at the least appreciate the work I did for Pearl. It was enough, I supposed.

"Zee food here, iz good, ya?"

She was a lovely young woman, broadly built and tall, her hands were rough and work-worn, but her smile was bright through thin lips, and her blue eyes sparkled.

"It is," I said, "very good."

We made our introductions. I introduced Anja, a new chambermaid, to my father, who delighted him with Italian words of greeting.

The three of us chatted for a while. Like a sweet dessert, it was a lovely treat to be treated with such kindness by another of the staff. Like us, Anja was new, and so something of an outsider. This closed group, as bigoted and prejudiced as those they served, opened easier to her German heritage.

Happy and kind, Anja endeared herself to me quickly. I might have a friend below stairs after all. Though such a friendship could never equal what I had with Pearl, no matter how many steps separated us.

The table talk turned to gossip as it so often did. Anja, new to the area, hung on every word, asking questions. As the others answered her, I heard the latest news, the terrible news of Pearl's dear Consuelo. Her name, her mother's name, was on everyone's tongue, more than their food. As the story unfolded, I understood. It was a tale of heartbreak.

I wanted to rush from the room immediately, rush to Pearl to tell her. Of course, I couldn't. The time would come when I could.

* * *

As our years together grew, I would often sneak downstairs at night when the house slept. Feeling like a specter in the Persian cotton nightdress Pearl had given me, I floated down to the rarefied air engulfed in the diaphanous material.

One time, her brother stepped out of his room, his door diagonally across from Pearl's own.

"Sis," he hissed at me, "what the dickens are you doing?"

I froze, hand on the crystal doorknob. With my dark hair, so like Pearl's, falling about my shoulders, robed in her nightdress, he could not tell the truth of the person in the musky light.

I shrugged my shoulders and made a sleepy sound of nonsense.

"Get back to bed," was all he said in reply.

I hurriedly did, ever so grateful for the striking resemblance to my dear friend.

Snuggled beneath her covers, we would giggle, wish, dream without sleep, gifting each other with the deepest parts of our souls.

Tonight would not be a night for laughter.

"Ginevra?" Pearl roused, squinting at me in the dark. "Is that you?"

I hurried to her bed and jumped in. I surrounded myself with the plush pillows that rose from it like little islands, a good place to hide should someone else come in.

"I, I have something to tell you," I said. She sat up.

"What is it? Why didn't you tell me when you readied me for bed?"

"I couldn't. Your mother and father were both awake, both in their rooms, they might have heard."

"You're scaring me, Ginevra." Pearl pulled me up to sit beside her. "Tell me right now."

I did.

"It is Consuelo. Her mother is forcing her to marry the Duke of Marlborough."

Pearl dropped her face into her hands. Her words muffled. "I knew it would come to this. They have been fighting about it for months."

I had been in Consuelo's company with Pearl and not a speck of this dirty linen had I seen on her pristine clothes, in her perfect manners. I pestered Pearl with my thick silence.

"Consuelo is in love. She is secretly engaged to Winthrop Rutherford."

It was my turn to cover my face. The strange lives of these people broke hearts as the chef did eggs, yet they clung to it.

"You have no idea, Ginevra, no idea just how malicious her mother is." Pearl squirmed out from the bed linens and faced me. "When we were children, she wasn't allowed to go to a school, not even the best private schools in New York. Alva insisted she was tutored at home by a governess, and later by two or three tutors at a time. Granted, she learned a great deal. I think she can speak at least three languages."

I nodded, taking her hand, squeezing as if to squeeze out more words from her. Her need to say them was in every huff of air she took.

"Alva has been a tyrant to her all her life. When Consuelo was young, Alva forced her to wear a steel rod against her spine, strapped to her waist and shoulders to ensure she learned proper posture."

I shuddered, "That is horrible! It is tor..." I struggled.

"Torture," Pearl finished for me. "It was, but that was not the worst of it. If Consuelo didn't like the clothes Alva picked out for her, if she found the courage to tell her mother so, she was severely reprimanded. 'I do the thinking, you do as you're told,' Alva would say to her. And then...then...," Pearl's lips trembled, her eyes grew moist.

"And then..."

"And then Alva would whip her, whip her with a riding crop."

The crop could have struck me, so sharp was the pain from her words, pain for Consuelo, pain for them all.

I envied these "cottagers" their life, their wealth, their beautiful homes, clothes, jewels. I wanted such a life for myself. Or did I? Hearing such things as this, made my wants as thin and elusive as passing summer clouds.

"As Consuelo grew to be so beautiful—"

"She is a true beauty," I agreed.

"Isn't she?" Pearl said, not a speck of envy spoiled her pride. "Well, her conniving mother knew that beauty would serve her well. Alva's been pushing members of royalty on her since she was as young as fourteen, fifteen. How better to become a true aristocrat rather than just a filthy rich American?"

"But Consuelo wanted none of it. She met Winthrop just this past winter. It was love at first sight, for both of them. They became secretly engaged, though I don't know why."

"What do you mean?" I whispered. It felt the only way to speak of such things; here with Pearl beneath the linens, we were mere specters in the dark of night.

"Well, Winthrop is from a very powerful family. He is directly descended from Peter Stuyvesant who was a governor. No, that's not right." Pearl closed her eyes, rubbed her forehead. "Director-General, that's it. He was the Director-General of New Netherland."

It was my turn to scrunch my face. "I never heard of this place."

"Oh, but you have. It's now called New York."

My eyes burst wide. "Why did not this man please Alva?"

Pearl shook her head. "Alva wanted a royal marriage for Consuelo and nothing less. And so, the staff is saying that Alva is forcing this marriage, Consuelo's marriage to the Duke?"

I nodded, my unbraided hair rustling on the pillows. "Yes, but they did not say how she is being forced. I did hear them say the Duke does not want the marriage either."

Pearl sat, steamily silent. The heat of her anger came off her in waves, as if she was a fireplace filled with wood in full flame. This anger—on Consuelo's behalf—overshadowed her own confusion and heartache.

"I will call on Consuelo tomorrow, first thing." She punctuated each word with a fist strike upon a pillow.

I slipped out of her bed and gently pushed her back down, covering her with the fine linens and tucking her in as my mother had once done to me. "Yes, tomorrow. For now, sleep."

I left her knowing she wouldn't.

PEARL

Ginevra and I didn't leave The Beeches, we hurried. As we approached Marble House, we slowed and stumbled. Though officially separated from her husband, Alva Vanderbilt had retained possession of their magnificent cottage. It had never looked like this before.

The staff scattered about in total disarray. Serious men, dressed in serious black, went in and out of the front door as we approached it. The Vanderbilt butler did not attend the portal, so we let ourselves in. More staff hurried around us, blind to our presence. In front of us rose the grand circular staircase with its fountain beneath.

"Come on," I hissed at Ginevra, pulling her by the hand when she hesitated.

Safe in an invisible cloak, we climbed the stairs and hurried down the hall to Consuelo's room. I knocked at the door.

"Please go away," Consuelo's weak response found us through the wood. We entered despite them.

"Consuelo, darling, it's me, Pearl." Darkness shrouded the room, curtains drawn tight, not a single lamp lit. Slivers of sunlight slipped in the folds of the drapes, dust danced in the beams. It looked so unreal, as dreamlike as the rest of the house.

"Oh Pearl," Consuelo cried softly, my name mangled on a sob. I rushed to her. Ginevra remained at the door. To guard us or out of respect? Either way, I was thankful.

I sat and pulled Consuelo to me. "What is happening? What is going on here?"

"Oh, Pearl," she whimpered again. Was that all she would or could say?

The words gushed out of her; a dam demolished. Her mother and Lady Paget—one of the 'Four Hundred' who had fallen on hard times, who now used her connections to make money as a marriage broker—had pushed them together, Consuelo and the Duke. Her mother had cajoled, begged, and then demanded Consuelo marry him.

"I r…refused, over and over." Consuelo looked up at me with her big brown eyes, there was so much there to see, so much that broke my heart. "I had never spoken to Mother like that in my whole life." Ginevra sniffed indignation. I agreed but said nothing.

"I told her that Winthrop and I would be married, even if we had to elope."

"Oh my. Good for you," I praised her for her courage, even knowing it would not have been well met.

"She locked me in, locked me in my own room." Consuelo slapped the bed upon which we sat.

I slapped my hand to my mouth.

"I wondered why I hadn't seen you these past few weeks. I thought you were away, that's what your mother has been telling people." At least those people who would listen. After her tryst with OHP, after word of the pending divorce came to light, the great Alva, became ostracized by many, but not all. "But your door is not locked now."

Consuelo shook her head. "No, my maid unlocked it, but only to tell me that my mother is ill, seriously ill."

Unkind words taunted my tongue; words of disbelief and manipulation, but I refused them. They would serve no purpose other than to feed Consuelo's discontent.

"How ill is she? How is she ill?"

"They say, the doctors say, she may have had a mild heart attack." Consuelo looked at me. Guilt turned her beautiful face into a gruesome mask.

I cast a look over my shoulder to Ginevra. I saw my skepticism upon her face.

"When they finally let me in, she really did look terrible…" I thought Alva always looked terrible, "…and when I sat by her, she said the stress of all this, with the Duke, was too much for her. She said it could kill her."

I had never longed to be one of the Great Triumvirate or Mrs. Astor than in that moment. If I were her peer, I would stomp into Alva's room and give her a good smack. How dare she manipulate this sweet girl like this? Especially after what she had done.

"What are you going to do?" I asked softly, refusing to heed my rebellious thoughts.

Consuelo shrugged; more tears came. She answered me as she dried them, "What else *can* I do? I will marry the Duke."

I could say nothing against her decision, no matter how against it I was. I would be her friend.

We stayed with her until she calmed…until she lay back on her silk-covered pillows and her eyes grew heavy.

Though my mother was no better than Alva was, she was no worse. Her attempts to control me as Alva controlled Consuelo were not as successful. I had my father to keep her from going too far. Though I wondered as Ginevra and I walked slowly home, gloomy in the bright morning, if Father wasn't around, would I be treated in the same manner? I knew my mother's ambition equaled and exceeded that of Alva Vanderbilt. What I didn't know was how far she would take it if she could. I knew only that my secrets, my painting, and my ambitions, could find me in a similar state. How far would I go to fight her?

My mother and her lascivious behavior, my struggle between Frederick and Herbert, the confusion and pain of both fell away. Consuelo and the world in which she struggled to survive took up all the space of my mind.

These men were the leaders of the country, the businessmen upon whose work the country worked and was fed. They had lifted the country out of its sorry state left behind after the War of Secession. These women were the bastions of good taste and deportment, at least on the surface of life. The homes they built were the finest in the country. They brought such beauty in their architecture and their art as few other places did. I knew they would stand the test of time, as did the chateaux and palaces they mimicked. They were a gift to all who would ever see them. Surely, these people deserved some respect for all they had accomplished; for all that they had given to Newport and their country. Were their true selves to be forgiven for it? Did what they achieve negate how they behaved? The question was a ghost that would never wisp out of the edges of my mind.

GINEVRA
1898

I waited for her beneath the beeches, thinking only of her arrival, not that of anyone else. When she returned and found I was not waiting for her in her room, Pearl would know exactly where I was. I didn't have to wait long.

Our embrace was warm and lingering. The time spent apart, forced on us, seemed longer every year though the days numbered the same. We were almost eighteen, just a few days away from it. Growing up meant growing more, dealing with more. There was no denying it as there was no seeing it coming.

We no longer climbed the tree that had held us so tenderly. We sat like the grown women we were on a blanket beneath the beeches, beneath the protective cavern that, like us, had grown and changed. It hid us now, more than ever.

Pearl laid back, her head on the blanket, and stared up into the sky. "I've finished school," she said. Where was her joy in saying it? She rolled over. "Well, I *might* be finished with school."

She teased me and she knew it. I heard it as clear as the larks singing above us. Her lopsided grin told me so. I poked her in the ribs, and she giggled as she used to when we were up in the tree.

But still Pearl said not a word.

"Tell me." I pulled her hair, hair that she now wore up every day, a mark of her change. "Tell me." I yanked harder.

Pearl did.

I gasped, I laughed, I hugged her. And I withdrew, enveloped in my maid's uniform, but only for a blink of time. She had spoken of it before, but only as one speaks of stars and dreams. Now she had done it. My joy for her was real and deep. She bathed in it.

"I'm not sure what Mother will say."

There it was, the note of sadness in her song of joy. I took her hand. A battle lay before her. It brought us to Consuelo and the battle she had lost.

Consuelo had married the Duke of Marlborough in November. Pearl had been there, as had everyone who was anyone in the lofty air of the upper east side of New York, all the "Fifth Avenoodles." I almost cried when Pearl told me Consuelo had cried, how so many thought they were tears of happiness.

"Speaking of men," Pearl rounded on me, giving me a yank of my hair, "have you met anyone while I was gone?"

The sun and its brightness went behind a wispy cloud, the same cloud passed across my face.

"No, no one really," I told her.

"But someone?"

"No, yes, but only…mostly simple men." I shook my head. I could not tell her.

Pearl took my chin in her hand. "And you are anything but a simple woman."

I smiled, then it slipped off my lips, away from me.

"I think I have seen too much… too much of your world. You have taught me so much of life. It is hard to settle for simple when you know there is more out there." I waved my hands about. Where were the English words for the Italian ones pounding in my head?

If I had met such simple men before—before Newport and before Pearl—I would have been more than happy to spend the rest of my life with him in his simple life. How can one be shown heaven then be told they must settle, once and forever, for purgatory?

I needed her to know, to see my feelings.

"It is a long des…deso-late, yes?"

Pearl nodded.

"A long deso-late road ahead for me, one with no end, no turns, no beautiful scenery. The sameness, it is…bleak. It will drive me mad."

Pearl hitched herself up on her legs. "I'm sorry if what I've done, teaching you, showing you, has brought you sadness."

I grabbed her fast and held onto her tightly. "Never say it again. I would not have it any different. I am so grateful."

"I will find someone for you," she said in my ear, then pushed me away, her face bright with the idea forming in her mind. "I swear I will. He may not be a rich man, not this kind of rich." She waved her hand at the house across the lawn, "But perhaps a well-to-do merchant, perhaps one who has traveled and seen something of the world. That is the sort of man you need. Leave it to me."

I laughed at her. "Have you become match-maker like Lady Paget?"

"Oh no." She pulled in her chin, face scrunching as if she had bitten into a lemon. "I'll be much better at it."

Together we laughed. Together we laid back down on the blanket.

"Have you been sketching?" she asked me after a time, when the birds grew used to our presence and swooped into our cave within the tree.

"Yes, some," I answered. In truth, I sketched all the time.

"Yet you haven't made anything for me since that beautiful dress."

Pearl sat up again. Her stare singed me with the heat of the sun.

"I want you to design a wardrobe full of clothes for me."

It was my turn to rise up. "And you would wear them?"

"Of course I would, silly, as long as they are not too outlandish."

"No, no," I assured her, "I want to stay...current. But I think I have ideas on how to make them better, eh, u-nick."

"Unique," she corrected me.

"Ah, *si*, unique."

"Good. I adore unique. I think they should be serious, clothing for a serious woman doing serious work."

I understood. She would not let go of her hopes. Neither would I. I nodded.

"Good," she said, "it's settled then."

Nothing was ever settled in this world of ours.

PEARL

I don't know why I chose that particular day to approach Mother. Being back in Newport, back with Ginevra, I was a different me, a better me. And I was a day away from turning eighteen, a day away from my "coming out."

Coming out. Such silly words. As if all young women existed in some impenetrable shadow until they turned eighteen. As if they weren't really people until then. Especially in those days, when more and more women felt as if they weren't real... and had begun to demand to be.

Mother had been in a tizzy about the affair for months and months. She sought out tizzy even when it did not find her. Living well didn't suffice, only living dramatically would.

It was my coming out, but I had little to do with her ebullience. Even the invitations, delivered by hand by our liveried coachman, didn't carry my name. Such invitations never did.

Mr. and Mrs. Worthington
At home
Friday evening, July 2
At nine o'clock

For all its vaguer, everyone seemed to know what it meant; it was a secret knowing of this insulated world. Mother had been jovial for weeks, full of ecstatic brightness I had only glimpsed here and there throughout my life, ever brighter as accepting responses came to our home. Surely her cheerfulness was welcoming, fertile ground.

Like many women of the age, my mother's bedroom served as her study as well as a private place to entertain a few ladies for tea. I found her at her desk, a magnificent piece of mahogany with trims of gold. I loved that desk, wished it for my own. Mother sat there, as I knew she would be, going over the last-minute details of the fete. Her corner room faced the back of the house. Its windows were a vista to nature's beauty that was our yard, our gardens, and the ocean in the distance.

Mother had arranged her desk to face in the opposite direction, to look upon the white and black marble fireplace with the stunning portrait of her. Painted by none other than Giovanni Boldini, an Italian painter renowned for his flowing style, he rendered a softness that made every woman he painted beautiful, whether they were or not.

"Pearl!" she greeted me with enthusiasm rarely tossed my way. "Come, look at the plans for the decorations."

For minutes uncounted, I indulged her. Not to feel excitement would be pretense. How could I not be excited by the addition of indoor trees upon which candles with pink globes would be festooned, the huge ribbons of green and pink that would be hung from the candelabras and draped to the four corners of the ballroom. It really was quite lovely. Amidst such glamor, I would be the guest of honor.

There are times when what the mouth and mind say denies the truth of the heart and soul. I wanted this moment that would be mine alone. Yet I still wanted more. The battle within raged on and I had no clue as to which side would win. Ginevra fought in a similar battle.

Mother seemed to have exhausted herself. She had barely taken a breath as she pointed out every little detail. She finally stopped to sip her tea. It was the moment.

I opened the letter clenched in my hand, the paper grew moist in my sweaty grip, a letter Mother hadn't noticed, though I'd made no secret of it.

"I have something to show you, Mother." My hands betrayed me, trembled as I unfolded the letter.

Mother snatched the paper from me, read it once, stared at me with a gaze narrowed and hard, blue eyes turned grey, and read it again. She dropped it on her desk. It had smothered the roaring flames of her enthusiasm. She was, once more, the mother I knew.

"Isn't it amazing?" I denied her face and all it said, I cared only of what the letter said.

It was an acceptance to Rhode Island School of Design in Providence, the capital city of Rhode Island, Newport's state. What began as a project for a group called The Centennial Women, a group devoted to raising money to exhibit works by women at the Centennial Exhibition in 1876, grew to such success, raising vast sums of money, that they set their sights in another direction.

It was Helen Adelia Rose Metcaffe, a Rhode Island native, who suggested the group put their funds into the formation of a college specifically to teach all facets of the arts. While not exclusively for women, the advancement of women artists was the school's primary focus. Mrs. Metcaffe had served as president until her death the year before. Then her daughter had then taken over the reins. It was one of the preeminent arts colleges in the whole country, and they had accepted me...me! I wanted to shout it from the rooftop.

"Who told you to apply?" Her dark stare found me as she rose and walked to the fireplace, stood beneath her portrait. Now two of her gave me a brittle look.

"No one *told* me to apply. I did have the encouragement and support of Mrs. Taligrin," I said, hoping the name of the headmistress of my New York school would carry some weight with my mother.

"She had no right to do so." My mother's beauty vanished beneath her anger. How horrified she would be to know how much older it made her look.

"Mother, very few women are accepted to Rhode Island School of Design, only those who exhibit a true talent. It is that fine a college, that prestigious. And I am to be one of them."

There came no praise, no gladness, nor pride. Only a warning.

"You waste your time with such matters. They will do you no good, no good at all."

The smooth curves of her face became hard edges as she gazed out the windows. She saw nothing of the beauty that surrounded us, only the "they" that lived around us.

"Look at the poor Jones girl," My mother took a step toward me, a finger pointed at my chest. I took a step back. "What was her name, Edna?"

"Edith, Mother, her name is Edith, Edith Wharton. And she is a very talented poet."

My mother snapped her fingers. It was a harsh crack. "Talented poet, indeed. And what has it gotten her? A first betrothal broke, after two years, no less. And why?"

Her pale skin, bleached with great care, flooded with blood. "Because her future mother-in-law found her too…intellectual."

The last word she spoke as if she called Edith a strumpet. She turned her back, turned to her portrait.

"You will not be attending. Tell them so."

"But Mother I—"

She spun on me like a whirlwind, her face a storm. "Tell them you will *not* be attending."

A boulder dropped upon my chest. I tried to breathe past its crushing weight but couldn't. Hope became an illusion. I took the letter. I retreated from her and the room.

I stiffened in the cold of the empty hall. The sounds of the servants on the back stairs came to me like mice in walls on a cold winter morning. For a few moments, I looked upon the message in my hands with contempt.

Not for long. Though the words swam beneath my watery gaze, they gave me what I needed most. Mother would not let me attend, but I had been accepted. I would most likely not attend, not next year at any rate. I held as tightly to that thought as I did the letter, that and the happiness Ginevra had shown for my accomplishment. She had been the champion of my cause, even knowing it may separate us for long periods of time, perhaps forever.

I went in search of my father, knowing the reception would be different. He would not go against my mother, not in this. It was too big a battle; it could end their never-ending war. It didn't matter. In this shallow world, I knew the joy of accomplishment for accomplishment's sake. He would celebrate it with me.

GINEVRA

We fluttered about her room like butterflies in a field of wildflowers, not knowing which blooms to choose, wanting to choose them all.

It was a rehearsal of sorts. Pearl had told me she wanted her hair styled in the new Gibson fashion, and I had spent days looking at the pen and ink drawings of Charles Dana Gibson. He claimed his drawings were a representation of thousands of American girls. He had, in fact, started trends—the wider, higher, more elaborate bouffant, the swan-hill corset with its straight busk inserted in the front to give women's body more of an 'S' shape when seen from the side.

Pearl had ordered herself just such a corset and we spent some time adjusting the gown I had made her to fit the new shape. The emphasis was changing. The fragile waif woman was fading away while the more curvaceous woman was finding her time. It was an omen, surely it must be.

I studied myself harshly in the mirror. I boasted nothing like the graceful thinness that these privileged women possessed. I knew they had much to credit their undergarments for the slim waist and barely perceptible hips. Did I not help Pearl don these very garments daily? Yet the glass before me made it clear, even with such assistance, my form would always be fuller, fleshier, built more for the physical labor it must do.

I looked down. The beautiful dress Pearl had so lovingly given to me that very morning—worn only in her room—stretched and wrinkled across my form as if it silently screamed for release from its torture on the rack of my body. It further denied me that which I so longed to be. Long and thin, not rounded and fleshy. It denied me one moment of gliding into a room, privilege in every slim and upright posture. I blamed my body for the lack of such an opportunity. It was a stupid distraction from the truth, but one easier to accept.

I envied Pearl in that moment… I hated myself for it.

I altered the dress to perfection. I began a trial attempt at the hair.

I sectioned it, twisted, and backcombed each section to create the illusion of more and fuller hair, rolled them back toward the main bun in the back center of her head, where I secured them with combs adorned with diamond chips. When all was in place, I picked out a few strands here and there, by the sides of her face, down the back of her long slim neck. The natural wave of Pearl's hair needed not a touch from the curling tong. The wisps of her bangs, parted in the middle made the perfect frame for her lovely face.

My work done, I turned her 'round to her vanity and its mirror.

Pearl blinked and blinked again. Her mouth opened then closed. It opened again and I worried. A useless worry.

Pearl turned and took my hand, "You have made me so very beautiful."

My shoulders dropped, releasing the tight pain that had been biting me as I worked.

I leaned down and pinched her lovely chin. "God made you so very beautiful. I only help him a bit."

Pearl jumped up, laughing, hugging me, and swinging me about until I laughed too. I almost laughed away the ghost of jealousy hovering in my shadow. Almost.

PEARL

I get to dance...I get to dance.

As protocol dictated, I stood beside my parents at the door to the ballroom, greeting each and every guest as they arrived, accepting their good wishes on my "adulthood." All I could think about was dancing.

So often in the last few years, I had attended such parties, mostly those of a more family-friendly occasion, thinking it cruel that *they* allowed *older girls* to attend, but did not allow them to dance. Oh, how I loved to dance. I had taught Ginevra every one of the popular dances of the time. Beneath the beeches, we would whirl and twirl as I taught her the waltz and the two-step. We laughed as we tripped and fell on each other, confused by who should lead and who should follow.

My dreams—my fantasies—were different from many of the other young women my age. Yet the desire, the longing, to be led about the dance floor, seemingly helpless, in the arms of a strong man, was a desire I could not deny. To feel his strong arms around my back as he looked into my eyes...

"Pearl, *dear*," my mother's insistence pulled me out of my daydream. "Please greet our guest. He's a friend of Mr. and Mrs. Havemeyer. This is Herbert Butterworth. Mr. Butterworth, our daughter, Pearl."

Herbert and I shared a smile. I prayed he could not see the tremble of my lips.

"*Enchanté, mademoiselle.*" Tossing back a thick wave of almost black hair, he leaned over and kissed my hand. As he straightened, my eyes fed upon him. He wore his swallowtails and pristine white shirt and tie in a way I had never seen, though every man there dressed the same.

"I...I...it's a pleasure to see you again, Mr. Butterworth."

"You know each other?" Mother pushed in, tried to break a moment that belonged solely to Herbert and me.

"Please call me Herbert," he said graciously to me.

"What a lovely greeting, isn't it, Pearl," my mother fawned all over him. Even from the corner of my eye, I could see her gaze eating him up. *Not this one, Mother*, I thought, *please not this one.*

"*Certainement*," I replied.

He smiled wide. His teeth were perfect, sparkling white behind full lips. "You speak French?" he asked me in that language.

I answered him in kind, never more thankful for my education, snidely grateful my mother spoke not a word of it. We spoke of his recent trip there and my own experience in Europe. The rest of the room fell away…

…until my mother poked my ribs with her sharp elbow.

"Ah, here is Mr. and Mrs. Havemeyer and their son Frederick now," she held out a hand to them, ignoring Herbert as he had ignored her, or because he had.

Oh, good Lord. My body grew warm and moist beneath my beautiful gown. Once more, I sat in the middle of the titter-totter.

Herbert took my hand again as if doing so would return my gaze to him from where it sat upon Frederick. Herbert leaned closer. "May I have the honor of your first dance?"

He asked for a great privilege. A debutante's first dance—and the partner she chose to dance it with—said much about them both. Mother had arranged for Willie Vanderbilt to partner me, and I had agreed. It seemed fitting, as we were childhood friends.

I knew all that but suddenly, didn't.

"Pearl, dear…," Mother began. She had heard. I didn't want to know what choice she would have me make. I made my own quickly.

With just a moment's hesitation, I answered him, "You may."

Herbert stepped away with a bow of his head to my parents, a quick glance back with those golden eyes of his. I didn't break his gaze, not even when my mother poked me again, not until she leaned toward me, raised a hand as if to pull up my long gloves, and pinched my arm.

"I said you look smashing, Pearl." Frederick stood before me. When did that happen? In his dark eyes, I could see myself—they were full of me. What a moment ago would have found me weak-kneed now made me squirm. What had I done?

"As do you, dear Frederick," I replied as he took my hand and, like Herbert, bowed over it. His golden-haired head reminded me of the gold in Herbert's eyes. "I...I'm so very pleased you've come tonight."

"I wouldn't have been anywhere else, I assure you." He spoke to me, yet his eyes skipped out to the room filling fast, a room of black and white and silk cravats, of silk and pearls and colors of a garden in full bloom. That skip... it was enough.

The faces swam before me after that, my smile was no longer forced. It seemed interminable until the small orchestra began its cacophonous warming up.

Then, he was there, standing before me with his long hand reaching out for mine. I took it gladly.

Herbert circled me around the room, my arm rested on his raised one, the opening move of the German cotillion. It was a natural first dance for a debutante. It paraded her around the circle of her guests.

I knew the sight we made together. I could see it in the bright blurry gazes as he whirled me before them.

I looked away from Frederick's tight mouth as if it wasn't there.

Herbert danced as if he was born to it. When it came time to face each other—when he needed to move me across the room, twirl me before him—he did so with all the mastery I had ever imagined.

It was my first dance. It was my first dance with Herbert, but not my last. I remember little else.

GINEVRA

I hid in the small upstairs pantry. From there, I could see through the open doors of the dining room and into the ballroom. I watched Pearl. She glowed beneath the praise of the many guests. She smiled with gratitude as so many women fawned over the beauty of her gown, of her hair. I felt my own glow.

Until he walked in. Until I saw her face when he did. To know someone truly is often to know them better than they do themselves. What I saw dimmed my glow, leaving nothing but spots of it in my eyes.

My gaze longed to linger on him, but my mind demanded I watch her.

When Frederick and his parents entered, when Pearl's skin paled, her eyes spinning, not knowing where to land, I watched my own battle stride across her face.

When Herbert took her hand, his other gesturing out toward the open space for dancing, I knew what he asked.

I closed my eyes and began to pray. It was not a thing to pray for.

I sighed as he took her to the dance floor, easily the most handsome young man there, though I didn't think he was as young as Pearl and me. He had a more mature look, a more lived look. I thought that perhaps he was in his mid-twenties. For all Pearl's beauty, for all that she was the center of attention, it was hard not to look at him, at his face. Together, they were heartbreakingly breathtaking.

Herbert knew the prize he had won. As he whirled her round, a tinge of arrogance spread over his superior smile, pinned his brows high upon his smooth forehead. My fingers prickled, my breathing came harshly, as if I breathed through a trap.

As one dance led to the next, as the many guests joined Pearl and her partner on the floor, I had to look away from them. My gaze fell and caught on Mr. and Mrs. Worthington.

To look at them, you would never know how little love existed between them, or that she gave herself to another. Their perfect smiles showed none of it. How very practiced these people were.

I watched a performance, as well-rehearsed as any musicale or opera. It was nothing but false gaiety. Would such a life truly make me happy? I was no longer sure. I didn't think I could be so many different people as each occasion called for it. I knew only how to be myself, though I was no longer sure who that was.

I was repulsed and yet filled with desire at their affluence, their monumental abundance of wealth, and everything it could afford them, which, of course, was everything. Envy and adoration vied for dominance in my mind, leaving a wasteland of confusion.

"Good evening, Ginevra."

He had snuck up on me, again. What a knack he had for it.

I dipped my head. "Good evening, Mr. B—"

Herbert held up a pointed finger and grinned.

I lowered my face and the grin on it. "Good evening, Herbert."

"Much better," Herbert cheered softly. He stood with his side toward the pantry door, the rest of him remained out in the party.

There we stood.

"Congratulations." The word burst from me without any help. One dark brow slanted crookedly upon his smooth face. "On first dance." I damned my continued failure to master English fully, tried again. "The first dance with the debutante. It is honor."

"*Grazie. Molto gentile da parte tua.*" Herbert replied.

Did he try to comfort me, speaking in my tongue, telling me I was kind?

My lips trembled in something resembling a fey grin.

Herbert shuffled a step closer. I heard his breathing. He gave me no choice but to look up.

"I might be a very lucky man," the golden eyes held my face in their warmth. "To know two such beautiful women, women who are always together." He licked his full lips then bit upon the bottom one. Did he have nothing else to say? It was a hope both for and against.

"Yes, many would say that makes me very lucky." Herbert swayed forward, rose up on the tips of his toes.

What did that mean? I drowned in an ocean of unknowing and in-experience, an ocean thick with desire if that was what it was called. I had never met it, not truly, ever before.

The room faded. It was just he and I. I forgot Pearl's name. The worst thing I had ever done.

"I hope you have a pleasant evening, Signorina Ginevra," Herbert said.

It was the first time I had ever been addressed so, how I would have been addressed all the time were we still back in Italy.

"*Grazie*," I managed, barely. A thief I could not name had stolen all other words from me.

He turned. I followed the left side of his body, the 'v' line from shoulder to waist. He turned back. His face said that he knew I still looked at him.

"I will see you again soon, I'm sure."

I stood in the wondering again—where his words put me—and watched him walk back, lost him in the swirl of people. Lost, as I was lost.

* * *

I no longer watched, could not, as I should have done. I should have been watching for any signal from Pearl that she had need of me. If I watched, I would have only watched him. I would have watched Pearl, and if her behavior was different with Herbert than it had been with Frederick. There had been others, but I knew it had come down to these two men. One I wanted for my own. I might as well have wanted to touch a star.

I laughed at myself, at my foolish desire, as I lay down to fitful sleep.

It took two days for the house to recover, for all the cleaning to be done, for the staff to return the house to its everyday condition.

I was on my way to Pearl's room to dress her for coaching when James, the first footman, stopped me on the stairs.

"Your father wishes to see you," he informed me, "in Mr. Worthington's library."

I stood like a statue, one with a jaggedly carved face.

"Go along with you," James said, retreating down the stairs.

I wasn't sure what I was most shocked by, my father's request to see me or where. I went rapidly.

I took one step in and the other stopped in mid-air. They were all there, the entire family. Annoyance splotched all over Mrs. Worthington's face, more emerged when she saw me in the door.

Mr. Worthington turned to follow her gaze.

"Ah, Ginevra, good," he said to me. Then to my father, "We are ready then, Felice, please show us."

His excitement was contagious. Pearl shared hers with me with a twinkle-eyed wink.

My father stepped over to something large, something covered in one of the fine linens used to cover the furniture through the long winters. He was a tall man who always seemed shorter, his head forever tucked down to his shoulders. Not today. He stood tall beside the mysterious item, the loveliest wisp of a smile on his lips. Without a word, he pulled off the linen.

I'm not sure which of us gasped the loudest, myself, Pearl, or—most surprisingly—Mrs. Worthington. Who would not be astonished by what we saw?

"Oh, I say," Mr. Worthington whispered with undeniable worship.

He stepped to the breakfront, as I now knew such pieces were called, and ran his hands over it with the same caressing touch that my father had touched the wood before he had formed this masterpiece.

The six-foot-tall breakfront boasted two glass panel doors; around each, the wood was carved in a row of perfect scallops. The crown was more elaborate: a lion's head rose up from the middle and crescent-shaped carvings curled away from it in either direction. But the eye could not travel far from the center, the beam between the glass. A man guarded at the top, a saint or a scholar with a flat-topped hat that curled at the ends and a book in his hands, each page finely carved and visible. The folds of his robe flowed with such realism, I could swear I saw it move. A precious dog curled at his feet. Downward the design continued, globes and shapes and more scrolls. My father's attention to detail, his perfection at it, astonished me. I had never seen anything like it. I had never felt so proud of him.

"Thank you, Mr. Costa. It is a beautiful piece. I shall be quite the envy of all my friends," Mrs. Worthington said, breaking the revered silence my father had spun on us. It was the highest praise this woman could give. The praise was short-lived. "You may leave us now. And you, girl."

My father didn't seem to notice the rudeness of her dismissal or the brevity of his triumph. I knew, for him, the creation was all the triumph he needed.

As we made our way below stairs, I held him with a hand on his shoulder. He turned.

"I am so very proud of you, Papa." The words gurgled in my tight throat, constricted with emotion. "Mama would be too."

He said nothing. He put his hand on mine. His mouth quivered but said not a word. He didn't know how to say such words.

Papa sat straight and tall in his chair that night as we ate dinner with the other servants. Words whirled around him as they always did, but he took no notice that none were directed at him, as few ever were.

When Mr. Birch rose, and we all followed, many left the table. The few that stayed behind, lingering over their coffee and private conversations, James and Charlie, the first and second footmen, took chairs beside my papa.

"Your work, Felice," Charlie said, pronouncing my father's name not only correctly but with respect, "that is a right fine piece of work. Well done, Sir."

"Too right," James agreed. "I had no idea you had it in you, old man."

It was a strangely formed compliment, but my father preened at their words, though I doubt either could tell.

"*Grazie*," my father said, dipping his head, corrected himself. "Thank-a you. Thank you both."

How glad I was that I sat beside him that night. It was one of the finest moments we ever shared in all of our time in this country. We would share it together forever in my memory.

PEARL

A switch had flipped. I did not know where the switch was, but above it lay my name.

It reminded me of that moment when all the candles and sconces in the house were replaced by gas lamps. There was so much more to see. Such was my life. There was so much to do, that I could do, and I reveled in it.

Invitations now came directly to me. I was an entity in my own right, not simply the 'family' in *To Mr. and Mrs. Worthington and Family*, but now *Miss Worthington*. They came in droves. I attended every one. I'm not sure why I continued to say yes, not because I wanted to, but because I could. Not once did I stop and ask why I didn't want to. I should have.

Young men flocked around me like bees on the first blooms of spring, as if denied the company of a comely woman for the length of a harsh winter. If I was honest with myself, and I tried to be, though I often failed, I had to acknowledge that some of the attention stemmed from my father's burgeoning fortune. Something had happened over the winter, an expansion that brought our financial worth up to the exalted level of the Astors and Vanderbilts. It brought my worth up as well, my worth as a bride, as a commodity.

I hoped some of the attention was for my own worth. For the beauty that I was often complimented on, that I sometimes believed. For my grace and impeccable manners that had been drummed into me, that had been secured by the inheritance of my father's quiet grace. And most of all for my intelligence.

It came as a surprise. I filled the role of coquette as well as a fish could fly. The loud false laughing that was fodder for a man's ego, the fluttering of my lashes as I caught the eye of a handsome young man across the room. No, I was not superlative at such comportment.

But I was learned, I was educated and informed, and if a man spoke to me of more weighty matters, I did not fade into the background but plunged in, head first. I did, much to my mother's annoyance, and some of the men as well, especially if I dare contradict them and from a point of knowledge. They would excuse themselves from my company quickly, never to return to it. Their absence went easily unnoticed.

A few seemed delighted with my knowledge and my wit. Herbert Butterworth was one such man.

Herbert seemed forever to be no more than a few steps away. At dinners, he often sat next to me. At dances, he was an ever-ready partner. I remember the first day he came to call, when he and I sat in one of the teahouses. It was in that moment that I truly felt like an adult. It was also when I learned who the real Herbert Butterworth was. Or so I thought.

Herbert took my arm as we strolled across the lawn of The Beeches. We must have made for a lovely sight: him in his navy blazer trimmed in gold piping, me in a soft yellow afternoon dress of layers of chiffon trimmed in lace, a parasol to match. For a sharp, flashing second, I thought to take him into the beeches. The notion passed quickly. It was my place—Ginevra's and mine. I could never share it with anyone else, except perhaps someday with my children and hers.

"Your cottage is magnificent, Pearl." Herbert stopped us at the edge of the lawn and looked back on my summer home. Genuine appreciation shone in his exquisite eyes. He was staying at Sherwood House for the season, with the Havemeyer family. While Sherwood House was a lovely cottage, I knew, with shameful pride, it could not compete with the grandeur of The Beeches.

"That's very kind of you to say, Herbert. It is one of my father's greatest joys."

"Your father is a remarkable man," he replied, looking down at me with those eyes. It was the best thing he could have said. The best thing he didn't say was that he knew Frederick had been here and on more than one occasion. Did they both know the titter-totter they both sat on?

I lead Herbert to a teahouse, all four doors flung open. A silver tray with an etched crystal decanter filled with fresh lemon water and the same etched crystal glasses waited for us, appearing as if by magic. In truth, by the hands of staff who possessed some magic, that of being invisible.

We had never been this alone before. I squirmed, slouched back, flung myself up, back straight. My hands twirled my glass without bringing it to my mouth. Herbert sat—or should I say slumped—in his chair, arms behind his head as he swam deeply into my opulence.

"How...how were your years at Harvard?" I blustered. It seemed a natural question, for I knew he had recently finished his education there. My own hopes of college, forever lurking in my mind, made my curiosity genuine.

"Wonderful," he replied, smile wide and bright. He leaned toward me as he told me of his experiences there. He spoke mostly of the mischief so rampant on the campuses of young men at college. As much as I wanted to hear about his classes, the academic environment, Herbert made me laugh with his stories until my eyes ran with tears.

Herbert stood, picked up his linen napkin, and towered over me. Ever so slowly he leaned down and gently dabbed my wet cheeks. The spark of his touch flashed through the whole of my body. I could not take my eyes from his face so close to mine, from his lips.

Such a look was far too forward, far too intimate. I broke it off with a soft "thank you," and picked up my serviette.

"Tell me, what are your plans now?" I had to turn the conversation. I had to defend against the onslaught of this powerful attraction. It was the proper thing to do, and I hid behind the proprietary. It was too soon. I wasn't ready.

Herbert returned to his seat. He did so with a previously absent stiffness.

"I'm really not sure," Herbert answered. "Father wants me to go into business with him, but I have little interest in business."

"What *are* you interested in?"

His penetrating look—his amber gaze fixed upon my face—answered the question. I dropped my eyes, lifted my glass, anything to hide the flush heating my face.

Herbert laughed, whether at the question, or me, I still don't know. He laughed, and it was merry, and I relaxed again, a bit. He threw his arms open wide, threw back his head to look up at the pure blue sky.

"I'm interested in living."

It was an answer I didn't expect, wasn't sure I could understand.

"I want to travel, to see the world, to experience the world and all it has to offer," he explained his sentiment. "My father is stingy, but still there is enough for me to do so."

"What about a profession?" I badgered; it was not well done of me, but it was me. I had always envied men their freedom to do whatever they wanted. It seemed wasteful to squander it.

I had asked the same question of Frederick as if the answer was a secret password for entry into my heart. His answer had stupefied me, "We'll see what comes along."

These young men who had everything seemed to want for nothing, not even purpose.

Herbert's lips formed a frown that was also a grin. "Professions are over-rated. Living, and living well, now that's what truly matters."

I could not fault him, nor Frederick, or even my brother, for being a product of the society in which they were born, in which they were raised. So many of the young men his age, with family fortunes that were, ostensibly endless, seemed to have the same unfocused, offhand approach to life. Had they not been bred to it? These vibrant men with the best educations would put it to little use if they had their way. While I, I who had longed to study, to contribute, to be...something...was denied the chance. I did my best not to bristle. Perhaps he saw something of it.

"And of course, a family of my own." Herbert leaned on the table toward me, his full lips opened ever so slightly, his penetrating eyes fixed squarely on me. "A wife with the same verve for life, a wonderful mother for my children. Of course, I want these things too."

Things. The word rumbled around in my mind but didn't latch. I could think of little else save those lips and those eyes. Still, the thoughts were insistent, the question ever pestering me pestered…is that all that awaits me?

Herbert and I sat and talked for the rest of the afternoon. He returned to join the family for dinner. Something physical, an intangible feeling represented by a bodily reaction, happened to me whenever he was near. I could not deny it.

As I lay my head on my pillow that night, the pestering words repeated in my mind until they became a scream…is that all that awaits me?

* * *

I was grumpy and difficult the next morning as Ginevra readied me for the beach. I was rude to her, and she didn't deserve it. My unsettled feelings came out as complaints. Mother's insistence that I continue to wear the older style of beachwear only added heat to the oppressively hot day.

Ginevra and I did our dance, getting me into the ridiculous clothes in the simple wooden shacks that served as dressing rooms at Bailey's Beach. They were a quarter of the size of my closet.

"Oh, these clothes are simply ridiculous," I snapped as she helped me into my beach attire, a floor-length black—black, for the beach, on steaming hot day—dress. The whalebone collar was so high and tight I could barely breathe in air already so thick with steamy moisture. Thick black stockings covered my legs. Heelless leather slippers encased my feet. My corset strangled my waist to the prescribed eighteen inches. Then the hat. It was festooned with flowers and feathers and was far larger than any other of my many others.

"It is bit of monster, *si*?" Ginevra said as she pushed in the long steel pins, gouging my scalp though she didn't mean to, to hold it tight to my hair.

Either blind or a saint, Ginevra was unruffled by my ruffled feathers. She soothed and calmed, though I didn't deserve it. I knew what she thought of the ensemble from a fashion point of view. It was always there on her face, as if she bit into something distasteful, whenever she dressed me in this costume, which was far too often.

"Is it not bad enough that I can't feel the sun, but to have to swelter beneath this...thing?" I rolled my eyes, gave a stomp of one foot. I regressed at least ten years with my tantrum.

Ginevra's reply was to lower the veil to hide my face from the damaging sun and to squeeze my hands into the tight gloves. Finished she stepped back, not saying a word. I think she did so to keep me quiet as well.

I hugged her.

"I'm sorry, Ginevra." I shook my head even as I continued to hold her. "I don't know what's wrong with me today."

"No to worry," she said. Her English was so incredibly improved, yet there were a few sayings that were uniquely a combination of her mastery of her new language and a hint of the old, expressions inimitably her own. "Sitting by the ocean is good place to think. Think on it."

I never knew where her wisdom came from, only that I was grateful for it.

I released her and headed for the door.

"Pearl?" she called me back.

I turned to find her, a grin full of half-amused irony all over her lips, as she held out my large black parasol to me. I laughed; it felt good.

"Go to the beach, Ginevra," I told her. "I'll instruct Morgan to take you back to the house so you can change. I know it's not your afternoon off but I'm giving it to you. No one should work in this heat."

"Thank you," she chirped, pleasure as bright as the blistering sun on her face. "I would love a swim."

I bonked her gently on the head with my folded parasol. Her swimming costume, one she had made herself, would actually be refreshing.

With her giggling in my ears, I stepped onto Bailey's Beach.

* * *

The small cove of Bailey's Beach sat at the very end of Bellevue Avenue, where it became Ocean Drive. The Fish's Crossways overlooked it from its high perch above. The same Smith who had bought so much of the land where our cottages now stood, had bought this beach as well, with a partner named Joseph Bailey. Even then it was beautiful, but so very primitive, nothing more than a field leading to sand. Mr. Bailey, I had heard, regretted the purchase, believing all it would get him was enough driftwood to keep him warm for the winter. It was, back then, in the middle of nowhere.

The cottagers used to spend their afternoons at Easton's Beach, closer to the center of town, but that changed when the mill workers from Fall River began going there as well. It was just a few years ago that my set turned to this beach instead, having no desire whatsoever to associate with people who brought their mid-day meal in buckets. They created the Sprouting Rock Beach Association, named for the large boulder that punctuated one end of the deep crescent-shaped shoreline. Another association that took a drop of blood to join.

As I stepped out of the small cabana, I wondered if I would see Herbert or Frederick or both. I wondered if I wanted to.

I stomped onto the sand with all the dissatisfaction I felt. I couldn't understand why this beach, this crescent-shaped, small plot of land, with seaweed always at one end and rocks at the other, was the 'chosen' beach. There were eighty-one outside cabanas and the dressing rooms were rough and tumbled wood shacks. It was far from the finest on this beautiful island.

'They' had not only chosen it; they had made it exclusive, more exclusive than anywhere else in Newport. Newcomers and climbers might work their way into the Casino, the men into the Reading Room, and the families into the Clambake Club. But it could take years—decades—to be welcomed into the Sprouting Rock Beach Association. According to the newspapers and tabloids, if one could ever believe a word of them, it was the most difficult and the most sought-after private club to join in all of American 'society.'

I suppose its physical attributes were not its finest characteristic; that distinction belonged to its clientele.

I sat on a blanket I pulled close to the ebbing sea, away from the others who did not seem to value it, watching the tide pull it farther and farther away from me. I sat and brooded. I sweltered beneath the punishing sun as I punished myself with thoughts. I floated outside myself, chiding myself for my ingratitude. I had a privileged life, highly privileged, yet these days the parts that didn't fit had a far more ill fit. I closed my eyes as if I could block them out. In the few seconds my mind was still, I heard the cries and gasps.

I looked round. Almost everyone was on their feet, even the elderly matrons who rarely moved from their chairs beneath their wide umbrellas. They stared and pointed to a woman in the water. Elsie Clews.

She was one of us, her father being Henry Clews, a powerful financier from New York, a friend to my father. His wife, Lucy Worthington as she was, was Father's distant cousin. As I craned my eyes against the flashes of light sparking off the ocean waves, I finally saw what everyone else did. Elsie dared to swim without stockings.

More and more cries of outrage rose up from the sand like castles, bursting from those far too old to understand. Men of all ages, though the older ones did so surreptitiously, gazed on, admiration as clear as the water before them, through which they could see her legs whenever a wave caught the end of her skirt, undulating it up and down.

My shock wore off quickly. My admiration never would. I jumped up and plunged into the water, wading closer to her. The delight on her face shone like the sun above our parasols.

"How does it feel, Elsie?" I had to ask.

Others might have asked how she had dared such an act. I need not for I knew her. I knew her to be of a like mind with myself, with Ginevra, and with other women looking for better, wanting better, wanting more.

When she turned to me, I saw tears glistening in her eyes.

"Glorious. Simply glorious," she whispered along with the whoosh of small waves. "My skin is tingling. My toes are ruffling in the moist sand."

She looked down at her legs and feet with disbelief, as if they belonged to someone else.

"Glorious," she repeated.

I smiled with her even as I left her to it. I knew what I would do.

* * *

When I stood in the bathing house the next day, I chided myself for my reticence. Elsie had not hesitated. She walked, sans stockings, with her head high, led by a wide smile. I simpered in fear.

Ginevra helped me dress, as she had the day before, but I dismissed her quickly, once more giving her the day to herself, sending her back to The Beeches. She could see what I was about; she could not try to stop me. I quickly re-entered our dressing shack, and just as quickly removed my stockings.

Already the sensation was marvelous. The bathhouses were exclusive, but they could not block out the air. The cool breeze found my legs beneath the black skirt of my bathing costume. I closed my eyes, remembering the child I was, running about with bare legs, grass tickling my feet. The memory was what I needed.

I opened the door.

How glad I was for the glare of the sun on the beige sand, for in its glare I could see little of the stares that greeted me. Those I could see, I ignored.

I entered the water and gasped. Its cool fluidity was unlike anything I had ever felt. The water-soaked sand beneath my feet mushed between my toes as if I stepped in creamy butter. I closed my eyes and luxuriated in the sensations and in my defiance. There would be a price, a hefty one, but it was one I was more than willing to pay.

* * *

My father took me to the Casino the next day, along with Herbert Butterworth. It had been two days since Frederick had called upon me, the same two days since my moment with the ocean.

My father had had an ugly tangle with my mother about it, who still wanted to punish me for my, in her words, "deplorable behavior" at the beach. He had triumphed in the end, extending the invitation to Herbert. I think Herbert regretted it afterward. I know my father didn't.

Tennis week in Newport was one of the highlights of the social season. The year after the Casino opened in 1800, it hosted the first national tennis championship, the United States Lawn Tennis Tournament. Of course, back then only the bluebloods were allowed to play. Brahmin Richard Sears won that first year, and the seven to follow. I saw pictures of him in his blazer, knickers, wool socks, and canvas shoes. He looked quite dashing.

Looks played as much a part in the tournament as did the tennis. It was one of the greatest opportunities for us cottagers to deck ourselves out in our finest and go about in them, to see and be seen in them.

Where one sat was almost as important. Seats in the Grandstand were status symbols claimed by birthright. Most belonged to the Vanderbilts and the Astors, the Belmonts and the Goelets.

The former Mrs. Alva Vanderbilt, now Mrs. Oliver Hazard Perry Belmont, attended. Some still ostracized her for her divorce and her quick marriage to the man of her infidelity. Alva laughed merrily in the face of them. I would have as well. She had not only retained ownership of Marble House, but she now resided in OHP's Belcourt, a sixty-room mansion she was completely renovating to her specifications. Just as miraculously, her mortally threatening illness had disappeared when her daughter had married the duke. Oh yes, she laughed often and well. I listened to it all that day as my father's recently enlarged fortune made it possible for us to acquire seats in the Grandstand now as well, rather than along the sides where we used to sit.

Today's tennis would be different from any other. Today women would compete.

My mother refused to attend; sticking to the antiquated notion that physical exertion was bad for the feminine form. As Wimbledon had done, the Casino had ceded to the pressures of the growing force of the suffragists, many of whom, surprisingly, were among the cottagers, and had allotted this day—one day—to a small ladies' championship.

As the women took to the court, there were as many cheers as there were jeers.

"Well, you have to give it to them. They must have known the reception they would receive," Herbert said in a low voice, though I'm not sure why he spoke so quietly. "It certainly takes courage."

I thought they looked remarkable, still lady-like in their crisp white button-down shirts adorned simply with what looked almost like a man's casual tie, their simple but full-length skirts. They fastened their long hair back tightly and, on their heads, sat the simplest of white caps, like those my brother wore as a child, fitted tight on the head with a small, curved brim to shade their eyes from the sun.

The battle in the stands, for and against these women, raged on as they began to play. Once begun, many closed their mouths to open their eyes.

These women played with all the grace and athleticism of the men, running cross-court, forward and back, hitting with precision. It was the most astonishing sight I had ever seen. They fought for every point with the determination of a soldier.

My wide-eyed gaze found Ginevra at the fence, it returned to her again and again. Her mouth never closed; her jaw hung open as if it were no longer attached to her head.

"Well," said Herbert between rounds, "they may not hit as hard or as far as men, but they do pretty well."

I wanted to ask him how well he could play if he had to do so in a full skirt and corset. Of course, I didn't.

"Thank you, Father," I said instead, taking my father's arm. "Thank you for letting me see this."

He put his hand over mine and smiled his small smile.

GINEVRA

It was a short walk for me, the three-quarters of a mile from the Beeches to the Casino. It was a lovely walk along the tree-lined road as carriages rumbled past, the smell of the ocean never far away.

The entrance was much like some buildings in Italy, with its stretched arched gateway. The man who created the Casino, Bennett I think his name was, allowed staff and Townies in, but only on special days, days such as this. I had been there a few times before, attending to Pearl, the only other way a servant could attend.

We couldn't do anything but watch. A hollow gesture then, but one I enjoyed anyway. I liked to watch, even if I must do it while standing along the fence. The players in their crisp white clothes glowed in the sun. Their exertions revealed what the body could do. I had seen them bowling once. It reminded me a bit of *bocce*, the game my father loved to play back home, with its precision of the rolling of small, heavy balls.

I met a few of the townsfolk as we stood along the rails; heads perched above like birds whose eyes flicked here and there. They denounced these wealthy people and their exclusivity even as they stood for hours watching them. A few I spoke to reacted with their own snobbery when they heard my accent, fading though it was. It was good they could not hear the cynicism in my voice then. Yes, most strayed from me... the English, Irish, and Germans. We Italians were still on the low rung. Most stayed away, but not all. I made a few friends, long-time Townies, a group of girls as eager to see the women play as I.

I watched Pearl as well, to see how she fared. I tried to lie to myself, convince myself that I didn't long to be on the Grandstand with her, draped in fineries, with my arm in Herbert's. I was not very convincing. My dark eyes once more turned green. They rarely strayed from my study of Pearl and Herbert. If I stared long enough, would I see their truth? One I needed to know desperately.

With her father on one side and Herbert on the other, Pearl stood in reality as she felt in her mind. She smiled, here and there. Her smiles were so often forced lately. She did her best, as did I, making the most of my afternoon off.

When the women took the court, I traveled to another world, as much as I had when my father and I boarded that ship. Any thought of men, of loving them, faded like the first dreams of slumber. They were women like me, strong women, women with muscles and flesh who were proud of them. They conquered that court as any soldier had ever taken a battlefield.

My head twisted back and forth, up and down, following the ball from one side of the net to the other, from the court to Pearl in the stands. Our eyes met as often as the racquets met the ball. In her face, I saw all the wonder I felt.

We were no longer alone.

It changed us even more.

PEARL

Without instigation, not a word or a note, Ginevra and I found each other beneath the beeches after dinner that night. What we saw that day demanded it. We had to meet in private, where mother's ears or those she employed could not hear. To speak of the shared experience made it all the more real. Our words ignited the images set so deeply in our minds. Though a fence had stood between us, we had experienced it together.

"I am in awe of what they've done, what they do," I said, lying back on our blanket, my gaze following my mind into the vast sky and all its possibilities.

We had talked so long, talked of every move the women had made, the late setting summer sun had finally bowed to dusk, and stars began to twinkle in the twilight, the patches of it we could see through the lush beeches.

"And me," Ginevra sighed as she too laid down beside me. "Such courage."

Her words hung heavy in the thick humid air. They struck me as if a heavy branch had fallen on my stomach.

"Am I a coward?"

Ginevra sat up fast, propelled by my question.

"You have done nothing cowardly," she insisted, a deep furrow plowing the flesh between her brows.

I shook my head; twigs and leaves snapped and rustled beneath it. "I didn't speak up to Mother, I didn't fight her."

"But you applied to college." Ginevra's insistence sounded like anger. "And you were accepted. You did that."

Had I told her how grateful I was for her? I hoped I had. I hoped I'd shown her.

I sat up. "And you have made some magnificent clothes...are designing ever more beautiful ones."

Ginevra had shared her sacred sketchbook with me on more than one occasion. Each time her flair, her mastery of design of fashion became greater. My request, for serious clothes for a serious woman, she had taken to an exquisite place. Her long jackets incorporating a diminishing bustle on a narrowing skirt were fabulous. Her incorporation of feminine touches kept the men's clothing-inspired outfits unique and feminine, comfortable and serious.

She shrugged but with a pleased smile and that shy dip of her head. "Where we to go from here?"

"That's the question, isn't it?"

Our gaze held, locked upon each other, locked on confusion that wore the same clothes, the same strangeness of our existence. She longed for wealth, for the elegant life I led. I felt restrained by it; it had become a gilded cage.

"You should have been born to this life, not me." I looked at my darling companion, not trying in the least to divest myself of the longing for her simple life.

She merely shook her head at me, said simply, "No. We only want what we no have."

Her wisdom was her own. Though I had taught her many things over the course of our years together, such insightfulness into the human condition was not one of them.

We hovered in the stillness, the poignancy of the moment. Around us, the night and all its creatures took their place. Crickets complained of the heat; owls hooted at them for silence. In the encroaching mist, the ever-present scent of the ocean settled in.

"Deciding is upon me, Ginevra," I whispered with a close of my eyes. If the world did not hear it, it would not be true; if I did not see the world, it could not see me. "Do I marry? Who do I marry? Or..."

"Or?" Her hushed whisper nudged me.

I threw my arms up, beseeching the heavens. "Or...something else. But what else?"

"Fate provides, we decide." It was the loudest murmur I had ever heard.

I rolled onto my side, dropped my head into the palm of my hand.

"Did you make that up?"

Ginevra snuffled. "No. I read somewhere. But it is true, no?"

"It is true." I studied her profile as she studied the canopy above us, now a silhouette against the gray twilight. "Sometimes it provides too much to decide and sometimes too little."

"Think of only one. Decide one, and then worry about the others." Ginevra didn't turn to me as she spoke. I dropped back on the blanket.

"One," I mused, rustling my fingers in the leaves that had fallen to the ground, thinning like brittle old paper. "I know I will probably marry. I do long for love and marriage and children especially. But who?"

"Who then?" Ginevra said stiffly, as rigidly as she lay upon the ground. Gone was the joy that had brought us there that night. Did she fear losing me?

"Frederick or Herbert. Herbert or Frederick." I said their names aloud. Deciding was truly upon me.

Ginevra sat up quickly, turned her body toward me. There was something in her face, in the small gap of her lips... something hung there, demons wrestled behind her eyes.

"What is it, Ginevra?" I took her hand. "There is nothing we cannot share."

I hoped to encourage; her face grimaced. She threw herself back down.

"No, it is... it nothing." Was it? "It is worse then, your deciding, yes?"

She could see me without any light. She always could. But did I see her?

* * *

Herbert dined with the family on our last night in Newport. I hadn't invited him. Perhaps Mother had. It was a congenial table, I think, for I forgot the flavor of the well-cooked veal and the tang of the wine on my tongue.

As Father stubbed out his cigar, Herbert paid his respects to my family.

I walked him to the door and out of it. I stood on the top step before the large doors, he on the one below. Our faces were level, his eyes bore into mine. I couldn't move, couldn't breathe. He lowered his face to mine, his lips to mine.

Their softness was everything their fullness promised. He moved them slowly, ever so slowly over mine. Who knew the touching of lips could tingle down my toes, could be the essence of human intimacy. Gently, his tongue opened my lips, gently touched the tip of my tongue with his.

I fell into his kiss. I tumbled and spun in a bottomless warmth and softness. I could fall like this forever.

GINEVRA

Our goodbyes were as tearful as ever, maybe even more so this year. That change, the threat of it that Pearl had spoken of once, threatened closer and closer. We could both feel it. We both worried over it. When she left, my worries would be my most constant companion.

I followed her carriage down the long drive and out the gate, watched it as it rumbled down Bellevue Avenue. I would see her, this Pearl, for as long as I could, for I didn't know which Pearl would return.

GINEVRA
1899

I barely knew her when she came back. Familiar features had taken on a haughty mask. I should have expected it. I think I did. The letters from her, far less than any year before, had dropped the seeds of it.

One letter, one piece of news was especially telling, above all the others. That letter I had carried in my pocket for most of the winter. That letter lay deciding at my door.

Pearl didn't rush to greet me. I saw her first when I followed Charlie who carried her luggage to her room, stuffed trunks for me to unpack. I stood in the doorway, watched her preen in her mirror. Only in the reflection did she see me.

"Ginevra, dahling," she said, spinning hesitantly from herself. If she knew she sounded like her mother she didn't seem to mind, as she would have in years gone by. Crossing the room, she did not embrace me. She kissed me on both cheeks with cold lips and held me out to look at me. It was a greeting so like her mother's, cold and dense in a cloud of perfume. In that moment, I thought I had lost her.

"Well, look at you. How... womanly you have become."

My body had changed, a buxom chest, wide hips, though my waist had stayed slim, even without a corset. But I hadn't, not the me inside.

I looked down, ashamed. A shame made worse by the changes in her. Taller than ever, she had not gained weight and her body had slimmed even more. Small breasts, straight hips, and her only curves were those made by her tight corset.

The Pearl inside had changed. She moved with such grace, such mature refinement. Pearl held her head straight and tall on her long slim neck, her nose high in the air where it had never been before.

"You look beautiful, Pearl," I said with all honesty, brushing away the concerns as we had brushed away the limbo of winter for the Worthington's return. "Betrothal suits you."

She didn't expect those words. I saw it in the way Pearl spun away from me.

"Thank you, Ginevra," she said, her words echoed hollowly.

Scratchy silence came between us. I filled it with the massive undertaking of unpacking. Pearl had brought back more dresses than ever. Would she no longer wear those I made for her? With them came more accessories and jewels than ever before. Of course, the ring was the greatest of all her newest items.

Pearl sat at her vanity all the while. I glanced at her here and there, as I whirled about the room. Her face looked sculpted out of stone.

I finished up, helped her change into a more comfortable afternoon dress, and made my way for the door.

"Ginevra?" She called me back. When I turned, I saw Pearl, my Pearl, standing before me again. I could have cried. She had changed, like so many things, but there was still something of the true Pearl remaining. "Tonight."

It was all she needed to say.

* * *

Below stairs, things were a frantic flurry. Even here, change was everywhere.

So many of the kitchen maids and chambermaids were new, driving Mrs. Briggs to distraction with their constant questions, with her overbearing demand for things to be done in just a certain way. So many of the previous maids had taken positions elsewhere, in factories and mills. There were more opportunities for them to do so than there had ever been.

I spent more time sketching and studying.

Greta was no longer with us, but Anja still was. I was pleased to see her even though she would only wink at me. For all the times we sat together at dinner, or on the odd servant's terrace on the stone roof, she kept our friendship casual when among the other servants. I didn't blame her, even for all the hurt it gave me. The new batch of servants was as filled with the English and the Irish as the last; Anja would not limit any new relationships with the newcomers by her relationship with an I-talian.

I had two friends, one from above stairs, one from below. To the world, both friendships didn't exist. I must be joyful for them, secretly in my heart. Better in secret than an empty heart altogether.

I helped in the laundry as Pearl took her nap. I would rather work, be useful, than retreat to my room, as Nettie would whenever Mrs. Worthington didn't require her services. Alone, in my room, my deciding grew too big; it left little space for me. My helping didn't seem to endear me to the staff much, perhaps a little. It made no difference to me; I didn't do it for them.

As the time for the staff dinner drew near, I thought to help in the kitchen and to get a drink of water, for the hot steaminess of the laundry always made me thirsty.

I opened the frosted glass door that separated the laundry from the cooking areas... and stopped, drew back a single step, far enough away not to intrude, close enough to see and listen.

My father stood in the doorway to the main kitchen, near the shelves filled with copper pots and pans of every size and shape. Beside him stood Mrs. O'Brennan, the assistant chef, taking pots down, putting others up. When she looked up, looked up at my father, I saw something that chilled my heart. She looked at him with familiarity and fondness.

I couldn't see my father's face, but I didn't have to. He spoke to her with such gentleness; he spoke to her in English. God grabbed my entire world and shook it until everything fell in different places, wrong places.

Many of his words were wrong. Mrs. O'Brennan only smiled and gently corrected him. When she didn't understand him, or him her, a look passed between them, a wordless communication. It troubled me more than their words, as much as the hint of smiles playing on my father's face.

Waves of emotion rolled on me—I rocked on them, heel-toe, heel-toe. I forgot my thirst, my step faltered as I turned away. I looked for something—anything—to quiet my mind.

PEARL

I waited for her beneath the beeches. For the first time, I worried she would not come to me. I knew my behavior toward her had been abominable. Ever since I had accepted Herbert's proposal, I had been trying to accept the life ahead of me, embrace it. Accept it I might, embrace it too, but it could never have affected how I treated her, how I spoke to her. It should never.

This way of life was like a pernicious illness; it infested every part of you. It was hard to turn from it once fully immersed in it, fully embraced by it. There was no medicine for some illnesses.

The winter had been a whirlwind. The instant I allowed Herbert to place the four-carat diamond on my finger, everything changed. We became "the" couple, the guests of honor at so many formal dinner parties, at cotillions and balls. From then on, I was freer from my mother than I had ever been in my life. The irony was, now that I was engaged, she wanted me by her side as she never had before, sought out my company and my companionship with far too much fervor. Did she merely want to step into my light, have some of it shine on her as well, or if, in the gesture, had I, at long last, earned her approval?

I cared little about the latter. I knew Mother's true colors and they would never change; they would never be a hue I found appealing. The freedom from her was something else altogether. It was what I longed for so often over the last few years. It was something I now reveled in. How can one not be changed when everything in one's life was changing? The trickier question, one that gnawed at me like a rat on spoiled cheese, was if I had accepted Herbert merely to be free of my mother?

"Hello, Pearl."

I jumped. I had been so entrenched in my thoughts I didn't hear the swoosh of the leaves as she pushed them aside to enter our cathedral, or the snap of the twigs beneath her feet as she approached. She was there, that was all that mattered.

I jumped up and ran to her. I gave her the embrace I should have given her as soon as I saw her. I felt her arms hesitate, had I lost her? When her arms, at last, rose up to encompass me, relief nearly broke my heart.

"I'm sorry," I said into her shoulder.

Ginevra said nothing. She held me tighter, pulled her head back to kiss my forehead, then held me some more. It was everything I needed.

I don't know how long we held onto each other. I know we were holding on to more than just our physical beings. We gripped our past with fisted hands; if we opened them, we'd both fly out, fireflies that had burst with light and escaped.

"When I am married you will be with me," I told her, still holding on to her, refusing to release the ties that bound us. "All the time, wherever I go. Mother won't be able to stop that any longer once I am a wife with my own home."

Ginevra's body became a stick in my arms. If she stood there, like that, long enough, she would grow roots.

I held her away from me but held her still. Her face was a canvas yet to see even a dot of paint. I splotched it with black, the darkness of fear, and a dingy blue of disbelief.

"Herbert has promised to take me to all the great museums around the world. And you will go with me." With the last words, I gave her a shake by the shoulders still in my hands. She finally spoke, though I wished she hadn't.

"Why him, Pearl?"

Now she was stone. So grey, I didn't see her lips move.

"Why H…him and not the other?"

GINEVRA

I thought I had lost her, lost her to the gayness, the surface frivolity that seeped down into them, like sparse summer rain on earth dried to dust. When she said those words, when she called me to our private place, I knew she was still in there. Still Pearl, but not.

I was still Ginevra, but not.

I had spent the winter studying, sketching, and sewing. I thought of her. And I thought of him. Especially after the letter came.

I remembered our last time beneath the beeches—mine and Pearl's—when we spoke of deciding. The news the letter brought, brought deciding to my door.

Should I tell her of Herbert's flirtations? Were they flirtations or just my dreams and hopes, my envious wanting, blurring my vision, making me see things that were not there? Or did he use his charms to win me over to ultimately win her? I didn't know. I didn't know how to know.

How much easier it would have been if she had chosen Frederick. The nattering in my mind would have been shut up. I could have simply let fate take me where it would. But she didn't, it didn't. The nattering grew louder, some of it slipped past my lips.

"Why H…him and not the other?"

PEARL

Ginevra turned to me. "Does he make you happy? Will this truly make you happy?"

How I wished she hadn't asked me these questions, not that question.

"He's a wonderful man," I said with truth. "He has been the very picture of respect and romance, more than any woman could want, could dream about. And he is so understanding of my love of art. He buys me books and books filled with beautiful images. Frederick cared nothing about art, only about those newfangled carriages, those engine ones."

Ginevra's silent stare accused me.

I tried to ignore it. She wouldn't let me.

"Is this truly what you want...will it make you happy?"

She questioned again, still waiting for an answer.

I left the question in the air, still so fresh and green with the early days of summer.

Together we lay back on our blanket to look at our stars.

"If you were a man, what would you do with your life?" Instead of answering her question, I asked one of her.

Ginevra laughed a little, a throaty laugh, a woman's laugh.

"I would have my own design house, as Worth does," Ginevra dreamed aloud. "I would sell my fashion, my clothes, all over the world."

"And every woman in the world would want to wear them."

She laughed again. "And you? What would you do if you were a man?"

I needed no time to think, to answer. "I would travel the world, go to all the great museums, but I would need no chaperone, no one to take me there. Most of all I would study art, learn its history, all its nuances. Perhaps I would have a gallery showing, in Paris of course, where I might be discovered as the next great talent."

"And you would," she whispered, fully in my dream world, walking there beside me. "Your eye, it sees the beauty and your hands recreate it."

We lay back with our dreams, our eyes closed, our hands clasped. In her grasp, I could feel the same need, the same longing I felt. We could not live in them forever. Life was about to happen. I would make sure it would happen with us together. I needed her to be sure. I lifted myself up and leaned over her.

I looked at her with all the intensity in my heart, all the love and all the loyalty. "Nothing will ever break us apart, keep us apart. I promise you."

Oh, how I wish I had kept that promise.

* * *

The newspapers proclaimed we were living in Gay Nineties. If so, it was Harry Lehr who brought us there.

Gone were the staid and somber manners as dictated by Ward McAllister, as gone as Mr. McAllister was himself. He had passed away two years before in the obscurity he caused by writing *Society as I Have Found It.* It was his last grasp for the same media attention the true "Four Hundred" garnered. It was a scathing work, denouncing the very people who had given him so much power and so much reign over the practices of their life. He hadn't named names, but the implied characters were too close not to recognize those he spoke of and those who knew them. Ginevra and I had laughed about his character, one he named Milly, a grasping climber who couldn't keep her skirts down.

Ousted from the very world he created, he died at his dinner table, completely alone.

Harry Lehr wore none of the chains of good manners, though he did often wear ladies' clothing, much to the consternation of most of the men. Tall and strong, a young and handsome blue-eyed blond, he came with no pedigree, worked as a wine salesman, yet his charismatic charm, his youthful, almost childish, vivaciousness was infectious.

From the moment Mrs. Evelyn Townsend Burden invited him to Fairlawn, her Newport cottage, he infiltrated himself into the good graces of the titular mistresses of our society, Mrs. Astor, Mrs. Belmont, and her triumvirate, none of them could get enough of him. They followed him into the world of the absurd, with monkeys as dinner guests and birthday parties for dogs. Tonight would be no exception.

Tessie Oelrichs and her sister, Virginia Fair, had, years ago, bought one of the most coveted plots of land on all of Newport. It perched above the Cliff Walk near the very tip of the peninsula. As heirs to a silver fortune, they had the means to do so. The cottage, Rosecliff, as it stood then, was far too sedate, could no longer compete with the grand mansions now surrounding it. Tessie set herself, and a vast amount of her inheritance to make it *the* cottage. That night, she would reveal it to us.

I arrived on Herbert's arm, a place where I had begun to feel more comfortable. His patience with my mother and her grand schemes for our wedding only strengthened my fondness for him.

"My word," he whispered, breathless, as we walked in, but, in truth, there were no words for what we saw.

The white terra cotta bricks that formed the exterior made the mansion look like something out of ancient Greece. To step inside was to step into a wonderland. The firm of Stanford and White modeled the cottage based on Louis XIV's Grand Trianon Palace at Versailles, but we never expected this... this was a palace in its own right.

Herbert and I walked about the H-shaped mansion as if we were tourists visiting a European palace of old. Through the arched entryway, painted ceilings rose twenty feet above our heads, before us a curving marble staircase rose in the shape of a heart. The opulence struck us dumb. The same could not be said for those in the ballroom. Conversation abounded, riotous laughter exploded, especially that of Harry Lehr. We followed it.

It was the largest ballroom in Newport, occupying the entire central area of the ground floor. It glimmered and shimmered, as did those who stood below its trompe-l'oel ceiling of painted clouds and its perfumed chandeliers. As I entered the fray, I couldn't help but think of Ginevra. Tonight, like so many that had come before, she accompanied me. Already I pictured us beneath the beeches glorifying the mansion, vilifying those who filled it that night.

For all our obscene opulence, you couldn't fault this clique of people, this minute elite segment of the populace, for their devotion to beauty and elegance, for their desire to not only acquire the best the world had to offer but to truly enjoy and experience it, to immerse themselves in it. These cottages—these palaces—were not false gods, but the true object of their adoration. They had the means to have the best life had to offer; they saw no reason not to.

Of all the sights astounding me that night, perhaps the greatest by far was the vision of Harry Lehr and Tessie Oelrichs flaying about on the dance floor to the sounds of Ragtime music, a highly syncopated, piano thumping sort of music, one I had never heard in the hallowed halls of Newport or New York before that night. Others, equally as exuberant, or perhaps equally as inebriated, crowded around. My mother, of course, danced openly in the arms of Lispenard Stewart. Those who watched laughed at their antics. I simply stared. Herbert laughed.

"Well, this looks like great fun," he said, surprising me. "Shall we give it a go?"

My nose crinkled on my face. I narrowed my eyes as if that would bring the man I knew into focus, that man would not, I thought, be so willing to participate in such distasteful goings-on.

When Reggie Vanderbilt grabbed his partner and hoisted her up on a table to dance on its top, Herbert slapped his leg with laughter. I could not. How strange it was that I, one who longed for change, couldn't embrace this one. Before me was the picture of hedonism and luridness for which the papers forever degraded us.

"Not for me, Herbert," I rebuffed the offer. As I did, a face in the crowd flashed into my gaze. "Oh look, Consuelo is here." I caught a glimpse of sanity in a sea of the insane.

Herbert unhooked my arm from his. "Go," he gave me a gentle push. "Go. I know how much she means to you."

How grateful I was for his understanding; I touched his cheek with it. "I won't be long. I promise."

"Take all the time you want," he replied. I took a step away. "But, I say, would you mind if I gave it a try?" he asked, pointing to the dance floor. "I'll find one of our friends who might partner with me."

It was forever done, partners dancing with each other's partners, but Herbert had never done so before. As his fiancé, his future wife, it would be something I needed to become accustomed to. I scratched away the itchiness his request brought out in me.

"Of course, dear," I conceded, turning away, making for Consuelo.

I could allow it; I didn't have to watch it. I threw myself into Consuelo's arms, forgetting, for a while, the depravity raging around us, forgetting about Herbert.

Like myself, my quiet friend found the night perplexing. They were half-mad, I think. We all were, but on what I'm not sure…the wealth, the ridiculously elegant affluence. Or perhaps just ourselves.

GINEVRA

If fairy tales were real, their reality took on the mythical at Rosecliff. It took the luxury of The Beeches and doubled it, tripled it. I could barely keep still in the maids' waiting room for the longing to walk about, to see more.

The butler's pantry where they kept us was a slim hallway away from the ballroom. Every loud guffaw, every thumping foot, every drumbeat of the wild music reached our ears. A few of the girls danced with each other in the small space. Nettie was there, silent and snobbish in her superiority. I tapped my foot along to the beat. I closed my eyes and imagined myself among them, as I had so often over the years, too often. In my mind, I wore a splendid gown, groomed to perfection, on Herbert's arm who whirled me about the dance floor as if I were his queen, as if I were the best of the best of them. The longing, the yearning... despised without escape.

The night wore on. I sneaked around the corner, sneaked a few peeks into the ballroom. Each time I found Pearl in conversations with her friends, not for her this glass-smashing ruckus. She needed no adjustments. Pearl looked as perfect as when she had left her room.

Here and there, I saw glimpses of Anja and James. Mr. Oelrichs had asked for the loan of their services; she didn't have enough servants of her own to cater to this many guests. Mrs. Worthington was only too happy to comply; she deluded herself that the asking made her a special friend of Mrs. Oelrichs. She would never give up her deluded dreams. They chose Anja for the young, attractive, hard worker she was. James was chosen, well, for being so incredibly attractive.

As he had grown from a young man into a man, or perhaps as I had grown into a woman, I found him more and more strikingly handsome. Charlie had continued to flirt with me, continued to try to charm me into strolling out with him. Charlie was no temptation. I could not say the same of James.

How well I remember those nights when Pearl taught me to dance beneath our beeches, moving to the chirp of the crickets, our shadows flickering in the light of our candles, warm winds lifting our hair, cooling the back of our necks with a touch that tingled. When I had closed my eyes, I imagined James' arms around me, not Pearl's. James' or Herbert's.

I turned away from the riotous party. Without purpose, I allowed myself a trip below stairs for some water, perhaps a bite to eat. I slipped down the first flight of stairs, turned onto the first landing… and stopped. As quick as I stopped, I hurried on, slipping past them as though I had seen nothing, though what I had seen I could never have unseen.

Harry Lehr sat on the top step to the next set of stairs, beside him, very close, another man, locked in Harry's embrace, their lips upon each other's.

There was no world where such men did not exist, nor women—for that matter—if rumors were to be believed. The innocent person I was, having lived as a child in my parents' home, the rest of my life in the confinement that was the life of a servant, I had never seen such things for myself. I would have lingered—watched—if I could, as one lingers before the bearded lady at a circus.

I hurried away unthinking, or thinking of what I had seen, seeing nothing else, not where I walked or who was there. That's when he found me.

"Ginevra!" The harsh whisper came from out of the dim light of a long corridor to my left, forming a 'T' with the one I walked through, leading to the kitchen.

I couldn't see who called. Murkiness blurred facial features, smudged them to the unrecognizable. I turned and walked toward it. It was my first mistake, but not the last.

As soon as I got close enough, he reached out to me, his hand a vice on my arm, pulling me against the wall.

"I knew this moment would come." Herbert stood before me, pressed me against the wall. His lips found mine.

I fell into his kiss, my first kiss, one that tasted of wine. I tumbled and spun in a bottomless warmth and softness. I could have fallen like that forever.

A part of me did, she saw me in his arms—my own hovered off my sides—saw me in this life, his life. In the moment, I forgot everything.

I forgot her.

Until I didn't.

What I saw was what I truly wanted to see, me in her life. Sitting beside her on a carriage in the parade, on the beach where surely the sand must be made of gold dust, or with a drink in our hands as we stood side by side at a fabulous party filled with the fabulous, with the Four Hundred.

My arms rose, so close to him, my palm brushed the smoothness of his silk evening jacket. My hands came up…

…and pushed upon his shoulders, pushed him away, but only a few inches.

Those eyes of his, already heavy with liquor, narrowed at me.

"What is it, Ginevra, why do you stop when you want so much to continue?"

"I can't. I won't." The words belonged to me as much as they did to him.

"Why, because of Pearl? It is perfect don't you see?" Herbert's lips, those that had just touched mine, spread in a crooked, lopsided grin. "I will have her intelligence, her brightness, and cool beauty as well as yours…your warm beauty and your fiery passion. All under the same roof. It will be so easy."

I shook my head so hard I heard the rattle of my tangled thoughts.

Herbert's fingers dug in the flesh of my upper arms like clamps.

"It is the way of us," he cajoled. It was the way of "them." "Pearl knows that, especially with that mother of hers." His chest puffed up as he snickered. "We are the captains of industry, rules don't belong to us, they belong to regular people. *We* are far from regular."

He was not the exception, but the rule, like all the other aristocrats that summered here. He fell fast and hard from the lofty perch I had placed him on.

"Y…you have not worked a day in your life," I spat the sour sting rising in my throat, burning my tongue. "You are the captain of nothing."

Darkness spread across Herbert's face; the snooty smile slithered out of his eyes like a snake going to ground. Were he not inebriated he would still not be able to shrug off the truth of his life. "She is but your mistress and you, her servant."

"No, oh no!" Whatever spell he had on me, he broke himself. "We are friends."

"Hah!" His guffaw was so thick with insult, I longed to slap my hands over his mouth, or perhaps just slap him. "*We* do not become friends with servants."

I had never heard prejudice in his voice before; now it was so loud it pained my ears.

"I will have you, Ginevra. I will have you both."

"I…" I opened my mouth to protest. I should have screamed. I didn't. It was my second mistake; one I would make again.

He plastered his lips against mine, crushing them, slathering my face with his spit, trying to pry my lips open with his tongue. The voice in my head screamed for help. That scream, a torment. No one heard it but me. How I hated for my first kisses to be this, nothing of the romantic gesture of my dreams, but a sickening violation.

I pushed at him, gaining only inches between us. I turned my head away to the light at the end of the hall, to the next hall where I needed to run. I would have run out of my skin if I could; I no longer wanted it. His hands, hard hands that moved all over me, had ruined it. Bile puddled in my mouth, gagging me. I couldn't get out from between him and the wall.

The light flickered. A shadow appeared. Then, a person. Anja!

I saw her silhouette in the light, her thin form rushing past with a large empty tray in her hands. I saw her step back quick; she'd seen something. It stopped her. I reached a hand out.

Herbert grabbed my head and turned it back, wrenching my neck as he crushed his mouth on mine once more. I tried to call out to Anja, to anyone, but it came out muffled. It sounded like a moan. He pulled back with a greasy grin on his face. Then he saw my hand. His gaze followed it.

"Hurry along, girl," he bellowed at her. She did.

In the diversion, I squirmed, almost finding release. I could not let him touch me more, could not let him kiss me, again.

"You will take your hands from me, Sir," I snarled beyond the quiver, one that had taken possession of my whole body.

"Or what?" His hands squeezed my buttocks. There would be bruises on every part of me.

I opened my mouth to nothing. Or what? A fine question, one for which I had no answer. I was but a shadow that could be replaced by any other. Nameless, faceless, powerless. That's what we were in this place, one of the most splendid on earth. Even as I began to drown, I found a buoy.

"I will tell Pearl…everything."

He sputtered laughter; spittle pinged my face.

"Then you are a fool. She'll never believe you."

I knew different. I knew the bond of our friendship, of our sisterhood. The knowledge gave me strength.

My hands, braced against the wall, came up quickly. Grabbing the back of his head by the hair, I yanked, even as my knee came up to blight his swollen genitalia.

As he howled, as Herbert bent double in pain, holding himself, I squirmed from out of the trapped corner. I ran, not to my father or Pearl's father or even Mrs. Briggs, as perhaps I ought to have done. I ran to Pearl.

PEARL

It was late into the night, well into the early morning of the next day before we took our leave from Rosecliff. I couldn't find Ginevra anywhere, though Herbert had assured me he had looked everywhere.

"She probably went back to The Beeches," he hurried me along. "I'm sure she knew you were all right before she did."

I believed him.

Ginevra wasn't in my room waiting to attend me, but her note was. The scratches on the paper were so maligned—barely legible—the words so intent, they frightened me. I ran to the beeches as they implored, still in my full evening attire.

"Ginevra?" I called as soon as the curtain of branches and leaves fell closed behind me. "Ginevra?" I said again; I saw her but didn't, not my Ginevra.

Rumbled and dirty smudged clothes covered her trembling body, her shirt half tucked in, half falling out of the tight waistband of her skirt. Strands of hair had escaped her bun; they floated around her as if she floated in water. Tear tracks slithered from her swollen eyes down her cheeks.

I dropped by her side, heedless of my gown—one of hers—so very frightened.

She looked up at me as if I were her savior or her mother, the whole of her expression pleading for salvation.

"What is it? What has happened?" I begged even as I held her close.

Ginevra told me, told me everything, every wretched word came out between more sobs. My mind went numb, stopped listening, started screaming, screaming against her words.

"How could you!" I jumped, snapping viciously.

Her head snapped sideways as if I had slapped her. I had.

"I thought you would pick Frederick. I did not think—"

"You've always wanted my life, you told me yourself." My body bumbled about our little clearing. I heard the crunching beneath my feet as if someone else stomped around. I felt my hands tearing apart the perfectly coiffed hair she had arranged for me, but I felt no pain...not from that. "You wanted my life and now you're trying to take it. You—"

"I said only I wanted life like yours, not yours." Ginevra was on her knees. "As soon as you made your choice, I no longer...it was him. He wants us both."

I heard and saw nothing of her, of my Ginevra, only someone who wanted to hurt me.

"Well you can't have it and you can't have him," I screamed as I ran from her, from the beeches, and across the lawn, tears of my own streaming out of my eyes, lost in the wind behind me. Yet even as I ran, thoughts, terrible thoughts of Herbert found their way in. I didn't believe her. I couldn't believe her. Yet, somewhere in the hurricane of my mind, a small voice warned me, *watch him.*

I threw my hands over my ears. I wanted to block out that voice, those words. I couldn't. I would heed my own warning.

GINEVRA

I picked myself up somehow. Somehow, I walked across the lawn and into the house on legs disjointed. I fell once, only to get up and start again.

I had to get to her. My heart tore apart into pieces of anger, regret, and sorrow. The anger bit me, deep inside. I should not have spoken to him, or smiled, or hoped, or dreamed.

Maybe I shouldn't have said anything to Pearl. Maybe I should have accepted my place as an object for these people to do with me as they wished.

The thought stopped me. I shook my head. I had to have said it, had to have told her.

In the house, I padded as quietly as I could to her room. I found her door closed. I reached for the handle. It wouldn't turn. Pearl had locked it, locked me out.

"Pearl, let me in," I whispered, knocking softly. "Let me help you undress. Let me talk to you."

"Go away!"

"Pearl, I—"

"Go away, damn you!"

I recoiled from the door as if she had thrown me out of it. I stood there, listening to the clocks and their arrhythmic ticking. I listened to her cry even as I cried.

As I lay my head down on my pillow, I don't know how long after, the tears were still flowing, but my thoughts cried out, refusing not to be listened to.

I couldn't let her marry such a man. I couldn't let her marry *that* man. I loved her too much. Even if it meant I would lose her, I wouldn't let it happen.

PEARL

The rest of the summer was cold without her, yet I could not release my anger. It was a tangled knot within me. She was still my maid; that incision I could not—would not—inflict upon us. But I could not say why; the why of it was far too elusive. It was there somewhere within me, but my grasp came away empty whenever I tried to reach for it.

It would have been so easy to let her go.

It could end the battle between Mother and me. I did not so much hate to lose as I loathed for her to win.

Ginevra would stay. I would stay with her, somehow. For now.

There were no meetings beneath the beeches. There were no long talks of our deepest feelings, our truest desires. They were never out of my mind. I couldn't abandon them for they were far too dear. I suffered in the purgatory between what we had been and what we had become.

I did that summer the one thing I set out to do, the one thing I told Ginevra I would do. I sent a letter to Rhode Island School of Design, not to decline their acceptance, but to ask for a deferment. With each word, I would forget. I would forget how she had wronged me, lied to me. As I wrote the letter, flashes of her smile, never more perfect than when she was proud of me, distorted the words I tried to pen.

The other thing I did, I did with no one knowing. I watched Herbert.

Another grand event was in the offing, hosted by Mrs. Fish and Harry Lehr in honor of a very special guest, the Czar of Russia. Bellevue buzzed for days about the presence of royalty, as if it made them royal too. Tiaras and glimmering jewels were in vast supply as we arrived at Crossways. How disappointed, how angry they were when the Czar turned out to be none other than Harry himself, dressed for the role, speaking with a hideous Russian accent. I saw it on their faces, the repressed frustration. I had no pity for them. Such is the price for worshipping false gods.

Herbert was as attentive as ever, getting me a drink, a bite to eat, checking on me if too much time passed while engaged with others. I didn't tell him about my letter. I knew he would understand, at least, I thought he would; he was a modern man after all. I would broach the subject to him after the wedding.

We spoke often of the growing suffrage movement, of women such as Harriot Eaton Stanton Blatch, who, with Susan B. Anthony, Elizabeth Cady Stanton, and others of similar courage, were publishing, in volumes, a *History of Women's Suffrage.* Herbert's comments were always ones of support. I knew he would support me in my intellectual endeavor, I was sure of it.

"Do you need another drink, dearest?" Once more, he appeared at my side just as I had taken the last sip of my drink as if he had been watching and waiting for the moment to serve me. In my mind, I cursed Ginevra again, for planting such plump seeds of doubt.

We danced the two-step, a whirling, exerting twirling of a dance. I could feel the moisture thick on my face when the song ended, as we all clapped enthusiastically at the orchestra's lovely rendition, at our own expertise.

"Please excuse me, Herbert, I must wash."

He kissed me on the forehead, no care for the beads of sweat on my brow. "Of course, my dear, of course."

In the brown marble and gold washroom, I dabbed myself dry, plied another layer of fine pale powder to my now dried face, smoothed a few errant strands back into my coif. I looked as I should, a woman of the age, what was it Twain had called it? Oh yes, the Gilded Age. And I was gilded.

I floated out, light as a feather on the warm breeze of my life. My worries seemed to have fallen away as Herbert and I had pranced upon the dance floor.

I left the small powder room, stepped lightly through the marbled corridor, and stopped.

Herbert danced with another. It was not that he danced that stopped me, but the way he danced.

I didn't know the young girl he partnered, but she looked younger than I. His bracing arm pressed firmly against the curve of her lower back, pressing her close to him, into him. She didn't fight him, didn't hold herself away as she should. Perhaps she was too busy looking up at him with adoring eyes. He looked down at her. There was no adoration there, only lust. I knew it as soon as I saw it.

I turned away, turned back into the powder room to wash my face again, to wash away the thoughts barging their way back into my mind. I convinced myself that my mind played tricks on my eyes, vision infested and diseased by Ginevra's confession.

I threw the thoughts away as I would anything poisonous and returned to my friends. The night no longer glittered; the stars no longer twinkled.

Herbert dropped me at my house. I almost asked him of the girl.

GINEVRA

I attended Pearl every day—five, six times a day. She allowed me to, in the way of "them," a stranger tending to their every need.

I had never known such aloneness, not even after mama died. This was different, for Pearl was still here, but she wasn't.

I tried to tell my father.

I went to his room with all intentions of doing so.

I wandered about his room, picking up his tools, putting them down. Picking up a new viola he was making, one that would have the most amazing back piece, he showed me the design. There would be an inlaid pattern of different types of wood, very small pieces, over a thousand of them.

"It is amazing, Papa," I said in English but switched to Italian. "Your talent grows the longer we are here."

Papa put down his work and stared at me. "Something trouble you?"

His English was much improved. I knew Mrs. O'Brennan had a hand in that. I was now only grateful to her for it.

The words—that night—it was all right there in my mind, on my tongue. Could he see them?

I couldn't get it out, couldn't tell my father of my shame. I had much to feel ashamed for, for I had dared to dream a dream that did not belong to me. Yet when I had tottered on the line between right and wrong, I had tilted as I should, as the daughter this man and my mother had raised me to be.

I was not the molester, yet I felt the dirt of it, no matter how often I washed. It was not only how a servant was made to feel, but women, all women. We were at the mercy of men, and they knew it. If we dared to defy them, we were wrong. How the world had come to be this way would forever remain a mystery to me.

Papa saw my struggle. He waited.

The haunting images of that night returned, floated into my mind as they so often did, silent and disturbing. They scared away sleep; they poisoned my food. I could not put those pictures in my father's mind.

I shrugged it off. "Nothing I cannot deal with," I lied.

Papa's head tilted; his gaze pierced. "You do what you have to do to survive in this world, Ginevra." He switched to Italian; his words flowed with his wisdom. "There will always be struggles. The strong overcome them."

Yes, they were wise words, true words. They didn't help at all.

I left him then and wandered about, running from the ghosts.

I would return to our place beneath the beeches as if it were a clock whose hands moved backward. Each twisted branch we walked on I walked on again, each feathery leaf a note of laughter, each broken twig the trust I had broken, each bird I frightened away Pearl.

I returned again and again. In truth, I waited for her. I waited in vain.

PEARL

The tennis tournament was upon us again and once more Herbert accompanied me. He was with me—with the family—almost every night. Almost.

As the players took the court, as their numbers dwindled down to the winner, socializing became the main sport of the day, and I a willing player. If I smiled enough, the smile would become real and hide the pain.

I grieved for Ginevra for all she had hurt me, grieved as if she had died. She had in a sense. But she had left a legacy, an endearing sense of consternation about Herbert.

From that night on, that gut-wrenching night, and the heightened awareness it brought me, I saw things differently. Or did I see things that weren't there? Which was the truth? The answer was as elusive as where the fog went after it rolled out each morning.

Through my new eyes, I saw Herbert's eyes watch my every move. I told myself it was proprietary protectiveness. I couldn't be sure. I tested it.

"Please excuse me, I'm off to the powder room," I whispered in his ear, straining up on tiptoes to do so.

He patted my hand, gave me a smile and a nod. I set off.

The facilities at the Casino were in the main building, the entrance under the archway. I entered the archway, but not the building. Instead, I hid in its shadows and watched Herbert.

Within minutes, he detached himself from the group of men he had been chatting with and made his way to a group of pretty young women. They were, in fact, women I knew myself, as did Herbert. There was relief there if I looked properly; he merely socialized with our friends. He was the flirtatious sort, but only flirtatious.

I could have seen him that way but didn't. Because of his face.

It had changed again, as it had on the dance floor that night. His eyes narrowed and softened, he licked his lips, and his cheeks flushed. He removed his hat and ran his hands through his thick hair.

What have I done?

* * *

Though I feigned tiredness, Herbert joined us for dinner the next evening. It was a quiet dinner with just the family and Herbert. There were no others to socialize with, no other women. It would be a peaceful dinner. At least, I thought it would be.

Mother entered the dining room last. She had chosen her moment of entrance with great care.

Sitting without a word, she acknowledged Herbert's gesture of pulling out her chair with a quiet nod.

I glanced at my father. His rough features twisted as did my thoughts. The answer came quickly.

Mother opened her hand, opened the letter she had folded up in it, and threw it on the table before me.

"I thought we were finished with this nonsense," she said, teeth snapping.

Without picking it up, I could see the distinctive crest of the scrolled lettering within a circle, *RISD*.

My hand flinched, ached to grab it, to read it, to see if they had agreed to a deferred acceptance. My hand moved a few inches and stopped.

"You opened my mail?" I snarled as she had to me.

Mother didn't deny it.

Instead, she glowered at me.

"I thought with all the changes in your life," her eyes flicked at Herbert, "that you had put this silly notion behind you."

"What is it?" Clarence grabbed the letter before I could stop him. Quickly he read it through. He was just as quick to laugh. "You, Pearl, *you're* going to college?"

I had never wanted to slap his dashing, pompous face more than I did in that moment.

I jumped up and around the table, snatching the letter from his clutches.

"I thought one of us should."

I tasted the flavor of nasty on my tongue. A small twinge of regret for having said it pinched me, a very small twinge, passing quickly.

Clarence had flunked out of Yale, though in truth I believe it was what he wanted all along. The real person hurt by it, by my words, was my father. His world overflowed with disappointment, no matter how he tried to pretend it didn't.

"What is this about, Pearl?" Herbert asked when I returned to my seat, a harsh whisper.

I shot my mother a stabbing look. I wanted to have this conversation with him, but at a time of my choosing, in a manner of my choosing. She had ruined that as she did everything else.

I told Herbert about my acceptance, about my mother's insistence that I decline.

"I thought that, well, I thought perhaps as your wife, as a woman of standing in my own right, that I could attend, with your approval, of course." The words rushed from me. I held my breath. I shrugged off the irksome irritation that I must ask for his approval at all.

"Well, that is quite an achievement, Pearl, to be accepted to college," he said amiably with a wide smile. His eyes narrowed ever so slightly, only I could see it. "I thought we were going to travel for a while and, of course, find a home of our own."

"Of course you would," Mother piped in, now she too smiled, a smile of triumph. "That's exactly what you should be doing."

"And, hopefully," Herbert put his arm around my shoulders. His touch was as tender as his voice, "Soon after we are married, we'll start our own family."

My mother clapped her hands together gleefully. My father stared at me. He saw my truth. I saw his dismay. There was nothing either one of us could do for the other. It was a high and thick wall surrounding us, built by those who delimited us.

Herbert continued to regale me with all the wonderful things we would do once we were man and wife. He tenderly talked me out of my plans. I thought I would have been surprised.

I wasn't.

GINEVRA

I packed her trunks as I always did. This year there was no talk of letters, no talk that began, "when I come back...when I see you next." I half expected her to fire me, to banish me from her sight as she had banished me from her heart.

Pearl sat like a stone as I swarmed around her, taking extra efforts to treat her belongings with great care. Without her seeing, I packed the suit dress I had designed and sewn for her during the long hours of the summer we spent apart. The one she loved so much. I didn't want her to see it until she arrived in New York. Without me there, her reaction would come freely, whatever it may be.

I followed Pearl and her trunks, in the arms of James and Charlie, out of the house and to the waiting carriage. I stood on the bottom step. Though she didn't look at me, I stared at her with a pleading gaze. I could have been one of the hobos with their tin cups that I sometimes passed as I walked along Thames Street, so deeply did my mind beg her to look at me, to say something to me.

Without a glance, she took James' hand, put one foot on the lowest carriage step...and stopped.

Pearl turned back. Her gaze fell on me, dropped on me. I saw something, something hopeful. Her lips parted, I waited for a word, any word. None came.

Just as quickly, her face darkened. It closed to me once more.

Pearl got in the carriage and shut the door...shut me out.

It would not be that last look that would warm me through the cold winter, but the one that came before, the one that had brought her a step back to me.

PEARL
July 1900

I was still engaged when we returned that summer, the plans for the wedding, one to rival any of our clique, were in its final stages. The date was set for the end of September, to take place here in Newport.

My sadness at not going to college remained like lint in my pocket.

The number of times I had surreptitiously watched Herbert being flirtatious mounted. But that's all I had ever seen, trifles. Powerful fripperies, if there were such things, effects as clear as the early summer sky.

My father had not raised me to be a fool. I knew in this stratified world, a flirtatious fiancé would more than likely become an adulterous husband. They thought it was their right, part of their birthright, as if their possession of wealth lifted them above the laws of morality. My opinions of such men came from my father, not my mother. Was it for the best? To be a bastion of decency often brought only loneliness and heartbreak in a world where the definition of decency changed as often as women changed their outfits.

It was *my* right to tolerate it or not. On that, I had still not made up my mind even as the date of our nuptials drew ever closer. I had never caught Herbert in an aggressive assault such as the one Ginevra had claimed he made upon her. I had not seen that one either. The opportunities for such disgraceful behavior were far too readily available. Confusion was the blood that pumped through my heart.

Herbert, college, my mother's life, my father's, *this* life. Which life? Ginevra and forgiveness. They were the ghosts that plagued me.

Selfishly, I needed my friend.

As Ginevra helped me unpack, I spoke to her. I had to.

"How...how was your winter?"

She spun as if struck, her lips quivered, her eyes filled with tears. Her body began to shake so much I thought she would fall. I ran to her, helped her to a chair. Ginevra hid her face, her tears, behind her hands. I moved them aside and knelt before her.

I talked to her. I did not talk of what had passed between us; I would not pick at a wound still open.

I talked of trivialities, nothing more than the social events through the winter. I didn't know any other way to start again.

Silence fell on us, we swam in it, our hands clasped, the connection reaching toward our hearts. I almost cried with the joy of it.

"I wrote to RISD, you know, last…last summer." It seemed wrong to speak of that time.

"You did?" Ginevra sat up, wiping her cheeks with her palms, her palms on her skirt. "What did you say?"

"I asked for a deferment."

She cocked her head to the side. "A de-fur-ment?"

She wouldn't know such a word. "Yes, it's when you ask them to hold your place—your acceptance—until you are ready."

"Did they give this?" Ginevra squeezed my hands so tightly my bones crushed against themselves.

Her jubilance was like jumping in the ocean at its warmest point in the summer. I felt terrible to turn it cold.

"They did, but Herb…my fiancé doesn't approve. He has grand plans for us to travel. Perhaps later." I said the words, but I didn't believe them any more than she did.

Ginevra stood and began to put my things away as if she could put away her palpable dejection, her worry. There weren't enough drawers and wardrobes for it all.

I asked her about her own dream, had she been drawing, designing. I told her about finding her gift, the lovely suit dress. I told her how often I had worn it through the autumn.

She dropped her head. I expected bad news.

"I have. A lot in fact."

It was my turn to squeeze her hands.

"Will you meet me beneath our tree tonight? Will you show me?"

She did not speak or could not. She took me into her embrace, and she nodded.

GINEVRA

We sat for hours beneath our beeches. The loneliness I had lived through last summer whooshed away with the wind as it sluiced through the tangled branches and the fluffy leaves.

Pearl studied my sketchbook as if it were the Worth catalog; commenting on what she loved and what she thought could be improved. She experienced my success, my growing talent, as if it were her own. In part, it was.

For a time, we were just...there—in our special place—together. In the united silence, we made our way through the bumpy ground that was rebuilding, not with words, but with being—tender, compassionate being. I would have stayed there the rest of my life if I could.

Pearl would still not admit that Herbert did what he did. I would still not say that he didn't. We put it aside, up on the high shelf of our lives that we would do our best to ignore, to let it gather dust and be forgotten.

I did not say sorry again. She did not speak of forgiveness. We were back together again. It was the best I could hope for; I should have hoped for more.

* * *

My world was clean and new again. Pearl was back in my life. For how long or how deeply, I didn't know. At that time, I didn't care. I saw only the beginnings of a path through prickly thorn bushes.

Pearl's words of encouragement, her complete faith in me and my designs, had given me such inspiration.

The night bell chimed for lights out. I swam too deeply in my inspiration to truly hear it. I left one candle burning as I made more sketches, as I changed the others as Pearl suggested; wonderful suggestions.

"*Whatt*...do you think you ah doing?"

Mrs. Briggs stood in my doorway. I hadn't heard her turn her key, open the door; there was no sound in my world of dresses.

"I...I am..." No matter what I said, it would make no difference. This woman's dissatisfaction with her own life ruled her completely.

"Give me that," she demanded. I clutched it to my chest and took a step backward. She stomped toward me and grabbed the book from my hands, her gnarled fingers turned page after page.

She laughed, at me, at them.

"You will learn to accept your place."

As quickly as she had come, she left. My treasured sketchbook in her hands.

* * *

Morning found me in silent mourning for my work and I could not hide it. Pearl reached out a hand, halting mine as I brushed her hair.

"Whatever is the matter, Ginevra?"

Her face was Pearl's face, my Pearl, though it had changed from a girl's to that of a woman. I told her.

"How dare she!" Pearl jumped from her chair. "Damn that woman."

Before I could stop her, she ran off. I followed. Down the back stairs and into the office Mrs. Briggs shared with Mr. Birch, barging in without a knock.

"You have something belonging to my maid." Pearl stood with hands on her hips, deep red splotches bursting and growing on her pale skin.

"Miss." Mrs. Briggs jumped out of her chair. "I beg your pardon. I wasn't expecting a visit from anyone above stairs."

I almost laughed. Even as Mrs. Briggs stood in the face—the fuming face—of one of her employers, she had to make her displeasure known. It was an unwritten rule, as powerful as the one that prohibited staff from certain parts of the family house, which demanded that Mr. Birch or Mrs. Briggs be informed before a family member came below stairs, as if they needed permission in their own home.

"This is no visit," Pearl snapped, unmoving. "Did you or did you not take something personal belonging to Ginevra?"

Mrs. Briggs' upper lip curled.

They stood toe to toe. Mrs. Briggs said not a word, not of denial or admittance. Clock hands stopped moving. Pearl didn't move, not even a flinch.

Mrs. Briggs moved first. She turned from Pearl, turned to her small desk, unlocked, and opened the top drawer. From there she removed my sketchbook, slapping it in Pearl's already outstretched hand.

We began to turn away. Pearl spun back.

"Never," she hissed, taking a step toward Mrs. Briggs, a sharp finger pointed at the housekeeper's face. "Never take something that belongs to Ginevra, or any of the staff, ever again. I don't care how long you have served this family, I will see you gone, my father will ensure it."

Mrs. Briggs said not a word. Her eyes narrowed to slits. Her lips formed a tight white line on her face.

"And if you punish Ginevra for this," Pearl held up the sketchbook, "or my retrieval of it, the same applies. Am I understood?"

Not a sound.

"I said, am I understood?" Pearl was a gladiator and I her ward. She commanded with mature authority, a magnificent force to behold. If she could only see herself, what might she do?

"I understand you perfectly," Mrs. Briggs finally replied.

Pearl smiled. It was a frightening sight. "Good," she said, hooking her arm in mine. "Come along, Ginevra."

I allowed my savior to lead me away in victory.

PEARL

Mother wouldn't accept my no to it. Once more, she planned a great fete for my birthday. It was the only one in the summer, the only one in the family that could be celebrated in Newport.

Between the engagement party—parties—that were held in our honor, I thought Herbert and I had been celebrated far too much already. I shied from the limelight as quickly and eagerly as my mother ran to it.

With Herbert on my arm, adorned in one of Ginevra's fabulous creations, I stepped hesitantly into the role of guest of honor that night and did my best to enjoy it.

Ginevra was never far away. I saw her peeking in time and time again. We weren't 'us' again, but we were on our way. Could my heart embrace complete forgiveness? Could my life embrace them both in my life?

I deserted these questions, lost them in the magic of the night.

There was magic of both sorts that night, the light…and the dark.

GINEVRA

Each time I slipped out to check on Pearl, she looked happier than the time before. Healing, as slow as it could be, had such power.

The night wore on. I peeked out once more. Pearl danced in the arms of that man. As he led her about, as he spun her around, he saw me. What was that saying? I had just read it in a new book taking the world by storm...*Dracula*, that was it, by a man named Bram Stoker. He coined an expression in that shivering work, and I shivered as I felt it...*if looks could kill*. Such was the look that man aimed at me.

I hurried away from it.

I hurried below stairs. I needed some water. I could barely swallow. I needed to be where there were more people. Such fear and rage did that man bring out in me. I fled toward safety.

I made my way to my father's room hoping he was still up. I found his room empty. I went in search of him, needing his quiet reassurance, but couldn't find him. I made to return upstairs.

That's when *he* found me.

"I don't know why you fight this, fight us," he whispered, it hissed like steam as he grabbed me by my upper arms, pushing me into the shoeshine room.

Herbert Butterworth shook me so hard. His face swam in my eyes. His words thumped in my ears.

"You told her, didn't you? Didn't you?" He shook me harder, pushing me deeper and deeper into the room. "But it did you no good, did it? She will still marry me."

He had pushed me into the darkest corner of the room, up against the stonewall and the metal table before it.

"I know you want me. I see you watching me. I know what I see is—"

"No, you're wrong." I pushed back. He laughed. "I watch Pearl, not you."

Herbert ran his fingers along the line of my jaw. I closed my eyes. "There's no need to lie to me, Ginevra."

His hand dropped to my leg. Groping fingers hitched up my skirts. The other fumbled at his pants.

Though his hands no longer held me, disbelief did. It shackled me.

He leaned against me; his naked flesh rubbed against mine.

"I *will* have you both. I deserve both of you."

They were the last words Herbert Butterworth would ever say.

GINEVRA
1900 Now

Every second is a blur. I stand by the body, the gun—still warm—in my hand. The voices creep towards me as I imagine old age does. There is a moment of escape, escape I could take. I don't. I don't know who had seen what, who had seen Pearl. For her, I stay where I am.

The first voice I hear is that of Mr. Worthington. He's first in the door, but barely. He stops as if struck, punched by the sight before him. His eyes dart from the body, to me, to the gun, to the body, to me.

"Ginevra..." he whispers my name. I'm not sure what I hear in it. Not condemnation. I think it's disbelief. I hang onto that. I know the best thing I can do is tell as much of the truth as I can. The tears I don't have to beckon come on their own.

"He tried...tried to r...rape—"

"Oh, my dear child." Mr. Worthington is by my side in an instant. His arms are around me. In this sympathy, I lose control, the grip I hold so tightly unravels. I collapse against him. Sobs rack my body. I can't embrace him with the gun still in my hand. I let it drop to the floor, metal hits wood with the sound of thunder. I grab onto him. My head spins, my legs tremble beyond stability. I crumble into the man I had respected since the moment I met him. I hide my face in shame. He leads me to a chair.

The other men, the other voices, reach us. Mr. Worthington stands between them and me—a shield.

He leans down to whisper in my ear, "We have to call the authorities, Ginevra."

I knew it as truth, but I'm living—floating—in a dream, a nightmare. I simply nod. I hear the gasps of the men at the door as if I'm at the end of a long tunnel and they stand at the other end.

"Birch, please send someone down to fetch the police, if you would. And ask Mr. Costa to join us." Mr. Worthington raises his hand, punctuates each word with it. "Just to join us, nothing more."

"R...right away, sir." The stalwart Mr. Birch has never sounded so flustered. He closes the door without instruction. A comfort.

The voices on the other side rumble against it, but it's too late, I think. They've all seen, the body, the gun, me. Mr. Birch bellows at them, "Stand back," with all the authority he owns. He owns a great deal of it.

Mr. Worthington crouches down before me. He takes my face by the chin, turning it one way, then the other. I know what he sees, why his face darkens with anger.

"We will make sure the police see this," he says.

I can't look up, but I must tell him. "There...there are other marks...in...other p...places." The tears still flow. My breath hitches between words.

"Oh, my dear," the sweet man lowers his head, drops it into the palm of his hand.

"We will...you will have to make sure they see those as well." He doesn't look up, perhaps he can't.

"I..."

I can't finish. The door opens and my father walks in. With a slowness—a stillness that creeps inside me like the cold wind as it blasts its way through winter—he studies the room, the body, me, the gun. His face is not so tender. I hope fear makes it so.

Papa walks to me. Now he sees my face. Now his changes. It churns with anger.

In Italian, he asks me, "What happened, Ginevra?" his voice quakes.

Mr. Worthington quietly steps away, steps to the door.

As I tell Papa in Italian, I tell him the lie, but even as I do, I wonder if and when I will tell him the truth.

"They've come, Ginevra," Mr. Worthington says, after opening the door to a faint knock. He stands beside us once more. "I will accompany you to the station," he says. "But you must not say very much, Ginevra. All I want you to say is that he attacked you and you defended yourself. When they ask for details, and they will, Ginevra, many, many times, I want you to pretend you don't understand English well. I want you only to say he attacked you and you defended yourself. Do you understand?"

I nod my head. I must act the part I have spent all these years fighting against, the unintelligent immigrant. I quickly whisper to my father all Mr. Worthington said.

"I go too," my father says, one of the few times I hear him speak English in front of Mr. Worthington.

"Of course, Mr. Costa, of course," Mr. Worthington assures him.

The police barge in as if the killing is happening in that moment, blackjacks in their hands. Mr. Worthington quickly says the words he told me to say.

I hear many words, many voices—the police, Mr. Worthington. I'm in the middle of a beehive. The buzzing in my head is a scream. Father asks me to translate but I can't. I can't understand myself. It is all too much.

The cold of the handcuffs is like a slap on my face. It snaps me back, but only for a moment. I realize what they are, what is happening. They take me by the arms. They stand me up. The world turns black.

* * *

I wake up in the cell. The gate isn't closed, isn't locked. My papa and Mr. Worthington are there. They rush to me as they see me wake.

Papa asks if I'm all right. I almost laugh. Instead, I nod my head, and with his hand, I sit up. Mr. Worthington reaches into the inner pocket of his swallowtail jacket. How odd it is to see him in it here. He pulls out a flask, removes the cap, and hands it to me with a quick look over his shoulder. My hands remain cuffed, so he puts it to my lips, tilts it back. I cough and sputter on the fire the liquid sets on my throat. I jut my chin out. I want more. He gives it to me.

Mr. Worthington squats before me, our eyes inches apart.

"I have insisted they take pictures, Ginevra, of your bruises, the marks...," he stumbles, looks up at my father.

"All, Ginevra," my father says. His bottom lip is trembling. The last time I saw his bottom lip tremble was the day we buried my mother. "You must expose, show, all of them."

I look at my father. He can't mean it. I look at Mr. Worthington who nods his head in silence.

"More," I say to him. He puts the flask to my lips, holds it there longer.

All those years I had wanted a photograph taken of me, as the Worthington's did every year. I will finally get my wish. I will suffer another violation to prove I was violated.

* * *

The steel bars clang to a close. I stand in the middle of the cell. My bug-eyed gaze flits from the small cot where I see fleas popping on it, to the damp stone of the other three walls, to the small slit of the barred window, set too high to see anything but sky.

I hold out my arms. They can almost reach from one side to the other. My arms shake as I put them back by my sides. How long will I be in this cell? Will the end of my days dwindle in such a place?

The memory returns. That moment I first stepped foot in my first room at The Beeches.

My legs crumble. My body falls on the infested mattress.

Ingratitude has its way in the end.

I wash as well as I can with the rag and bucket of water they give me. Yet as I put the scratchy wool prison gown once more on my body, I still smell the awful odors. Odors from others who had worn it, perhaps the last thing they wore.

All I think about in this moment are the beautiful dresses Pearl gave me through the years. I think about how wonderful I felt when I wore them. I wonder if I will live to wear them again.

PEARL

I wake. Sweat saturates me. As if his form escapes the prison of my mind, his face hovers before my eyes. I rub them hard, but he will not disperse. I stare at him. His face constantly changes, from the handsome one to the gruesome one, from the seducer to the defiler.

My body shakes with hate and fear. Some of the hate is for myself, for what I did and did not do, for what I believed and what I should have. I brought him into our lives. I didn't listen to her. I allowed myself to be carried off on a journey I knew, in the depths of my heart, was not for me.

I had bitten a piece of Mother's poison fruit and all its false promises, its false life.

I am the guilty one.

As I lie here, I begin to pray, not for me, or him... but for her. *Please, dear Lord, if this specter must haunt me for the rest of my life, I accept it, I welcome it. But please, please save her.*

* * *

"I'm sorry, Miss, I'm not sure I understand you."

Frank Morgan, our chauffeur stands between the carriage door and me, sweltering in a morning sun already set to blister. His aging face, though still handsome, twists and pinches at my choice of destination.

"You do understand me, Mr. Morgan, and you will take me there." I use the voice I had heard so many of the powerful women of Newport use. I channel Mrs. Astor and Mrs. Vanderbilt. "I am a woman of twenty-one years, and you work for me. You will take me where I tell you to."

I have never spoken like this, and though my voice quivers, I refuse denial of my demand.

Mr. Morgan, as ever in his long livery coat and breeches in forest green velvet, his tall top hat, looks up to the main house, looks to see if anyone—my mother—watches us. No one is.

"Very well, miss, to the jail it is." He steps aside, opens the carriage door, and helps me climb in, gently holding the edge of my long black skirt. It is the façade of mourning I must wear. The carriage shakes as he takes his place on the driver's bench. My hands shake as they grip the book I grasp so tightly in my hand. The book I bring to Ginevra.

It is a short journey along the full northern portion of Bellevue Avenue onto Spring Street and around the corner to Marlborough Street. The solid square building looks daunting, frightening, as it should for a jail. Bricks painted white does little to dispel the impression. It stands beside the First Methodist Episcopal Church of Newport. I wonder if those trapped within can see its tall bell tower, if looking at it brings any solace. I hope so.

With Mr. Morgan's help, I step out of the carriage, blinking in the brightness, climb cement stairs with shaking legs, and enter the building. Once more I blink, this time in the murkiness. The foyer is small. A well-locked door stands before me. Just to my right, a barred opening where a uniformed policeman sits on the other side. He looks at me, strangely, but says not a word.

"I am here to see Ginevra Costa," I say with as much surety as I can muster. It isn't much. Now, inside this building, the one housing those who are accused but cannot afford bail, are held till they are put to trial. Its presence of doom invades me. I will not turn back.

"This is no place for a lady like you to be, Miss." The guard rises and looks down his crooked nose at me, face striped by the shadows of the bars.

"It is Miss Worthington," I say, using the power of my name for one of the few times in my life. "She is my lady's maid. I have every right." As I speak, I pucker my lips as I had seen Mrs. Astor do on many an occasion. I discover puckered lips don't quiver as much.

"She murdered your fiancé," he says, bordering on impertinence.

"All the more reason." I'm growling now.

He angers me. How dare he speak to me in such a way?

"Now unlock that door and let me inside." I point, keeping my hand outstretched, waiting for his response. He stares at me, gauging me.

With an unenthusiastic nod, he does as he is told.

He brings me to a small room, three walls of more white brick. The other wall is made of bars and a gate. With obvious reluctance, he opens the gate and gestures in.

"Wait here, Miss," he says, it's a grumble.

Even as a visitor, to be so confined...I squirm, I itch to run. I almost cry thinking of her here day and night, for a week now. I hear the rattle of chains.

She's here. Ginevra stands outside the gate, her hands manacled together by metal cuffs. I bite my lip to stop the tears. I have never seen her so pale; her lovely olive complexion looks yellow. She's so thin, her lovely curves barely discernable. All those years she longed for the slim body so in vogue, she has attained, in the worst possible way. The worn, drab grey prison frock hangs on her like a sack.

The guard frees her hands from their restraints and lets her in, locking the door, locking us in. I rise, move to her, but stop.

"Some privacy, if you please," I say to the guard, still standing just outside the gate.

"Ten minutes, no more," he replies, and moves off, though I think he does not go very far.

I rush to her side, throw my arms about her. Ginevra drops her head on my shoulder.

"You should not be here," she mumbles, sobs, into me.

"There is nowhere else I should be."

GINEVRA

Pearl puts the book down on the scarred wood table between us. I almost laugh, almost.

I smile even as tears pinch the back of my throat. It was the old, tattered version of *Huckleberry Finn*, the book I the first book she used to teach me to read.

"Are you eating, Ginevra? Are they feeding you well?"

Pearl reaches across the table to take my hands. I try to pull away, ashamed of the marks the cuffs put on them, but she holds me firmly.

I nod. "There is plenty of food. I...I don't have much of an appetite."

"Well, you wouldn't, would you," she says.

"Why have you come?" I whisper. How I fear her presence will somehow give the truth away. It must stay hidden, buried as deep as I can bury it.

Pearl pounds me with her stare. "I've come to see my dearest friend. It is the right thing to do." Her eyes tell me her words are for the benefit of those who may be listening.

"How is my father?" I have to ask; unsure I want to hear the answer.

"As well as he can be, I think," she replies. I nod, knowing with my father how hard it is to tell.

"My father spends a great deal of time with him."

My breath hitches on a sob. Such news as this truly helps me. So different, yet so alike, I know my father will find comfort with Pearl's father. It is the best I can hope for him.

Pearl squeezes my hands, still in hers. "He's hired a lawyer for you, Ginevra, one of the best, from New York."

I shake my head. I can't help feeling it is the wrong thing to do. How many difficulties it will cause with the other families, the other important families. "Your mother must be fit to be tied."

Pearl smiles a little, shrugs her slim shoulders. If her mother is angry, Pearl is enjoying it.

"I don't think it will matter. I don't think it will help." Helplessness is all I know.

"It will. It must," she insists.

Her courage, her loyalty, is a never-ending stalwart surprise, a gift.

"I've also come to give you this book. I know how much it means to you." This meaning, this truth, is for me. I hold to it tightly.

With a quick glance to the hall outside our cage, she slips two fingers in the book, pulls out a folded piece of newsprint.

"Look," she whispers, lips barely moving, eyes flitting everywhere.

She opens the book, lays the article on the other side of it, blocks it with the cover, and taps the newsprint. The headline, large and bold, is easy to read. Repeating acts from days of old, we bend our heads over it:

MRS. CRANE OF GAINESVILLE, OHIO, SET FREE ON CHARGE OF MURDER IN SELF DEFENSE.

"They will not believe me as they believed her." I drop my back against the steel chair.

"Why ever not?" Pearl asks sharply, her eyes rove the paper as if the key to my freedom hides on it.

I tut at her hope. Or is it her guilt blinding her?

"I am, was, a servant—"

"A lady's maid." She cuts me off sharply.

"A servant still." I shake her off. "And he was the son of a rich and powerful man. It is my word against that of a privileged ghost. The ghost will win."

* * *

The lawyer and Mr. Worthington sit on the other side of the table from me this morning, waiting.

They wait for me to say something. I don't know what words to use.

In the long hours of confinement, I had rehearsed the story, fixing it here, changing it there, and practicing it so it would make sense without making too much sense.

Now they flee me. At the moment I must say them, they betray me.

"Could I have a drink of water?" I ask, wrangling for time for the studied words to return.

The lawyer, Mr. Fonsworth, beckons the guard. The guard goes grudgingly to fill my request. We wait; they stare at me. I stare at my hands. Glass in hand, cold water sliding down my tight throat, I look back at them.

"I want you to take your time, Ginevra," Mr. Fonsworth says. Old and gray and a bit hunched over, there is, however, something about him that is commanding, fortifying. "But you must give us all the details."

His emphasis on "all" tells me he knows some of the details will be difficult to speak. There is only truth in that.

I begin my tale.

* * *

They stare at me in silence. It is a prod upon my tongue.

"It...it was not like the first time, the first time Mr...he touched...me," my hesitation is not an act; my fear is true. "He—"

"Wait...what?" Mr. Worthington balks.

"This man accosted you before?" this from Mr. Fonsworth.

They look sideways at each other.

"What happened and did anyone see you?" Mr. Fonsworth asks.

I nod. I tell them of that time. I hang my head as all the pain that came after rush back into my memory. There is no need for lies in this tale.

PEARL

I hide around the corner of the jailhouse. As soon as I see my father and Mr. Fonsworth leave, as they get in my father's carriage and pull away, I rush in.

The guard is not pleased to see me, not pleased Ginevra has another visitor. I don't care. I stand with arms folded across my chest, asking him if I should call my father and the lawyer back. He lets me in to see her.

She looks worse than ever. Ginevra tells me she had to tell the "story," the whole story, to them. She tells me how hard it was. She didn't have to. I can see it in her red, swollen eyes, her ravaged face, her hands twisting in her lap.

Ginevra tells me the details of her "story" and the response. I too see where the weak point is. But it's not true.

I'm shaking my head. She's still talking but I'm no longer listening. "I must say something."

Ginevra stood so fast her chair flew over. Her hands are on me before I look up. I hear the guard barreling toward us.

"Say nothing, nothing," she hisses at me. "It is done. I have made the story."

I'm shaking my head. The guard is almost on us.

"Promise me, Pearl," she raises my hands to her, kisses them, "for all that we once were, promise me."

In her eyes, I see all our moments, all her love. I make the promise.

* * *

As I walk home, not caring who may see me leaving the jailhouse, not caring about much save Ginevra, I take no notice of the others strolling about around me. Until I almost walk into them.

A highly ranked married couple. I make my apologies, which they accept with practiced casual grace. We take our leave. I turn and watch them walk away. They smile at each other, laugh with each other. I know they are both having affairs with others. I believe they know it too. Yet they chose to live the lie, chose to live as liars.

The thought stops me. Perhaps it is the choice I must make myself.

* * *

Yet another day I sit across the metal table from her. I come more and more often as the date of the trial draws closer and closer, drawn to her repeatedly. This time she is the strong one as if she came to console me.

I try to speak of silly things, of gossip, the kind we used to laugh at together. I talk of my mother's antics and how terrible she is behaving. It is a foolish attempt at foolish conversation. I find it hard to say what I need to say. At last, the words come.

"I'm so sorry, Ginevra." The tears flow, racking my body. I can do nothing to stop them even if I want to. "My dearest, dearest friend. I should have believed you. For that is what you are...the dearest and truest friend. I shouldn't have..." I cannot finish.

I reach my hand out blindly. She takes it.

"You were in love. Love blinds. I thought I was in love." She hangs her head; something runs up her spine and she shivers. "I saw it with my parents, how blind they were to each other's faults. It is the curse of love, *si*?"

"I love you," I lament, for it is true. I love her as I would love a sister, far more than I love my brother or my mother, and yet I abandoned her at the most crucial moment. I had become one of them, I see it clearly now. The riches, the lifestyle, all they said about us in the newspapers. I let the glittering wave of it carry me away on its golden tide. But the sea was not golden, it was only the reflection of the sun, and the clouds have come out, come to stay.

The guard comes. He tells me I have to leave.

"You are not alone, Ginevra. Please remember. Please know how sorry I am."

Ginevra smiles at me, eyes glisten. "I know, *mia cara amica*, I do know."

The guard shuts the bars between us. In this moment, I realize what I must do.

"I will get you out of here."

Ginevra's face falls. My words reveal too much for she knows me too well.

"Pearl, please do not do…"

I walk away before she finishes.

GINEVRA

Alone again in my cell, my eyes weep silent tears. If not for the bars around me, I could have been back in my room in the hidden floor of The Beeches, crying myself to sleep as I had so many nights. Except this time, they are tears of joy. Pearl's words touch the deepest part of me, the heart that still beats, if too quickly. Her loyalty, her expressions of love—no, not expressions—the truth of her love fills my frightened soul.

Whatever happens to me I will know I lived this life as a true friend, as a person loved. It will have to be enough.

Even as the warmth of dear Pearl's love blankets me, my mind catches on her last words, and I am full of fear.

PEARL
AUGUST 1900

For two months, I relive that night in my dreams. I know I will for the rest of my life.

For almost two months, Ginevra has sat in a cell. Finally, the trial is beginning.

Each day my father, Ginevra's father, and I take the Ferry to Providence. Each day Mother screams at us not to go, not to shame us. Each day we take a carriage to the Customs House on the corner of Weybosset Street. Each day we enter the mean-looking granite building with its metal domed roof to sit and listen, to worry and cringe as the State makes its case against Ginevra. Each day we sit on the hard benches directly behind Ginevra. My presence on her side brings more than one mean-spirited word our way.

The large room reeks of wood, sweat, and desperation. The tall windows sit high up the walls. They're open, but the breeze, what there is of it, doesn't reach us, does little to dispel the heat and gloom.

Anja is called to the stand. I grab the hands of the two men on either side of me. They don't know what I do, that Anja had seen the first assault Herbert had made on Ginevra. They look at me brimming with hopeful excitement as if I am a stranger. It doesn't matter, it is short-lived. The prosecution calls her. I don't realize what that means.

Mr. Tanner, the current Attorney General of Rhode Island, is trying the case himself, no doubt for the notoriety it brings him.

He stands at his table, a hunched back, gray-haired man well into his seventies, yet his eyes burn with intensity and intelligence.

"Miss Schneider, can you tell us what you saw on the evening of July the twenty-seventh of last year at…," he puts his glasses to his eyes, looks at the papers on the desk before him, "…at Rosecliff?"

"Vell, I saw a lot a things that night. It vas party, you know."

The people packing the gallery snicker. The twelve men of the jury do not. The judge bangs his gavel for silence. He gets it.

Mr. Tanner looks over the top of his glasses at Anja. "What did you see—specifically—when you went downstairs at one point?"

Anja squirms. She knows exactly what he wants her to talk about. Everything about her—the slump of her body, the clamped lips—says she doesn't want to. She must.

"It vas dark and I vas in a hurry." Anja tries to preface her tale. I think she does well.

Mr. Tanner is out of patience. "Did you see Miss Costa that night downstairs?"

Anja nods. "I did."

"Was she alone?"

Anja will not go where Tanner wants her to unless he pulls her by a leash.

"No."

"Who was she with?"

"Mr. Butterworth, as vhat vas."

"Did you see them kissing?"

"No."

"Did you see them in an embrace, holding each other?"

"Vell, I saw hem holding her, that iz for sure."

Mr. Tanner moves to the front of the table. He pushes, looks at the men in the jury box, then back to Anja.

"Did Miss Costa call out to you? Did…she…call…for…help?"

His staccato delivery delivers drama; each word pounds her.

Anja shifts in her seat as if she sits on pins. She looks to Ginevra; her eyes fill with tears.

"Your Honor?" Mr. Tanner prods.

"You must answer the question, Miss," the judge instructs Anja.

She shakes her head. "No, she…she didn't call to me, she did not calls out."

A gasp shutters through the courtroom. My hope is dashed.

"I'm done with this witness, Your Honor."

Mr. Fonsworth stands up so quickly Mr. Tanner is not in his seat yet.

"Miss Schieder, do you know the defendant well?"

Anja shrugs. The corners of her mouth twitch. They can go either up or down. "Pretty vell, not as vell as I should." It is her way of apology. I knew it, as did Ginevra, who gives Anja a small smile, as best she can.

"And have you ever known her to be a woman of low morals? A loose woman?"

"No!" Anja yells, slaps her hand on her mouth as she cowers at the judge. "Geenevra iz a lady, a true lady."

"Have you ever known her to dally with any of the men of Newport society?"

Anja is shaking her head before Mr. Fonsworth finishes his question. "No, never. She does not even have a boyfriend, even vith those who vould vant her to be."

Anja puts fisted hands upon the rail before her. They shake as she squeezes.

"Just one more question, Miss." This time it is Mr. Fonsworth who walks around to the front of his table. "On the night in question, you testified that Miss Costa did not call out to you... with words." Here he looks at the jury. "But did she make any gesture towards you?"

"Yes, yes," Anja slips to the edge of her seat. "Her hand, her arm, I saw it, reaching out."

"Reaching out as if for help?"

Mr. Tanner jumps up. "Objection, Your Honor, leading."

Anja doesn't wait for the judge's ruling.

"Yes, for help. She needed help."

The judge bangs his gavel. "Strike that," he yells, turns to the jury. "You will not take that answer into consideration."

What useless words. They heard it; how could they dismiss them from their minds?

"I'm finished with this witness," Mr. Fonsworth says as he retakes his seat.

Father leans down, whispers in my ear.

"It was a good cross-examination," he says, "the best he could do."

I nod. I pray. I know all we need is enough doubt.

Mr. Tanner calls the arresting officer to the stand, Officer Callaghan.

An Irishman, I think bitterly, knowing their feelings about Italians.

Officer Callaghan describes the scene, the gun, and the body at Ginevra's feet. It is damning, especially the last question and answer.

"Did Miss Costa tell you that anyone had seen Mr. Butterworth assaulting her, pushing her into the room?"

"No, Sir," the burly man answers. "I asked her the very same questions. She said no one saw them."

It isn't enough for Mr. Tanner.

"So, in a house—a mansion—filled with guests and servants, not a single person saw anything that took place between them?"

I almost stand up...almost yell out. Only the presence of my father beside me stops me.

"No, not a single soul," the policeman replies.

The men of the jury turn to Ginevra, look at her with hard eyes. I have never felt such frustration.

Mr. Fonsworth stands. "May I approach the witness, Your Honor?"

The judge nods. Mr. Fonsworth moves to the witness stand, the officer in it, with grainy photographs in his hand. I knew what they were, what they showed.

"Have you seen these pictures, Officer Callaghan?"

"I have. I was there when they took 'em."

"What do they show?"

Now the mutton shunter is not so quick to answer, but he must.

"They show the defendant."

He's being pedantic. Mr. Fonsworth will have none of it.

"What does it show about the defendant?"

"It shows her all bruised up."

"Like she had been struck, perhaps more than once?" Mr. Fonsworth asks as he walks to the jury, as he passes the pictures out for them to see. They are repelled. I see it clearly.

"Yes."

"How do you think she suffered these bruises?"

Officer Callaghan shrugs with a sneer. "I don't know. I didn't *see* her get 'em. Maybe she did it to herself. Or maybe she likes that kind o' thing."

"How dare you?" I cry out, my father holds me down. The courtroom erupts again.

Mr. Fonsworth returns to his chair, his body reeks of disgust.

The judge bangs the gavel. "Court is in recess until tomorrow morning at eight."

I cry the entire journey back to The Beeches.

GINEVRA

I sit primly, quietly, just as Mr. Fonsworth told me to do, showed me how to do. It is torture.

To hear me talked about so badly, each word is like the stab of a dagger. I want to jump up, I want to cry out, I want to turn around to my father and tell him not to listen. That he hears these things is the worst thing of all.

I keep my face as blank as I can; it is a great struggle. The other lawyer is finished, he tells the judge on the second day of the trial. It is our turn. It is my turn.

"Are you ready?" Mr. Fonsworth leans toward me, whispers to me.

My anger helps me. I nod repeatedly.

I take the stand. I swear on the Bible. I pray that my lies, that they are to protect another, will be forgiven.

Mr. Fonsworth is tender as he questions me, questions that give my side of the story, my experiences, the first time, and most especially the second.

"How was the second time different?"

"He...he was different. He was mean...angry."

I begin the story.

"I had been upstairs, in the pantry outside the breakfast room. It is done, you see, the maids stay close in case their mistress needs help with dresses and hair." My hands flay about. I know what they say. I drop them into my lap and squeeze. "He...Butterworth saw me, saw me peeking in the ballroom checking on Miss Pearl. Right away he stared at me, angry."

"Why? Why would he be angry at you?" Mr. Fonsworth asks.

"I...I had told Pearl, of the first time. She must have told him." I shrug, trying to shrug away those days from my life. I can't look at Pearl. I know the pain these words cause her.

"Ah, yes, I see. Continue."

"When he saw me, when I saw Pearl no longer need me, I left. I went downstairs for some water, to maybe see my papa. He must have followed me, but I didn't know, didn't hear. My father was not in his rooms. He didn't like it when the house was full of guests. I was on my way back upstairs when…when…" My throat closes. I cannot even will it open.

"It's all right, Ginevra," Mr. Fonsworth reaches out a hand and pats my fisted hands. "We are here to protect you."

His kindness is almost too much. I have to finish. I rush out the rest.

"He pushed me into the shoeshine room. It is the room next to the gunroom. He—"

"You're absolutely positive?" Mr. Fonsworth cuts me off to ask, to accentuate my answer. "Is the gun room immediately next to the shoeshine room?"

"It is. The Worthington's will tell you so."

I hadn't planned it, but the jury turned to look at Pearl and her father. They see their nods.

"Go on, Ginevra," Mr. Fonsworth prods me gently.

The room falls into silence. I fall into its abyss. Somehow it helps. I feel it is just Mr. Fonsworth and me.

"He grabbed me and…and touched me. He said many things, bad things, about me, about Pearl. He ripped my blouse open. The b…buttons flew, popped off. Now I get angry, for what he was doing, for what he has done to us. I start to push back. He grabbed me by the arms," I show them, crossing my arms so each hand can grab the top of the opposite arm, "and he shook me, shook me so hard, it was…I lost my breath. He yelled at me, told me I was nothing, yelled at me to just do what he wants. He threw me against hard stonewall, banging my head. The pain…it makes me angrier. I pushed back. I kicked him, very hard. He let go and I ran out the door."

I stop for a minute. I am breathing very fast. Tears drop on my lap. I wipe my face.

The worst is coming, the middle of the story that never happened.

He followed very fast, too fast, pushing me into the next room, the gun room. It was a mistake, yes. For both of us. I grabbed a gun and he laughed at me. Telling me I would not shoot him, that I was a coward. I...I held the gun to his face, tell him to get away from me.

"With his face to me, he backed out of the room. Out the door, he walked backward, in front of the door to the shoeshine room. I wanted him to go the other way, toward the kitchen. I—"

Mr. Fonsworth holds up a hand, "How far away is the kitchen from where you are?"

I lift one shoulder and close my eyes to think. "It is after the big laundry room that is after the gun room."

"And was anyone in the kitchen?"

"Yes, many, but they were very, very busy. Rushing in and out. Lots of cooking."

"Did you cry out to them? Did you cry for help?"

"I...yes...no, I didn't. But...but we were yelling so loud at each other. They didn't hear. They couldn't. I could hear banging of pots and pans and trays over our yelling. The house was filled with noise."

It is the weak part of my defense. They had told me so the first time I told them my story. I do my best to stress just how noisy it was.

"I yell at him to get away, to go, but he doesn't. Then...then..." I shake my head, "I don't know what happened, all went very fast. He grabbed my arm, my wrist, the one with the gun. He twisted me around, my arm and the gun are behind my back. Pushed me...he pushed me, back into shoeshine room. We moved so fast, almost running, we slammed into table, hard against my legs." I can't talk fast enough. I want to vomit it out. "My legs, the pain is like fire. He put his other hand on the back of my head and slammed it down on the table, marble table, bending me over. I get dizzy. He let my head go. I felt his hand fumbling...f...fumbling with his pants, pulling up my skirt. He squeezed...clawed my...my..." The pain, the humiliation of this mostly true moment rushes at me. I feel the gagging fear, the help-lessness. I want to scream, to run, just as I did then.

"Your buttocks," Mr. Fonsworth helps me.

I nod. "It feels...it felt like he was tearing my skin. But my hand...my hand..." I reach it out as if the gun is there, "my hand is still holding the gun. When he squeezed me…I…I squeezed it!" I yell the last words, blasting them like the shot of a gun; they tumble away into a horrifying silence.

Mr. Worthington's eyes are moist. His are not the only ones.

Mr. Fonsworth looks at me. "I am so very sorry, my dear."

He believes me, as does Mr. Worthington and my father. So much of it is true that they can. I look at the jury.

O Dio mio let them believe me, for her.

We reach the end. My face is dripping with tears. The judge gives me his handkerchief. I nod my thanks, wipe my face, and my nose. I feel raw and naked. I am as violated with the telling as I was with the doing.

It is the other lawyer's turn. I twist and squeeze the judge's handkerchief in my lap. My nails dig into my own hands. I must keep my emotions there. I cannot let the jury see too much of my anger, the fury that burns my blood. Mr. Fonsworth advised me not to let it show. I can feel the heat pumping through me.

Mr. Tanner stands up. His first question is an arrow pointed straight at my heart.

"You testify that you told your mistress about the first incident with Mr. Butterworth. What was her response?"

I want to hang my head, shake it, turn away. I can do none of those things.

"She did not believe me."

I glance quickly at Pearl. Her body curls forward, tears wet her face as her father puts an arm around her shoulders. It is as painful for her to hear as it is for me to say.

"Isn't it true that you didn't want to be a maid?" Mr. Tanner looks down at the papers in front of him. "That you wanted to design clothing?"

Damn Mrs. Briggs.

"Yes. Who does not want for better?"

"Your Honor?" Mr. Tanner looks to the judge, who looks down at me.

"Just answer the questions, Miss, nothing more."

I nod.

"You wanted more than better, didn't you?" The old man with the mean face walks around to the front of his desk, takes a step toward me. "You wanted Miss Worthington's life, Miss Worthington's fiancé?"

"No!" I yell.

The judge bangs his gavel; Mr. Tanner doesn't stop.

"And everything that happened between you was consensual…you agreed to it, wanted it? That's why you didn't cry out when you saw Miss Schieder, why you never cried for help."

"No! No!" My voice, so loud, so harsh, carries over the banging.

Mr. Tanner is yelling now. "Herbert Butterworth wanted it to stop. He didn't want you any more…," he raises his voice even higher, "…and that's why you killed him, isn't it?"

"No!" I jump up as I scream. "I didn't want him, not ever. I shot only to stop him, to save myself, not to be r…raped. I would never have done that to Pearl."

The judge yells at me to sit down, to be quiet. I refuse.

"She is more than my mistress, my employer, she is my dearest friend!"

"Enough!" the judge screams now. The courtroom is shocked silent.

I look at the faces of the men in the jury. I don't know if they hear my words or only see my anger. There is no sympathy in their faces, their hard eyes.

"I'm done with this witness, Your Honor," Mr. Tanner says, walks to his chair, and sits down. He looks very pleased with himself.

"You are dismissed," the judge says.

I can barely walk from the chair. I almost fall as I step down. I can barely see through my tears. I stumble to my chair beside my lawyer. He says nothing but takes my hand. He doesn't look at me.

PEARL

We stand outside the courthouse waiting for a carriage to take us to the ferry. My father and Mr. Fonsworth whisper to each other. Their efforts to keep me from hearing are useless.

"I don't know if Ginevra's testimony helped her case or hurt it," Mr. Fonsworth murmurs.

"She seemed to give the right responses," Father says.

The lawyer nods, "But it was the way she said them. I told her to keep her emotions under control."

"And just how was she to do that?" I charge my way into their conversation, a soldier on a battlefield. "She was almost violated and that…man implied that she wanted it, that she killed Herbe…him in cold blood. Should she have been a meek and mild woman succumbing to whatever is said to her?" Outrage fuels my tongue.

My father rubs my arm, "No, my Pearl. But when a jury sees such emotion, such anger, it is easier to believe the things she's accused of."

"It makes no sense," I cringe.

"No, it doesn't, Miss Worthington, but it is the truth," Mr. Fonsworth tries to calm me. "What we need is someone to speak on her behalf."

"But there's no o—" Father begins.

"I will speak for her," I say, I declare.

"Pearl!" Father yelps. "You cannot—"

The carriage pulls up. I make for it. "Later, Father," I say, get in the carriage, and sit back. The discussion, here and now, is over.

GINEVRA

The cell in the Providence jail is even smaller than the one in Newport. Other women cry, scream, and beg for help. It wells up all around me. I try to cover my ears with the thin, stained pillow, but it doesn't work. I hear their pain as loud as I hear my own.

"You have a visitor," the guard says with pure displeasure.

I uncover my head. My father stands on the other side of the bars.

There is no visitor's room here. We speak through the bars. I run to them, to him, as much as I can. His hands cover mine as they grip my cage.

"Why have you come, Papa?" I ask him in Italian. I want no one to hear our words. "You shouldn't be here, shouldn't see me... like this."

Papa stares at me as if he's never seen me, as if he's seeing me for the first time. He struggles with words, struggles with emotions, as I have never witnessed.

"I came..." his voice cracked and caught, "...I came to say I am sorry."

I flinch in surprise. "You? You are sorry? For what, Papa?"

He hangs his head, even as he still holds my hands, hangs it so low it falls between his long arms.

"I was not the father I should have been." He looks up. A single tear trails slowly down his face. "I should have watched out for you more... better."

I realize he had just heard the story of what happened to me, the true parts... a father hearing how a man abused his daughter. It is a thing that should never happen to any father.

"Oh, Papa, it was not your fault," I say, I mean it. "Please do not blame yourself. There was nothing you could have done to stop it."

"I could have kept you home. We should have stayed in Italy."

I shake my head, a pendulum. "If we had, I wouldn't have lived in such luxury. I wouldn't have met Pearl, wouldn't have all she has given me."

Papa's head pops up. "What? What has she given you?"

I smile. I tell him of the years beneath the beeches, of the many nights of magic there. I tell him of my dream of being a designer, how many of Pearl's clothes are my creations, how she has let me believe I can be what I dream to be.

Papa is tearful again, but I can see it comes from my happiness, and his gratitude.

"Whatever happens, Papa, I will always love you. Always love you for bringing me here."

His arms reach through the bars, and he holds me as best he can. It's the best he ever has. It's all I need.

PEARL

Long past the time when I should have been asleep, long past the time the house has gone to sleep, I slip out of my room.

I check, but my father is not in his bed. I didn't expect him to be.

On the pads of my bare feet, I walk down the cold marble stairs to his library. He stands in the middle of the room, directionless, yet so elegant in his velvet smoking jacket, one that accentuates his broad shoulders—shoulders I have stood on the whole of my life. I will remember him looking like this.

"Can't sleep either, Father?" I disturb his reverie.

He turns, looks at me for a long time without saying a word.

"No," he finally says, walking toward me, "I can't sleep. I can't sleep because of you. Why must you take the stand? What can you say other than she is your friend, was a good worker? Why, my Pearl?"

Even now, as my actions disturb him so, I am still "his Pearl." The question I had been asking myself since we left the courthouse earlier is answered. My decision is made.

"I think you should sit down, Father."

He stares at me a moment and then sits in his high-backed, winged chair by the window.

I sit on the ottoman before him.

I tell him everything, not the story of Herbert that he's heard all along, but the real story.

As I tell him, his face turns red, purple. His hands clench into fists. Every muscle in his body becomes stiff and rigid. By the end, he is shaking. If Herbert were still alive, Father would kill him.

"We have to fix this."

"No," I shake my head, "*I* have to fix this."

GINEVRA

As soon as the judge takes his seat, Mr. Fonsworth stands up.

"Your Honor, I call Miss Pearl Worthington to the stand."

I spin in my chair. I want to jump from it to stop her. I don't know what she's going to say, and the fear sickens me.

The courtroom buzzes like bees in a nest disturbed.

Pearl stands and passes through the swinging gate on her way to the stand.

"Pearl, don't, please." The words fly from my mouth.

"Quiet, please." The judge bangs his gavel, his eyes on me. Pearl gives me a small smile over her shoulder as she continues forward. She's wearing the suit dress I designed and made for her. She takes the oath.

Mr. Fonsworth asks her all about me, about our relationship. Pearl, as calm as I've ever seen her, answers with brightness and command, no one can question the truth of her words, of us.

"Thank you, Miss Worthington," Mr. Fonsworth says. "You may step down."

Pearl doesn't move, instead, she says, "Don't you want to know what I saw that night?"

The court gasps as one, a wave barreling onto the beach.

Mr. Fonsworth is confused, and it shows. He didn't expect this from her. He recovers quickly.

"*Did* you see something that night?"

Where there was none for the near hour he questioned her, there are tears now. They are as real as she is.

"I saw Herbert, I saw him. I followed him following Ginevra below stairs." She stops. My stomach heaves into my throat.

"I saw him push her up against the wall, I saw him forcing kisses on her."

Quietly, Mr. Fonsworth prods her for more. "What was Miss Costa doing?"

"She…she was pushing him away, telling him to stop."

Pearl is reliving it. I can see it in her eyes. I can see her pain.

"What did you do then?"

I can't breathe. I pull on the high collar of my gray prison dress but still can't find any air.

Pearl hangs her head, covers her face with one of her hands.

"I walked away. I was so ashamed, so humiliated by his behavior. I was in shock. But only for a few minutes." She's sobbing now. As he did with me, the judge pulls out his handkerchief from beneath his robe and hands it to her.

"I started going upstairs, to get my father, to get Ginevra help. But…but halfway up the servants' stairs, I heard the gunshot. For a few moments, I was afraid to go and look, I didn't know who would be shot, who may be dead."

Pearl raises her head, looks squarely at the jury.

"I feared most that he had killed Ginevra. Before I could move again, my father and a great group of men, overtook me on the stairs, got to the room before me. I couldn't see. I heard Ginevra's voice and knew she was alive. I felt such relief."

Mr. Fonsworth knows the whole courtroom is spellbound. He asks his next questions very slowly.

"Do you believe Mr. Butterworth deserved to be dead?"

Mr. Tanner is on his feet. "Objection, Your Honor."

Before the judge can speak, Mr. Fonsworth does.

"Withdrawn." He looks at Pearl once more. "Do you believe Miss Costa killed Herbert Butterworth in self-defense?"

Pearl turns to me, bestows a tearful smile upon me. "Absolutely. I have no doubt of it whatsoever."

The room explodes. People are on their feet, yelling for Pearl, against Pearl and her words, for and against my innocence.

The judge is banging on the gavel so hard I think he's going to break it.

"Fonsworth, Tanner, to the bench," he yells above the ruckus.

They stand before him. He whispers, but not soft enough. Those of us closest, Pearl and me, can still hear him.

"Mr. Tanner," the judge directs his words to the Attorney General, "do you want the case to go to the jury, or do you wish to retract the charge? Between the pictures and Miss Worthington's testimony, a highly regarded witness, I'm not sure if you have a case. At least not one free of doubt."

Every gaze in the now silent courtroom watches as Mr. Tanner stares at the all-male jury. He can see how they are looking at me, at Pearl. Yes, they are all men, but they are all merchants and townies, they are the registered voters of Newport. The aristocrats are New York citizens and so not allowed to serve, though Pearl told me some had tried. He stares at them for a long time. It feels as long as I have lived in a prison cell. He turns back to the judge.

"Drop the charges, Your Honor."

I drop my head to the table. I can't control my sobbing. I feel a hand on my shoulder, look at it, know it as my father's, and grab on to it to keep me from fainting away.

Once more, the judge bangs his gavel.

"The charges against Miss Costa in the matter of the State of Rhode Island versus Miss Ginevra Costa have been dropped by Attorney General Tanner." The judge turns his pale blue eyes on me. For the first time, I feel he looks at me as a human being. "You are free to go, Miss Costa. This court, and all its officers, apologize to you for the hardship it has caused you and your family."

PEARL

As two pairs of fathers and daughters, we return to The Beeches together. For the entire journey home—the carriage ride, the ferry ride—I refuse to let go of Ginevra's hand, her father keeps the other for himself.

We don't talk much. What is there to say? What do people say in the wake of a hurricane? There is wreckage, but there is survival. One will haunt us for the rest of our lives. We can only hope the other, the survival, will someday overcome the haunting.

"I'm guessing you could do with a good meal, Ginevra?" My father breaks the taut silence. We all laugh, if only a little. "You will dine with the family tonight, you and your father."

For all my father has done for Ginevra, for Mr. Costa—the cost of the lawyer, the daily absence from his own business affairs—this is by far the most tender thing he can do for them. It is a great honor few servants ever experience.

I squeeze Ginevra's hand harder. She smiles softly at my father and gives a small, simple nod of her head.

We dock in Newport and enter another carriage, our carriage with Mr. Morgan on the reins. As we turn onto Bellevue Avenue, we see them.

People are rushing south, away from the town center, toward the cottages. Hundreds of them, clogging the avenue.

"What is going on here?" Father sits forward, sticks his head out the carriage window. It is the worst thing he can do.

They see him. The yelling starts as well as the cheers. As in the courtroom, the world seems divided by support for Ginevra and against her.

"Newspapers," Mr. Costa says. He understands first. I have no time to be amazed by his English. "They follow them."

As we come up to our cottage, we can barely make the turn into our drive, so many people stand before it. Among them, lots of men with notebooks, and many more with cameras. It is as Mr. Costa knew it to be.

Mr. Morgan drops us at the door, and we rush in, hoping to get away from the madness. Instead, we entered it.

"What have you done?" Mother's screech fills the marble foyer.

She is as I've never seen her, hair unpinned and unruly, sticking out in all directions, clumped where she's tangled it with hands fisted to white. Her morning dress is in remnants, blouse hanging out of her skirt in places, top buttons no longer in existence, skirt creased in bunches, twisted and gripped. She runs at me, grabs me, shakes me.

"You have ruined us, ruined us forever!"

I can't speak, can't breathe.

"Leave her alone!" my father yells, steps between us, pulls Mother off me by her shoulders.

"She has ruined us!" she still cries out, pelting my father's face with her spittle. "Why did she do it? Why did she say those things?"

"Because they are true," Father says calmly as if it will help. It doesn't.

Mother shakes him off, stumbles round in a vortex of confusion and anger. Her hands twist once more in the nest of her hair.

"She didn't have to say it, she didn't have to speak. The girl is nothing but a servant."

Mr. Costa flies up the five marble stairs from the door foyer to the grand one. He frightens me with his quickness, with his rage.

"She is my daughter. She is innocent girl."

He slaps my mother into silence by the force of his emotions. She staggers back from it.

We wait, the four of us, wait to see what she will do, what other horrid things she will say to us. I never expected it.

Suddenly calm, eerily calm, Mother steps to me, locks her eyes with mine. In a voice I don't recognize, she speaks to me, and only me.

"You are dead to me."

GINEVRA
SEPTEMBER 1900

For days, weeks, we hole up inside the house. We can't go out. The crowds won't leave. Every day there are more of them, more newspapermen and photographers. If they even glimpse someone in a window, anyone, the bulbs flash like summer heat lightning.

The staff complains constantly to Mrs. Worthington, who screams at them; to Mr. Worthington, who tries to convince them it will all die down, to give it time. But they can't do their jobs. Those who are married and live in the small houses just outside the wall can't get in. Delivery carriage drivers whip the people back in order to make their way past the gate.

Life—all our lives—are in limbo, neither coming nor going. Days stretch out endlessly before us. I hear the Worthington's fighting about leaving, about returning to New York. Mrs. Worthington screams for it. Mr. Worthington will not run away.

"I have never been, nor will I ever be, a coward," he tells her.

Days and nights blur, turn to weeks without notice.

Pearl and I can't even go to our trees, not in the daylight. The south wall is too low. They line up, three rows deep, just waiting for a glimpse of anyone.

We read together in her room. I help below stairs. My guilt for what they are all suffering makes me do it. Most are so much kinder to me now. I sniff at the irony. I must suffer violation, almost hung as a murderer, in order to gain their respect, their kindness. I no longer want it. Only Mrs. Briggs stays true to herself. She hates me more than ever. I don't care.

I creep up to my room, having spent hours in the kitchen, helping Chef Pasquale, helping the kitchen maids clean up until the room sparkles like new. I exhaust myself. It's the only way I can sleep.

I open the door to my room. Even without lighting a lamp, I see the piece of paper on my bed. I rush to it, grab it, read it.

Pack your things, say goodbye to your father, and meet me beneath the beeches. P

I stand there for a long time. I read it over and over. I know what it means but am unsure what it means to me. Words tumble in my head like the small rocks at the beach pulled forward and backward by the surf. At last, one word speaks louder to me, the loudest of all.

Freedom.

* * *

I enter Papa's room, my bulging bag in my hand.

He sits at his desk facing outward, toward the door, toward me, as if he is waiting for me, waiting for this moment.

I take a step in. Papa stands and takes a step toward me.

I drop my bag and rush into his open arms.

We stand there for the length of a life, for the embrace may have to last us that long.

"I will write to you, Papa, all the time," I sob against his still firm chest. He squeezes me tighter.

"I may not have shown it," he says in Italian, kissing the top of my head, kissing my cheek, more kisses than he has ever given me, "but you are the greatest joy of my life."

I can't leave him, I can't.

The words in my head torture me. He has no one without me. Or does he? For the first time, I am grateful for what I saw between him and Mrs. O'Brennan. I pray there is something real for him there. I can't bear the thought of him alone.

"You will bring me greater joy; I know you will." Papa steps back, but only a few inches, gazes deeply into my eyes, eyes that are so like his. "You will do great things, live a great life. There is no greater joy for any parent."

I pull him to me again; sob again, knowing I have to leave, have to rush away from this pain.

I do, somehow, I do.

I'm at the door. I look back. I have to.

Papa is smiling. I will remember him that way always.

I turn.

"Ginevra?"

He stops me. I turn back.

"Your mother would be so proud of you."

Somehow, I smile past my tears. I nod with wrenching gratitude.

It was the best thing he could have said to me.

PEARL

It is almost three months since I killed my fiancé. Most nights I wake in a sweat. The dreams are so real, the visions keep repeating that moment again and again.

I don't remember why I chose that night, that moment—of all the moments I watched him, wondered about him—to follow him. It was as if something compelled me to do so.

I snuck behind him, on tiptoes so my heels would not clatter, holding my skirt up and close so that it would not whoosh. I was so quiet I heard him—heard them—too easily. I followed their sounds, his repulsive anger, her mewling. Or did she moan? I snuck my head around the threshold of the shoeshine room.

They were plastered together. His hands, his lips, were on her. She touched him, my Herbert. He pulled at her skirt, at his pants. She didn't seem to fight. Dizziness, nausea overtook me. I swayed barely able to stand on my feet. My vision blurred through the lens of tears, tricking me for a moment. But only a moment.

"I will have you both."

I heard Herbert's words as if he stood at one end of a very long tunnel, and I at the other. I emerged from the mist.

From hating Ginevra, I could think only of saving her. I think I became someone else. I remember little of the minutes, the seconds after I saw them, saw him.

Somehow, I moved to the gunroom and put a pistol in my hands. Someone, some part of me, went back to the shoeshine room, back to the nightmare.

In the time it takes the eye to blink, to put finger to trigger, I raised the gun and began to squeeze. My hand swayed; I closed my eyes. I fired the gun without aim. Someone, a dark part of me, fired the gun without a moment's hesitation.

PEARL

With two heavy cases, one in each arm, I slip down the marble stairs. I don't look back to my room, to the pink and green loveliness that had watched me grow, heard me laugh and cry. It is only a place. they are only things. I will have my own.

The sleeping house watches me as I slip down the ground floor gallery, toward the Conservatory and its door to the terraces. I hear the gurgle of the fountains I love so much. I will miss the sound greatly. It gave me peace when there was little for me to find elsewhere.

"Do you have any money?"

The voice jumps out at me from the dark corner. I drop my bags with a yelp. I inch forward.

I see my father in the dim light of the moon streaming through the glass walls.

"How...how did you know?"

My father chuckles as he stands up, as he comes to stand before me.

"Because I know my Pearl. I know what she wants, what she dreams of, what she deserves."

I throw myself into his arms as I had throughout my life. I pray silently that this is not the last time I will feel his strength around me.

Father puts his lips to my forehead, leaves them there as the clocks tick, as the fountain runs. I close my eyes to the feel of it.

I don't know how many minutes later—is it really only minutes—when Father pulls back, reaches into his pocket, and pulls out a pouch. He takes my hand and places in it my palm. I can feel a thick roll of bills, I can only imagine of what sort.

"Go, my Pearl," he says, once more in our embrace. "Go show the world what my Pearl can do."

They were the best words I could hear. They give me the strength to release him, to release this life and head for the new.

"I will, father, I promise you."

I pick my bags up again and head for the door. He stops me with his words.

"No matter where you go, no matter what you do, you will always be my Pearl…always and forever."

I turn back to him. I see his tears match my own.

"I will be, Father…always and forever."

GINEVRA

"Pearl!" I hiss as she finally enters our place beneath the beeches. Though I hadn't been waiting long, it felt too long.

She drops her bags, throws herself in my arms.

"Are you ready?" she asks.

"Yes...no...yes...ready for what?"

Pearl pulls back. I can see her shining face in the patches of moonlight the beeches allow to reach us.

"Are you ready to live?"

I laugh. I can't help it. I have followed this glorious woman for the majority of my life. I would follow her anywhere.

"*Si*, yes, I am. I am ready to live. But how? Doing what?"

Pearl struts a circle around me, twigs snap beneath her feet, leaves flutter, disturbed by the short train of her dress. They lift up into the breeze, fly away free.

"I am going to college, to the Rhode Island School of Design." she smiles mischievously. "And so are you."

"Me?" I gape at her. "Me? In a college? Where?"

Pearl runs to me. Grabs me again.

"Why, to the very same college. They teach art, Ginevra, all forms of art. Sketching, drawing, painting...and fashion!"

"No!" I can't believe her words, for the first time in our lives.

"Yes!" she cries.

"But...but how will we pay for it...how will we live?"

Pearl pulls out a pouch and hands it to me. I can feel the thick wad of money in it.

"We have this from my father," she tells me, even as she's reaching into her reticule. She pulls out another pouch. This one jangles. "And we have this from my mother."

She puts that one in my other hand. I bounce it on my palm; the tinkling of jewels matches the twinkling of the stars. I look up at her. At the same time, laughter blurts from us.

Together we look up, look around. I know, like me, she is remembering all our times here. I know she is thinking the same as me...all our dreams, those we talked of for hours here, are just a few steps away.

"You saved me, Ginevra," she whispered as I would in church.

Even in the dark, her confusion is clear to see. "No, Pearl, you saved me."

I kick the ground. I know how I had saved her. What she had done for me was different.

I turn. We stand face to face.

"No, Ginevra, you saved me from becoming my father."

I gasp with understanding. Pearl was never going to be like her mother. She would have lived a life of looking the other way, waiting home alone at night and wondering, of knowing the truth and all its pain, with little to do about it. As her father did, as he may continue to do.

We pick up our bags and take them.

PEARL

"To the ferry, if you please, Mr. Morgan," I say to our driver. He looks anything but pleased. He will do as I say. "We'll get the train in Fall River," I whisper to Ginevra. I want none of the servants to know. My mother can't find out.

We climb into the carriage. It begins to turn away.

Together we look back as we pull away from The Beeches, my summer home, the only home Ginevra has known for the last six years.

We stare at it. That's when we see; that's when we hear.

My father stands in the Conservatory still, as still as the statues surrounding him. Even in the dimness, we can see his eyes never leave the carriage. I know they won't until he can't see it, see us, at all.

On the warm night breeze, we hear the sound. The mournful, beautiful sound of a violin.

GINEVRA

We are two young women, dressed much alike in the simple clothes of a shopgirl. We look like the sisters we have become.

Sitting across from each other, I snicker as Pearl rubs her fingertips together, an automatic reaction to the grubbiness of seats in lower class, not the private car she has always been accustomed to.

Her nose crinkles.

I laugh. I can't help it. "It will be dirtier and smellier out there, out in my world."

Her gaze catches mine and holds. I know I smile. I feel it all over my face. I see her own smile born on her lips grow in her eyes.

Pearl slumps down, wiggles her way deeper into the shabby chair. "Sounds wonderful."

Our laughter is lost in the whistle of the train as it pulls away from the station.

THE BEGINNING

Dear reader,

We hope you enjoyed reading *Gilded Summers*. Please take a moment to leave a review, even if it's a short one. Your opinion is important to us.

Discover more books by Donna Russo Morin at https://www.nextchapter.pub/authors/author-donna-russo-morin

Want to know when one of our books is free or discounted? Join the newsletter at http://eepurl.com/bqqB3H

Best regards,
Donna Russo Morin and the Next Chapter Team

The story continues in:
Gilded Dreams by Donna Russo Morin

To read the first chapter for free, please head to:
https://www.nextchapter.pub/books/gilded-dreams

Author's Note and Acknowledgements

It has been a life-long pleasure to live in the shade of these magnificent mansions, to mark and celebrate some of the major moments of my life in glorious Newport, Rhode Island, and to play with my children—now grown men—beneath the beeches.

The Beeches as rendered here is, in fact, The Elms, the summer 'cottage' of Mr. and Mrs. Edward Julius Berwind of Philadelphia and New York. Designed by Horace Trumbauer under the direction of the Berwinds to model it after the French Chateau d'Asnieres outside Paris, The Elms construction was completed in 1901 for a cost of $1.4 million dollars. Its interior and exterior have been depicted with detailed accuracy under the auspices of The Beeches. However, the Berwinds, for all that history has recorded them, are nothing like the inhabitants of The Beeches.

The interesting lifestyles, including those concerning love, marriage, and the suffrage movement have also been depicting in accordance with historical records. And while there have been famous murders committed among the rich and mighty in this community, none took place in this era, among these specific people.

Loving Newport as I do, I have been a member of the Newport Preservation Society for many years, attending some of the most informative, inspiring, and enjoyable events in these glorious mansions.

I am indebted to the Society for all their support and collaboration on this book, as well as to the Newport Historical Society.

As I have with every book I've ever written, many of the characteristics of many of the characters are based on family, friends, and myself. This book is no different. Felice Costa is based on my paternal grandfather, Michele Galiano Russo. My grandfather was, in fact, a violin/viola player and maker who came to this country, just as Felice did. One of his violas is on exhibit at the Smithsonian Institute. Though he passed from this realm to the next when I was only eight years old, I have heard many lovely tales of this tall, quiet man. Among them is that he often played in Newport and for the very rich. There is a breakfront exactly matching the description of the one in this book residing within my grandfather's descendants. We have been able to trace it as having once resided in Newport; exactly how it came to be in our family is still a mystery.

To my grandparents, I applaud you for the courage to make the hazardous journey, to create lives in a new land, and to make my birthplace a land where dreams belong to those who believe and work hard, as they taught me to do. I will be forever grateful.

And to Grandpa... I hope you played for me.

It has been a life-long pleasure to live in the shade of these magnificent mansions, to mark and celebrate some of the major moments of my life in glorious Newport, Rhode Island, and to play with my children—now grown men—beneath the beeches.

The Beeches as rendered here is, in fact, The Elms, the summer 'cottage' of Mr. and Mrs. Edward Julius Berwind of Philadelphia and New York. Designed by Horace Trumbauer under the direction of the Berwinds to model it after the French Chateau d'Asnieres outside Paris, The Elms construction was completed in 1901 for a cost of 1.4 million dollars. Its interior and exterior have been depicted with detailed accuracy under the auspices of The Beeches. However, the Berwinds, for all that history has recorded them, are nothing like the inhabitants of The Beeches.

The interesting lifestyles, including those concerning love, marriage, and the suffrage movement have also been depicting in accordance with historical records. And while there have been famous murders committed among the rich and mighty in this community, none took place in this era, among these specific people.

Loving Newport as I do, I have been a member of the Newport Preservation Society for many years, attending some of the most informative, inspiring, and enjoyable events in these glorious mansions. I am indebted to the Society for all their support and collaboration on this book, as well as to the Newport Historical Society.

As I have with every book I've ever written, many of the characteristics of many of the characters are based on family, friends, and myself. This book is no different. Felice Costa is based on my paternal grandfather, Michele Galiano Russo. My grandfather was, in fact, a violin/viola player and maker who came to this country, just as Felice did. One of his violas is on exhibit at the Smithsonian Institute. Though he passed from this realm to the next when I was only eight years old, I have heard many lovely tales of this tall, quiet man. Among them is that he often played in Newport and for the very rich. There is a breakfront exactly matching the description of the one in this book residing with my grandfather's descendants. We have been able to trace it as having once resided in Newport; exactly how it came to be in our family is still a mystery.

To my grandparents, I applaud you for the courage to make the hazardous journey, to create lives in a new land, and to make my birthplace a land where dreams belong to those who believe and work hard, as they taught me to do. I will be forever grateful.

And to Grandpa...I hope you played for me.

About the Author

Donna Russo Morin is the internationally bestselling author of ten multi-award-winning historical novels including **GILDED DREAMS: the Journey to Suffrage,** the sequel to **GILDED SUMMERS**.

Her other award-winning works include **PORTRAIT OF A CON-SPIRACY: Da Vinci's Disciples Book One** (a finalist in *Foreword Reviews BEST BOOK OF THE YEAR,* hailed by Barnes and Noble as one of *'5 novels that get Leonardo da Vinci Right'),* **THE COMPETITION: Da Vinci's Disciples Book Two** (EDITOR'S CHOICE, Historical Novel Society Review), and **THE FLAMES OF FLORENCE,** releasing as #1 in European History on Amazon.

Her other titles include **THE KING'S AGENT,** recipient of a starred review in *Publishers Weekly,* **THE COURTIER OF VERSAILLES** (originally released as **The Courtier's Secret**), **THE GLASSMAKER'S DAUGHTER** (originally released as **The Secret of the Glass**), **and TO SERVE A KING.** She has also authored, **BIRTH: ONCE UPON A TIME BOOK ONE**, a medieval fantasy and the first in a trilogy.

A twenty-five-year professional editor/story consultant, her work spans more than forty manuscripts. She holds two degrees from the University of Rhode Island and a Certificate of completion from the National Writer's School. Donna teaches writing courses at her state's most prestigious adult learning center, online for Writer's Digest University, and has presented at national and academic conferences for more than twenty years. Her appearances include multiple HNS conferences, Writer's Digest Annual Conference, RT Booklovers Convention, the Ireland Writers Tour, and many more.

In addition to her writing, Donna has worked as a model and an actor with appearances in Showtime's *Brotherhood* and Martin Scorsese's *The Departed.*

Donna is expanding her writing talents and has begun writing for the screen including the adaption of her ***Da Vinci's Disciples Trilogy***. The pilot has thus far won four awards.

Her sons—Devon, an opera singer; and Dylan, a chef—are still, and always will be, her greatest works.

www.donnarussomorin.com

Gilded Summers
ISBN: 978-4-86745-045-1

Published by
Next Chapter
1-60-20 Minami-Otsuka
170-0005 Toshima-Ku, Tokyo
+818035793528
30th April 2021